W9-CPA-393

Praise for *Virtual Girl*, the John W. Campbell Award–winning novel by Amy Thomson

"Definitely not your usual girl-grows-up story. An entertaining and observant look at human beings from a computer's point of view. A diverting and highly promising first novel."

—*Locus*

"A promising debut novel with a decidedly different point of view."

—*Science Fiction Chronicle*

"A very good book in many ways and a superior first novel. Absorbing and suspenseful."

—*Aboriginal Science Fiction*

"A coming of age novel for the cyberpunk era . . . with a depth of compassion not found in . . . most. "

—*Denver Post*

"An excellent first novel. Grabs your attention and doesn't let go."

—*Kliatt*

"Steeped in tradition with a '90s sensibility, state-of-the-art technology, and a complexity of characterization reminiscent of Shelley."

—*Minneapolis Star Tribune*

The Color of
DISTANCE

Amy Thomson

ACE BOOKS, NEW YORK

THE COLOR OF DISTANCE

An Ace Book / published by arrangement with
the author

PRINTING HISTORY
Ace trade edition / November 1995
Ace mass-market edition / July 1999

All rights reserved.
Copyright © 1995 by Amy Thomson.
Cover art by Linda Messier.
This book may not be reproduced in whole or in part,
by mimeograph or any other means, without permission.
For information address: The Berkley Publishing Group,
a division of Penguin Putnam Inc.,
375 Hudson Street, New York, New York 10014.

The Penguin Putnam Inc. World Wide Web site address is
http://www.penguinputnam.com

Check out the ACE Science Fiction & Fantasy newsletter
and much more on the internet at Club PPI!

ISBN: 0-441-00632-9

ACE®
Ace Books are published
by The Berkley Publishing Group,
a division of Penguin Putnam Inc.,
375 Hudson Street, New York, New York 10014.
ACE and the "A" design are trademarks
belonging to Penguin Putnam Inc.

PRINTED IN THE UNITED STATES OF AMERICA

10 9 8 7 6 5 4 3 2 1

To Dr. Jane Smith, Dr. Robert Ireton, Dr. Jane Uhlir, and to the Swedish Hospital for saving my life. This book and all my subsequent work would not be possible without them.

Acknowledgments and sincere thanks are due to:

Eleanor Arnason, Octavia Butler, Mary Gentle, Ursula K. Le Guin, and Carol Severance, for their inspiration.

To my agent, Don Maass, and to my patient and long-suffering editor, Ginjer Buchanan, without whom this book would never have arrived in your hands.

To the friendly, professional, and helpful staffs of the Seattle Public Library, and the Suzallo and Odegaard Libraries at the University of Washington, who patiently helped me on all sorts of oddball quests for information.

To Dr. Gordon Baker and Jack Haldeman for information on anaphylactic shock.

To the Government of Costa Rica for their farsighted conservation of their rain forests, to Wildland Adventures of Seattle for helping me get to see the Costa Rican rain forests, and to Patricia Maynard for her help and enthusiasm while I was there.

To Jane Hawkins, Vonda McIntyre, Andy Hooper, Kate Shaefer, and Steve Berry of the Novel Group Workshop, who saw this book pass before their eyes over and over and over again. Their insistence on excellence, accuracy, and good punctuation are what have helped bring out all that is good in this book.

To my second readers: Jon Singer, Ian Hageman, John Hecht, Edd Vick, Rich Dutcher, Ctein, Bruce McDanel, T-Om Seaman, Terry Garey, and Scott Barton. Their support, feedback, and ideas were endlessly helpful.

To Kim Graham for her wonderful reference sketch of the Tendu, and for her rendering of the stick figures in chapter 3.

To Anetta Pirinen for her lightning-fast Finnish translation and to the Ethiopian Community Mutual Association of Seattle for correcting my Amharic.

To Bruce Durocher for his encouragement, enthusiasm, and moral support.

To Margaret Organ-Kean and Kris Wheeler for emotional support during the final crunch.

And to Rosalie the Wonder Cat, who bore all of this book-writing nonsense with exquisite feline martyrdom.

O n e

ANI WAS GATHERING tender bibbi shoots when a patch of white on the distant forest floor caught her eye. She pointed it out to Kirito, and her sitik, Ilto. Curious, they climbed down to investigate.

The patch of white turned out to be two unusual animals lying on the forest floor. At first the two strange animals didn't even seem to be alive. The white shell that covered them was made of something that had never lived. The covering was flexible, like the shell of a lizard's egg, only much tougher. Kirito's sharpest knife could barely cut through it.

The first creature they uncovered was dead. Kirito pierced its skin with a wrist spur, taking a few cells into her allu to see what kind of animal it was. Her ears lifted in astonishment. Pink with surprise and excitement, she beckoned urgently to Ilto. Kirito linked spurs with Ilto, sharing her discovery with him. He colored as excitedly as she had, and began helping Kirito free the other creature from its tough white covering.

Ani's ears lifted in surprise. Ilto was rarely surprised or excited anymore. Over the past couple of years, he had become listless and apathetic. Her sitik's withdrawal worried her. She was his bami. Ilto had chosen her from among all of the other tinka. He'd raised her, training her to fill his place in the tribe some day. But Ani wasn't ready yet. She still needed him. She was afraid he would decide to die, leaving her unprepared to be an elder. Perhaps this new creature would restore his interest in life.

While Kirito and Ilto were busy cutting open the covering on the second animal, Ani examined the dead one. Its odd pinkish-tan skin was very strange—smooth, like hers, but dry like a lizard's. It lacked any protective slime and was covered with sparse hair, like the fuzz of an ika flower. She had never seen an animal with fuzz on its skin before. She wondered what purpose it served.

Ani sank a wrist spur into the creature. It was even stranger inside than outside. Its cells made no sense at all, which was strange, since the corpse was very fresh. She should still be able to read its cells.

Ilto chittered quietly to get her attention. She looked up to see what he wanted.

"This one's alive!" he said, the symbols flashing across his body almost too quickly to read. "Help us take this thing off its body!"

Puzzled, she helped them strip the covering from the second creature. This one was darker brown, with a finer, sparser covering of hair. It was smaller and more delicately built. Ilto lifted off the hard shell encasing its head. Underneath the masklike head-covering was a flat, uninteresting face with a fleshy nose like a bird's beak, and a small mouth with fat, swollen lips. The hair on its head was thick and long.

Stripped, the creature was ugly and clumsy-looking. It was at least three hand-spans taller than any Tendu Ani had ever seen. Its thick, awkward feet had tiny, weak toes, useless for climbing. The creature's blunt claws were as impractical as its absurd toes. It lay there, laboring for breath like a dying fish. How could such a poorly adapted animal manage to survive?

Wondering if its cells tasted as alien as those of its dead companion, Ani reached out to sample them with a wrist spur. Ilto caught her arm before she could pierce its skin.

"No," he told her. "Let us make sure it's safe first."

"It's going to die unless we stabilize it soon," Kirito warned.

Ilto flickered agreement. "Which of us is going to do it?"

Kirito rippled blue-grey longing, then brown embarrassment at her selfishness.

Ilto held out a clenched fist and flushed faintly purple. They were going to kenja for the privilege.

They put their hands behind their backs, counted to four, then held out their hands. Kirito's hand was cupped into the mouth position, Ilto's fist was flattened into a leaf. Mouth eats leaf. Kirito had won the right to work with the new creature. A ripple of deep green satisfaction crossed her skin.

Ilto and Ani stood watching as Kirito linked with it. She concentrated hard, her nictitating membranes half-covering her blank, unfocused eyes. Gradually the creature's labored breathing eased, and became steady.

Kirito removed her spurs from the creature, took a deep breath, and looked up at Ilto. "I've helped it a little, but I need to do some deep work to stabilize it. Will you monitor me?"

Ani's ears lifted, this time in surprise. Deep work was dangerous. She remembered the first time she had attempted it. She had become so attuned to the bird she was working on that her heart began to lose its rhythm and her metabolism fluctuated wildly. Despite Ilto's careful monitoring and rapid intervention, she'd been in a coma for a full day. It had taken six days for her body to return to normal. Now Kirito and Ilto were going to attempt deep work on a creature whose cells were unrecognizably bizarre. It was dangerous, even for them, the two most senior elders in the village. An orange thread of fear flowed slowly down Ani's back.

"Are you sure you want to do this, Kirito?" Ilto asked her.

"I'm ready," she said. Her skin was a calm, resolved chartreuse. "Kiha can fill my place if I die."

"So am I," Ilto told her. "Ani is also ready to become an elder."

The stinging stripes on Ani's back tightened.

"No, siti. Not yet," she pleaded, her words pale grey with dread. "There's so much more to learn. I'm not ready yet."

Vertical bars of negation flickered across Ilto's chest. "If I die now, you're ready to be an elder," he told her, turquoise with pride and fondness. "Everything else I know you can learn for yourself."

"We must hurry," Kirito said, with a tinge of impatience. "The creature is weak and won't remain stable for long."

"Don't worry, Ani. I won't die," Ilto said. "Not today. I want to understand this new animal first."

Ani looked away, not wanting to see any more of his words. Ilto brushed her shoulder with his knuckles and turned to monitor Kirito and the new creature.

Ani loaded her blowgun and stood watching the forest around them. The afternoon thunderstorm had moved on toward the mountains, and the still air was a huge warm exhalation of rot, leaves, and the distant sweetness of flowers blooming high above in the canopy. Up in the trees a gudda lizard boomed out its throbbing call. Distant cries answered it. She scanned the branches. She wasn't expecting anything to happen. Few predators were foolish enough to attack a Tendu, but it was always wise to be prepared.

Thrashing and a wet snapping noise made her glance down. Kirito was now the same strange, flat shade of brown as the creature. Convulsions racked her body. Her left leg was bent at an odd angle, broken by the force of her convulsions.

Every muscle and sinew of Ilto's body stood out as he strained, trying to bring Kirito back into harmony. He was white with fatigue, and he was failing. If he didn't break the link, Ilto would follow Kirito down into death.

The bones of Kirito's left forearm snapped as Ani watched. Ani tore Ilto's spur out of Kirito's arm, breaking the link between them. Ilto cried out in pain, his skin a wordless rush of intense colors. A final violent convulsion racked Kirito's broken frame, driving her bones through her skin with a rush of brilliant red blood. She lay still, her skin slowly fading to the silvery pallor of death. The humid air was filled with the salty, hot smell of Kirito's blood and the swampy reek of her voided bowels.

Ani shook Ilto's arm and patted his face in an attempt to rouse him. When Ilto didn't respond she linked with him, flooding his body with her presence, forcing him to perceive something other than Kirito's pain. At last Ilto acknowledged her presence, sending her feeble reassurance. She broke the link.

Ilto lay still for a while, looking up at her, his hand lying limply in hers. He had come so close to dying! He sat up very slowly, refusing Ani's offer of assistance. Ochre with concern, Ani watched him struggle to sit up. Finally Ilto made it. He sat very still for a few moments; then he reached over and brushed the shoulder of Kirito's corpse sadly.

"I will miss her," he said in somber grey. "We shared many memories. Now I'm the only one in the village who remembers that far back."

Ilto touched the new creature on its forearm. Blood trickled from the spot where Kirito's spur had penetrated its skin. Before Ani could stop him, he linked with it.

"Siti! No! You're too weak!" Ani reached out to snatch his arm away, but Ilto broke his link with the creature before she could do anything. He looked down at the strange new animal and the ruin of Kirito's corpse. A grey cloud of grief flowed over his skin as he stood up.

"Kirito succeeded; it's stabilized," he told her. "It will live until we can take it back to the village for more work." The words on his skin were pale and indistinct with exhaustion. Ani could barely understand him. She brushed his shoulder with her knuckles and Ilto turned to look at her.

"Forgive me for breaking the link, siti, but I thought Kirito was going to take you with her."

An indistinct pattern of negation rippled across Ilto's chest. He staggered and then sat, his legs too weak to support him.

With an effort he focused himself. "I need your strength, bai." He flushed a washed-out shade of brown, embarrassed by his need. He held his arms out to her, spurs up.

Ani linked spurs with Ilto, joining with him in the healing communion of allu-a. Ilto's blood was sour with fatigue and his energy reserves were dangerously low. She sent sugars into his depleted system to give him energy. Then she broke down the poisons in his blood. Once the fatigue toxins were gone, she scanned him more closely, looking for more subtle problems. It was then that she tasted a faint taint in his blood. It disturbed her, but Ilto broke the link between them before she could investigate further.

"No, bai," he told her gently. "You've done enough. I was

following Kirito down to death, and you brought me back. You are as skilled as any elder, and better than some of them."

Ani looked away, frightened by the implications of his praise. She looked back at him. "I don't want to lose you, siti. I'm happy being your bami. I'm not ready to become an elder."

"You've been ready for a long time now," he told her. "Don't worry about me. I'll be all right." He sat up then, still a little pale, but better. He needed food, fruit and meat, before he would be ready to travel. Ani pulled several bright blue tumbi out of her gathering bag and gave them to him. Juice ran down Ilto's chin as he bit hungrily into the sweet fruit. Ani helped him over to the base of a nearby tree, settling him between two massive, buttressed roots.

"We passed one of Hanto's na trees a while back. I'll go get some narey and honey," she told him. She leaped up the tree and bounded through the canopy until she came to the thick-trunked na tree. A swarm of tilan buzzed curiously around her as she reached the tree, but they drew off when they recognized the familiar scent of her tribe. The Tendu's na trees were carefully guarded. If the bees had not recognized her, they would have descended in a cloud of stinging fury. Few creatures intruded into a tilan-protected na tree more than once.

Ani paused to catch her breath. Allu-a with Ilto had tired her. She pulled two more tumbi out of her satchel, eating one and breaking the other open for the tilan. The bees clustered thickly on the fruit. Misty grey regret clouded her skin. Normally she would have fed them honeydew straight from her wrist spurs, but she was still drained from healing Ilto.

She climbed into the hollow tree trunk, descending past humming chambers of tilan hives until she reached the pool of water at the bottom of the tree. Even though her need was urgent, she felt a little guilty taking food from an elder's tree without permission. At least this was Hanto's tree. The young elder respected Ilto. She would be honored to have helped him.

Hanto took good care of her trees, Ani noted with admiration. The tilan were prosperous and the glow fungus illuminating the inside of the trunk was healthy. The water in the pool in the tree's base was clean and pure. The narey swimming in its depths would be plump and strong.

Ani slid into the dark, rich water, feeling the vibrations of the startled narey as they rushed to bury themselves in the bottom of the tank. She dove after them, reaching down into the thick, oozing sediment with both hands, grabbing a wriggling narey in her claws and stopping its struggles with a quick sting from her spurs. Ilto was popular as a mate. This might even be one of his own offspring. Ilto could easily repay Hanto with narey from his own thriving brood.

Ani paused at the rim of the reservoir to lay a small clutch of infertile eggs to feed the remaining narey. It wasn't necessary, but Ilto had taught her the virtues of generosity. Once the narey was butchered, she wrapped it in a fresh leaf and put it in her satchel. Then she gathered several large honeycombs from the tilan hives. She ate one, sucking out the sweet honey, and leaving the waxy, indigestible comb for the tilan to eat and recycle back into their hives.

Renewed by her snack, Ani set off, swinging through the trees at a dangerous pace, hurrying back to Ilto. It was dangerous to leave him alone when he was so weak.

She needn't have worried. Ilto was sitting where she had left him, munching on handfuls of bibbi shoots from his gathering bag.

A good meal restored them both. Ilto sent Ani back to the village to fetch some help. It took twelve Tendu to bring the new animal and Kirito back to the village. Ilto was still too exhausted to do much, so Ani had to organize everything. She half-expected the elders to scold her for telling them what to do, but they followed her orders without question or comment. Their quiet acceptance of her ability to assume command bothered her. It meant that they agreed she was ready to take Ilto's place.

They laid the comatose animal on the sleeping platform in Ilto's room. Ani shooed off the curious villagers and helped her exhausted sitik into bed. The new creature was safely in stasis, and could remain like this for half a month if they fed it nutrients and fluids through their allu.

The next morning, Ilto ate an enormous meal, then set to work. He spent the next four days squatting beside the animal, eyes half-hooded, unaware of his surroundings, lost in intense

communion with the new creature. Ani monitored him, working in shifts with other elders so that she could rest and eat. She
had to keep herself strong in order to provide Ilto with the
strength he needed to continue his deep communion.

Ani watched as Ilto studied the minute details of the new
animal's bizarre physiology. A full day passed before he began
changing the new creature. First Ilto altered its body processes
so they would not react so strongly to foreign substances. That
was easy to do. Next, he improved its sight and hearing, so that
it could see better in the dark, and hear nearly as well as a
Tendu. Then he puzzled out how to make its toes grow long
enough to be useful without causing the rest of its bones to
change. That was hard, but it gave him the knowledge he
needed to create a skin that adequately protected it from the
hazards of the forest.

The skin was the most difficult part. It had to shield the
creature from all of the things its own body could not, yet still
be able to co-exist with, and draw nourishment from, the body
it covered. When complete, the skin would extend through its
digestive tract and down into its lungs, protecting it from foods
that might make it sick and the unseen proteins in the air that
had nearly killed the animal before they found it.

Ilto made its skin capable of showing emotion. Ani doubted
the creature was intelligent enough to make use of such a gift,
but she decided not to share her doubts with Ilto. She was even
more dubious about his decision to give it the same protective
stinging stripes as the Tendu, but Ani couldn't bring herself to
say anything. Ilto was happier than she had ever seen him, alive
with the joy of a challenging task. The bright, sweet tang of his
joy filled her allu as she monitored him. The elders spoke of
him in shades of awe and admiration. It was like watching a
legend come to life.

Ilto emerged from communion in the middle of the fourth
night. He was so weak that Ani had to help him into bed. He let
some of the elders give him strength, ate a little kayu mush and
yarram, and fell into a deep, healing sleep. Ani piled the leafy
bedding over him to keep him warm and moist. She made sure
the new creature was all right, then burrowed into her own bed
and fell asleep.

Ilto woke Ani late the next day, eager to resume working with the animal. Ani managed to make him wait until she had fed him a big meal. She wanted him to rest another day, but he was determined to continue.

Ilto's frenetic pace was wearing him down. Despite the enormous and frequent meals Ani forced him to eat, and the nutrients that she poured into his body through her allu, the flesh was melting off Ilto's bones.

The strange taint in his blood grew stronger as well, but Ilto was too obsessed by the new creature to stop and heal himself. He refused to allow Ani to try to clear it out of his blood. Concerned, she turned to Ninto, the one elder who knew Ilto better than she did.

"He's pushing himself too hard," Ani told Ninto, "but he won't rest."

"He's as stubborn as an old kular," the tall, slender elder agreed.

Blue and green amusement flowed over Ani. She had no trouble seeing Ilto as a spiny, irascible anteater.

"There's no arguing with him when he's like this," cautioned Ninto. "He was like this when I was his bami. I don't think I remember him ever changing his mind, not in all the years I've known him. Once he makes up his mind to do something there's no arguing him out of it."

Ani suppressed a brown flush of embarrassment at Ninto's glancing mention of her relationship with Ilto. Most elders raised only one bami, and once it was ready, its sitik either died or left the village. But an elder had died without a bami to succeed him. The village chief chose Ilto's bami, Ni-ne, to fill the dead elder's place. Ni-ne became the elder Ninto. Ten years later, Ilto selected Ani as his second bami. That made Ninto her tareena.

Ani had been with Ilto for many years. Trees they had planted during their first year together now spread their leaves in the sunshine at the top of the jungle's canopy. But Ninto had been there before her. She knew Ilto as both sitik and fellow elder. Ani and Ninto were the only tareena in the village. It was an unusual relationship, and it set Ani apart from the other bami.

Ninto brushed Ani's shoulder affectionately, and set aside the gathering bag she was weaving. "I'll see what I can do," she reassured her.

Ilto was linked with the new creature when they came in. Ninto joined the link and gently pulled Ilto out of allu-a.

Ilto turned brilliant yellow with irritation. "Can't you see I'm too busy to be interrupted!" he flared at Ninto. "I thought I trained you better than that!" He launched into a long tirade about manners, lecturing Ninto as though she were still a bami.

To Ani's surprise, Ninto listened politely. Only a tiny blue flicker of amusement running down Ninto's back showed she paid absolutely no attention to Ilto's scolding. Ani's ears lifted, and she fought back her own amusement.

"Kene," Ninto said, when Ilto was done, "you are being selfish."

"In what way am I being selfish?" Ilto asked, his words stiff and formal in response to Ninto's use of his title.

"You are neglecting the future of our village by mistreating your bami."

Ani sat up, insulted. "He is not!" But her words went unnoticed. A cautionary pattern flared briefly on Ninto's back, telling Ani to be still.

"Look how thin and tired she is. You're asking too much of her." Ninto motioned to Ani, who came forward out of the shadows.

Ilto linked with Ani. She could feel him probing her physical condition. Brown shame coursed over his skin as he broke the link.

"You're right," he told Ninto. "I will put the creature into jeetho tomorrow." Grey regret clouded his words.

"Not tomorrow," Ninto said. "Give Ani a day of rest before you work any more with the new animal. The creature's stabilized. It can wait another day."

"But—" Ilto protested.

Ani, realizing that by giving her a day of rest Ilto would also be resting, interrupted him with a touch on the shoulder. "Please, siti, I won't be able to do it tomorrow. I'm too tired." She turned a pale, sickly white, hating herself for the lie she was telling. "I'm sorry, siti." That much, at least, was true.

Ani glanced at Ninto's back, and saw a faint ripple of approval.

"Ani will rest tomorrow. We will put the creature into jeetho the day after tomorrow," Ilto announced, never admitting he had changed his mind.

Ani glanced over at Ninto, impressed with her skill at manipulating Ilto. She hoped someday she would be that clever. Ninto met her glance and flicked an ear at her.

"Ilto is right," Ninto said when Ani followed her out to thank her. "You are ready to become an elder. You handled that well." A mist of regret clouded the colors of her words. "I'll miss Ilto when he goes."

"I think Ilto will die rather than leave the village," Ani said.

"Does it matter?" Ninto asked. "Either way, he will be dead to us here."

Ani disagreed. She wanted to know Ilto was alive somewhere in the world, even if she never saw him again. She said nothing. Ninto was an elder, and one didn't argue with elders.

Ninto brushed her knuckles across Ani's shoulder. "Thank you for letting me help." She paused, and there was a flicker of color on her chest as though she was about to say something else. Instead she turned and climbed down the trunk.

That afternoon, Ilto took Ani and a tinka to help gather food for the evening meal. Their hunting went well. They killed two plump, scaly mityak and an unwary young moodar, its feathers bright with courtship colors. The tinka found a rotting log full of grubs, and gathered a bag full of bardarr berries. They would eat well tonight. Before returning, they paused to lay out a paste made from yarram and mashed dindi roots as bait to attract mantu. Back at the village tree, they rewarded the tinka with a strip of dried yarram each and a share of the food they had gathered, and returned to their room.

They ate steadily. Every time Ilto paused, Ani handed him some particularly choice delicacy. She wanted to be sure he ate as much as he possibly could before they started working again on the new creature. Ilto also pushed her to eat. At last, her stomach tight and bulging, Ani could eat no more. Ilto sent her to bed. Exhausted, Ani burrowed into her warm, moist bed of leaves and fell asleep.

Ninto woke her. The rank smell of sickness filled the room. Ninto's skin was clouded with worry. Ani glanced over at Ilto. His breathing sounded ragged and rough and his skin had the flat, silvery sheen of sickness.

"He drugged you to keep you asleep, and then started working again on the new creature," Ninto said. "A tinka found him. Since it couldn't wake you, it got me. Ilto won't let me help him. He keeps breaking the link."

Ani linked with Ilto. The alien taint in his blood was stronger than ever. She recognized it now. Some of the new creature's cells had gotten into his body, and were attacking Ilto.

"Can you do anything?" Ninto asked.

Startled by the question, Ani looked at Ninto for a long moment before replying. If this was beyond Ninto's skills, then it was probably beyond hers. She would try, though. She was willing to do anything for Ilto.

"It will be deep work," Ani said. She had never been monitored by anyone other than Ilto.

"I'll monitor you," Ninto said, answering her undepicted request.

Ani linked with Ninto and closed her eyes. Ninto's presence in the link felt so much like Ilto's. It reassured her as she reached in through the link to sample Ilto's blood.

With no warning at all, the link broke. Ninto eased Ani back into balance, then gently eased out of the link.

Ani opened her eyes and sat up. She reached out to Ilto to try again.

Ilto's eyes flickered open. His hands moved away from hers. "No, don't," Ilto told her, his words pale under the deathlike silver sheen of his illness. "It might make you sick. I'll take care of myself. The creature is ready; start the changes and put it in jeetho."

"Siti, please—" Ani began, but Ilto's eyes closed and he slid back into unconsciousness. She looked at Ninto, hoping for help.

"He told us not to interfere," Ninto said, her skin olive-grey with resignation. "There's nothing more that we can do but let him be and hope he gets better on his own." She picked up a tumbi and handed it to Ani. "Now, eat. You'll need your strength. We've got to put that thing in jeetho before Ilto recovers enough to start tinkering with it again. I've asked Hanto to look after Ilto while we're busy."

A large group of mottled brown mantu were feeding placidly on the bait they had left the night before. Ninto and her bami, Baha, helped Ani gather about two dozen of them. The mantu retreated beneath their oval shells as they were picked up.

Back at the village, they hauled an enormous trough from one of the storerooms. Pulling a mantu out of her gathering bag, Ani pried up the horny operculum that sealed the base of the shell. She sank her spur into the soft, yielding flesh beneath, injecting it with an enzyme that began the process of turning the mantu into jeetho, and put the shell in the trough. Ninto squatted beside her, and began stinging the mantu she had gathered.

The mantu flesh began melting as the enzyme took effect. Baha removed the shells, opercula, and any undissolved organs from the slimy grey mass. Nothing of the mantu would go to waste. The shells would eventually become feast platters, the horny operculum would be made into tools and ornaments, and the organs would be fed to the narey.

At last the gathering bags were empty. Ani leaned against the side of the trough. She felt drained and slightly dizzy from the effort of producing so much dissolution enzyme. Normally they only needed a few mantu, but the new creature required a huge batch of jeetho.

After stopping to rest and eat, they resumed work. The jeetho was now a translucent grey jelly, covered with a frothy black scum which they skimmed off. Once the jelly was clean, Ani stuck her wrist spurs into it and injected another trigger chemical. She stirred the jelly, tasting it with a wrist spur. The jelly began to stiffen and turn a faint pink. Ninto stuck a spur into the mass and flushed approvingly.

"You can leave it now," Ninto said. She brushed her knuckles across Ani's shoulder. "You did well."

Ani turned and glanced inquiringly over at Ilto.

"He's better," Hanto told her. "He'll be weak and shaky for a while, but he will recover. He's a strong old kular. Just don't let him play with that again," she said, gesturing with her chin at the new creature.

By morning the jeetho was transformed from a grey jelly into a reddish mass, striated with veins. The surface rippled as air rushed through its primitive respiratory system. Several simple hearts pulsed rhythmically inside it. It was ready to receive the new creature.

Ani injected the strange animal with a trigger chemical to initiate the changes laid down by Ilto. Then they stung the jeetho once again, and laid the animal on it. The jeetho softened, and the new creature began to sink down into it. As Ani and Ninto watched, veins began growing into the creature's skin.

This was a risky time. The creature would either live or die, depending on how well Ilto had done his work. Could it survive inside the jeetho? Ani stuck a spur into the creature, monitoring its adaptation. Its complex heart beat slowly and strongly in a strange one-two rhythm. The level of oxygen in the creature's blood dipped as its face was covered, then rose again as the jeetho took over the task of supplying it with oxygen.

Once she was sure the new creature would survive inside the jeetho, Ani broke her link, pushing its arm into the clinging red jelly. The strange animal inside would be fed and nourished by the jeetho until its metamorphosis was complete. She stung the jeetho one last time. In a couple of days the jeetho would develop a tough, leathery skin.

Ani and Ninto hid the creature in a storeroom. When the jeetho's skin hardened, they concealed the new animal in one of Ninto's na trees, where it would not tempt Ilto while he recovered.

T w o

J∪NA AWOKE TO darkness and confinement. She was inside some kind of damp, leathery sack. She tore her way out and found herself staring down at a fifty-meter drop. She moaned and clutched the tree branch she was on, her claws sinking deep into the bark. *Claws?*

Her fingernails were gone. Instead sharp, catlike claws protruded from the ends of her fingers. Her skin was a brilliant orange. Juna closed her eyes, hoping that when she opened them again, her hands would be back to normal. But she could feel her claws pulling against the tips of her fingers. This was an incredibly vivid and realistic nightmare.

She rested her forehead against the rough bark of the branch. The last thing she remembered was lying on the ground in the middle of an alien rain forest, struggling to breathe through her constricted airways. She had been dying of anaphylactic shock. Before that had been the flyer crash, followed by a forced march through the jungle in a desperate attempt to make it back to the Survey base. Now she was fifty meters up a tree, hanging on for dear life to a slippery, wet branch as big around as her thigh. A steady warm rain was falling. This wasn't a dream. She was alive, impossible as that seemed. She clutched onto that thread of hope, and felt her terror ease.

Why had she survived? Humans were profoundly allergic to every living world the Survey had found. This world was no exception. The air was loaded with pollen, molds, spores, and microscopic organisms. They couldn't infect humans, but their alien proteins caused violent allergic reactions. Test animals from Earth exposed to the atmosphere usually died within hours.

Tears pricked the inside of her eyelids as she remembered the slow, painful deaths of the others. Catherine, the tall, elegant pilot, had died in the crash. The rest—Hiro, Yanni, and Shana—had died of anaphylactic shock when their filters failed. Oliver had been the last to go. She had been holding him in her lap when the first symptoms struck her. She remembered the agony of her own itching eyes and swelling throat before she blacked out. It was a terrible way to go.

Juna opened her eyes. Her skin was the grey of wet clay instead of its familiar dark brown. Fleshy red spurs protruded from the insides of her arms just above the wrist. They looked swollen and angry, as though they should hurt, but they didn't.

A slight breeze played over her scalp. It felt oddly cool. Juna pried her claws from the branch and ran a hand over the top of her head, and sighed with regret. Her hair was gone too.

The branch swayed in a sudden gust of wind. Her stomach tightened, and her claws dug into the branch until her fingers ached. Her skin flared orange again as a fresh burst of fear blossomed in her stomach.

Juna took a deep breath and let it out. If she lost control, she would never get out of this tree alive. She fought back her panic. As it subsided, her hands faded to pale green. The strange color changes seemed related to shifts in her emotional state. *So much for mah jongg and poker,* Juna thought to herself with a nervous laugh. She shook her head. She had to get down to the ground before she fell apart completely. *Focus on getting down*, she told herself. *Worry about everything else later*.

Juna inched carefully backward over the shredded remains of the leathery sack she had clawed her way out of. How had she wound up inside it? At last her groping feet found the trunk. She turned to face it, fighting a sudden surge of terror as the tree swayed in a fresh breeze.

Clinging to the huge trunk made her feel a little more secure. Juna paused to consider her next move. It was then that she saw the alien.

The biologist in her awoke and began observing the alien, her fear forgotten for the moment. It stood on a branch below Juna, watching her calmly. It resembled an enormous tree frog, except for its large fanlike ears and high, domed forehead. The alien was pale green, and completely naked, except for a satchel of woven grass slung over one shoulder. Its eyes were golden, with vertical, catlike pupils. On the inside of its arms, just above the wrist, were bright red spurs resembling the ones on her own arms.

She looked like the alien, Juna realized. Was it responsible for her transformation? If so, how had it been done? The creature seemed far too primitive to be capable of such a feat.

A ripple of brilliant blue passed over the alien's chest. The color moved so fluidly and swiftly over its body that Juna glanced around, looking for a blue light source. Another blue ripple passed over the creature, and Juna realized that the alien was changing its skin color with uncanny speed and control. It was an eerily beautiful sight.

The alien stepped back on the branch, and sat down. It patted the branch in front of it, gesturing toward her with a limp hand. Clearly it was inviting her to join it.

Juna hesitated, wishing that Kinsey or one of the other Alien Contact specialists were here. She had forgotten most of the Contact Protocols she had learned at the Academy. She looked at the alien. It was waiting to see what she would do. What did it want with her? Could she trust it?

She didn't have much choice. She was lost in a jungle on a strange planet. Her chances of surviving were much greater if this alien helped her. Besides, finding such a creature was an incredible coup. Juna imagined the fuss that her appearance back at base camp with the alien would cause. Her fear eased and she smiled. Carefully, her new claws sinking deep into the bark as she fought a renewed surge of fear, Juna climbed down to meet the alien.

An explosion of yellow spirals appeared on the alien's chest as Juna settled herself against the trunk of the tree. It beckoned her closer but she refused to move. Getting this far was terrifying enough. She wanted to sit somewhere that felt safe for a while.

The alien came toward her, walking easily on all fours. It settled itself only a couple of meters away. Reaching into its satchel, it took out a large yellow fruit, holding it up so she could see it. It bit into the fruit, chewing and swallowing with ostentatious enjoyment. The alien flushed a deep shade of turquoise. Then it took another fruit from its satchel, shuffled forward cautiously, and extending a very long arm, set the fruit on the branch within Juna's reach. It moved back and finished the fruit it was eating, never taking its gaze from her.

Juna looked from the fruit to the alien. Her stomach growled. She was ravenous. Moving slowly, she picked up the fruit. Blue and green flowed over the alien's skin, like ripples over the surface of a pool. Juna examined the fruit. It was soft and pulpy, like a papaya, and smelled sweet. Her mouth filled with saliva. She hadn't been this hungry since she was a child in the refugee camps.

What the hell, Juna thought, *I'd rather die of food poisoning than starvation.* At least it looked more appetizing than some of the things she had had to eat when it was a choice between starving and eating filth. She bit into the alien fruit. It was delicious, the flavor falling somewhere between banana and papaya, with a hint of hard-boiled egg. She glanced down. Her skin was brilliant turquoise.

"Good," she said. "It's good."

At the sound of her voice, the alien's delicate ears fanned wide. A cluster of purple shapes passed over its skin. They reminded her of grapes. That triggered a sudden, vivid memory of harvesting grapes in her father's vineyard. She remembered the dusty sunlight, the rich, winey taste of the fruit. It seemed so far away now, as though it had happened in someone else's childhood. Juna took another bite of the yellow fruit. Its intense sweetness, so different from the tart tang of remembered grapes, brought her back to the present.

The alien watched Juna intently as she ate. When she was finished it eased forward on the branch, holding out another fruit.

Juna took it from the alien's fingers and tore off a piece. She held it out to the alien, returning the gift. A complex zigzag pattern flickered across the alien's chest as it accepted the offer. It ate the fruit, then reached out again, fingers carefully curled, and brushed the backs of its fingers across the knuckles of her outstretched hand. The gesture seemed formal. It waited expectantly.

Hesitantly, Juna reached out and brushed her knuckles across the back of the alien's hand. Its skin felt cool and moist.

The alien visibly relaxed. Rapid explosions of turquoise and azure flickered across its skin. Juna sighed in relief. She felt as though she had crossed a barrier, gaining the alien's trust. It was a good beginning.

When Juna finished the second fruit, the alien got up and ambled to the end of the branch, beckoning her to follow. It bounded across a two-meter gap to the next tree. Then it turned and looked at her, flushing purple, its ears lifted.

Juna climbed as far out on the branch as she dared. It bowed under her weight. A wave of sick dizziness overwhelmed her. She looked across the gap at the alien, then down at the distant ground.

"No," she said. "I can't do it." She shook her head and backed away from the end of the branch, her skin blazing orange with fear. What would she do if the alien abandoned her?

The alien beckoned to her with the same limp-handed gesture, dark green ripples passing over its body. Juna shook her head and backed farther up the branch.

The alien turned bright yellow and leaped lightly across the gap. The impact of its landing shook the branch. Juna cried out and dug into the tree limb with her claws, fighting for balance. The alien reached out to her. She reached up and grasped its hand. Despite the cold wetness of its touch, the strength of the alien's grip reassured her. The sick dizziness began to ease.

"Thank you," she said, knowing it didn't understand her.

Before Juna realized what it was doing, the alien levered her onto its back. She started to struggle, then froze, afraid she would knock them both off the narrow branch. The alien leaped across the gap between the trees with Juna on its back. It released her as soon as they were across. Beckoning her to follow, it set off again.

Juna followed the alien. She wanted to get down onto safe, firm ground where she could cry and shake for an hour or so, but that wasn't an option. *This is no harder than the obstacle course at the Survey Academy,* she told herself. She focused on the details of the climb, finding footholds, pulling herself up, proving both to the alien and herself that she was capable of surviving.

The alien waited for her by the main trunk. As she drew closer, it leaped nimbly up the trunk to another branch about six meters higher and about a quarter of the way around the tree. It paused again, watching, as Juna clambered up the massive trunk. As soon as she reached the limb where the alien waited, it bounded to the end of the branch, pausing at the gap between the trees.

Several thick vines bridged the space between the branch they were on and the next tree. The alien purpled and raised its ears in what was becoming a familiar, inquisitive gesture. It swung hand over hand across the gap, as though the sixty-meter drop didn't exist, then sat waiting for her on the other side. Juna looked at the vines, and then up at the alien, then back at the bridge of lianas.

"All right," she muttered, "but if I fall and kill myself, it's your fault."

She grabbed hold of the vine and let herself swing down. It sagged, but didn't break. Her stomach tightened and her heart beat wildly as she crossed hand over hand between the trees, but she made it over in one piece. The alien reached down and helped pull her onto the branch. As soon as Juna was settled, it turned and bounded off again.

Juna lost all track of time on that terrifying trip through the treetops. Twice, she nearly fell to her death. Each time the alien was there to steady her, or pull her back onto the branch. Then it continued on as though nothing had happened. Finally, the alien paused and beckoned her close. It smeared a sticky liquid on Juna's back. When it was finished, it leaped across the gap, beckoning Juna to follow.

A cloud of brightly colored, loudly buzzing bees swarmed

around Juna as soon as she landed on the next tree. Juna ducked and hid her head between her arms. These same bees had attacked her when she was out collecting specimens for the Survey. They had clustered so thickly on the faceplate of her helmet that she couldn't see to climb. This time, the insects merely hovered briefly and then buzzed off again.

The alien turned the bright red spurs on its wrists upward. The bees clustered on its arms. Looking closer, Juna saw a sticky, golden fluid oozing from its wrist spurs. The insects appeared to be feeding on the secretions. After a minute or two the alien gently shook its arms and the bees flew away.

Several other aliens sat on another branch, staring at Juna. Brilliant patterns rippled over their bodies. She looked back at them for a long moment. Then her guide brushed her shoulder with its knuckles and beckoned her on. She turned to follow, and stopped short in amazement, her exhaustion forgotten.

She was in one of the most remarkable trees she had ever seen. The limb she stood on was half a meter thick, and fifty meters from the ground. The bark was worn smooth from the passage of many feet, and its sides were bearded with ferns and moss. The trunk was at least a dozen meters in diameter, rising from thick, buttressed roots. The trunk split into a many-branched crotch about forty-five meters from the ground, forming a great bowl a dozen meters across. In the center of the crotch was a round hole big enough to drop a piano through. The edges of the hole were worn smooth with use. As she watched, an alien emerged from the trunk of the tree, joining several other aliens seated beside the hole, busy weaving baskets. They stopped and stared at Juna as she approached. She felt naked under their unreadable gaze.

Excitement broke through the wall of her fatigue. No wonder the Survey team hadn't seen these people. Their villages were indistinguishable from the surrounding forest.

Ignoring the stares of the other aliens, her guide beckoned her toward a series of steep steps leading down into the gaping hole. Clouds of bees filled the air. The tree vibrated with their humming. At last her guide helped her onto a platform about two meters wide.

She turned and looked down into the heart of the hollow tree.

It reminded her of a gigantic seashell. Four steep ramps spiraled down the inside of the tree. Arched doorways branched off it at regular intervals. Aliens climbed up and down the ramps on mysterious errands; others clustered in doorways eating and socializing. The walls glowed with a soft blue radiance that illuminated the tree's interior. The glow came from a fungus growing on the walls. She touched its soft, velvety surface, wondering what form of bioluminescence caused the glow. Her fingers came away powdered with faintly glowing blue.

Juna looked down into the depths of the tree for a dizzying moment. A distant pool of water reflected the blue glow of the walls and the far-off gleam of the sky. The tree smelled of damp wood and leaves, tinged with the faint sweetness of honey. There was a sense of order and tranquillity about this beautiful, strange place.

The tree teemed with life. Iridescent bees swirled in shafts of watery sunlight. Small lizards scuttled out of her way, and thousands of insects filed up and down the trunk of the tree, carrying bits of leaves and litter. She startled a tiny, slender serpent, no bigger around than her little finger, and perhaps twenty centimeters long. The snake hurled itself into the air, gliding away on brilliant ribbed wings.

About a fifth of the way down, they stepped onto a narrow balcony and entered one of the many low doorways that opened onto the central cavity. The door passed through a half-meter-thick wall opening onto a room shaped like a wide slice of pie with the tip cut off. It was a good-sized room, bigger than the common room in her group marriage's house. She felt a small twinge of regret, as she always did, at anything that reminded her of her failed marriage.

Two small, deep windows set into the meter-thick trunk provided more air than light. The same glowing fungus that illuminated the rest of the tree covered the low ceiling, filling the room with shadowless blue light. Coils of rope and nets hung neatly from pegs by the door. Shelves growing out of the walls held a variety of baskets, gourds, and leaf-wrapped bundles. The only things marring the sense of neatness and order in the room were several large insects that scuttled purposefully over the glowing ceiling. The floor stepped up to form a raised platform across the wide end of the room. Three aliens were seated on the edge of the raised platform. Their ears spread wide as Juna came in.

One of the seated aliens beckoned her closer. It was painfully thin; its color seemed faded and it moved slowly. She wondered if it was sick. It motioned her to sit with a flat, economical downward gesture, its fingers partly curled. She sat, facing the gaunt alien. Her guide squatted beside her, its long, slender toes splayed wide for balance.

The sick alien examined her hands, turning them over and looking at her palms. Then it pinched her fingertips, one after the other, forcing her claws to extend. It hurt. Juna tried to pull away, but the alien's grip was like iron, despite its frail appearance. It examined the red spurlike swellings on her wrists, and ran its fingers lightly over her back. It even spread her legs and examined her genitalia. Juna remembered showing sheep at farm fairs as a teenager. She knew now how those sheep felt as they were being judged. She suppressed the urge to struggle. Her life depended on these aliens. A hostile move now could be fatal.

At last the examination ended. Her guide and one of the other aliens got up and left the room, pushing through a crowd of curious onlookers at the door. Juna suddenly felt very weak and shaky. She rested her forehead on her knees as the shock of all she had been through today caught up with her. She wasn't giving them a very good impression of the human race, Juna thought, embarrassed by her weakness. With an effort, she mastered herself and sat up.

The two remaining aliens watched her in silence; faintly luminous patterns flowed over their skins like the reflection of waves in a pool. The frail alien motioned toward a pile of gourds. More patterns flickered over its skin. The other alien got up and brought the sick one a gourd. The sick alien lifted the lid, pulled out a thick honeycomb, and handed it to her.

Gingerly, Juna bit into it. Thick, sweet honey dripped down her chin and gushed into her mouth. She chewed, sucking the sweet syrup out of the comb. She swallowed the honey and spit the comb into her hand. Her skin turned purple as she looked

inquisitively at the alien. It handed her an empty leaf. Juna set
the chewed wax on it. Bees began clustering on the wax,
probably taking it away to use again.

The sweet honey hit her system with a rush of energy. Her
head cleared, and she felt much less shaky. She brushed the
emaciated alien's hand with her knuckles, hoping that her skin
reflected her gratitude. Its ears fanned wide in surprise, and it
looked at its companion, flushing purple. A wash of patterns
flickered over the companion's skin, too fast for Juna to follow.
The sick alien watched, then flickered patterns back.

Watching, Juna realized that those patterns had meaning.
The aliens communicated visually. Her heart sank. If the aliens'
language was visual, it would take a long time for her to learn
to communicate with them, especially without her computer.
The Survey was scheduled to leave about two and a half
Earth-Standard months after the flyer crash. Juna had no idea
of how long she had been unconscious. If she didn't get back
to base soon, she might be marooned here forever. Her throat
tightened in fear at the prospect. She had to move swiftly. If she
couldn't get an alien guide in a few days' time, then she was
going to have to set out on her own.

The other aliens returned bearing large leaves piled high
with food, and several big gourds full of water.

Juna's stomach growled. The aliens' ears lifted and they
looked at her, purpling with curiosity. Embarrassed, Juna
blushed. Her skin turned a deep, rich brown, almost its original
color. Pale blue and green waves of color washed over the sick
alien. Was it laughing at her? Juna shrugged, and blushed a
deeper brown. The sick alien laid a reassuring hand on her
shoulder. She smiled and brushed its hand with her knuckles
again. She was beginning to like these people.

Her guide offered her a gourd brimming with clear water.
Juna drank deeply. The water was flat, with a faint acidic tang.
So much had been going on that she hadn't realized how thirsty
she was. The aliens drank, then splashed water over their skins.
Juna sluiced water over herself, washing away the sticky
honey.

The aliens began eating. Her guide picked up a small purple
fruit, smelled it, and handed it to her. Juna picked it up, and

examined it. She didn't recognize it, so it was probably yet another species new to the Survey. She smelled it, in case this was expected. The fruit had a rich, complex odor, aromatic and sweet, like a fine wine. The sick alien touched her arm with its knuckles. She glanced up. It held out a similar fruit, and showed her how to peel and eat it. It tasted like one of her father's finest botrytic Rieslings, only without the alcohol aftertaste.

The food was delicious, but the textures and flavors were disconcerting. One fruit smelled and tasted like custard with cinnamon, another fruit resembled fresh crab. Juna sampled the pale grey meat. It tasted sweet, as though marinated in fruit juice, and salty, with a faint hint of cheese. It was odd, but not unpleasant. She wondered what kind of animal it had come from.

The aliens urged food on her until she couldn't eat another bite. The meal made a huge difference. She no longer felt as if a strong wind could blow her away. When everyone was finished eating, her guide poured water into a bowl made from half a gourd and presented it to each person in turn. They rinsed their hands and arms, and splashed their faces to wash off the remains of their meal.

When that was done, the sick alien held its arms toward Juna, spurs up. It wanted something. Unable to understand, Juna shook her head. The alien reached out and grasped her arm just above the wrist. Its touch was cool and firm. Then its wrist spur pricked her arm, and she was unable to move. Fear surged through her as she fought this sudden paralysis. As quickly as it had come, her fear was washed away. Juna knew she should be terrified, but she couldn't reach her fear. Her guide grasped the sick one's other arm. Their wrist spurs joined. A third alien linked wrist spurs with her guide.

It was like being trapped in warm ice. She could feel a presence moving through her like a chill in the blood. It felt as if slimy hands were fingering her flesh from the inside. Enmeshed in a cocoon of passivity, she could only sit in paralyzed terror as an alien presence took over her body.

Once, in the refugee camps, five older boys had held her down and taken turns raping her. She had been only eight. This alien violation brought it all back—the shame, the humiliation, the helplessness. Anger surged up inside her. She hurled her rage against the alien presence inside her. It was all she had left to fight with.

Then a wave of unadulterated pleasure swept aside her rage as easily as though it were a feather in a breeze. She drifted in a warm sea of euphoria, divorced from her body. Nothing mattered anymore. She drifted happily into unconsciousness.

Juna awoke. She was half buried in a pile of moist leaves. Two aliens slept in piles of leaves on the other side of the room. She remembered the cold presence investigating her body from the inside, and she shivered despite the humid warmth of the tree.

Then she remembered the wash of pleasure that had wiped away her resistance. She sat, shivering, naked, and terrified by how easily the aliens had taken her over. And she had enjoyed it.

She had to leave. Better to die, starving and lost in the jungle, than to remain here and endure more violations like that.

She gathered what she could: a flint knife, a water gourd, a small net, and a braided coil of stout cord, and placed them in one of the aliens' shoulder bags. Then she collected all the food she could find and put it in another bag. Slinging them both over her shoulder, she began the long climb out of the tree.

A couple of aliens watched as she walked up the ramp toward the giant tree's exit. She tensed, waiting for them to sound an alarm or try to stop her. They merely watched her incuriously. Juna didn't stop to question her good luck. She reached the entrance hole and climbed out. It was night, and a heavy rain was falling as she emerged into the great bowl of the crotch. It was almost totally dark.

Juna paused. Her initial, driving terror had subsided and now she could think. Once she was free of the aliens, what then? The Survey base camp was located on the coast. The flyer had been 600 kilometers north and east of the base when it went down. A sudden solar storm had blocked radio reception, making it impossible to contact base camp. After several days with no sign of abatement, they decided to try to walk out.

They had walked about ninety klicks toward the coast. The
aliens couldn't have carried her very far. She was probably
within a few kilometers of where she had collapsed.

Juna closed her eyes, remembering the photo maps of the
region. A large river lay to the north. They had crossed it in the
flyer. The streams in this area drained into it. If she followed a
stream, it would lead her to the river. She would follow the
river to the sea and then head north up the coast until she
reached the base camp. It was a long shot, but if she didn't
starve or get killed by a predator, it might work.

First, though, she had to reach solid ground. She wanted to
travel as far as she could by daylight, in case the aliens came
after her.

Juna groped her way down the tree, feeling with her hands
and feet for footholds. It was a long, terrifying climb. The
humid, velvety blackness of the night was easing toward dawn
by the time her feet touched the damp leaf litter of the forest
floor.

She stood for a long moment embracing one of the massive
buttress roots of the tree, her face resting against the bark, her
heart hammering, not quite believing she had actually made it.
She turned and groped through the dim gloom of the pre-dawn
forest, then worked her way downhill until she came to a small
stream. There she knelt and drank deeply, then bathed her face
and hands.

As Juna washed her face, she wondered what the other
members of the Survey team would make of her grotesque
transformation. Would they even recognize her as human? She
shook the excess moisture from her hands. Better to worry
about that when, and if, she ever made it back to base. She felt
her throat tighten in fear, and shook her head. She couldn't
allow herself to panic, not if she wanted to reach the coast
alive.

Dawn was beginning in earnest. Juna could see more than
vague shapes and shadows. She paused to eat and continued on.
She had to move quickly; the aliens might be following her.

Exhaustion overtook her near twilight. She ate several of the
small fruits in her satchel, and finished off the last of the dried
meat. Then she curled up between the buttresses of a tree,
covered herself with leaves, and fell asleep.

Three

JUST AFTER DAWN, Ilto woke Ani with the news that the creature was missing. Ani was relieved that the stupid, clumsy thing was gone. At least Ilto wouldn't be making himself sick working on it. When Ilto began gathering supplies to go after it, she realized that it wouldn't slip out of their lives that easily.

Ninto and Ani managed to convince Ilto to stay in the village and let them search for the new creature. They found its trail around midmorning. Its distinctive rank scent, like wet feathers on a dead bird, made it easy to track. Ani's nostrils contracted at the smell, and she exhaled sharply in disgust. Fortunately, she didn't need her nose to follow the creature. It left a visible trail of broken branches and disturbed leaf litter. It had half a day's lead on them. They would have to hurry if they wanted to catch up with it.

They paused in a morrin tree for lunch, picking several handfuls of the dark, sweet berries. Ninto found some grubs inside a rotting log. Their sharp, sour flavor tempered the berries' sweetness.

"You don't like the new animal, do you?" Ninto asked Ani as they were eating.

"It killed Kirito and it's killing Ilto," Ani said. "If Ilto dies, that will be two elders gone in two months."

"Ilto is the oldest Tendu in the village. It's time for him to make room for you. He has chosen to die instead of leaving the village. Don't blame the new creature for Ilto's choice."

Ani looked away, not wanting to see her tareena's words, but Ninto brushed her shoulder with her knuckles, and she looked back.

"Besides," continued Ninto, "I want to get to know my tareena better in the years I have before I leave the village and let Baha take my place. Perhaps when you're an elder, you'll stop worrying so much about what the other bami think, and be my friend."

Ani turned deep brown, ashamed that Ninto had noticed her shyness and embarrassment. "I'm sorry, kene," she said, using Ninto's formal title, "I meant no offense."

"It's all right, Ani," Ninto said. "It's difficult having a tareena. It hasn't been easy for me either, watching someone else fill my place with Ilto. But I like being an elder, and Ilto is very proud of you. I promised him that I would watch over you after he dies. I want to be your entoo when you become an elder. Will you let me?"

Ani turned magenta with surprise and amazement. Ninto was highly regarded by the other elders. Her offer of support and sponsorship when Ani became an elder was an unexpected honor.

"I would be honored, Ninto, but I hope—"

"That Ilto doesn't die," Ninto finished for her. "He will, Ani, and soon. He loves the village too much to leave it. He's healing himself more out of pride than because he wants to live. He'll choose the date for his funeral as soon as he's sure that the new creature will live. Now let's find the new creature and bring it back before Ilto starts looking for it himself."

After scattering the remains of their meal, they found the creature's trail. They nearly lost it at the first stream they came to, but Ani scented its rank odor on some overhanging leaves. It had headed downstream, walking along the bank and wading when the bank became too overgrown to walk on.

After following the stream for an hour, they were certain enough of the creature's trail that they began to leapfrog each other. One of them would move ahead and check for the scent, and call back to the other when it was detected. The one behind advanced two or three yai ahead and found the scent trail. This enabled them to move much more quickly. The scent grew fresher as the day progressed.

They paused at sunset for a quick meal of fruit and mealy-tasting dried pingar, then tracked the creature until Ani, still exhausted from caring for Ilto, became too tired to continue. Ninto killed two gudda pups for dinner. They finished eating, built a nest of leaves and branches in a bondra tree, and fell asleep.

Ninto woke Ani before dawn. They ate several handfuls of dried pingar, drank deeply, and set out again. Refreshed by a night's sleep and some food, they made good time. Ninto found the creature's sleeping spot. The rank scent was very fresh. They were close.

Then Ninto scented a pack of taira. The large predatory lizards were also trailing the new creature. Ninto quickened her pace, bars of pale orange anxiety flaring on her back. Ani followed. The clumsy thing didn't stand a chance against a pack of taira. Ani rather hoped that they killed it.

They heard the high-pitched yips of a taira pack on the hunt, and hurried toward the sound. The new animal was standing against a tree, bright orange with fear as it fended off several of the big lizards with a stick.

The taira were in no hurry. Half the pack lay watching as the others harried the creature. They knew they had the advantage of numbers and time.

The new creature let the end of its stick drop. Immediately, a taira charged, snarling fiercely. The new animal hit the attacking taira on the side of its head, just below its ear. The speed, force, and accuracy of the blow surprised Ani. The taira fell, and the creature hit it again. Bone crunched. The rest of the pack drew back, uncertain.

Ani looked at Ninto. "Now?" she asked.

Ninto flickered acknowledgment. The two of them turned bright red and charged from behind a tree screaming and hurling sticks, stones, rotten fruit, and anything else they could pick up off the forest floor.

The taira fled, falling over each other in their haste. Millennia of association with the Tendu had made such flight instinctive. The new creature backed between the buttresses, and stood, stick in hand, ready to defend itself.

Ani backed away and squatted so as not to threaten the creature. Ninto moved forward, grasped the tail of the wounded taira, and dragged it backward, until it was out of the new animal's range. The new creature sat down, its stick across its knees. Ani doubted that it would attack unless they tried to capture it, but it wasn't willing to let go of its only means of defense.

Ninto chittered to get Ani's attention. She was crouched over the taira, hands sticky with blood.

"It's dying, Ani. Come help me."

Ani got up slowly, and crouched beside Ninto. The taira were a part of Ninto's atwa, and she was responsible for their welfare. Ninto was trying to build up the population in the area so as to bring down the numbers of the puyu before they ate the bark off all the saplings in their territory.

"Can you save it?"

"I think so. It's strong, but it needs deep work. Will you monitor me?"

Ani looked at the new creature. It was still sitting there, its stick across its knees. Could she trust it not to attack while she was monitoring Ninto? She remembered the crack of the stick as it struck the taira. Clearly the creature was capable of killing, but it hadn't attacked her or Ilto.

Ani flickered her assent. They linked, and Ninto entered the taira. Ani monitored the balance and flow of Ninto's body. Ninto healed torn flesh, soothed swollen tissues, and knitted the cracked skull together. The taira was strong, so Ninto was able to draw on its reserves of fat and protein to help heal it.

The healing complete, Ninto and Ani withdrew. The taira was hungry and had a noticeable dent in its head, but it would survive to sire more cubs during the rainy season. They waited until it got up and trotted off into the forest, shaking its head in irritation.

The new creature was gone, but its fresh trail was easy to follow. They caught up with it around midmorning, sliding down out of the trees. The new creature stopped and turned orange with fear, holding its stick crossways, ready to defend itself. They squatted down out of range of the stick. Ani reached into her bag and pulled out a ripe tumbi that she had found while tracking. She rolled the fruit across the leaf litter to the creature. It picked it up and ate it. When it was finished, Ani and Ninto picked up their satchels and beckoned to the new creature to follow them. It sat down, refusing to move. Irritation forked like yellow lightning down Ani's spine. She beckoned again, more emphatically this time. The animal sat there, shaking its head in a gesture of refusal.

"What should I do now?" Ani asked Ninto.

"I don't know. You could sting it and carry it home, but it would be a lot of work, and it would probably run off again as soon as it got the chance."

"I can't just leave it here. Ilto wants it back."

Ninto just shrugged. "You brought it back to the village once before. Try gaining its trust. Find out what it wants and see if you can help it."

The creature picked up a small stick, and beckoned to Ani and Ninto. It cleared away the leaf litter, exposing the red clay below, and drew a stick figure.

Then it drew a second, smaller stick figure.

It pointed at the first drawing, then at itself, back and forth several times. Then it pointed at the second drawing and at the two of them.

Ani and Ninto watched, ears wide with curiosity and puzzlement. The new creature repeated the gesture over and over again.

"It's trying to say something," Ninto said.

Finally it picked up a green leaf, put it beside the second drawing, then put a brown one by the first drawing. It concentrated hard, and slowly began to turn brown. Then it pointed from itself to the drawing.

"I think I understand," Ani said, "The first drawing is itself, and the second drawing is a Tendu. See, those things on either side of the head are supposed to be ears."

"Then what's that stuff sticking out of its head?"

"When we found it, its head was covered with long fuzz, like an ika flower."

Concentrating hard, Ani copied the stick-figure Tendu on her skin, and then superimposed a picture of a Tendu over it. Then she did the same for the drawing of the new creature, superimposing an image of what it had looked like when they first found it. The image was hazy and indistinct, but the animal seemed to understand. It bobbed its head vigorously and made more guttural noises. It smoothed over the drawings in the dirt, and started another.

Ani recognized a group of Tendu and a group of new animals. Then the creature drew itself standing with the Tendu. It pointed to the drawing and then to itself, several times.

"Yes," Ani said, "I understand." She copied the picture on her own chest, superimposing a realistic image of the new creature over the stick figure inside the oval. Ani then displayed the vertical pattern of black bars of agreement on her chest. She made them very large and simple, as though she were talking to someone far away.

The animal nodded in response. It drew a line from the group of Tendu with the new creature to the other new animals.

It pointed from itself to the group of new creatures, back and forth. Ani watched, confused; then Ninto touched her on the shoulder.

"I think it wants to go back to its own kind," Ninto said.

"We can't do that," Ani replied. "We have to take it back to Ilto, and we don't know where its people are."

"After Ilto dies we can take it back. Ask it where its people are."

Ani touched the new animal on the shoulder to get its attention. She pointed at the two drawings, and nodded to show she understood. Then she turned an interrogative shade of purple and spread her ears to show she was asking a question. She pointed at the drawing of the new creatures, and then pointed in all directions. The animal watched attentively, but didn't seem to understand what she was trying to ask it. Ani picked up the stick, and drew ovals full of new creatures all around the group of Tendu. Then she stood the new creature on the drawing of the Tendu and pointed at each drawing of new creatures, flushing questioningly at each one.

The animal bobbed its head again. It smoothed the dirt with its hands, looked carefully up at the canopy, and began to draw.

Ani recognized the Tendu and the new creatures right away, but she didn't understand the rest of the drawing. She shook her head, imitating the animal's gesture to show that she didn't understand. The creature bobbed its head up and down. It walked to the stream, picked up a double handful of stones, and laid them down on the jagged lines to the left, until it had a line of small piles of stones. It uncapped its water gourd and began sprinkling water on the outside of the line to the right until a small puddle of water formed on the heavy clay soil. Then it poured a small stream of water into the forked line that ran through the middle of the picture. The water trickled slowly along the line, flowing out to join the puddle. The creature tapped the forked line with the stick, then walked over to the stream and dipped the point of its stick in the stream.

"The river!" Ani said, understanding breaking through the clouds of her confusion. "That line is the Kiewa River, Ninto. Then those lines must be the mountains, and the puddle is the ocean. Its people are on the coast near that big point of land!"

"You know, they may be at Lyanan. That's almost twenty days away from here. What is it doing so far away from its people?" Ninto wondered.

Ani rippled a pattern of purple clouds. "Who knows?"

"Well, let's try to convince it to come back with us for a while. We can't do anything until after Ilto dies. Then we'll find a way to take it back to its people."

The rain clouds were beginning to build for the afternoon downpour by the time all the explanations were finished. Out of respect for the creature's reluctance to climb, they walked back. It was a long, weary trip, and Ani was relieved when they climbed up into a fruit tree at the end of the day for dinner. Ani showed the new creature how to pick fruit while Ninto went hunting. The elder returned an hour later with a necklace of small birds hanging limply around her neck. She held them up.

"It was the best I could do," she said, browning apologetically. "Everything else was protected."

"It's a thin time of year to be out in the forest," Ani agreed. It was going to be a meager meal. Ani set about plucking the birds. To her surprise, the new creature ate only one of the birds, and that with visible distaste. It handed the rest to Ani and Ninto.

"Could it be sick?" Ani wondered.

"I don't know," Ninto replied. "I'll check it after dinner and see."

But when Ninto reached out to link with the animal, it drew back with a loud cry. It backed away, terrified and ready to flee. Ani and Ninto retreated, and after a long, tense period, the new creature relaxed and rejoined them in the nest. Even then, it kept its arms tucked tightly against its sides. It slept curled up on itself, like a baby bird in its shell. Most Tendu slept lying flat, unless they were cold.

"I could check it now," Ninto offered, her words glowing in the darkness.

"No," Ani replied. "It's frightened of allu-a. If it realized what you were doing, we could never get it to trust us again. Let it sleep."

It rained hard all day, clearing just before they arrived back at the village, footsore, weary, and hungry. Ilto greeted them happily, glad the new creature was back. He looked much better; clearly he had successfully healed himself of the alien taint in his blood. Relief flooded over Ani. Ilto wasn't going to die.

Several other elders were there, all old friends of Ilto's. He reached out to link with the new creature, eager to show off his work. It pulled away with a loud cry, shaking its head, intensely orange with fear.

"Siti, the new creature won't link," Ani explained. "I don't think we could bring it back if it ran off again."

Ilto sighed wearily. A grey cloud of sorrow passed over his skin. "Then I have only a few more matters to attend to before I die. We'll need to arrange for a funeral feast."

"Siti, please—" Ani began.

"No, don't argue with me. I'm tired. It's time for me to go. You'll be a good elder. Will you take Ninto as your entoo?"

Ani gave a faint flicker of agreement. Ninto would care for her during werrun, and sponsor her when she became an elder. It still seemed to be an impossible prospect. Even now, Ani couldn't imagine herself as an elder. She wasn't ready, didn't want to be ready.

"Good," Ilto said. "You couldn't have a better one. There is one more thing I need to ask you. Will you take the new creature as your atwa? No one else knows it as well as you do. No one else could do it."

Stunned, Ani could only manage a weak pink ripple of astonishment. She hadn't really thought about her choice of atwa. She had been too busy looking after Ilto and the new creature to think about such things. The thought of choosing an atwa upset her deeply. It was as though choosing an atwa would be agreeing to let Ilto die. She still didn't want to accept his death.

The choice of an atwa wasn't lightly made, either. Her life would revolve around it. She would spend the rest of her days looking after the plants and animals in her atwa, keeping them in harmony with the other atwa and with the rest of the forest.

She had always assumed she would become a member of the Tainka atwa. It was Ilto's, and she was the most familiar with it. The idea of taking this creature as her atwa shocked her. The thing had no place here, and she hated it for what it had done to her sitik.

"But siti, it's killing you!" Ani said. "How could I accept it as my atwa?"

A ripple of deep burgundy irony passed over Ilto. "Ani, I knew the risks, but I chose to save the creature's life. I chose to risk my life transforming it, even though I knew it was dangerous. Besides, I have healed what it did to me. My death is my choice. I don't want to leave the village, and live and die alone in the forest. I want to die here, where I have lived so long. I am a part of Narmolom. I don't want to live anywhere else."

Ani looked away, bars of negation flickering rebelliously across her skin. Ilto touched her arm, wanting to say more.

"Ani, please see what I have to say," he told her, when she looked up. "The new creature is valuable, important. It's different from any other animal I've ever seen or heard of. Who knows what important things we might learn from it? There is no one else who can do it. The elders have chosen their atwas and are busy with them. The other bami are not ready."

"Neither am I!" Ani blurted. "I'm not ready to be an elder, siti! I don't know enough!"

Ninto touched Ani's wrist. "Of course you do, Ani. You know more than I did when I first became an elder. You link as well as any elder in the village. You're ready."

"Ninto's right," Ilto added with a gruff red tinge. "You've been ready for a long time, but I've been selfish. I wanted to do something special before I died. Healing the new creature was it. I've lived long enough to know the creature will survive. Let me go, bai. I've taught you everything I can. I can't wait until someone else is ready to carry your burden."

Ani flushed deep brown with shame and looked away. "I am sorry if I have added to your burdens, siti."

"Of course not, bai. I have had much joy from you and Ninto both, more than my share should have been." He turned azure with pride. "I am pleased with you."

"You won't be alone, Ani. I'll help you as much as I can," Ninto told her.

Ani thought it over. She could either accept graciously and ease her sitik's pathway to death, or make his passing difficult and more painful with her intransigence. After he died, she would take the creature back to its people. Then she could go back to being a simple, settled village Tendu with an atwa like everyone else's.

So for reasons that had nothing at all to do with the new creature, and everything to do with her love for her sitik, she accepted the burden he laid on her. She would wonder, in years to come, how she could have given her future away so easily, but at that moment, the relief in her sitik's eyes was worth everything in the world to her.

F o u r

JUNA EASED FORWARD and watched, astonished, as the blood flowing from the lizard's wounds slowed to a trickle and its skin closed over the wound. She glanced at the aliens; they were completely entranced, their spurs stuck into the lizard, and each other. Clearly they were responsible for this almost miraculous healing. How had they done it? The researchers back at the base would be fascinated. Juna wished that she could record what was happening.

Then fear and caution overcame her amazement. She didn't want to be there when the aliens came out of their trance. She picked up her bags and stick and fled into the forest.

The aliens dropped down out of the trees in front of her a couple of hours later. Juna backed away and stood ready to defend herself with her staff. She wasn't going to let them keep her from going back to base camp. The aliens moved back also, flushing green and blue. One of them pulled some fruit from its bag, and offered it to her. Juna looked at it for a long moment, her stomach tight with hunger. She took it. She had nothing else to eat, and she was too familiar with starvation to refuse.

When Juna finished the fruit, the aliens picked up their bags and motioned to her to follow them. Juna shook her head, refusing to get up. The lizard attack had shaken her confidence, but she wasn't going to follow these aliens until she knew what they wanted with her.

The aliens conferred with each other, washes of pattern and color appearing and disappearing on their bodies. They seemed uncertain about what to do next.

Juna picked up a twig, and beckoned to the aliens. Brushing aside the leaf litter, she began to draw in the red dirt. The aliens watched curiously, ears wide, as she drew a stick figure representing herself, and another figure representing an alien.

Several hours later, after a number of drawings and much gesturing back and forth, they reached a tentative agreement. Juna wasn't sure how much of what she was trying to explain they understood. As best as she could tell, they knew she was trying to get to her people. The aliens recognized the peninsula where the base was located. They would guide her back to base camp, but they had something they needed to do back in their village first.

Juna thought it over. By now, she was fairly sure that these were the same aliens who had found her the first time. If so, they had saved her life again. These two days alone in the forest had made her realize how slim her chances were, traveling alone. A guide back to the base would greatly increase the likelihood of getting there alive. Besides, it would be best if she arrived at camp with some aliens. Despite her exhaustion and hunger, Juna smiled. The A-C specialists would be halfway to hyperspace when they found out they had a real sentient species to study.

Juna got up and, through pantomime, indicated she would follow them back to their village. When they tried to get her to travel through the canopy, Juna refused. It was a tense moment, but the aliens agreed to walk. The knot in her shoulders eased. Winning this tiny concession gave her a sense of control. Perhaps everything would work out after all.

Toward evening, the aliens stopped and built a temporary nest of branches and leaves in the crotch of a tree. Juna helped one of them gather fruit. The other one vanished into the jungle and returned with several small birds dangling around its neck on a cord.

With a glance at the alien for permission, Juna picked up one of the birds. It was small and brown, perhaps twenty centimeters long from beak to tail. There was a showy patch of green iridescence at its throat.

Juna lifted a wing with a forefinger, exposing a brilliant red underwing with a dark eyespot. It must be spectacular when courting, she thought. It wasn't a species she recognized, but then they had only catalogued a tiny fraction of the species on this planet.

The alien touched her on the shoulder, and she handed it the bird. She felt a pang of regret at not being able to catalogue the bird before it became dinner.

It was growing dark. Her guide fished out a tightly woven basket. Inside was a chunk of wood covered with glow fungus. The alien hung the glowing wood on an overhanging branch. It cast a surprisingly bright light over the nest. The aliens skinned the birds, handing three to Juna. She ate one of the scrawny, raw birds, and then filled up on fruit.

After dinner, one of the aliens grasped Juna's arm and tried to link with her.

"No!" Juna shouted, backing away and scooping up her bag. She would jump out of the tree and kill herself before she would let them violate her again. The aliens stopped. Glowing blue and green patterns washed across their skin as they beckoned her back into the nest. Juna shook her head. She held her arms out, spurs up, then shook her head, tucking her arms against her sides and flushing bright orange. She repeated the gesture several times. At last the aliens understood. They tucked their arms against their sides also, and huddled on the far side of the nest, ears fanned expectantly.

Cautiously, Juna climbed into the nest. Blue and green paisley patterns moved slowly across the aliens' bodies as she did so. One of them reached out toward her. She flinched from its touch, but the alien only brushed her shoulder with its knuckles. Juna relaxed a little after that, but kept her arms tucked tightly against her sides, and slept curled in a tight, protective ball, terrified that they would try something while she slept.

A driving tropical rainstorm woke Juna shortly before dawn. It was a long, sodden miserable hike back to the village. It rained hard most of the day. The footing was treacherous. She slipped and fell several times. In the middle of the afternoon, the rain stopped suddenly, as though it had been cut off by a switch.

They reached the village about an hour later, and went directly to the sick alien's room. The sick one seemed pleased to see them. It reached out to link with her. Juna pulled away, shaking her head. One of the aliens who had brought her back intervened. A long discussion followed. Juna watched, too tired to try to comprehend what was being said. She wanted a hot meal, a bath, and a soft, comfortable bed, in no particular order.

At last the discussion was over. Another cold meal of fruit, honey, greens, and raw meat was served. Juna looked at the cold, raw food, longing for a hot plate of couscous, or a big bowl of her father's pea soup. Still it was better than tiny bird corpses, and it beat starving. She ate, poured a couple of gourds of tepid water over herself, and burrowed into the warm, rotting mass of leaves that was her bed. She fell asleep immediately.

The next few days were agonizing. Juna endured an endless round of poking and prodding by curious aliens. They fingered her ears and manipulated her hands, holding them palm to palm against their slender four-fingered hands. Patterns flickered rapidly across their skins as they discussed her.

All of them attempted to link with her. Juna's guide stopped them, but several times Juna had to fend off the insistent aliens herself. The first day of this was interesting, the second day tedious. By the third day, Juna's patience had reached the breaking point. When an alien tried to examine her, she brushed its hands away, gently but firmly. The aliens persisted. At last, unable to take any more, Juna huddled against the wall, her hands over her ears and her head between her knees. Her skin burned bright orange, and she felt the strange lines of goose bumps rising along her back.

"Leave me alone, leave me alone!" she moaned, tears welling behind her eyelids. It reminded her of her first visit back to her mother's people, how the village children had poked and prodded at her in her foreign clothes, only this time she didn't have any relatives to shoo away the curious. She was more alone than she had ever been before.

A gentle hand brushed her shoulder. She brushed it away. When it rested on her shoulder again, Juna looked up angrily, ready to fend off another curious alien. It was her guide. She looked around. The other aliens, except for the sick one, had all left. Her guide led her to a small storeroom near the bottom of the tree. In the room was a pile of empty gourds lying with their lids askew, stacks of dried seaweed, a bundle of hollow reeds, coils of rope, neatly folded nets, empty baskets, and a big mound of dry grass. A beetle scuttled out over her feet as she stepped inside. The alien hung a mat over the door and left her alone.

Juna inspected the wall for insects. She found a section that seemed free of visible crawling creatures, leaned against it, and closed her eyes, savoring the solitude. She longed to wake up and find that this whole experience had been nothing more than an exceptionally vivid nightmare, that she was safe in her bed back at the base. Memories of home washed over her with a sudden poignant intensity. The thick milky light falling on the neat, whitewashed walls of her father's house. The wide stretch of vineyards curving up and away toward the green fields of the satellite's artificial sky. The sweet smell of hay in the barns, and the small comforting sounds of the horses in their stalls. All of these returned sharp and clear to her in this alien place, filling her eyes with fresh tears.

Juna shook her head. She needed to think of something else besides how homesick she was, or she would go crazy. To distract herself she imagined the reaction at base camp when she strode out of the jungle, accompanied by a pair of sentient aliens. Kinsey, the Alien Contact specialist, would kiss her feet in gratitude. A-C Specs were probably the most frustrated people in the Survey. They spent their entire careers as supercargo on Survey ships, doing scutwork, writing theoretical papers, and hoping that someday someone would discover an alien race.

Humans had so far discovered only three alien races. Two of those had been long extinct. The third, the Sawakirans, had fled human contact, whole cities vanishing into the wilderness. The few Sawakirans that humans contacted died a few hours later. It was not entirely clear whether the deaths were from fear,

sickness, or suicide. The Survey put the Sawakirans' planet on
the proscribed list and left them alone.

Kinsey would cut off his right arm for the chance to be
turned green and live in a bug-infested tree with a bunch of
smart frogs. All Juna wanted was to go home, take a nice hot
bath, eat food that had been cooked first, and talk to people she
could understand.

Tears of self-pity welled up. Juna shook her head, angry at
herself. Tears wouldn't change things. It was time for her to
stop acting like a frightened child and start acting like a
scientist. She had been given an incredible chance to study an
alien race. This discovery could make her career; she shouldn't
waste time being homesick.

First she needed to learn to communicate. She reviewed
everything she had learned about the aliens' language. The
patterns on their skin seemed to carry information; the colors
showed the emotional content of their words. Blues, particularly turquoise, were associated with pleasure, and greens with
approval or agreement. Reds and oranges were related to anger
and fear. Purple was connected with curiosity and questions.

She could now recognize a few very simple words: yes, no,
food, water, their term for her, and some names. "Yes" was a
series of three horizontal bars. "No" was three vertical bars.
Food was a colored dot or circle inside a green oval. Water was
a series of three vertical dots, usually blue or green. Her guide's
name-symbol looked like a connected pair of blue spirals. The
alien who had accompanied Juna's guide in the forest had a
name sign resembling a complex triangular looped knot. The
sick alien's name-symbol consisted of three sets of concentric
circles, like ripples from a raindrop falling into water. The rest
of the aliens' language was an incomprehensible blur of
colored patterns.

"How am I ever going to keep any of this straight?" she
wondered aloud to the glowing, bug-infested walls. There was
nothing permanent to write on, nothing permanent to write
with, and no way to explain what she wanted to the aliens. If
only she had her computer. Every Survey-issue computer came
with sophisticated linguistic analysis programs hard-wired in.
But her computer was lost, along with her suit and everything

else she had been carrying when she collapsed. It hadn't been much: a compass, some hard-copy maps, a knife, some rations, a canteen, a standard-issue first aid kit, and, of course, her computer.

Well, she would simply have to do the best she could. The aliens had learned a few of her gestures. Perhaps they could invent a common pidgin that would serve until she got back to base. Then the experts would take over, and she could go back to being the xenobiologist that she was trained to be.

Juna visualized the few alien symbols for which she had meanings, repeating the meanings out loud to engrave them in her mind. When she was too tired to think anymore, she curled up on the dry grass and slept.

The next morning, she went in search of her guide. She had decided to call the alien Spiral until she learned its real name. Spiral was sitting on the edge of the raised platform in the room it shared with the sick alien. It was weaving a large basket. The sick alien was buried in its bed of leaves, asleep or unconscious. A complex pattern flickered across Spiral's chest when Juna came in. The alien beckoned her closer and gestured to a broad leaf heaped with fruit, meat, and honey. Juna sat and ate, watching Spiral work. The basket it was weaving was over a meter long, and oval, like a large cocoon. The weaving was intricate, full of strange patterns. Juna wondered what it was for.

Spiral had completed several rows of basket work when the sick alien stirred and made a low, creaking noise. Spiral squatted next to its bed. Colors flickered over the aliens' skins as they conversed. Spiral brought over the basket and handed it to the alien. The sick one examined the basket, and turned deep green. It was pleased. Spiral helped the alien out of bed and over to the edge of the platform. It picked up the basket and began working on it.

Spiral picked up several woven grass shoulder bags, handed two of them to Juna, and slung the others over its shoulder. Then it led Juna out of the tree and into the canopy. The alien seemed to have grasped how frightened she was of falling. They moved slowly, Spiral helping Juna across the difficult spots, until they came to a heavily laden fruit tree. As they picked fruit, Spiral began teaching Juna to climb, guiding her foot to a more secure perch or pointing out a hand grip. The alien was a good teacher. After an hour, Juna was moving with more confidence through the tree.

Sometime around noon, rain clouds began building in the skies overhead. Spiral handed her bulging bag of fruit to Juna and left, motioning that she should stay in the tree and wait.

Juna settled herself into a comfortable, secure perch and watched life in the treetops unfold around her. Off in the distance, a bird called over the clamor of the jungle, letting out a long, mournful hoot with a rising note on the end. Back at the base, they called them pooo-eet birds, after the sound of their call. Closer by, a troop of squirrel-sized lizards glided from branch to branch. Long loose flaps of skin between their front and back legs billowed out like sails. The lizards hung from the branches by their tails, eating plump purple fruit, red juice staining their lips. As Juna watched, a baby lizard's head poked out of its mother's pouch. It nibbled at the bottom of the fruit while its mother ate the top, pausing occasionally to peer wide-eyed at the world around it.

These lizards were marsupials, like the large grazing reptiles the Survey team had found on the great central savanna on the other side of the mountains. These were the first marsupial lizards recorded in the jungle. She wondered if they followed the same reproductive pattern as the savanna reptiles. Juna's fingers flexed. If she had her computer, she could record their picture for the Survey. Nine months wasn't long enough to sample more than a tiny fraction of the species on this planet. With so little time, each new species was important.

A large black pooo-eet bird landed heavily in the tree, causing the lizards to scatter and regroup on another branch, scolding the bird with high-pitched, liquid notes. The bird pulled branches toward it with the claws on the bend of its wing, and fed greedily on the plum-sized fruit. The bird tossed a fruit into the air and caught it in its enormous red beak.

Juna laughed at the bird's antics. It eyed her suspiciously, then dropped from the branch, spread its broad, stubby wings and flew heavily off into the next tree. It preened itself, then shuffled its wings into place and began letting out mournful pooo-eet calls. This close, the bird's calls were painfully loud. Juna hefted an overripe fruit, preparing to throw it at the bird and scare it off.

The calling ended with a sudden squawk as the bird went limp and began to fall. Spiral leaped from a nearby tree and caught the bird as it fell, then grabbed a passing branch and swung up onto it. The alien pulled a long, down-tipped dart out of the bird and held it up triumphantly. Then Spiral swung back up to the tree from which it had shot the bird, and retrieved a reed blowgun about a meter long. It gave the blowgun a quick twist, and the long tube collapsed into itself, making a package about as long as Spiral's hand. The alien stuffed the bird and blowpipe into a bulging bag, and swung easily through the trees to where Juna was sitting. Then it pulled the bird and several limp lizards from its satchel, showing them to Juna. Spiral turned a brilliant blue and the symbol for food appeared on its chest.

"It's good food?" Juna asked, nodding to show that she understood.

A cool, moist gust of wind shook the treetops, and a few loose drops of rain spattered them. The alien stuffed its prey back into its satchel, and beckoned Juna to follow. There was a great crack of thunder, a brilliant flash of lightning, and then the rain began. It fell as though poured from buckets, pounding against the green canopy with a sound like falling gravel. A stiff wind made the trees sway sickeningly, sending a shower of leaves and debris to the forest floor. To Juna's immense relief, they climbed down to the ground and walked back to the village instead of crossing through the wet, storm-tossed branches of the canopy. It was a cold, weary trek. Juna was shivering when they reached the village.

Sheets of water cascaded down the inside of the village tree, splashing into the pool at the base of the trunk. Villagers filled water gourds or played, leaping about under the sudden waterfalls, splashing and calling to each other.

Ripple, as Juna had decided to call the sick alien, was seated at the door to their room, watching the other villagers enjoy the rain. Much to Juna's relief, the sick one's room was dry and warm. She sat in a miserable shivering huddle, longing for dry clothes and the warmth of a fire. Ripple came up to her, purple with curiosity. The alien felt her skin, then beckoned her to one of the piles of leaves that served as beds. Scooping a hollow in the pile, it gestured that she should lie down. When she did so, Ripple heaped leaves around her. The mound of damp leaves, heated by its own decay, was more warm and comforting than Juna would have believed possible, though she still would have preferred a nice hot fire. She remembered her mother's village, sitting in a circle of aunts, grandmothers, and cousins around an open hearth, warmed by good food, the tight web of kinship, and the fire itself. Her shivering stopped, and comforted by that distant memory of belonging, she fell into a light doze.

A touch on her shoulder awakened Juna. It was Spiral. Ripple and several other aliens sat on the edge of the raised ledge. Mounds of meat, fruit, greens, and honeycomb were laid out on leaves. They were waiting for her to join them. Juna got up, picking bits of decayed leaves off her damp skin. Spiral handed her a water gourd, and she washed herself off before sitting down to eat.

There was enough food for fifteen people or more, instead of the six or seven aliens in attendance. Meat from Spiral's recent kill as well as several other kinds of meat, some familiar and some new, had been neatly sliced and arranged in patterns on a large polished shell platter. Three large baskets heaped with fruit, and another leaf piled with dripping honeycomb were set out with the meat. Sheets of leathery-looking dried seaweed, smelling of salt and iodine, two baskets heaped with mixed greens, and a large gourd bowl filled with a starchy brown mush completed the feast.

The sick alien picked up a sheet of the dried seaweed. Reaching into the bowl of mush, it scooped up a gobbet of it and put it on the seaweed, folding it into a neat package. Ripple passed the completed packets to the guests. The guests waited until everyone had one, then began eating.

Juna bit into her package of mush. It was sour and faintly bready, like her mother's injera, but there was also a sharp cheddar cheese taste, with a hint of iodine and a salty tang like soy sauce. It would, she thought with a sudden surge of homesickness, go well with her father's Burgundy. She closed her eyes, feeling tears prickle as she remembered her home, with its neat rows of vines filing off into the distance. Would she ever see it again?

She opened her eyes. The aliens were looking at her, purple with curiosity. She blinked back tears and took another bite, concentrating only on the taste. It was delicious. She flushed turquoise, and nodded to show the aliens how good she thought it was. They relaxed, and began talking among themselves, handing her other foods to try.

Juna finished first. She was full, but the aliens kept pushing more food on her. They continued to gorge until their flat bellies bulged. Instead of water, they washed their food down with large gourds of sweet fruit juice. They chewed on great chunks of honeycomb, spitting out the chewed and sucked comb. Brilliantly colored bees settled on the chewed combs and began eating the wax.

At last the aliens were full. They leaned back, stroking their distended bellies, letting out a chorus of loud rumbling belches that sounded almost human. Juna laughed. The aliens looked at her, ears raised in curiosity.

Embarrassed, Juna blushed brown. Blue and green ripples burst across the aliens' skin and they belched again. Juna's embarrassment deepened, and there were more ripples from the aliens. Spiral touched her arm, and turned a dark blue. A pattern rippled across Spiral's chest. The other aliens' ripples died away. One by one, they touched Juna's arm, in apparent apology. Juna nodded at Spiral, and then belched. The aliens rippled again, and Juna laughed with them.

After that, the aliens relaxed, flashing symbols among themselves and occasionally to her, though she couldn't understand them. She decided to try communicating with them in their own language. Picking up one of the large leaves that they had used as dinner plates, she reached up and rubbed her finger across the ceiling to pick up some of the glowing blue fungus on her finger. Then she smeared three lines of the glowing blue substance across the leaf. The seated aliens watched her as she touched Spiral on the arm. Holding the leaf so that the lines were horizontal, she nodded, then turned the leaf so that the lines were vertical, and shook her head. She repeated this several times, then Spiral nodded, and flashed an explanation to the other aliens. Their ears went up, and they looked at her, deeply purple. They began talking among themselves in shades of pink and purple.

Juna watched and waited. She had created a stir among the aliens. One of them flushed purple and held out a fruit, its ears raised inquisitively. Juna turned her leaf so that the lines were vertical and shook her head, refusing the fruit. A blue and green ripple of amusement passed across the aliens.

Another alien offered her a gourd of water. She turned the leaf so that the lines were horizontal, and drank a few sips. She offered the gourd to another alien. The horizontal bars of agreement appeared on its chest. She handed it the gourd. The alien took the gourd from her and drank.

Her attempts at communication became a game. The aliens offered her things, and she would accept or refuse them. Juna learned the symbols for several kinds of food, the symbol for basket, and what was probably a verb for *show* or *offer*, or perhaps *try*. She wrote approximations of these symbols on leaves with the glowing blue fungus, much to the amusement of the aliens.

Then a complex pattern appeared on Ripple's chest, and the alien held out its wrists, bright red spurs pointing upward. Juna panicked for a moment, thinking that it was asking her to join spurs, but it ignored her, looking instead at the other aliens. It was asking something of them. The aliens turned a soft, misty grey. One by one horizontal bars flickered across their chests as they agreed.

Spiral touched Juna lightly on the shoulder, and pointed to Juna's bed of leaves. It indicated that she should lie down and sleep. Then it left her and joined the other aliens. The game was over; she had been dismissed. Juna watched as the aliens linked arms in a large circle, and abandoned themselves to their strange communion. It reminded her of the two aliens healing the lizard in the forest, only there was a ritual solemnity to it.

Juna yawned. The huge meal on top of a long, stressful day had made her sleepy. She burrowed deeper into the warm, moist pile of leaves and slid down into sleep.

The next morning Spiral nudged Juna awake, beckoning for

her to follow. Juna followed the alien down the inside of the trunk to the pool at the tree's base. Spiral dove in. Juna, eager to rid her skin of the rotting leaves from her bed, plunged in too. The tepid water felt wonderful. Curious, she dove for the bottom. The pool was surprisingly deep, at least three and a half or four meters. The bottom was soft mud. Something wriggled under her questing fingers. Startled, Juna shot toward the surface, emerging with a splash that drew curious stares from the aliens seated around the pool. She swam to the edge of the pool and sat on a low ledge.

Spiral emerged a few moments later, carrying a fat, wriggling burden. Juna thought it was a fish. When Spiral handed it to her she realized that it was an enormous tadpole. It was the size of a large house cat, mud-brown, with an oily, iridescent sheen. Its tail was horizontally flattened like a dolphin's and its eyes were large and golden, with vertical catlike irises. The hind legs were strong and well-developed. Beneath the translucent skin, the small dark lump of its heart pulsed slowly and steadily behind its gills. It was soft, slippery, and cool, like the mud at the bottom of a lake.

Juna wondered what species it was, and how closely related it was to the aliens. She wished again for her computer, so that she could catalogue the tadpole. So much knowledge was slipping through her fingers without it.

The tadpole wriggled wildly, slipped out of her grasp, and fell back into the pool with a soft plop. Spiral shot after it, caught it with both hands, and stuck a wrist spur into it. It ceased wriggling and lay motionless. Spiral handed it to Juna, and dove into the depths of the pool.

A small, dark green alien climbed down to the edge of the pool, carrying a bulging satchel. Juna watched curiously. There were at least a couple dozen of these smaller aliens in the village. They were darker in color and lacked the red stripes that ran along the back of the others. Juna had never seen them change color. The larger aliens ignored them. They moved quietly in the background, cleaning up, helping prepare meals, and carrying things. They puzzled Juna. If they were juveniles, where were their parents? If they weren't juveniles, what were they? A related, less intelligent species? A neuter form, like worker bees?

The small alien pulled handfuls of food scraps out of its satchel, tossing them into the pool. The calm surface churned and boiled as hungry tadpoles gobbled the food scraps. They devoured it all—meat, fruit, vegetables, even the huge, tough leaves that the aliens used as plates. Juna opened the mouth of the limp tadpole in her lap, revealing sharp, predatory-looking teeth in front, and flat, powerful molars in back. They certainly had the dental equipment to eat almost anything.

There was a sudden surge in the water as Spiral caught a feeding tadpole. The alien stung it with a wrist spur and flung it toward Juna. Spiral watched her until she had hold of it, then dove again, emerging with another tadpole in its grasp. It caught nearly a dozen tadpoles, then climbed out and began butchering them with a wooden knife. The alien flung the offal into the pool, where it was eaten as soon as it hit the water. Juna was shocked that the aliens would eat tadpoles, then reminded herself that some humans ate monkey meat. The tadpoles must be some sort of related species. Perhaps the worker species was trading some of its young for the protection afforded by the aliens. She shook her head; it was a nice theory, but it didn't feel right to her. Clearly she was missing some important piece of the puzzle.

When the tadpoles were reduced to bite-sized pieces, the alien wrapped the meat in a large green leaf and carried it back to their room. Then they went out into the canopy. Juna spent the morning gathering fruit, while Spiral hunted. They returned with heavy, bulging bags full of game and fruit.

Back in the room, preparations were under way for a feast of epic proportions. There were large leaf-lined baskets full of meat and fruit, and leafy platters piled high with honeycombs. Even Ripple was busy helping out. Its color looked better today, and it no longer seemed as weak. Perhaps the circle last night had something to do with it. Could the other aliens have been healing it? Were they celebrating the alien's recovery?

Juna was set to work helping the dark green workers fill baskets with food and carry them up to the top of the tree, where some of the elders oversaw the food's arrangement.

There was an air of subdued excitement, and much bustling about as they chittered loudly and flickered to each other.

Juna was sitting in the crotch of the tree arranging a platter of food, when she heard a scream. She looked up. In the next tree, the largest snake she had ever seen was coiled around a worker. The alien's legs quivered and gave an occasional reflexive twitch, but already its head had disappeared inside the serpent's huge maw. The worker's skin turned silvery white as Juna watched. The other workers had scattered. They huddled in frightened groups, watching the snake consume its prey. Several of the larger aliens glanced up and then continued with what they were doing.

Juna clung to the branch, watching the worker disappear down the throat of the snake. She couldn't believe what she was seeing. The death of this alien apparently meant no more than the death of a mouse or a bird to the rest of the village. Juna looked away as the snake, with the feet of its prey still protruding from its mouth, slithered off. Juna left the half-finished platter for someone else to arrange, and walked to the end of a branch. She was sickened by what she had seen.

She stared off into the jungle. Why had none of the others tried to save the alien? Clearly they couldn't be juvenile forms of the aliens; she couldn't imagine any intelligent species allowing its children to die without lifting a hand to save them. The aliens seemed to regard the workers as expendable. So much for her protection theory. So what was really going on here? She looked at the now-empty branch where the snake had been, and shuddered. It had been a horrible death, made more horrible by the fact that no one had lifted a hand to help the little alien.

A great, hollow booming resonated throughout the tree, interrupting Juna's thoughts. The feast was about to start. Looking down, she saw several aliens pounding hard on the huge buttresses of the tree with large sticks. Clouds of bees streamed out of the tree like iridescent smoke.

After the bees dispersed, a group of aliens climbed out of the tree's great hollow. They wore garlands of flowers or necklaces of shells, teeth, or fish scales. Some even wore necklaces made from the strung-together corpses of tiny dried birds. Others carried sprays of branches. Juna found herself wondering if there was any way she could trade for some of the necklaces, especially the one with the dried birds. It would be a treasure trove of specimens.

The aliens moved with slow solemnity, seating themselves in a large circle around the tree crotch. Then another group of slightly smaller aliens followed them out of the hollow tree, their bodies plain and undecorated. Each one sat behind and slightly to the left of the decorated aliens.

Finally, Spiral and Ripple came out of the tree, seating themselves in the gap made by the others, in a slightly higher and more visible spot. The other villagers turned to look at them as they arrived. The huge, unfinished basket was set before Ripple. Clearly, he was the guest of honor. Spiral beckoned Juna over to sit with them.

If this was a celebration of Ripple's recovery, it must be an important event. The entire village was present, almost eighty adults, with a dozen or so workers busy serving them. Brilliant patterns flickered over the aliens' skins—blues, greens, and softer pastels occasionally muted with grey.

Something strange was going on. Ripple wasn't eating. Spiral seemed withdrawn and remote, picking at its food, despite Ripple's obvious enjoinders to eat. Though they were guests of honor, neither of them seemed very happy.

After the aliens were sated and the workers had cleared away the remains of the feast, Ripple rose and addressed the assembled villagers. The brilliant, flowing patterns were extremely lovely, even though Juna couldn't understand any of it.

When Ripple finished speaking, each of the decorated aliens stood up and addressed the gathering, then came forward and laid its decorations in the large basket in front of Ripple. Halfway through the speeches a soft rain began falling. The aliens ignored the rain and went on speaking.

The speeches went on for most of the afternoon. Juna sat there, warm rain drumming on her naked skin, bored out of her skull by the endless, incomprehensible ceremony.

At last every decorated alien had spoken. Ripple rose again, beckoning Spiral to its side. Another speech ensued as Juna sat shivering in the rain. Then Juna was summoned forward and displayed to the assembled audience. When the speech was over, Ripple walked out onto a high branch and jumped off. Juna heard a distant, wet thud as the alien's body struck the forest floor far below.

Numbed by hours of boredom, Juna stared at the spot where Ripple had stood, unable to believe what she'd just witnessed. She peered down at the distant forest floor. Ripple's mangled body lay there, a bright splash of red beneath it, its limbs twisted, its head at an impossible angle. Swallowing hard, Juna looked away. Spiral sat hunched and grey beside her. The other aliens sat, watching Spiral expectantly, ignoring Ripple's fallen body.

After several minutes, Spiral rose and addressed the assembly in somber tones of grey and black. When Spiral was done, the enormous unfinished basket full of decorations was set in a sling and lowered to the ground. The villagers and Juna climbed down and stood around the corpse and the basket. They watched as Spiral cut open the dead alien's stomach and placed a dark brown, fist-sized lump inside it. Then Spiral gently placed the mangled corpse in the basket, on top of the decorations. The alien covered the corpse with fern leaves, and methodically wove the basket shut.

The other villagers had known that Ripple was going to die. The whole ceremony had been in honor of Ripple's suicide. Juna sat down heavily on a tree root. First the death of the worker, and now this. She felt suddenly very alone as she realized how deep the gulf between her and the aliens was. Juna felt a sudden, fierce longing for the safe familiarity of home.

Five

Ani FINISHED WEAVING the basketwork coffin shut and stood up. Four villagers slung the coffin between two stout poles and began carrying it away. Ani followed behind the casket, and the rest of the village fell into procession behind her, walking through the forest to the site where Ilto would be planted. The villagers set the coffin down near the hole that had already been dug to receive his corpse.

Beside the hole lay a huge pile of leaves, branches, and rich black humus. She watched as the other bami lined the bottom and sides of the grave with the leaves and compost, then laid the coffin in the trench. Once the coffin was settled in place, the villagers defecated on it, leaving a last bit of fertilizer to help the sapling that would contain Ilto's spirit. Then they covered the coffin with more humus and rotting leaves, piling branches on top of the low mound to anchor it in place.

Ani stood numbly by as the others piled branches over the grave. The coffin was beautiful, woven tightly and well by hands that had known him. Ilto himself had worked on it. At the farewell banquet, Ani had sat quietly through the memorial speeches and the presentation of the death gifts. She made the required speeches, and gave the required gifts. She planted the na seed in Ilto's stomach. All of it was done properly; none of it comforted her.

There was an empty place inside her now that nothing could fill. Next year a pale green na seedling would reach toward the canopy from Ilto's grave, holding his spirit inside it. Someday the tree would shelter her narey, and those of her bami, in its cavity. In seven or eight generations, it might shelter the entire village. Thinking about that was supposed to comfort a bereaved bami. It didn't. Ilto was dead. Ani would never feel his presence or see his words again. The future stretched before her, grey and empty. A seedling na tree was nothing beside that.

Someone touched her shoulder. Ani looked up. It was the new creature. Unable to contain her anger at it any longer, Ani flushed red and hissed at it. The new creature backed away and Ani slipped back into numbness. Then Ninto was at her side, reminding her that the rest of the village waited for her to pile the last few branches on Ilto's grave, bringing the funeral to an end. Automatically, she completed the ritual. Ninto led her away from the grave, and escorted her back home. She followed, lost in her grief.

When they arrived at the village, Ninto led her back to her room. A third bed was laid on the platform.

"You should stay with me until you are through werrun," Ninto told her.

"Thank you, Ninto," she flickered, grateful that she would not have to face the empty room where she and Ilto had lived for so many years.

"Go rest," Ninto said. "Tonight you will begin werrun."

"So soon?" Ani asked, surprised by how quickly things were happening.

"The village will be in ming-a until the empty place among the elders is filled," Ninto said, "It's best not to wait too long to bring things back into balance. Now get some sleep."

Ninto ordered her to bed as though she were a very young bami. It reminded her of her first days with Ilto. The memory sent fresh arrows of grief through her. Ani burrowed into the fresh bed of leaves. She wanted to go to sleep and wake up and find that Ilto was still alive and that the new creature had never arrived. Ninto squatted beside her and grasped her arm.

"Do you want me to help you go to sleep?"

Ani ached to feel nothing for a while.

"Yes."

There was a faint prick as Ninto made the link, then sleep blotted out the world. It seemed only moments later when Ninto shook her gently awake.

"Ani, it's time," Ninto said as she sat up. Ninto helped her up, and escorted her to a waiting group of bami. They led her to a quiet pool in a nearby stream, and bathed her. Ani remembered bathing Kirito's bami only a month before, when he underwent werrun. They had laughed and splashed, and been full of joy for Kiha, who had sat gravely during their celebrations. Ani had joked about mating with Kiha when she became an elder, and they had laughed. Kiha was the elder Kihato now. He had become stiff and formal after werrun and their friendship had faded. Now it was Ani's turn. She sat there like a stone, unable to share in her friends' joy at her upcoming transformation. The openness of her grief shamed her, but each moment that passed took her farther from the happiness she had known as a bami, and moved her toward a difficult and lonely future.

Her friends saw her grief, and it puzzled them.

"You've been a bami longer than any of us; there are elders who became bami after you did. Aren't you ready to become an elder?" her friend Kalla asked.

"I still miss him," Ani said. She was being rude, speaking of the dead, but now that Ilto was gone, she felt as though a part of her were missing.

The other bami's laughter subsided, and they each linked with her briefly, tasting her sadness, and sharing their fondness for her.

"I'll miss you all," Ani said when the link was broken.

"You make it sound as though you were dying," Baha said.

"No, but I've seen other bami go through werrun. They change. When I'm an elder I'll be busy running things. Things will be different between us."

"We'll catch up to you in a few years," Kalla said in reassuring tones. "Someday we'll all be elders together. It won't be long. You'll see."

"And then you'll all be vying for my favors in the mating pool," Baha said, preening shamelessly.

Kalla splashed him, and soon the quiet pool resounded with a huge water fight, with Ani caught in the middle, watching the others' skin ripple with vivid laughter.

At last, tired and panting, the bami emerged from the pool. Kalla draped a necklace of dried bakim around Ani's neck, their iridescent blue wing cases gleaming in the dusk. One by one, the other bami came forward to adorn her, until she was covered from ears to hips in brilliant necklaces made of flowers, seeds, shells, small birds, and insects. Safely hidden by the muffling decorations, Ani repeated Ilto's name over and over again.

When they were finished decorating Ani, the bami led her gravely and ceremoniously back to Ninto, who waited with the other elders.

The elders led her back to the tree, descended to the bottom, and formed a circle around the rim of the tree's reservoir. The brief joy that Ani felt during the water fight had dissipated. She felt as numb and lifeless as a rock. The long ritual, with its rhythmic calling, dancing, and celebrations, flowed over her like water over a stone. She performed the required actions, and said the things that needed to be said, automatically. None of it touched her. It was as though she were watching the ritual happen to some other bami.

At last, Ninto came forward, arms outstretched for allu-a. Ani came forward and linked with her. Now the real transformation would take place. She felt Ninto's presence inside her, moving through her, coaxing forth the hormones that would bring her into full adulthood.

She would not feel the effect for several hours. Then she would sink into a deep coma for a couple of days, and awaken as an elder. Ninto led her up the tree to her room. A huge meal was laid out. Ani picked at it. She would need the energy during werrun, but her stomach was filled with grief. She couldn't eat, and she was getting sleepy. It would be good to sleep. The oblivion of sleep seemed like a release. The thought of living without Ilto was too painful to bear. She wanted to fall asleep and never wake up.

Ani hardly noticed when Ninto eased her onto the bed. She

fell asleep as quickly and easily as a stone sinks into a deep pool.

Strange visions troubled her sleep. She tracked Ilto through the forest, following his scent through the trees, and over the ground. She searched for what seemed like days. Her body ached in odd places. She was cold, tired, and hungry.

At last she came to a wide beach. Ilto's footprints stretched before her in the sand. They led to the ocean. His footprints marked the water where he had walked, stretching out to the horizon. She wanted to follow, but the water would not bear her weight. She would have to swim after him, but the water was unimaginably cold. It swirled over her ankles. The cold made her heavy and stupid. She would have to hurry before she became unable to continue. She took a step into the frigid ocean. A wave swirled up to her knees and then slipped back down the beach again. It pulled at her legs, drawing her into the ocean.

She felt a sudden warmth, as if the sun were shining on her back. She sensed a presence somewhere behind her. It felt like Ilto's. She turned around, looking for him, wondering how he could be so close when his footprints stretched out to the horizon. She stepped from the icy-cold sea. Where was he? If she closed her eyes, she felt as though she could reach out and touch him. She took another step up the beach, chittering a loud, urgent summons, flashing Ilto's name sign over and over again. She found nothing, only the presence near her, inside her, like allu-a. She ran up the beach to the forest's edge, then turned and looked behind her. Ilto's footprints were gone. The ocean was smooth again, and the only footprints on the beach were her own.

She cried out again, squalling like a frightened tinka. Ilto was gone. He was dead. She was alone. The realization terrified her. Without Ilto, she was nothing.

A hand brushed her shoulder. She looked up. It was Ninto. She recognized the presence in her dream now. It hadn't been Ilto; it was Ninto. Her presence felt like Ilto's.

Ninto reached out to her, beckoning. Ani glanced back at the ocean one last time, then reached out and took Ninto's hand and followed her into the forest. There was a nest in one of the trees. Ani laid down beside Ninto and fell into a deep, peaceful sleep.

Ani's eyes opened. Ninto was sitting beside her bed. Baha and the new creature were with her. Ani took a deep breath, smelling the rank odor of sickness. Ilto must be sick again, she thought, and she tried to get up to go to him. But she was too weak. She realized that what she smelled was her own sickness, and remembered—Ilto was dead; she was an elder now.

Ninto flushed a pure, brilliant pale blue. "Welcome back, Anito. You survived werrun. For a while we thought you were going to follow Ilto."

Hearing an elder's suffix attached to her name startled Ani. She tried again to sit up, and failed. She was weaker than a newly hatched lizard pup. Ninto and the new creature moved to help her, with an ease that spoke of familiarity. She looked down. Her skin was stretched tightly over her ribs.

"How long have I been asleep?"

"Eight days. You nearly died." Ninto rubbed her cheek ruefully. "I should have waited. You hadn't eaten enough, and I didn't realize how deeply you felt your sitik's death. You didn't want to live. I had to go in and bring you back."

"I saw it," Ani said. "I was following Ilto and you brought me back. I'm an elder now." She tried to stand, and Ninto pushed her back down.

"No, Anito, you're too weak. Drink first, and eat." Ninto turned to the new creature. "Bring food and water," she said in large, plain words.

The new form of her name struck her like a blow. She couldn't accept the fact that she was an elder. She still thought of herself as Ani.

The new creature got up and brought over a leaf cone full of mushed kayu, and a large gourd of water. Washes of blue and black and green flickered over its skin as it handed the water to her.

Ani took the gourd and drank deeply. She was extremely thirsty. There was very little left for her to wash with, but she poured it over her head anyway, washing away a little of the rank smell of sickness. She handed the gourd back to the new creature, thanking it as though it could understand. To her surprise, the creature responded with a garbled wash of colors.

Ani gestured at the creature. "Why does it keep changing colors like that?" she asked Ninto.

"It's trying to talk. It's very intelligent, you know. All the time you were sick, it watched over you. It copied what I was doing, and I let it take over since it was so capable. It bathed you and changed your bedding when it got foul. It even warmed you with its body heat while I was linked with you. It helped save your life."

Ani looked at the new creature, and it offered her the leaf cone full of mush. Ani took it with a nod, and began to eat. She felt vaguely embarrassed by the new animal's help. It was her atwa now. She should be taking care of it, not the other way around. She flickered her thanks, and the creature flushed blue with pleasure, and then began that incoherent flickering again.

"It understands!" Ani said.

"It knows a lot of words," Ninto said. "It was a game we played while you were sick. I'd make pictures on my skin and then show it the pattern. Then I'd tell the creature to bring me whatever it was that I asked for. It learns quickly. Now eat. You need your strength."

The sweet mush was nutritious and easy to digest. Ani could feel energy coursing through her blood before she finished it. The new creature supported her while she relieved herself into a wide round gourd. Her wastes were thick and strong-smelling, full of sickbed poisons. The new creature covered the gourd with a lid and set it aside. Then it brought over a huge, brimming gourd full of fresh water, and held Ani upright while Ninto and Baha sluiced water over her.

Even the mild exertion of standing left Ani shaking and light-headed with fatigue. The new creature picked her up as easily as though she were a basket of feathers, carried her to a freshly made bed of leaves, laid her on it, and piled the leaves over her. The new creature's strength startled her. It was easy to forget how strong it was.

"Sleep, Anito," Ninto said. "You're through the worst of it, but it will take several days for you to recover." She shook her head. "I've never seen anyone have such a hard time during werrun."

My name is Anito, I am an elder now, she thought, but she was too tired to speak. Anito closed her eyes and fell into a deep, profound sleep.

The next few days were a round of sleep, food, and water. Always when she awoke, the new creature was waiting by the bed. Once, Anito woke in the middle of the night to find the creature asleep on the floor beside her. The new animal's patient concern puzzled Anito. There was no reason for it to do this. Anito had treated the creature with disdain and active hostility before she had undergone werrun.

Anito was now indebted to the creature. It was an obligation that she hated. As soon as she was able to travel, she would take the creature back to its own people. Then she would have discharged her obligation to the new creature, and be able to return to the village and choose another atwa.

S i x

Juna HEARD A rustle at the door, and looked up. Knot came in, followed by its apprentice, whom Juna referred to as Bird, because its name sign resembled a bird. Their gathering bags bulged with fruit, greens, and meat. They unloaded their bags and sat beside Spiral's bed.

Knot examined Spiral, running a hand over its torso, gently pinching a fold of skin. Juna leaned forward, eagerly watching for some sign of recovery. Then the alien linked with Spiral. It broke out of the link, ochre in color, and motioned to its apprentice. They talked for a few moments. Then Knot motioned to Juna to lie next to Spiral in bed. Spiral's skin felt icy cold. Juna curled around the alien's body, warming it. Knot piled the warm, moist leaves over them, and then linked with its apprentice and Spiral.

It was a long link; Spiral twitched several times, moving its head as though questing for something in its sleep. It chittered, and then lay still for a few moments, breathing heavily, then let out a long, low moan, and lay still, its breathing quiet and calm. Knot and its apprentice unlinked.

"Food," Knot said, in response to Juna's attempts to ask how Spiral was. "Need food. Talk later."

Juna helped Bird prepare and serve the food. The two aliens

ate a huge meal. As they were finishing up, a rustling came from Spiral's bed.

Spiral's eyes slid open. Juna leaned forward, her heart leaping with sudden hope. Spiral tried to sit up. Juna slid an arm around the alien's shoulders and helped it sit; then Knot sent Juna for food and water.

Juna brought a gourd of water and a rolled leaf full of mush. She wanted to let Spiral know that she was glad it was awake, but her skin produced only meaningless blotches of color. Spiral drank and washed, then handed the gourd back to Juna, thanking her. Juna tried to reply and failed. Spiral lifted its ears and drew back its head in surprise.

Spiral turned and said something to Knot. Juna recognized the name sign they had given her, but the rest was incomprehensible. Knot replied. Spiral lifted its ears even higher, turning a deep, surprised purple. It gave Juna a long, considering look. She offered Spiral the leaf cone full of mush. It took the cone from her and ate greedily.

When Spiral finished the mush, Juna helped the alien relieve itself, and bathe. Then she picked Spiral up and carried it over to a fresh pile of leaves. The alien was as light as a small child, despite the fact that it was only a few inches shorter than Juna. She remembered how light her mother's body had been after she had died from malnutrition and cholera. She had looked like a bundle of sticks held together by skin. For a moment, Juna was angry at the alien for living when so many people she cared about had died.

The alien recovered rapidly. Three days after Spiral awoke, the alien told her that they would leave in another couple of days, and took her down to the storerooms to collect the supplies needed for the trip. Juna was busy filling gathering bags with packets of dried food when Spiral pulled the helmet from Juna's suit out from under a pile of gourds. Juna stared at it in disbelief for a few seconds. She had thought it was rotting in the jungle where she had collapsed.

She turned to Spiral, and flushed a deep purple. She pointed at the helmet, then gestured to the rest of the storeroom. Spiral watched her, head cocked, ears spread wide. Finally it flickered understanding, and tossed aside more dried grass. Underneath was Juna's suit. She lifted it up and examined it. It was beyond repair, sliced to ribbons and covered with mold, but it reminded her of all she had left behind. Tears welled up. Juna dropped the suit, then knuckled away the tears before they could spill down her face. The salt in her tears stung her fingers, and she put them in her mouth. The minor annoyance served as a poignant reminder of how alien her body had become.

Spiral held out Oliver's helmet and suit. Juna picked them up, remembering Oliver's collapse, his breath wheezing in and out of his lungs. What had happened to him? Could he still be alive?

Juna pointed from her suit to Oliver's, turning a deep, questioning purple. The alien watched her, and shook its head. On its chest two figures in suits appeared. They were lying on the ground. Green aliens appeared; the suits faded away. One of the figures was pink, the other brown. Spiral pointed from Oliver's suit to the pink figure on its own chest. As Juna watched, the pink figure turned pale silver, the color of death. The aliens carried the brown figure away, leaving Oliver behind. Spiral pointed to Oliver's suit and shook its head again.

Oliver was dead, Juna realized. Oliver had been the tough one, the survival expert, but she had outlived him. He had been so patient with her, always giving her a word of encouragement when things were tough. She remembered his compassion when the botanist Hiro, their final surviving crewmate, had died. Oliver had held him, talking gently, soothingly, as Hiro's breathing grew more and more labored. Then, after they had laid Hiro out and covered his dead body with leaves, he had held her, letting her cry out her grief and fear. Remembering, Juna was unable to stop the stinging tears of grief and loneliness.

A cool hand brushed her shoulder and she looked up. It was Spiral, ochre with concern.

Juna felt suddenly angry. She didn't want the alien's concern. She wanted to be home again and safe. It didn't understand; it couldn't understand her. It was an alien.

Then she remembered how Spiral had hissed at her during the funeral, when she had tried to offer sympathy to it. She smiled. Neither of them understood the other. At least they had that in common. She clasped the alien's hand.

"Thank you," Juna said aloud. She tried to make her skin express her thanks, but produced only garbled waves of color.

The alien flushed dark green. It picked up Oliver's suit, folded it, and held it out to her. She smiled and took it. She would take the suit back with her, so that the Survey could give it to his family.

Spiral rummaged through a pile of nets. It pulled out her pack and Oliver's. Juna opened them, taking out ordinary human artifacts, which were priceless treasures now. There were maps, her multipurpose knife, a first aid kit, a radio, sealed packages of rations, extra clothes, a canteen, a tent. Down at the bottom, folded into a compact oval, was her computer.

Juna turned on the radio. There was nothing, not even static. She opened the case with the screwdriver on her knife.

"*Färrädäbenge!*" she muttered in Amharic, when she had pried the case open. The radio was packed with fluffy black mold, the chips blackened and useless. She tried Oliver's radio, but it didn't work either. Spiral picked up the useless radio and examined it, ears wide with curiosity. Juna frowned; allowing the alien to examine the radio was a breach of Contact Protocols, but she could see no tactful way of stopping it.

Juna unfolded the computer. It came alive with a polite chime as she activated it. Relief flared on her skin. At last she could record her observations. The computer would be a powerful tool to help her unravel the aliens' language. Spiral's ears lifted and it flushed pink in surprise. Juna smiled, then frowned as she realized a working radio would be more useful than a working computer. The Survey had tried for years to incorporate a radio into the nanocomps, but they needed too much power, especially on a planet like this, where radio reception was problematical at best. Even if the radio had worked, she probably couldn't have reached the base. At least she had her computer.

Juna brightened the screen and peered at the familiar menu of configuration options, a status report on the computer's condition, and the time and date.

"Perkele!" Juna muttered in Finnish as she saw the date on the computer screen. It was much later than she had thought. She checked the activity file, fighting back a wave of fear. The clock had not been reset since she had first arrived on board ship. In desperation she scrabbled through Oliver's pack, and checked the date on his computer.

The clocks were running within a second of each other. The survey flyer had crashed in the jungle sixty-four days ago. Base camp would be dismantled in a week's time. In another three days, the mother ship would leave orbit. If she didn't hurry, she would be marooned here forever.

Seven

ANITO PAUSED TO catch her breath. They had been traveling for five days now. Ninto had been right. She should have waited a few more days before leaving. Her body was still changing, drawing on her scant energy reserves. Even the creature's cautious pace exhausted her. Her body ached all over. She wanted to hide somewhere and sleep for a week.

During the allu-a Ilto did with the new creature on its first night in the village, he had dampened its panic response, and improved its reflexes. It no longer froze in terror when it looked down, but it was still learning to trust its new reflexes. Driven by the sudden urgency that blossomed when the creature found that noisy dead-but-alive box, it learned quickly. Every day it traveled faster, moved with more confidence. Unfortunately, the new creature was learning faster than Anito was healing.

Anito's tired body protested as she leaped to the next tree, where the creature was waiting for her. Slanting bars of golden light pierced the canopy. It was getting late. Anito could smell the rich sour scent of a nearby tree full of ripe geramben. She was intensely hungry. If they stopped here for the night they would eat well with relatively little effort. Tomorrow morning they could gather supplies for the next few days of the trip. It would give her a chance to rest and recover her strength.

Anito put a hand on the creature's shoulder, communicating by gesture and skin speech that they would stop here. She led it to the geramben tree, showed it how to recognize which fruit were ripe, and left the new creature to gather fruit while she hunted. Hanging her bag of gear on one of the branches, she took with her a gathering bag and her blowgun and darts.

The hunting was good. Here in the wild spaces between village territories there were no restrictions on what she could kill. She soon bagged two fat ooloo and was stalking a garban when she smelled the other Tendu. He was male, and had passed this way very recently. She shot at the garban and missed, then began tracking the Tendu, following his scent through several trees. She heard a rustling behind her and then something brushed her shoulder. Startled, Anito leaped up to another branch before looking back. It was the Tendu she had been tracking. He was taller than any Tendu she had ever seen. Judging from his height and the length of his muzzle, he must be extremely old. Ripples of laughter coursed across his body.

"I am Ukatonen," he told her. "What takes you from Narmolom so soon after werrun? You should be home resting."

Anito drew back her head in surprise. He had the fourfold name sign of an enkar. The enkar passed from village to village, settling disputes. They were hundreds of years old, and reputed to have strange powers. They moved through the forest more silently than the wind. He had approached her without her knowing; that hadn't happened since she was a tinka. He even knew what village she was from. She was impressed and a little frightened.

Anito had seen only a few enkar. One had come after their last chief elder died. She had chosen Ilto to fill the chief elder's place. Once in a while, one would show up at the village, stay a few days, and then move on. They were treated with great respect and given the best that the village had to offer. To do otherwise would mean great loss of face for the entire village.

"What's your name?" Ukatonen asked.

"You don't already know?"

The enkar rippled laughter. "If I did, then I might know why you are out here in the wilderness so soon after werrun. Your sponsor should be ashamed."

"Ninto tried to make me stay!" Anito protested.

"Then why didn't you listen?"

"I had a promise to keep. It involved my atwa."

"It couldn't have waited a few more days?"

"No," Anito told him. "But I was going to spend tomorrow morning resting and gathering supplies for the rest of the trip."

"Stay with me tonight," Ukatonen offered. "My nest is already built, and it would be easier to enlarge it than for you to build a new one. I can help you gather supplies tomorrow. Where are you going?"

"To the coast, near Lyanan."

"In that case, we can travel together. I'm heading there also."

Anito paused. It was tempting. The new creature was terrified that its people would leave it behind. If they did, then Anito would be stuck with it as her atwa. The enkar could get them to Lyanan faster. Anito would learn a lot traveling with an enkar. Besides, she couldn't refuse the enkar's offer without causing her entire village to lose face.

"Thank you, en," said Anito, using the most formal form of address, "but I'm not traveling alone. My companion is—unusual. It might give offense. Perhaps you should meet it before you decide whether to give us the gift of your company."

Ukatonen's ears went up. "This sounds interesting. Please lead me to your companion."

It was growing dark when they reached the geramben tree. The new creature was watching two hananar birds flutter in their courting dance, the female's golden throat feathers gleaming in the fading light. Disturbed by their approach, the two birds flew away, piping alarm calls as they went. The new creature turned toward them, giving Ukatonen a good look at its flat, small-mouthed face and tiny ears.

Ukatonen's head went back and he flushed an excited pink. "What kind of creature is it?" he asked Anito.

"I don't know. We found it dying in the woods. Saving its life cost the lives of two of our elders. One of them was my sitik."

"Why are you taking it to the coast?"

"Its people are near Lyanan. I'm taking it back to them."

The new creature approached, purple with curiosity, occasional flickers of ochre concern blotching its skin. Anito flushed a reassuring deep blue and the creature relaxed.

"It speaks!" Ukatonen said in excited tones of dark magenta on bright pink.

"Not really," Anito told him, "but it can communicate, and it understands some of what we say." Anito felt the weight of her exhaustion. She longed for a big meal and a chance to rest. "I mean no offense, en, but I am very tired, and the creature doesn't travel well after dark. Could we go to your nest? I can tell you more about the new animal when we get there."

"What?" Ukatonen said. He had been watching the creature with an excitement so intense that he glowed. "Oh, of course. I apologize. Here, let me help carry some of your things." Blue-green amusement rippled down Anito's back. She liked this enkar. His fascination with something new reminded her of Ilto.

Ukatonen had built himself a neat and cozy nest at the top of a tall quinjara tree. He hung a chunk of glowing fungus on a branch to provide some light and began enlarging the nest to accommodate his guests. When Anito moved to help, he told her to rest. Relieved despite herself, Anito settled her aching body against the branch.

The new creature nudged her gently, and offered Anito a geramben. Anito refused. It would be rude to eat before the enkar did. The creature offered her the fruit again. She could see that it was concerned for her. She must look as tired as she felt.

"Go ahead, Anito," Ukatonen said. "You need to eat. Save your formal manners for banquets."

"But—"

"I'll eat when I'm done."

Anito accepted the fruit, peeled it, and bit into it. It was delicious. She flushed a brilliant turquoise, and closed her eyes, savoring its sweetness. This was a truly exceptional strain. She should save the seeds. She opened her eyes and saw that the new creature was also eating. Anito glanced anxiously at Ukatonen, but he was busy weaving branches into the end of the nest. Anito let the creature go ahead and eat; she was too tired to stop it.

Ukatonen finished the nest and beckoned them into it. Anito settled against the leafy pile with a contented ripple of weariness. She wanted to sleep till next month. Ukatonen sat down beside her, spurs upward, asking for allu-a.

With an effort Anito shook herself awake. Her arms felt as heavy as boulders. She could barely summon the energy to clasp arms and link with the enkar. Ukatonen's presence rushed over her like the current of a river. Anito was caught up and swept along by his strength. Even Ilto, whose presence had been as warm as the sun and as constant as the rain, could not compare with Ukatonen's strength. Ilto had taught her to read other living creatures, but she had never been able to read herself this clearly. Every cell of her body stood out in sharp focus. Anito wondered whether this new clarity was due to the changes brought on by werrun, or Ukatonen's skill.

She relaxed and allowed Ukatonen to clear the fatigue from her blood. After five days alone in the wilderness, contact with another Tendu felt wonderful. She hadn't realized how lonely she had been until she felt Ukatonen's presence within her. Even so, it was strange to be in allu-a with a Tendu who was not from her village. She had linked with strange bami only a few times, when her village was on migration. It had felt all wrong, like finding a tumbi fruit on a yaminay vine. That wrongness had frightened her. With Ukatonen, she was too overwhelmed to be afraid. She had no choice but to yield to his power.

At last Ukatonen broke the link. Anito, dazed and bemused by the compelling force of his presence, sat motionless for a few moments, gathering her scattered thoughts.

"Anito, are you all right?" Ukatonen asked, putting a hand on her shoulder. His words were tinged with concern.

Anito touched the enkar's hand to reassure him, flushing a faint brown in mild embarrassment. "You have a very strong presence, en."

To Anito's surprise, Ukatonen browned in embarrassment. "I spend too much time alone."

Uncertain what to say, Anito rippled a deep blue wave of reassurance at the enkar.

Ukatonen handed her a geramben fruit. "You must eat. The strength I gave you won't last. You need food and rest to rebuild your strength." The enkar began butchering the game they had killed. He handed rich juicy pieces of meat to her and the new creature to eat while he prepared the meal. Anito ate until her stomach hurt. Still, she felt restless and hungry.

"Here," he said, rummaging in his bag, and coming out with a large sheet of yarram. "Chew on this, it'll ease your craving."

Anito shook her head, startled that he would offer her such a delicacy. "No. I'll be fine. Really." Despite her denial, Anito's nostrils flared at the scent of the dried seaweed, and her mouth watered.

"Go ahead. You need it, and we're headed to the coast. It's not so precious there. Your sponsor should be feeding you plenty of yarram and bibbi. You need a lot of it just after werrun."

Brown with embarrassment, Anito took the yarram. Ninto had placed a packet of yarram in her pack the night before she left. Anito had quietly slipped it underneath a pile of hunting gear, ashamed at being given so much of this delicacy. She tore off a piece of the tough, leathery seaweed and began to chew. Her restless hunger faded, and she felt better than she had in days.

"Tell me about Narmolom. Is Ilto still the chief elder?" the enkar asked.

Anito's skin darkened to a stony grey. "He was my sitik. He died saving that one's life," she said, gesturing at the new creature. Her old resentment flared for a moment; she was surprised at its intensity.

Ukatonen touched her arm with his knuckles. "I'm sorry to hear that. He was wise. He would have made a good enkar."

Negation flared on Anito's skin. "He loved Narmolom too much to leave it."

"Do you know who will succeed him?"

"No," Anito said. "No one knows, en. Everyone thought it would be Kirito, but she died before he did." With a flicker of shame, Anito realized that she had been so shaken by Ilto's death that she hadn't thought about what it meant to the village as a whole.

"When I am through at Lyanan, I will go to Narmolom," he told her.

"Thank you, en," Anito said. She spoke in the complex, formal patterns of high speech. Even though she was barely out of werrun, she was an elder representing her village before an enkar. "We will be grateful for your presence. May it bring us into harmony."

Ukatonen straightened, and suddenly, despite the feathers clinging to him from the birds he had plucked and cleaned, he was every inch a powerful, mysterious enkar. "May harmony be achieved," he replied in high speech so formal that it took Anito a moment to understand it.

Now that she was an elder, Anito was going to have to pay attention to such things as formal speech. A cloud of regret rippled over her skin as she thought of the formalities and manners she would have to learn. None of it interested her in the slightest. Ilto had tried to teach her the manners that she would need to know as an elder, but the knowledge ran off her like wet mud in a rainstorm.

"Tell me about the new creature," Ukatonen said.

Anito told the enkar everything that had happened since they found it dying in the forest. Ukatonen watched Anito speak, eyes bright, ears wide, taking in her words the way a leaf drinks in sunshine. When Anito was done, Ukatonen sat beside the new creature. It was curled into a tight ball against the side of the nest, one arm over its face, the other arm extending across the floor, wrist spur pointing up. Before Anito could stop him, the enkar linked with the new creature. The enkar flared pink with excitement and broke the link. The creature slept on, undisturbed.

"You shouldn't have done that!" Anito was angry, her words tinged with red. "I promised it that no one would link with it. What if it woke up? I could never get it to trust me again! That creature is my atwa until I get it back to its people. I don't want to have to tie it up and carry it to Lyanan!" She realized that she had just spoken sharply to an enkar, and browned in embarrassment.

To Anito's surprise, Ukatonen's brilliant pink color faded to a subdued muddy blue, half reassurance, and half embarrassment. "I am sorry, kene. I only looked at its cells. I don't think I disturbed it."

Anito looked up, startled. Ukatonen had addressed her with the formal title of an elder. It was the first time anyone had done that.

"I'm on my way to Lyanan," he went on, "because the enkar have heard about a group of strange creatures tearing up the forest. Your creature sounds like the ones on the coast. Perhaps it can help me understand what's happening out at Lyanan. If these creatures are your atwa, you may be obligated to help repair the damage they have done."

"I don't know anything about the other creatures on the coast," Anito replied. "I have no control over the creatures at Lyanan. I only know about this one here. I'm not ready for such a responsibility, en. I don't even know how to be an elder yet."

Ukatonen placed his hand on Anito's chest, deep blue with reassurance. "You know more about these creatures than any other Tendu alive. I hadn't even seen one before I met you. I know it's a great deal to ask of you, but someone must take responsibility for bringing things back into balance. That is the most important thing about being an elder, Anito."

"But how can I bring things back into balance? I'm barely out of werrun, and I'll be a stranger as well. No one will listen to me."

"We won't know how to balance things until we see what's happened. And people will listen to you. They have to. After all, these creatures are your atwa. You know more about them than anyone. You have already taught me a great deal that I didn't know, kene. I am obligated to you for that."

A cloud of grey regret crossed Anito's skin. Already the web of debt and obligation that entangled every elder was beginning to bind her. It would never end, she knew. The rest of her life would be spent incurring debts, and paying them off.

"You won't have to fix everything by yourself," Ukatonen assured her. "You'll have powerful allies. I'll help, and so will the other enkar. The villagers will listen."

Anito flickered her thanks, trying not to think of all the

obligations she would create in the process of bringing the new creatures back into balance.

"It's been a long, difficult trip. Your body needs rest. You should sleep, kene," Ukatonen said. He lifted the glow-fungus off the branch where it hung, sprinkled it with nutrient solution, and put it back in its gourd.

Anito settled herself between the new creature and the enkar, and fell asleep.

E i g h t

JUNA WATCHED SPIRAL and the new alien discuss her, wishing that she could understand what they were saying. Her name sign was the only recognizable word in the complex blur of skin-speech patterns. Juna shook her head. She was too tired to even try to follow what they were saying. She gave up and went to sleep.

The next day Spiral told her they would remain here for a while. Whether that meant an hour, a day, or a week wasn't clear. When Juna protested, Spiral merely turned over and went back to sleep. The new alien, whom she had dubbed Lizard since its name sign resembled a stylized lizard, stopped her attempts to waken Spiral.

When it was clear that further protests would get her nowhere, Juna sat with her computer, working on the aliens' language. After about an hour the low power warning came on. Juna sighed. Oliver's computer was wadded up in her pack. She pulled it out and told it to get ready to receive data. When it extruded the proper ports and cables, she linked the two computers and backed up her files. Then she put her own computer in one of the mesh gathering sacks, and climbed to the top of the tree, where she tied the computer securely to a sunny branch and left it to recharge.

When she got back to the nest, Lizard was examining Oliver's computer. Spiral was still sleeping soundly. Lizard handed the machine back to her, then pointed up at her recharging computer. "*Something something not good,*" it told her in skin speech.

Juna shook her head. She didn't understand. Was the alien talking about the computer, or something else entirely? Had she done something to cause offense? Were they bothered by her computer? A surge of fear passed through her. She hoped not. It was essential. Without it, she had no way of communicating with the aliens. Still, Lizard didn't seem troubled by the computer he'd examined. She shrugged. If it was important, it would come up again.

So who, or what, was Lizard? It was larger than any alien that she had seen thus far. Was that due to age, nutrition, gender, class, or racial differences? Spiral seemed respectful, even deferential to the other alien. Spiral's colors were subdued, and it spoke to Lizard in complex patterns. The computer indicated a possible correlation between levels of formality and the complexity of the patterns used. It certainly seemed logical.

Why was Lizard coddling Spiral? Was Spiral sick, or was this a mating ritual? What did it know about her people? When would they start traveling again? Each passing day made it more likely that she would be marooned here.

Lizard touched her on the shoulder, interrupting her reverie. It nudged the computer and pointed to her, ears wide, purple with curiosity. Juna picked up the computer and pulled it out into a wide flat surface, then instructed it to assume a large-display format. It smoothed out into a rectangle and went rigid. Lizard ducked its chin, flickers of magenta surprise crossing its skin. Juna smiled at the alien's reaction.

Leaning the computer against the side of the nest so that Lizard could see it, Juna called up the visual linguistic program she had been working with earlier.

"Computer," she told it, "display symbol for food."

The aliens' word for food appeared on the screen. Lizard turned completely pink. It looked at her and back at the computer in amazement. The symbol for food appeared on its chest, and it picked up a piece of fruit and put it in front of the computer. Juna picked the fruit up.

"Computer, display gratitude symbol and affirmative symbol."

They soon ran through all of the words Juna knew, and then she began questioning Lizard about the immense collection of unknown words that she had recorded.

They worked all day, with a break for lunch when Spiral woke. Then they continued on into the evening. It was very exciting and productive. Lizard tripled Juna's stock of known words. The alien was much more attentive and patient than Spiral. Perhaps it was less bored with her.

Lizard woke Spiral for another meal around sunset. Juna, still tired from the exertion of the trip, fell asleep after dinner, her head swimming with alien words.

To Juna's immense relief, they started traveling again the next day. Lizard assumed leadership of the group, determining their direction and pace. Although they started earlier in the morning, they stopped more often to rest.

They moved through an endless green gloom. Every day the sun rose, dispelling the heavy nighttime fog. The thick canopy filtered the few hours of morning sunlight into a dim greenish glow. Rain clouds began gathering around noon. Every afternoon it rained for a couple of hours.

Juna had no idea how far they traveled. Even with her compass, the jungle seemed directionless. The days were all alike. Without her computer she would have lost all track of time. How many more days before they got to base camp? Would she be too late?

Lizard paused often to teach her a new word or show her a new plant or animal. Her computer, wrapped around her neck to keep her hands free for climbing, recorded everything. Her stock of words grew. Soon she could understand most words pertaining to basic survival and could identify many concrete objects, especially if they were not alive. The aliens spoke slowly and clearly to her, but conversations between Lizard and Spiral were still impossible to follow.

The computer was also constructing a phonetic analogue to the aliens' patterns. Having verbal keys for the aliens' words made it much easier to learn to think in their language. She now had names for people and things that had some connection with the aliens' visual language. Spiral became Anito, Lizard became Ukatonen, and Knot and Ripple became Ninto and Ilto. Ukatonen's name for her was Eerin, which meant "stone speaker." It was a reference to her computer, which the aliens thought of as a stone.

Her attempts to make her skin form meaningful patterns remained fruitless. By controlling her emotions, she could change her skin color, but she still could not make her skin produce patterns. The best she could do was make a cloudy dark blob appear on her chest.

One night about ten days after Ukatonen had joined them, the alien touched Juna's arm, indicating that it had something to say to her. Juna looked at it and nodded.

"You speak with skin?" Ukatonen asked her, touching her on the chest.

Juna concentrated and made a dark blob appear on her chest, then shook her head no.

"You want speak?" it asked.

Juna nodded yes.

"You want speak, I teach," it said.

Juna nodded again, suddenly hopeful. It would be wonderful to be able to converse freely, without the clumsy interface of the computer.

The alien held out its arms, red spurs upward. "You want speak, you must *allu-a*." The computer had no analogue for what the alien wanted, but Juna knew immediately what it meant. She shook her head, flushing bright orange, and backing away, to emphasize the depth of her refusal. Her stomach was heavy with disappointment.

"Why fear?" it asked her. "No hurt. You learn speak with us."

Juna shook her head, unable to explain her fear of allu-a.

Anito touched Ukatonen's arm, and began talking to the other alien, explaining something about Juna's unwillingness to link spurs with them.

Juna stretched the computer out into a display screen. The aliens broke off their discussion and watched as the computer became a smooth, rigid rectangle alive with color. Juna touched the aliens' arms as a signal that she wanted to speak.

"Translate," she told the computer. She selected the word *allu-a*, and tied it to the word *link*. "I link before. Was bad. I fear link," she said.

Ukatonen looked at Anito, its ears raised in a question. Anito said something in reply. Juna recognized the word for "link" joined with the odd little hook that indicated past tense, and the name signs for herself, Ninto, and Ilto, and guessed that Anito was telling Ukatonen about that first link.

"Why link bad?" the computer translated for Ukatonen.

"Not want link. Cannot leave link," Juna said, frustrated by the limited vocabulary available to her.

Ukatonen looked back at Anito. Anito explained something to Ukatonen. Yellow irritation flickered down Ukatonen's back.

"You link with me, it not bad. You can leave. I show you how. You learn speak. Link good. Learn fast. You not need stone-speaker," Ukatonen said, pointing its chin at her computer. "You *t'al* me." The symbol for *t'al* resembled a stylized braid. It was a word that she had a phonetic for, but no definition.

"What means *t'al*?" Juna asked.

"You leave village alone. Ninto, me find you. You *t'al* us. You come back to village with us," Anito explained. "Your people want find you. I say we go. You *t'al* us. We go your people now. You link with us. You *t'al* us."

Juna untangled the meaning from the semi-translated hash the computer made of their words. *T'al* either meant believe or trust. She entered the possible meaning into the computer for it to cross-check against other recorded occurrences of the word. The response was "Possible. Not enough data to confirm."

She had trusted the aliens when they said they would take her back to her people, and now Anito was taking her there. She had gone back to the village with Anito and Ninto. She had trusted Anito enough to go with the alien alone in search of her people.

Juna rubbed her forehead. If *t'al* meant what she thought it did, Ukatonen was asking her to trust it while it rummaged around inside her and changed things. It was asking a lot, especially if she was only a few days from base camp.

"No," Juna replied. "My people find me soon. Not need learn speak you."

A ripple of olive disappointment washed over Ukatonen's skin. The alien's ears drooped. Its expression was comical, but Juna was too tired to manage much more than a weak smile.

"You want link, ask me," Ukatonen offered.

Juna nodded, and crumpled the computer into a small ball. She'd done all she could. Her brain was worn out from trying to understand and communicate with the aliens. She was exhausted by the physical demands of the trip. Once she got back, she'd turn the aliens over to Kinsey and go back to being a biologist. That is, if the Survey's doctors could make her look human again. Juna's throat closed tight with fear for a moment at the possibility that she would look like an alien for the rest of her life. Then she shut her mind firmly against contemplating that possibility.

Three days later, the forest ended abruptly at a set of rocky cliffs overlooking the sea. In some places the jungle actually hung out over the cliffs in a tangle of branches and long streamers of dangling roots and vines. Juna smiled, remembering how they had winched her down a cliff in a sling seat so that she could collect samples of canopy biota. She had been terrified the whole time. If she had known then what she'd have to face . . . She shook her head, an ironic smile on her face.

They followed the wide arc of the coastline north. On the second day, she began recognizing landmarks she had seen from the flyer. Anticipation alternated with fear. Would the Survey team even recognize her? What if they didn't?

The sun was low on the horizon when Juna spotted the gleaming silver radio beacon. She climbed down to the ground and ran toward it, stumbling heedlessly over sharp rocks and rotting branches, calling out as she ran. She burst out of the jungle and stopped. Where the camp had stood there was now only a wide plain of baked soil and black ash. It was all that was left after decontamination procedures. Only the gleaming radio tower remained, marking the spot for future expeditions. Base camp was gone. The Survey had left.

Juna knelt to examine the soil of the burnt-over area. The rains had washed the ash into gullies and depressions. She shook her head: That ash contained most of the nutrients needed to sustain a rain forest, and it was washing away. Near the edge of the forest, where the soil wasn't baked hard, plants were sprouting to cover the area, some of them well established. She estimated that the ship had been gone for at least three weeks. Was the mother ship gone as well? Had the *Kotani Maru* made the jump to hyperspace? Could they still come back for her? Juna walked across the burnt-over clearing, mind carefully held blank. She didn't know yet. She wouldn't know until the *Kotani Maru* failed to return her distress call.

Juna's hands shook as she plugged the computer into the radio beacon and transmitted her identification code and a distress call.

There was no reply. She checked the connections, made sure there was enough charge in the radio's massive solar-powered batteries to punch her message out into space. Everything was working, her transmission was going out. She told the computer to repeat the transmission over and over until it received a reply, and settled back to wait. If the ship had left orbit, it might take hours for her message to reach them, and then more hours for her to hear the ship's reply.

She looked around. Except for the radio tower, there was no sign that humans had lived here. Ukatonen and Anito wandered over the burnt ground, their legs covered with blackened soot, their skins grey with unhappiness. Had the *Kotani Maru* vanished into hyperspace? Was she condemned to wait twenty or thirty years before the nearest human outpost heard her distant pleas for help?

Juna set her jaw. She looked out over the surging ocean toward the horizon. The setting sun turned the sea pale gold. She would not despair until dawn, she decided. If she didn't hear from the *Kotani* by the time the sun came up tomorrow, then the ship was gone.

Her left foot throbbed. She had cut it on something in her hurry to reach base camp. She should have been more careful. Even a minor injury could be serious if she was marooned here.

Tears welled up in her eyes. She mustn't give up hope. She had until tomorrow.

Juna leaned against the base of the tower, thinking of as little as possible. Anito came up and examined her injured foot. Yellow streaks of irritation exploded on the alien's chest like miniature lightning bolts.

"You bad foot," it said. "Not good. Get sick." It squirted a clear, sticky substance from its spurs, and rubbed it into the cut on Juna's foot. The throbbing faded.

"Where your people?" the alien asked her.

Juna shook her head, fighting back her fear.

"Gone?" it asked next.

Juna shrugged. She didn't know how to explain what she was waiting for. Radio and starships were beyond the scope of these aliens' lives. Juna pointed at the setting sun, and then moved her arm in an arc until she pointed at the eastern horizon; then she pointed at herself and patted the ground. She would stay here until dawn. Anito thrust its head forward as it tried to figure out what Juna was trying to say, then nodded to show that it understood.

"You stay here. I get food."

Juna nodded and sat back against the base of the tower, waiting. She called up her report and reviewed it, trying to keep her mind busy with details so she wouldn't think past dawn. She barely noticed Anito's return. She was too anxious to eat more than a couple of bites of fruit.

It was several hours past sunset when the speaker on the radio tower crackled to life.

"This is the Survey exploration vessel *Kotani Maru* calling Dr. Juna Saari. We are currently 13.5 A.U. from your planet. Our estimated transmission lag time is one hour, fifty-two minutes. Our time remaining before hyperspace transition is two and a half days. We are unable to return to pick you up, but we will report you as marooned to the Survey." There was a brief pause. "I-I'm sorry Juna. We'll push them as hard as we can for you. This message will repeat."

The sound of another human voice jolted Juna out of the light doze she had fallen into. She listened, her heart soaring. She wasn't lost after all. She had gotten here in time. Then the meaning of the message sank in, and her heart dove. She was trapped here, in this alien skin, alone with these slimy aliens. The message began repeating, driving the realization home with mechanical relentlessness.

"Damn!" she shouted, striking the tower with her fist. It gave out a dull metallic gong. "Damn," she said again more quietly, rubbing her bruised hand. She reached over and cut off another repetition of the message, fighting back tears as she spoke the command.

She sat for a moment, getting herself under control. Then when she was ready, she reactivated the computer, this time to record a message.

"*Kotani Maru,* this is Dr. Juna Saari. I am in good health, although somewhat changed." That, she thought, was an understatement. "My prospects for survival are excellent, even without my suit. Tell Kinsey that I've got some intelligent aliens for him. A full report follows. Computer, transmit message and append report."

She sat back while the computer transmitted the verbal and visual report she had prepared for the Survey, and contemplated her situation. She was stuck here for several years at least. But her discovery of the aliens would give top priority to a return mission.

Still, it would take the *Kotani* eight months to get back to Earth. Then, once the news got out, there would be an incredible academic turf battle as every A-C specialist on the planet vied for a spot on the return expedition. A ship would have to be yanked from its schedule, prompting another squabble. Add in the time necessary to outfit the expedition and brief the crew, and then the months it would take for the ship to actually get here. It would be years.

Juna shook her head. Years without simple human contact and the sound of human voices. Years alone. She finally let her stinging tears flow.

The next transmission woke Juna. It was Kinsey, the ship's Alien Contact specialist, full of questions, most of which she couldn't answer, and useless orders on how to deal with the aliens, most of which she had already violated. Juna sighed, wishing Kinsey weren't such a by-the-book idiot. But then, anyone with a lick of sense stayed out of a discipline with so little future. Perhaps when he read her report, he would understand how helpless she was down here.

After Kinsey was through, Takayuki Tatsumi, the head of the life sciences team, began questioning her.

"What does it feel like down there? What does it smell like?" Tatsumi wanted to know.

She could feel Tatsumi's longing to be on the planet, able to wander around without a suit, able to touch, smell, and taste things. She was living the dream of every Survey tech.

Juna wanted to shout at the radio, to tell them it wasn't worth the isolation, the loneliness, the discomfort. Their envy made her angry, and worse, it made her feel ashamed. Hadn't she wanted this too? To shed her bulky, uncomfortable suit and be able to touch and smell an alien world? Dreaming about such things while sitting comfortably around a table in the lounge was cruelly different from the reality of her situation.

"It smells like a jungle," Juna told him, "hot and wet and full of things rotting." She paused, trying to control her bitterness. They were hungry, as she had been, to experience another world. It was why they were all here, in the Survey, instead of at home, surrounded by friends and family. She described the smells and tastes of the food she had eaten, both good and bad. She was longing for a hot meal, as much as the Survey team was longing to taste alien food.

Juna cued the computer to continue. There were more questions, all variants of "What does this smell/taste/feel like?" She answered them as well as she could. She clung to their human voices. Soon she would be the only human for hundreds of light-years. She wanted to savor every moment of human contact left to her, even when their questions were stupid or impossible to answer.

At last the questions came to a close. Personal messages would follow. She paused the computer, and drank deeply from her water gourd. All of this talking was a strain on her voice. She had become used to the aliens' silence, and spoke only rarely.

She corked the water gourd, and told the computer to continue.

"Juna, this is Ali." The sound of Ali's deep voice, with its lilting accent, brought fresh tears prickling at the back of her eyelids. She paused the message, suddenly overwhelmed by memories of Ali's ebony skin, the feel of the tribal cicatrices on his chest, the sharp, warm smell of him. She wanted to curl up in his arms and cry for a week. Glancing down, she discovered to her surprise that her skin had turned a rich, metallic shade of gold. She cued the message to continue. ". . . I saw the pictures of what's happened to you, and I'm sorry. You were so beautiful. I'll miss you."

Ali continued on, telling her how much he would miss her lovely body, and filling her in on what he had been doing after she disappeared. Juna sat, the words flowing over her in a meaningless murmur of sound. He was saying goodbye. His words burned deeper than her tears. Even though this relationship was only a shipboard convenience, she had expected a little more from him than this self-centered farewell. It hurt more than she would have expected. She looked down at her transformed body. No wonder he was pulling away. No one would want her, not when she looked like this.

Ali's words left her too drained to listen to the other messages. She dictated a brief request for hypertexts on tropical rain forest biomes, jungle survival, and a variety of anthropological and linguistic works, as well as a complete Survey inventory of the rain forest biome. Then she curled up at the base of the tower and fell asleep.

Dawn brought more messages, from friends and co-workers, and a steady transmission stream of hypertext books on the data line.

There was a note from Alison, her closest friend on the ship. Alison was in her seventies, and was retiring after this trip. Juna would miss her.

"You seem so changed that I fear for you," Alison told her. "I know that the next few years are going to be very hard for you, all alone amongst aliens. Be strong, and remember that there are people who love you back home.

"I'll drop in on your father as soon as I can and make sure that he's all right. When you get back to Earth, come and visit. Tell me stories of the forest and the aliens."

Juna felt a surge of gratitude well up in her. Juna had brought Alison home on leave a few years back. Alison and her father had had an affair, and still remained close. Juna suspected that Alison was keeping an eye on her for her father. She was glad that Alison would be there for him while she was away.

Padraig, who carried on a continual flirtation with all of the women, and most of the men, regardless of age, looks, or marital status, said:

"You should never have let that handsome alien kiss you. I'm downloading a file of things to make you smile. I hope it helps. When you get back, come kiss me, and I'll turn you into a handsome prince. Be well, *m'acushla*, be well."

Juna laughed in spite of herself. They had been lovers, briefly, before she settled in with Ali. They were still close friends. Perhaps it would have been better to be one of Padraig's dozen lovers than to have paired off with Ali.

Anger at Ali flooded Juna. She hoped that the waste evac tube on his e-suit would get stuck shut on a hot day.

There were several other messages from good friends. Then there was an official communication from Chang, the Morale Officer. Juna grimaced. Chang had been on the *Next Great Leap Forward People's Generation Ship*. A Jump ship retrieved the crew about ten years ago. Almost all of the crew had joined the Space Service; it was the only place where they didn't feel completely lost. Rumor had it that Chang landed her present berth because they wanted to get rid of her groundside. Juna could believe it. Chang was a stolid, humorless, by-the-book sort, and shipboard morale was high more or less despite her.

"Juna," Chang said in her message, "on behalf of myself and the entire crew, I want to extend our most sincere regrets about the misfortune that has befallen you. I assure you that Captain Rodrigues and myself will make every possible effort to expedite a return expedition. I urge you to abide by the Survey nonintervention guidelines, and to be a credit to the Survey's century-long tradition of cautious, nondestructive exploration. I will be downloading all of the Survey regulations pertaining to alien contact and environmental quarantining. I trust that you will do your best to obey them. Sincerely, Mei-Mei Chang."

Juna rolled her eyes, and switched off the sound, leaving the computer to record the rest of her messages. She got up and went into the forest. Finding refuge high in the branches of a tree, she listened to the clamor of the forest, and the distant, barely audible hush of the surf. The forest was a refuge now, from lovers she couldn't touch, from the uncomfortable comfort of well-meaning friends, and from the impossible expectations of the Survey. The green shade soothed her sun-blasted eyes, and the humidity eased her dry, drawn skin. She must have a touch of sunburn. She scratched at her itching skin, wishing an unpleasant fate on Morale Officer Chang.

The branches nearby swished and rustled, sending a shower of dead leaves pattering to the forest floor. It was Anito. The alien swung down beside her, touching Juna's shoulder to get her attention.

"People come?"

Juna nodded.

"When people come?"

Juna shook her head, then waved her arm as though gesturing at something very far away.

Anito made some response that Juna couldn't interpret. Her computers were out at the radio beacon, one controlling the radio, the other recharging in the sun. She shook her head, indicating that she didn't understand.

Anito touched her itching back. "Skin bad. *Something something* not do."

Juna shook her head. She didn't understand what Anito was trying to tell her.

Anito squirted a cool liquid on her skin and the itching eased. Juna flushed lavender with relief. Anito handed her a large, sloshing gourd of water, which she drained, wishing for more. The alien then fished in its satchel and gave her a brilliant red fruit that tasted rather like a sweet honeydew melon, and a chunk of raw meat wrapped neatly in a large leaf. Juna nodded her thanks, and the two of them ate in companionable silence.

When they were through, Juna got up to return to the beacon. Anito followed her, pausing briefly to refill her gourd from the tank of a large bromeliad, using a hollow green reed as a siphon. Just as Juna was about to push through the tangled brush at the hem of the forest, and emerge onto the rocky, sunlit cliffs, Anito stopped her.

"No. Skin bad. You make more bad."

Juna shook her head. She didn't understand. She needed to contact the ship before they started to worry. There was no way to explain this to Anito, though. She started out again, but the alien moved in front of her, blocking her way.

"No go," Anito insisted. It flushed a pale white, and pointed at the sun. "Sick you get," Anito told her in emphatic tones of dark brick red.

Juna pointed insistently out at the beacon. She had to go.

"Wait. Rain come, you go. Skin not bad then."

Clouds foretelling the afternoon shower were already beginning to build. It wouldn't be more than a couple of hours before it started to rain. Juna needed a rest. Anito led her to a clear jungle stream and the two of them bathed and wallowed in it until the first fat drops of rain began to fall.

Juna returned to the beacon and began answering more questions from the Survey team. Many of them were impossible to answer. She had been too busy surviving to take notes. Still, she documented the bee-fungus-tree ecosystem that the aliens lived in, and she described what new animals and plants she could remember. She would have to start keeping better records.

The sun was a big red ball breaking through the clouds on the horizon when she heard from the ship again. She checked the computer's clock. The radio lag time had stretched another twenty minutes each way, and her last contact with humanity was growing more tenuous with each passing minute. It was Morale Officer Chang again. She sounded suspicious about Juna's two-hour disappearance. Juna listened unhappily to Chang's inquisition. She had one more day before her last contact with humanity for several years would vanish. She didn't want to spend that time in petty wrangling with Chang. She listened politely, trying to say nothing that would trigger a tirade.

When Chang's lecture was over, Juna repeated the reason that she had given them when she had returned, that Anito had advised her against coming back sooner, for reasons she didn't entirely understand. No, the alien had not threatened her. Juna believed that the alien didn't want her to get sunburned. Then Juna returned to answering the backlog of questions from the Survey crew.

It was fully dark when she finally signed off for the evening. She was exhausted, her skin felt raw, and her back hurt from sitting too long in one position. She picked up Oliver's computer, which she was using as a spare, and headed into the forest. Anito was waiting for her with a glow basket on a stick to light their way. She followed the alien through the velvety darkness. The forest shimmered with the sounds of insects and the cries of nocturnal animals. Something close beside her let out a deep, rumbling roar. Juna started, and looked at Anito. A glowing ripple of laughter flowed silently over the alien's body. Anito lifted a large overhanging leaf, and holding the light up, beckoned to Juna. Huddled on the underside of the leaf was a small green frog with enormous black eyes. Juna nodded, and Anito let the leaf drop. A few minutes later they heard the little frog roar again. Juna wondered whether the noise was to frighten predators or to attract potential mates.

They walked for a couple of hours until they came to an enormous tree. They climbed it and were greeted by a group of aliens as they reached the multibranched crotch. It was another alien village. Juna's shoulders slumped. She was too tired to cope with more alien diplomacy tonight.

Anito led her to a large room near the base of the giant tree, where Ukatonen and a group of nearly twenty aliens were waiting. Juna sat between Ukatonen and Anito. Ukatonen began to speak. It was a very formal speech. Ukatonen's skin-speech patterns were very complex, and its gestures were stiff and stylized. Juna concentrated on staying awake, but even so, she was dozing off by the time the food was served. There were several different kinds of seaweed, fish, honey, and a number of new kinds of fruit. One fruit, which looked like a large purple peach, was horribly sour. She set it aside after one bite, to the amusement of the local aliens, who ate the sour fruit with obvious relish.

After the meal, curious aliens clustered around Juna. They

poked and prodded her, examining her hands and ears, their own ears wide and their skins deep purple with curiosity. These aliens handled her much more roughly than the people of Anito's village. Juna bore it stoically, flinching away only when something threatened real harm. Finally she gave Anito and Ukatonen a pleading look. Anito noticed it and said something to Ukatonen, who addressed the rest of the aliens. Then Anito led her up the tree to their room. Three fresh leaf beds were laid out for the travelers. Juna crawled into the moist warmth of the nearest one and fell asleep.

Juna's skin was tender and sore when she awoke the next morning. It was vaguely reassuring to know that not all of Anito's magic potions worked perfectly. She would have been more reassured if her skin didn't feel two sizes too small. She got up and washed herself off, then sat back to think over her situation. She was going to be stuck here for a very long time. After three weeks of trying, she still couldn't control her skin coloring well enough to "speak" skin speech. It was proving to be a serious handicap. Now that she was stuck here, she needed to speak the aliens' language. That meant linking with Ukatonen.

Juna swallowed, her throat dry with fear as she remembered the violation of that first link. If only there were some other way; but the problem was physical, and only a link would fix it.

Ukatonen came in bearing breakfast. Fighting back the orange glow of her fear, Juna touched Ukatonen on the shoulder to get its attention, and extended her arms, spurs uppermost. Their eyes met. Ukatonen flushed a dusky purple, like shadows on a ripe plum, its ears spread wide.

"Talk want you?" it asked her. "You want allu-a?"

Juna nodded. Part of her wanted to run screaming, but she fought down her fear. She needed to be able to speak with the aliens. Her life would depend on it.

"You trust me?"

Juna nodded again. She had to trust the alien, and endure the violation of linking.

"Good," the alien said, turning a dark, reassuring blue. "You no fear me. I not hurt you."

It was all she could do to keep from pulling away as Ukatonen reached out and laid its arms over hers. Her fingers shook as she grasped the alien's forearms. She closed her eyes, afraid to watch as its slender four-fingered hands grasped her wrists. Then their spurs touched, connecting with a slight prick.

Entering the link felt like diving beneath the surface of a warm pool. There was a faint sensation like surface tension breaking, and then Juna was inside herself. It was a blind world, full of sound—the rush of blood through her veins, the swish-beat of her heart, quickened by her fear, the gurgle of her stomach. She could taste it as well, the rough, dark tang of her blood, the soft furry-peach feel of her skin, and the coppery tang of the alien skin that protected her. Juna could feel/taste it extending down through her gut, and into her lungs, filtering out the deadly alien poisons. She could sense her fear, bright, and sharp, flavoring the link.

Then she became aware of Ukatonen's presence. It felt like the current of a mighty river. Terrified, she struggled, but the alien's presence swept her up and carried her along, helpless as a leaf caught in the current. She watched as Ukatonen's presence pooled up at the barrier between her human and alien skin. He was male, she realized, without really knowing how she knew. Her skin tingled and stung. It was like taking a bath in champagne, only on the inside of her skin. She felt the alien presence move through her, pooling briefly in her aching muscles and stiff tendons, leaving them loose and relaxed. It cleared away the bitter traces of stress and fatigue that clung to her even after sleep. Then Ukatonen's presence receded from her body like a wave from a beach. A cool ghost of the alien lingered for a moment. Juna opened her eyes and the ghost disappeared like the sheen of water on the sand after a wave recedes.

Juna stood up and stretched. She felt fresh and pure, like one of her mother's starched linen festival shirts fresh from the clothes presser. Her skin no longer felt as if it had been sandpapered. Taking a deep breath, she stretched again for the pleasure of feeling the ease in her muscles.

Holding out her right arm, she spelled out her name in turquoise letters edged in black, then made her name creep up her arm, across her chest, and down her left side, vanishing as it reached her left knee. She pictured a flower, and a flat, crude flower appeared on her skin. She concentrated, trying to make the flower look more realistic, and the image improved. It was strange, watching pictures appear and disappear on her skin. She couldn't feel the images, but she knew exactly where they were on her body without looking. She visualized an image and it appeared. It was as easy as lifting her arm.

She looked up at Ukatonen, who rippled approval. "Hungry?" he asked her.

She was ravenous. "Yes," she thought, and horizontal black bars of agreement appeared on her chest. "Food," she thought, visualizing the green oval symbol for food, and the sign for food appeared on her chest. Ukatonen handed her a basket of fruit, and some chunks of honeycomb.

"I go bring more food. Come back soon," the alien told her, and left.

Juna played with making skin speech while she ate, practicing big and little signs. The versatility and responsiveness of her new ability was amazing. Anything she could visualize would appear on her skin. Even though she could make her skin "speak," Ukatonen had not given her instant knowledge of the aliens' language. She could skin-speak only those symbols that she knew well enough to visualize. Juna sighed, thinking of all of the memorization that she had to do in order to become fluent in the aliens' language. Still, she felt relieved that Ukatonen hadn't violated her trust by tinkering with her mind. She wondered what limits the aliens had when they linked. Clearly it took energy. She was extremely hungry after linking, and she noticed that the others always ate big meals before and after allu-a.

Juna finished her breakfast and was wishing for more when Anito came in carrying a leaf cone full of freshly filleted fish. The alien handed some to Juna.

"Thank you, Anito," Juna said in skin speech.

Anito's ears lifted and it flared a surprised pink, fading to a questioning purple.

"Ukatonen," Juna said, and held her arms out, spurs upward. It was a trifle crude, but Anito understood what had happened.

The alien flushed a deep, concerned ochre. "Not good," Anito said. "Ukatonen get sick from allu-a with you. I fix."

Ukatonen returned a few minutes later, carrying more food. Anito grabbed his arm and began flickering away at him, too fast for Juna to follow. Ukatonen looked at Juna, ochre concern tingeing his skin. He handed her a leaf-wrapped package of meat and seaweed, and told her to eat. The two aliens settled themselves in a corner, and linked spurs. Juna ate a third of the meat and seaweed, wrapping the rest up and setting it beside the water gourds. Anito and Ukatonen would be hungry when they unlinked.

She needed to get back to the radio beacon. There was so little time before the ship went through transition! Her need to be at the beacon was a hot ache. She wanted to spend every minute she could there. It was her only link to humanity, and it would soon be broken.

Could she find her way back to the beacon alone? She looked at the two aliens, locked into their strange communion. There was no way to tell how long they would stay like that. It could be ten minutes, it could be all day.

Juna went out and tried to talk with the other aliens, but she didn't know enough skin speech to get very far. The aliens of this village weren't interested in trying to talk with her. They brushed past her impatiently, ignoring her questions. A few seemed outright angry, flattening their ears against their heads and hissing at her like cold water on red-hot metal. Not since the funeral had an alien treated her with such hostility.

Juna wondered what she had done to deserve their anger. Had she committed some alien faux pas? She couldn't think of anything she had done to offend them. Perhaps they were afraid of her because she was an alien to them. Or maybe they were angry at her because of something the Survey did. There were just too many possibilities. She would ask Anito or Ukatonen about it later.

Juna climbed out of the trunk of the tree, emerging into the bowl formed by the huge tree's branches. She glanced up through the branches of the canopy, checking the weather. Fleecy white clouds were already gathering. Soon the sky would be clouded over. In two or three hours it would rain. She needed to be on her way.

She climbed to the topmost branches of the village tree and looked out. The forest fell away toward the distant blue expanse of the sea in monotonous green humps and bumps, broken occasionally by a bright burst of flowers, or the stark grey branches of a dead tree.

Juna could see the beacon off to the north, a slender silver gleam set on a rocky promontory, surrounded by an empty, blackened expanse where the forest had been burned away. If she hurried, she could get there in an hour and a half. She settled her net bag more firmly on her back, checked her water gourd, and set off.

She moved steadily through the canopy, pausing now and again to check her bearings. When she was only fifteen or twenty minutes from the beacon, Juna stopped to rest in the topmost branches of an emergent tree. She ate one of the sweet red fruits left over from last night's feast and admired the view. The sea was a sheet of silver, dappled by shafts of light breaking through the majestic grey clouds heavy with the day's rain. A fresh sea breeze gently rocked the branch on which she was seated. She felt like the queen of the forest here. Why did the aliens spend all their time buried in the gloom of the canopy, when they could be up here in the fresh air and sunshine? Were they agoraphobic? Did they hate the sun?

It was time to go. Juna tossed the last fruit pit out into space and shouldered her bag. Just as she was swinging down to the next branch, an immense shadow tore out of the sky like a black thunderbolt. Something sharp struck her shoulder, knocking her from the branch. She fell, tumbling. The tree branches seemed to move past her with preternatural slowness as she fell. She reached out and grabbed a passing branch.

There was a wrenching jolt. Pain shot up her arm. She wasn't falling anymore. Time moved normally again. For a moment, Juna just hung there, too shocked to move, not quite able to believe that she was alive. She reached up to grasp the branch that she clung to with her other hand, and felt a sharp pain in her shoulder. Setting her teeth and grunting with the pain, Juna pulled herself up onto the branch.

Something warm oozed down her back. She reached back
with her good arm. Her hand came away sticky with blood. She
probed higher with her fingers and found two deep scratches in
her shoulder. What the hell had hit her? She felt as if she'd been
struck by lightning out of a clear blue sky.

A black shadow crossed the sun, too quickly for it to be a
cloud. Juna looked up in time to make out the form of an
impossibly large raptor gliding above the treetops. She recognized it immediately. She had spotted several of them during
trips over the jungle in one of the Survey flyers. They were
massive, powerful creatures with a leathery wingspan of over
five meters. She had been impressed by the raptor, but, with
typical human arrogance, believed that it couldn't harm her,
and so had dismissed it. Now she knew why the aliens avoided
the topmost branches of the canopy.

Juna took a deep breath. It was over. She was all right. Her
shoulders hurt like hell, one injured, the other strained, but she
was alive. Settling herself securely in a nearby crotch, she took
out her med kit and doctored the wound. It was awkward and
painful. The wound was in a hard-to-reach place and it hurt to
lift her arm. Still she managed to clean it and cover it with
antiseptic fleshfoam. Then she climbed slowly and painfully to
the ground and walked the rest of the way.

The first drops of rain began to fall as she reported in. She
summarized her activities of the night before and documented
her link with Ukatonen, and how it had given her the ability to
depict skin speech. The physiology people would be fascinated
by what had happened to her, as would the Alien Contact
specialist and the linguists back home. The more excited they
got, the sooner they would return for her.

Then she turned to the messages she had received. There
were several hundred K of personal messages and mail. They
would be precious and painful. Juna decided to shelve them for
later. She needed to attend to business. The ship would make
the jump to hyperspace just past midnight, and she had a lot
more information to send in before that happened. She sat in
the pounding downpour and dictated reports for a couple of
hours. Her voice was rough and hoarse, and the wound on her
shoulder throbbed. Something touched her wounded shoulder.

She jumped and looked around. Ukatonen and Anito were standing there.

"Come," Anito told her, beckoning her to follow.

Juna needed to take a break; her voice was wearing out. She signed off and followed the aliens into the jungle. When they were safely ensconced in a large tree, Anito touched the fleshfoam covering her wound.

"What is on your arm?"

"Bird hurt me. I fix hurt," Juna explained.

"You allu-a with me. I fix better," Anito told her. The alien held out its arms to Juna, indicating that it wanted to link with her.

Juna shook her head. Linking still terrified her.

Anito persisted, flickers of yellow irritation crossing its ochre skin. Ukatonen watched them talk, saying nothing.

Juna shook her head again, rubbing at her itching eyes. If she gave in to Anito, all of the aliens would want to link with her, and there would be nothing of herself left by the time they had satisfied their curiosity.

Anito touched her arm again, pleading with Juna for a link. "Shoulder bad. You get sick."

Juna shrugged off the alien's touch and looked away. She was tired of telling the aliens to keep out of her body. Her shoulder burned and her eyes itched. She sneezed as she got up to go back to the beacon. Her head felt thick and heavy. What a time to be coming down with a cold. She couldn't get sick, she had too much to do. . . .

Anito grabbed Juna's arm and jerked her around so that she was looking at the alien.

"Sick you! Bad sick you!"

A picture appeared on Anito's chest. It was a picture of Juna, before the aliens rescued her, dying in the forest. Then the alien superimposed a picture of Juna as she looked now, with two red scratches on her shoulder, and flickered between the two. Then Anito's skin turned silvery-pale. The sick elder, Ilto, had looked like that after it died. Anito extended its arms again, asking for a link.

The alien had always accepted Juna's refusals to link before. Something else was going on. Juna rubbed at her itching eyes

and tried to think. She felt terrible. She hadn't felt this bad since
her suit had been breached. Her skin flared orange as a sudden
surge of fear jolted through her. She was on the verge of
anaphylactic shock. She looked at the two aliens. They knew
what was happening to her. Anito was asking for permission to
save her life.

"Yes," Juna said in skin speech. "I understand." She held out
her arms to Anito, wordlessly requesting a link.

Anito's skin turned a deep, reassuring dark blue, as it
grasped Juna's arm with one hand. Ukatonen took the other
arm, and the two aliens linked with her. Juna was inside the link
so quickly that she barely had time to be frightened.

Anito's link felt less controlled and subtle than Ukatonen's.
There was less sense of focus, of flow and control. It was clear
that Anito was younger and less experienced. Juna could sense
Ukatonen hovering in the background watching over the two of
them in their link.

Despite Anito's youth and lack of subtlety, the alien was a
competent healer. Juna's eyes stopped itching within seconds.
Her head cleared, and her sore throat eased. She felt a warm
tingling in her shoulder, and a sudden tightness as the edges of
the wound closed over. She felt the pain lift from her bruised
muscles as Anito's presence healed them. Something in the
flavor of the link made Juna aware that Anito was female. She
became so involved in sorting out what it was that made
Anito's presence so ineffably female that the breaking of the
link caught her by surprise.

Juna sat for a few minutes, disoriented by the sudden shift
from linking to not-linking. It was like being awakened in the
middle of an extremely vivid dream. There was an unreal
feeling to allu-a. She blinked a few times and took a deep
breath. Her throat was no longer sore, her eyes weren't itching,
and her breathing was clear. Anito had saved her life again.

"Thank you," she said at last. "I not know I sick."

"You not go in top of tree again?" Ukatonen asked her.

Juna shook her head, then remembered to use skin speech. "I
need feed my talking stones," she said using the aliens' term for
her computers. "They need sun."

Anito and Ukatonen conferred.

"Next time you need feed talking stones, one of us goes with you," Ukatonen said.

Juna looked from Ukatonen to Anito and back again, wondering what she should do next. Ukatonen got up and headed out toward the radio beacon. Anito and Juna followed. Ukatonen squatted beside the computer, and looked at Juna, ears raised inquisitively.

Ukatonen placed his hand on the silver radio tower. "What this is?"

Juna frowned. This was going to be hard to explain. "I talk to my people. My people very far. This tower sends talk."

"How you talk?" Ukatonen asked, ears wide in puzzlement.

Juna shrugged. "I show you."

She signed on, checking the chronometer and the estimated lag time. The link with the aliens had taken less than half an hour, she noted with surprise. Subjectively it had felt much longer. It was actually about 1500 hours. There was time for one last exchange with the ship before it jumped to hyperspace and left her here. It was time to introduce the aliens to the humans and vice versa.

Juna began updating the ship on her activities since the break, explaining that Anito and Ukatonen were with her. She paused and looked at Ukatonen, who watched her, ears spread wide, deep purple with wonder.

"How they hear you?" he asked.

Juna thought of trying to explain how radio worked, with her limited vocabulary, and shook her head. "Hard tell you," she explained, hoping she was using the right words.

"I talk them?" Ukatonen asked.

"You talk me, I tell them what say you. Good?"

Ukatonen flickered agreement.

Juna set up the computer for visual and vocal recording, guided Ukatonen within range of the computer's camera, then nodded to him to begin.

"Formal greetings, Eerin's people. I am Ukatonen, an enkar {untranslatable social status term}. I speak to you through Eerin. The village of Lyanan {untranslatable village place name} is in {untranslatable} because the {long list of plant, tree, and animal names}"—here Ukatonen pointed to the burnt, black gap in the green forest—"is through your actions, no longer there. The village is angry. What may be done to bring {untranslatable}?"

Juna sighed. This was going to be difficult. She looked at the charred expanse of burnt forest, destroyed during normal Survey sterilization procedures before leaving the planet. It helped ensure that no Terran bacteria survived to contaminate the planet. If the Survey had known about the aliens, they would have acted differently. It would be up to her to make reparations.

"The alien sends formal greetings from its people, and wants to know what we are going to do about that piece of forest that we burned down. Apparently it belonged to a nearby village. I will do what I can to make reparations. Please advise." Juna sent along the visual clip of the alien's speech with her translation for their computers to analyze.

Juna nodded at Ukatonen. "It's done," she told him.

Ukatonen's ears spread wide. He watched the radio intently, waiting for a reply.

Juna touched Ukatonen on the shoulder. He looked at her.

"My people are far," Juna said, gesturing into the sky. "They not speak—" She paused; duration was one of the aspects of skin speech that she didn't understand. She pointed at the sun, which was a low, bright spot behind heavy clouds. "It be night when they speak back to us."

Ukatonen's ears spread wide again. "Where your people? How they hear you?"

Juna hesitated. It was against Contact regs to explain space travel to such low-tech people. She had half a dozen plausible cover stories, but she simply couldn't bring herself to lie to Ukatonen.

So going slowly, groping painfully for the words that she needed, she explained that their planet circled a star, and that her people were from another star, and had traveled there in a ship. She had to use rocks as visual aids, but eventually the aliens understood.

Ukatonen shook his head. "Not can be," he said, deeply purple. Anito, watching, echoed his words.

"It true. My people do," Juna insisted. "I speak my people.

That"—she pointed at the silver radio tower—"throws my—" she paused, not knowing the word for "voice," or even if the aliens had such a word in their language—"words to them. They understand my words; they talk back." She pointed to the tower again. "That catches their words and shows them to me."

Ukatonen looked from the tower to Juna and back again, and turned an odd shade of puce, probably indicative of doubt or disbelief. "Not can be," Ukatonen repeated.

"My people can do," Juna insisted.

Doubt, wonder, and a tinge of fear rippled across the alien's skin. "When your people return?"

Juna shrugged and fought back a sudden surge of fear and grief. She shook her head. "Many, many, many—" She paused, and pointed to the eastern horizon, sweeping her arm across the sky to the west, the pattern for sun on her chest.

Ukatonen supplied what Juna hoped was the term for "day."

"Many days," she said. She tried to explain what a year was, gesturing to the rocks she had used to represent their sun and planet, but Ukatonen shook his head.

Juna searched for the words to explain, but couldn't find them. She picked up a pebble. "My people's ship," she said.

Ukatonen rippled understanding.

"My people leave." Juna moved the pebble farther from the planet. "They go so far and—" Juna picked up the pebble and threw it. It landed several meters away. "Now they can't hear my words. I can't hear their words."

Juna picked up another, fist-sized stone. "My people's sun." She picked up another rock. "My people's world," she said. She picked up the ship pebble and placed it beside the rock representing her home planet. "My people leave your sun, go my sun. Then they come back." She picked up the ship pebble and tossed it back toward the aliens' solar system. "Many, many, many days."

Ukatonen turned puce again.

"My people can do," Juna insisted. "This day, my people hear my words. When the sun is there"—she pointed at the eastern horizon—"my people no longer hear my words. I wait many, many, many days before they come back. I am—" She paused, not knowing the word for "alone" in the aliens' language. She flushed a dark, funereal grey and looked away, as the depth of her isolation sunk in.

Ukatonen's knuckles brushed her shoulder. Juna looked up. Anito was gone; she and Ukatonen were alone beneath the gleaming metal tower.

"I am like you," Ukatonen said, "Always one person. Never with others. I understand. I am *enkar*," he said, using a term that Juna didn't understand, though she had seen it before. "Enkar are always one person."

Ukatonen got up and walked back over the rocky expanse of the cliff into the jungle. Juna stared after the alien until he disappeared into the solid mass of green. She returned to her reports feeling as though a tight cord binding her heart had been released. She worked steadily, updating and finishing reports on the aliens and their ecosystem. She finished her work as the sun touched the horizon.

She stood up and stretched, feeling empty. Every detail in her log had been transferred to the ship, she had answered all of the questions she could. The Survey had everything she knew about the aliens. She got up and walked to the edge of the cliff. Clouds of seabirds whirled to and fro, riding the rising air currents. One of them rose up from beneath the edge of the cliff, hanging a couple of meters in front of her, holding its position with tiny movements of its iridescent blue-grey wings and tail. It wasn't a true bird; its face was scaled and it had a toothy lizard's snout instead of a beak, but it filled the place of a sea gull in the ecosystem. It regarded her with its beady, enigmatic black eyes for a moment, then slid away on the wind, arcing out over the ocean until she lost it amongst the other birds.

Her mother would have loved to see that. She had always gloried in birds, especially seabirds. Juna remembered that when they still lived on Earth her mother used to take her to the coast. They would sit on the cliffs, watching the birds fly. They would hover just as this bird did, on the strong updraft from a windward cliff. She remembered her mother, standing near the edge of a cliff, the wind streaming back through her sun veils, laughing at some hovering bird.

She turned back to the radio tower. She had a little over an hour before her final transmission window closed. She wanted to send a letter to her father, and take care of as many personal details as she could before the ship entered transition.

"Father, this is Juna," she dictated. "The good news is that I'm still alive. By now the Survey has told you the bad news. It's going to be a long time until I see you again. I miss you, and Toivo, and Danan. I won't be entirely alone. There are aliens here. They're very strange, but I think we will come to understand each other better. The world is beautiful, and I'm the first human ever to survive without an environment suit on a living world.

"The aliens here are like zero-gee trapeze dancers, only more graceful and agile. I've gotten very good at climbing. I had to, in order to keep up with them. I spend most of my time in the trees now."

Juna paused, not quite knowing how to say the next few necessary words.

"If I don't come back, please give my extra Survey pin to Danan. I know he'd like to have it. Keep half my money for Danan, and the other half should go to you and Toivo.

"Just before I wrote this letter, I stood on the cliffs and watched some birds flying out over the ocean. It made me think of Mama. Please put some flowers on her grave for me. Tell Toivo and Danan that I love them. I love you too. Take care of yourself."

Juna replayed the message. There was so much that she wanted to say, but she was tired and drained by the long reports she had filed. She thought of her father, stocky and slightly bowlegged, as he walked between his vines. Tears rose to her eyes. He was getting old. Would he still be there when she came home?

She sent other messages, to family, friends, and to her ex-wives and husbands. Survey members shouldn't bond with the system-bound. She hadn't been able to keep up with her group marriage. She was away for years at a time, and the marriage couldn't stand the separation. Still, she cherished the memories, and from time to time she would visit, to catch up with her former spouses and to see how the children had grown.

Her computer's chrono chimed softly, reminding her that she had twenty minutes left. After that, her messages wouldn't reach the *Kotani Maru* before it made the jump to hyperspace. She finished her last letter and sent it only a few minutes before her transmission window closed. Then she got up and walked to the cliff edge again. The sun was a red ember on the horizon. As she watched, it sank below the sea and vanished. Juna went back to the forest.

Ukatonen and Anito were waiting for her. They beckoned her on, their words glowing like fireflies in the dark jungle, to the nest they had built in a tree near the edge of the forest. Juna was relieved that she wouldn't have to face a village full of curious aliens tonight.

"When your people speak back to us?" Ukatonen asked her when they were settled.

Juna shrugged. It would be almost two hours before the ship responded to Ukatonen's translated message.

"We eat, go out and wait. Their words come," Juna told them.

She was so exhausted that she was almost looking forward to the *Kotani Maru*'s final transmission. At least then she could get some sleep.

They ate, washed themselves in a nearby stream, and filed out to the radio beacon to await word from the ship.

Twenty minutes later, Kinsey, the Alien Contact specialist, signed on, telling Juna that he wanted to speak to Ukatonen. He paused for a couple of minutes, so that Juna and Ukatonen could prepare themselves, then began.

"My name is Arthur Kinsey. On behalf of the Solarian United Government, the Interstellar Survey, and the Interstellar Survey Vessel *Kotani Maru*, I accept your formal greetings, and offer you ours in return. We deeply regret the destruction of the forest. If we had known that there were intelligent aliens with land-rights to that section of forest, we would never have disturbed it. We will do our best to make reparations for such damage when we return. We thank you for the care and healing of Dr. Saari, and ask that you continue to treat her well until we return. We will do our best to repay you for your efforts in this matter. Our people live very far away. We estimate that it will be four to six of your years before we are able to return, but we will return for Dr. Saari, and to learn more about you. Until then, we wish you peace and prosperity. Thank you. This is Arthur Kinsey signing off."

Juna frowned, and glanced up at Ukatonen, who was leaning against one of the beacon supports, ears spread expectantly. This was going to be very hard to translate.

"The person who is speaking sends greetings from all of my people. We apologize for burning (here Juna appended as much of the detailed description of the forest as she could remember). My people will try to make this better when they come back for me. He also thanks you for taking care of me, and says that my people will be very grateful for that. He says that my people live very far away, and that it will be many, many, many days before they come back. He also says that we want to learn more about your people. He asks you to teach me about your people so that I may teach my people when they return. He hopes that you have good hunting and much good food until they come back. He thanks you."

Ukatonen looked puzzled. "That was very strange," he said at last.

Juna touched him on the shoulder. "I not do a very good job. I don't have the words. I try again when I know more," she offered. "This person knows only what I have told him about you. Your people and my people are very different."

"Yes," Ukatonen said with a glowing ripple of amusement. "I see that."

Juna smiled and rippled with shared amusement, then turned back to the radio, to listen for more messages and instructions. The two aliens touched her shoulder and slipped back into the forest.

Following his message, Kinsey downloaded the Survey's alien contact protocols, and noninterference guidelines for alien cultures. Juna rolled her eyes when she saw them. They were completely impractical. She had broken the rules on food and personal contact only minutes into her first meeting with Anito. Her explanation of space travel to the aliens was in direct violation of the technology transfer dictates, as was using the computer in their presence. These guidelines were for someone with a Survey base to retreat to between contacts. She simply couldn't follow them.

She also was not empowered to make treaties, or agree to reparations. Juna sighed. She would be returning to the radio beacon periodically to send updates to the Survey satellites so that they would have a complete record in case she was lost or killed. She needed the goodwill of the neighboring village. To get that, she might need to make up for her fellow humans' mistakes.

After Kinsey's report, Morale Officer Chang came on with another of her sententious little speeches. She expressed deep concern over Juna's link with the alien, and ordered her not to do it again. Juna turned down the sound. Leaving the computer to record her messages, she got up and walked to the edge of the cliff. Sitting cross-legged near the edge, she looked out at the quiet alien night. The shadows of shy night birds flickered past her as they emerged from their holes in the cliff-side and flew out to sea to fish.

The sea was phosphorescent tonight. The waves glowed green as they struck the shoreline. Out at sea a school of fish left a trail of brilliant green streaks in the water.

She used to come out here in her environment suit, before she had been lost, just to watch the stars and the ocean. How different it all seemed, now that she wasn't trapped inside her suit. Then she had been hot and stuffy, unable to feel the night breeze. The clatter and hum of the base's machinery, and the whirring of her suit had drowned out the cries of the birds and the shimmering sounds of the insects.

It was a beautiful night. Only a few clouds obscured the heavens. Juna looked up at the stars. Sol with its jeweled necklace of colonies, and the bright, diseased gem that was Earth, was not visible. It could only be seen from the planet's northern hemisphere. Just as well, she thought to herself. If she could see Earth, she would yearn for it even more.

She began to hum a tune her mother had loved, an old tune from before The Collapse. Her mother had learned it as a child, and passed it along to her daughter. It was about a bird called the albatross, one of the first Antarctic birds to die as the ozone hole spread north. The long-winged, graceful birds spent nine months flying alone over the open ocean, returning to the same mate every year. Juna sang to herself about going away and coming back again, about someone waiting for her return. As she sang, her grief eased.

She fell silent, watching the stars. She heard the sound of surf pounding against the cliffs, the thin high cries of the night birds, and the sound of her own breathing. The computer chimed, signaling the time that the *Kotani Maru* made the jump. She was alone now, an alien on an alien world. She got up and walked into the jungle, where Anito and Ukatonen slept. She would parcel out the news and messages from the Survey ship, making them last as long as she could. They would be the only human voices she would hear for years.

N i n e

"It's crazy," Anito told Ukatonen as they watched the new creature making noises at a box built into the base of the strange tree made of silvery death-colored stone. "When it found out that its people went away, it went crazy."

"But where did Eerin's people go?" Ukatonen asked Anito, referring to the new creature by the name he had given it.

Anito disliked the name. She didn't believe the new creature was intelligent enough to deserve a name. The enkar had even started calling the creature by the same pronoun used for a female Tendu. It made the creature more like a real person. As far as she was concerned, the new creature barely qualified as an animal, and should be referred to as such.

"I don't know," Anito said. "They're gone. Isn't that enough?"

A ripple of exasperation passed over Ukatonen's body. "You're an elder now. It's time to start thinking like one. You must think past today. What if the new creatures come back and destroy more forest? What if they've gone somewhere else and are destroying the forest there? Remember, these creatures are your atwa. Whatever they do, you are responsible for it."

Anito looked away, angered by the unfairness of it all. She had only taken on the new creature to humor Ilto. Now she was responsible for things that had happened far from her village.

Ukatonen touched her gently on the shoulder. Anito looked around. "Someone must find out what happened here and how to stop it from happening again. Someone must be responsible. But this isn't a load that you can carry alone. We'll do it together."

Anito looked away again, fighting back a dark red wave of anger and frustration. She looked out over the black ashes of the destroyed forest. She had never seen anything like this. Lightning would sometimes take out three or four trees, or a mud slide would clear out a patch of hillside, but never had she contemplated such an expanse of devastation. It still felt like an impossibility, even as she looked at it. She thought about this happening somewhere else, to some other village, to her own village, and the venom sacs on her back tightened in anger and fear.

Ukatonen was right, something had to be done. She looked at the enkar. He was watching her, ears spread expectantly.

"What do you want me to do?" Anito asked.

"Stay here. Look after Eerin. Find out where her people might have gone. I'll go to Lyanan and see what can be done about this." Ukatonen gestured at the blackened devastation before them. His skin turned grey with grief at the destruction.

Agreement and sympathy passed over Anito's body. Ukatonen touched her on the shoulder and disappeared into the forest.

Anito walked across the blackened remains of the forest, feeling exposed and vulnerable. The new creature was silent, its skin grey with sadness. It looked up as Anito approached, but otherwise remained motionless.

The new creature's left foot was bleeding. Anito squatted down and examined the foot more closely. The sole was cut from running across the sharp rock of the cliffs. If the cuts weren't treated, the creature would get sick.

The creature was too stupid to take care of itself, Anito thought with a sudden burst of irritation, and it wouldn't allow her to link with it even for healing. Anito synthesized something to speed healing and keep the creature from getting sick.

"Bad feet, you," she told the new creature in simplified speech. "Not good. Get sick."

"Where people?" she asked as she rubbed the healing substance into the creature's feet.

The creature shook its head. Its grey color deepened.

"Gone?" Anito asked.

The new creature's shoulders moved up and down. It shook its head, pointed at the sun, then swung an arm in a wide arc until it was pointing directly east. Then it pointed at itself and patted the ground.

Anito pondered the creature's gesture. It wanted to stay here. Anito nodded to let it know that she understood. She told the creature that she would go find food and come back. The creature nodded its head and leaned back against the silver tree, closing its eyes.

Anito walked back across the horrible expanse of burnt forest. A lavender ripple of relief flowed across her body as she felt the dim, cool safety of the forest enfold her. Fortunately the burnt patch of the forest was on the edge of Lyanan's territory. She could hunt in the wild lands without worrying about disrupting the balance of the village's atwas. They had been disrupted enough by the new creatures. She swung up into a red-barked tavirra tree, and headed into the wild lands to hunt.

Game was sparser than she had expected. The village had probably shifted its hunting pattern to make up for the loss of their forest. Anito set out some snares, picked some ripe red yarra berries, and gathered a variety of greens. Her snares yielded a pair of ground-dwelling leang. She surveyed the birds with a critical eye. They were small, but they would do. Night had fallen by the time she returned to the clearing with food.

The new creature refused to leave the deathstone tree to eat. It felt wrong to eat in the middle of such devastation. Just thinking about it made Anito's throat dry and tight. She set the food down and walked back into the forest.

Anito settled herself in the crotch of a half-charred tree to eat and keep watch over the new creature. She had been watching for a while when she heard a sound from the deathstone tree. She slid farther out on the branch. The new creature sat up excitedly and did something to the sharp-cornered box at the base of the tree.

Anito swung down out of her tree, and moved quietly toward

the deathstone tree. A murmuring sound, like water gurgling, was coming from the box. It was like the sounds the new creature made, only deeper in pitch. The new creature listened, then made noises back to the box.

Anito watched and listened intently. What was the new creature doing? Was this some kind of mating ritual? Why would it try to mate with a box? That made no sense at all.

The new creature was always making noise. It made a lot of noises to the strange, half-alive speaking stone that it carried, and the stone responded. It made noises at the stone and the stone then spoke to Anito and Ukatonen in skin speech. They spoke skin speech to the new creature, and the box made noises. Was this some form of communication? If so, it was very inefficient. It would scare away any animals that you were stalking, and tell every predator in hearing range exactly where you were.

Anito returned to the familiar refuge of the forest to think over this strange new idea. She lay along a branch watching the new creature. Something very odd was going on here. How could a dead object like a box talk? It wasn't even half-alive, like the speaking stone. Was there something in the box, some kind of animal? She had never heard an animal that sounded like that. Had the new creature captured a spirit, as in the old stories?

Like a shadow, Ukatonen appeared on a nearby branch.

"How is Eerin?" he asked, his words enlarged to be visible through the thick fog and the pre-dawn gloom.

"The new creature is fine."

The enkar swung over and joined Anito on her branch. "Have you found out where her people are?"

"No, but I think that those noises it's making are like skin speech. It 'talks' to the box, and the box talks back. How could a dead thing like a box talk, en?"

"I don't know," Ukatonen said in mauve hues of puzzlement. He sat silent, eyes hooded, lost in thought.

At last, unable to contain herself, Anito touched his shoulder. "What is it, en?" she asked him. "What's going on? Is it spirits, like in the stories?"

"I don't know, kene," he told her. "I have lived a long time and I have never seen a spirit. Spirits live here," he said, touching her forehead. "Not out here among us."

"Then what is the new creature doing?"

"Perhaps Eerin really is talking to her people."

Anito turned a doubtful shade of puce. "How could it do that? It says that its people are far away."

"I don't know," Ukatonen admitted, "but you've seen that strange talking stone that she's always playing with. I don't know how it works, but it talks, both in Eerin's language and ours. I spoke to the villagers last night. They said that the new creatures have many dead-but-alive objects, like that box, that do many strange things. These new creatures are very odd."

There was a noise from the deathstone tree. Anito and Ukatonen leaned forward, straining to see through the thick morning fog. The two of them swung silently down to the ground and crept closer, skins the mournful color of the fog around them. The new creature was completely absorbed in the strange noises from the box. They could walk right up to it, Anito thought scornfully, and the new creature wouldn't notice until they touched it. The box talked for a long time. The fog began to thin. Ukatonen touched Anito's shoulder and motioned with his head, and the two of them slipped back into the forest, silently as the fog itself. The creature never even looked up.

Ukatonen acted strangely subdued when they reached the trees. He sat hunched in thought, his eyes locked on the figure under the strange deathstone tree. At last he blinked, shook himself, and looked at Anito.

"I had a hard time believing some of the villagers' stories, but now—" He paused. His skin flickered several times as though he was about to say something.

"I don't know what to think," he said at last. "It's very strange." His skin had a faint tinge of orange fear to it. Anito felt the venom sacs in the red lines on her back tighten.

Ukatonen held up a gathering sack. "I brought you some food. Keep an eye on Eerin. Bring the creature back to the village tonight. I want the elders to get a good look at her."

Anito flickered agreement and settled back into the crotch of the tree to watch the new creature. It remained sitting under the

strange death-colored stone tree, heedless of the burning sun
and its exposed position. Anito found herself scanning the sky,
looking for the black shadow of a koirah. They usually hunted
in the mornings, before the clouds gathered. The new creature
was protected by the strange death-colored stone tree that it sat
under, but Anito still felt anxious. The sky remained a blank
blue slate, so bright it made her eyes ache. As the morning
progressed, heat began to rise off the scorched plain. The air
danced in bright waves over the ashes. Anito's skin was dry and
her throat ached with thirst. Duty held her to this hot, dry spot,
though she longed to retreat to the coolness of the inner forest.
She shifted uncomfortably on the branch. How could the
creature stand the heat and the terrible glare?

At long last the new creature got up and headed for the
forest. Anito glanced anxiously at the pale bright sky, but there
was no sign of a koirah. That didn't make it safe. Koirah
sometimes came diving down out of a seemingly empty sky.
Fortunately, the big flying reptiles were rare, and they preferred
to pick their prey out of the top branches of the canopy.

The new creature reached the forest safely. It was sitting
unhappily on a branch, scratching itself, when Anito swung up
beside it.

"People come?" Anito asked.

The new creature nodded.

"When people come?"

The creature shook its head and gestured wildly.

"Don't you know?" Anito asked. "You've been talking to
them for a long time."

The creature shook its head again. It couldn't understand her,
Anito realized. It was too busy scratching to follow a conversation. Anito examined the creature's skin. It had the dry, dull
look of a serious sunburn.

"Skin bad. Don't go out until it starts raining."

The creature shook its head once more.

A trickle of yellow irritation forked down Anito's back. If the
new creature's skin was too badly damaged, the creature would
be vulnerable to the things that made it sick. She synthesized a
sunburn cure in her allu-a and squirted it on the troublesome

new animal's back. Then she gave it food and persuaded it to
stay in the cool gloom of the forest until it started raining.

When the rains came, the new creature returned to the
silvery deathstone tree. It stayed there, talking and listening to
the box at the base of the tree until it was dark. Anito met it at
the forest's edge, and followed the scent trail Ukatonen laid
down to guide them to the village of Lyanan.

Anito could feel the hostility of the village as soon as they
reached the tree. Tilan bees hovered around them, unwilling to
trust their unfamiliar scent. The village elders' greeting was
terse and rudely informal. Nevertheless, Anito greeted them
with all the politeness due their station, not one feather's-
weight more or less. It was what Ilto would have done.
Glancing over, Anito saw a tiny ripple of approval trickle down
Ukatonen's arm.

The enkar stepped forward and fanned his ears wide,
commanding the attention of the entire village with this one
small gesture. "I am assisting Anito in the matter of the new
creatures, and I appreciate the kind welcome you have given
us."

A faint brown stain of embarrassment passed over the
villagers. Ukatonen had neatly and gently shamed them for
their rudeness. The subtlety of the maneuver impressed Anito.

Ukatonen went on with his speech. "Although Anito is
young, she was well-raised by one of the finest inkata I have
known, the chief elder of Narmolom. He judged Anito to be
capable of accepting this challenging and difficult atwa. I have
traveled with her and the new creature for almost a month and
I agree with his judgment of this fine young elder."

Anito raised her ears in surprise at Ukatonen's words.

The enkar turned and gestured at her to come forward.
"Please, kene-sa, tell her all of the stories that you have told
me. Tell her everything that you have observed about the new
creatures. This is her atwa, and she needs our help to bring it
into harmony with the rest of the world."

Ukatonen stepped back, leaving Anito alone in the speaker's
position. The elders looked at her expectantly, waiting for her
to speak. She felt suddenly very small and frightened. The

weight of the elders' gaze fell upon her like the coils of a huge matrem snake. She needed to act before it crushed her.

"Kene-sa," she said, using the collective, formal title of the elders, "I am eager to hear what you know about the new creatures. I need to understand these creatures before I can work with them. Please give me your help." She stepped back beside Ukatonen, out of the speaker's position, wishing that she had delivered a more impressive speech.

Ukatonen's knuckles brushed her shoulder; out of the corner of her eye she caught a flicker of reassurance and approval.

Lalito, the chief elder, stepped up to the speaker's position. "We will try to help you. Please, be welcome and eat." She picked up a basket full of neatly folded packets of yarram and held it out to the two of them. Ukatonen took a packet, then Anito stepped forward and took two packets, one for herself, and one for the new creature. A ripple of surprise fluttered over the assembled villagers at this gesture. Ukatonen thanked Lalito calmly, as though Anito had done nothing unusual.

The ceremony over, everyone sat down and began eating. Ripples of laughter and flickers of conversation passed across the villagers' bodies. Anito felt suddenly homesick for Narmolom. She was a stranger here. She wanted to be home again, learning to be an elder in her own village, with an atwa she understood. She longed to be a part of things instead of an outsider.

Ukatonen brushed her shoulder. "You did well," he told her. "The villagers are on your side now."

Anito looked away, embarrassed by his praise. "It was your doing."

"I merely said good things about you. You proved them to be true."

"How did I do that?"

"By not being angered when they were rude. By not trying to be more than you are. You showed them a courageous young elder, coping well under enormously difficult circumstances. They sympathize with you now. They want to help."

"But I only did what was polite. Any well-raised Tendu would do the same in a similar situation."

"Exactly," Ukatonen said. "You proved that you were smart and well-raised."

"What should we do about the new creatures?"

"For now? Keep this one healthy; watch, and learn as much as we can. The more we know, the better we will be at dealing with them if they return."

After dinner the villagers crowded around the new creature and began examining it. They were much less gentle than Anito's people had been. In Narmolom it had the sponsorship of a revered chief elder. Here it was one of the creatures who had willfully destroyed part of their home. It would take more than a lifetime before the destroyed forest was back in harmony with its surroundings. The entire village would have to work to restore it, neglecting other important work. It was little wonder that the Tendu of Lyanan were angry.

Anito watched the new creature anxiously, but it bore the villagers' mistreatment bravely and without apparent anger. Anito was impressed with its patience and forbearance. At last the creature looked at Ukatonen and her. Anito knew the creature well enough to recognize that look. It was tired and wanted this to stop.

Ukatonen brushed Lalito's shoulder. "The new creature is tired, kene," he said politely. "She needs sleep. May I please take Eerin upstairs and let her sleep?"

Lalito flickered acquiescence. There was no polite way to refuse a request from an enkar, not without losing face in front of the entire village.

"I'll take the new creature up to our guest quarters, en," Anito offered. She felt uncomfortable in the presence of all these hostile strangers, and wanted a chance to be alone.

Ukatonen flickered acknowledgment, and Anito beckoned to the creature. She led it up to the guest quarters at the top of the tree, just below the rooms where the tinka slept. The creature crawled into the nearest bed and fell asleep almost immediately.

Anito squatted against the wall and watched it sleep. Its deep, regular breathing sounded loud in the quiet room. It was noisy even when it was asleep. She should never have agreed to take this creature as her atwa. It brought nothing but trouble.

Anito shook her head. It was a gesture she had picked up from the new creature, she realized, flushing beige with disgust.

It was more than half a month since they had left Narmolom. Watching the villagers talk, she found herself longing for home. She was tired of coping with strange creatures and strange Tendu.

Ukatonen came in. "I was wondering why you didn't come back down," he said.

"I wanted to be alone for a while."

"You miss your village, don't you?" Ukatonen said. "I'm never lonely until I'm among people. I can spend months alone in the forest and never notice, but if I spend the night at a village, I suddenly feel alone." Grey sadness clouded his skin briefly. "It's watching them all together, gossiping and telling stories. They share something that I don't. It can be hard, not having any place you belong."

"Don't you ever feel at home anywhere?" Anito asked him.

"Sometimes," he said. "In the wild lands, there are moments when everything is in harmony. I feel at home then. When I spend time with the other enkar, we share something. It's not like a village, but . . ." A ripple of blue-grey longing crossed his skin. "It's been a while since I've spent time with the other enkar. I've been living like a trader, traveling from village to village."

Anito felt honored by the brief glimpse he had given her of what it was like to be an enkar. She brushed his shoulder with her knuckles. "I'm sorry, en. Would you like to link with me? Would that make you feel better?"

Ukatonen touched her shoulder with a ripple of regret. "Thank you, Anito," he said, "but you need to listen to the villagers tell about the new creatures. Perhaps later."

They rejoined the village elders, who were sitting around the edge of the pool talking. A few were linked in allu-a over in the shadows. Conversation ceased as Ukatonen and Anito joined the group.

"Please tell us about the new creatures," Ukatonen asked.

A rainbow of responses erupted, mostly in shades of anger and fear. Ukatonen held up his hands, and the flickering colors dimmed.

"You, Korto," he said, pointing at one of the elders. "You and your bami were the first to see them. Tell me what happened."

Korto moved forward into the speaker's position. She ducked her head shyly at the enkar. "The afternoon rains had started to fall. My bami and I were on our way to South Point beach to gather yarram and lyarrin, when we heard a strange sound. We looked out at the ocean, and a large white thing floated out there, making a growling noise. At first I thought it was one of those giant teatari that the lyali-Tendu tell of, but it didn't have long arms. It came right up onto the beach. It opened up a hole in its belly and some new creatures came out, five of them, I think. They were all white, like they were sick. They walked up and down the beach, and climbed up onto the cliff. Then they went back and climbed into the big thing's belly. After a while the growly creature began moving up the path to the cliff. It didn't have legs; it moved on silver strips of stone that rolled along the ground. It was very heavy and left deep tracks in the beach sand. I sent my bami to the village to tell them what was going on.

"Once the big white thing was up on the cliff face, other creatures got out. They made holes in the rock, and filled them with something. Then there was a loud noise. It shook the ground and the trees, scaring all the animals. I—" Korto flushed deep brown. "I ran away, en. The noise frightened me. That was all I saw."

"Thank you, kene, you did well," Ukatonen told her, deep blue with approval. His praise only deepened her embarrassment, but Anito saw an azure circle of pride flare on her back as the young elder returned to her seat.

"Who saw the creatures next?"

Flickers of conversation passed across the assembled elders like wind through the trees. Two elders stepped forward. One of them said:

"Lalito sent us to see what Korto had found. We went to the cliff. They were making the deathstone tree that they left behind. Other new creatures burned away all of the plants on the cliffs. Then they put a thick sheet of something that was clear like water, only harder, down on the ground. It began to swell, until it looked like a bubble, only much bigger. It was at least eight yai across, en, and as tall as the canopy. The end of the bubble was connected to the big white growly thing. They began pulling things out of the thing's belly, and making big boxes inside the bubble. There were at least a dozen of the creatures, en. They took off their white coverings when they were inside, and we could see that they had brown skin and fur on the tops of their heads, like an ika flower. They wore coverings under the white coverings. They were very strange, en. They would capture and kill things, but not eat them. They took them apart, en, but they didn't eat them."

"What else did they do?" Ukatonen asked.

Lalito stepped forward into the speaker's position.

"They flew through the air in noisy creatures made of stone," the chief elder said. "They gathered all kinds of plants and insects. They wrapped whole trees in that clear stuff, and then poisoned everything inside. Then they cut the trees down and picked all of the dead things out of them. After they caught and killed a couple of tinka, we moved to a tree on the far side of our territory. There wasn't enough food. Several elders chose to die or leave so that the rest would have enough to eat. We have moved back to this side of the territory, but they burned some of our best forest. We lost five young na trees, and many of our most productive fruit trees.

"We cannot afford to have a village as large as we had before. Our bami are going to have to wait for years before they can become elders. There is no place for them to fill. It will be many years before we are back in balance. Never have I seen such a terrible calamity, en! I don't know what to do!"

Ukatonen ducked his chin, and sat, staring off into space for a long moment.

"Your troubles are not new," he said at last. He held up his hands to dim the ripple of disbelief that ran across the villagers. "While the new creatures are something we have never seen before, other villages have lost large portions of forest, sometimes larger than what you have lost. Their forests were destroyed by fire, storms, floods, mud slides, or earthquakes. Those villages have come back, and so will yours. The enkar know of your trouble. They have sent me to help you. Others will come. We will show you how to restore your ruined forest.

In a few seasons you will have more food than before. I will
speak to the sea people on behalf of the enkar, and ask them to
provide you with more food until then. The sea people owe the
enkar many debts. They will provide the food. Send some of
your people to the mountain tribes, and trade dried yarram for
food. I grant you permission to hunt the wild lands as though
they were your own lands for nine seasons. After that, you will
not need them."

"But, en," said Lalito, "we will owe the enkar a great debt.
How shall we repay you?"

"By sending your elders to become enkar, instead of letting
them die, or by sending us some of your young and gifted
bami."

Lalito turned a dull orange. "What you ask is a great
sacrifice, en. You want us to send our tired old elders to you.
They will die alone and friendless. You ask for our bami, our
future. You ask us to send them out into a strange, harsh world,
away from the village that raised them. How can we do this?"

"My life," Ukatonen said gently, "is not empty. I have lived
long and well. If sometimes I am alone, far from people who
know me, then I also enjoy my friends more when I see them.
And I have friends in many places. Every village welcomes me.
It is not a bad life. It is full of interesting things." He paused.
"If you do not wish my help, or the help of the plants and
animals that I carry, then I will go, and you may solve your
problems by yourself." He got up to leave, ignoring the protests
and pleas of the villagers.

Lalito caught at his elbow. "Please, en. We meant no offense
to you or the other enkar. It's just that we will miss our people
when they go to you."

"Your elders would be dead, and there are always tinka eager
to become bami," Ukatonen said. "But I thank you for
accepting my offer. Those you send to us will not regret it.
Tomorrow, I will begin helping you rebuild your village. I must
go and rest now." He turned and left the pool.

Anito, not wanting to face the villagers alone, followed him.
He seemed preoccupied and angry.

When they reached their room, Anito touched him gently on

the shoulder. He turned and looked at her, the red glow of his anger fading.

"What's the matter, en?" she asked.

"Nothing that I can change," he said, a mist of regret clouding his words. "It is hard, sometimes, talking to people in the villages. They see things so differently."

Anito remembered his earlier words. He was tired and lonely. It must be very hard to be an enkar. They spent so much time alone. She was glad that she had her village to return to, where she would be among her own people. She missed them so much. "Would you like to link with me, en?" she offered, holding out her arms.

Ukatonen turned an affectionate sea-green. "Yes I would. Thank you."

They entered the link, their presences swirling around each other. Anito allowed herself to feel all the loneliness bottled up inside her. She felt Ukatonen do the same. The bitter tide of loneliness that filled them drained away as they basked in each other's presence. Ukatonen's power and skill and Anito's youth and energy flowed together until they were in harmony. At last they broke the link. They sat for a moment, savoring the well-being and closeness they felt and then got up and went to bed.

When Anito woke the next morning, she thought that she was back at Narmolom. Then she sat up, and realized that home was still far away. A wave of sadness clouded her skin. It was the sense of balance and harmony left over from last night that had fooled her into thinking that she was home. Ukatonen was up, probably talking to the villagers. She rose and went out to the wild lands to gather breakfast for the three of them. She caught a fine big ponderi in a nearby stream. It would make an excellent breakfast, and she could save a fillet to give as a guest gift to Lalito. She watched the shifting patches of brown, green, and black fading as the fish died, hoping she could read the future in its skin, as the enkar were said to do. She saw nothing but a dying fish.

The new creature was sitting on the edge of the sleeping ledge when Anito arrived back at the room.

She held out the leaf cone full of fish. "Hungry?" she asked.

"Thank you, Anito," the creature replied in clear, understandable skin speech, as it reached out to take some fish.

Anito almost dropped the leaf cone. She looked questioningly at the new creature.

"Ukatonen," the creature said, holding out its arms as though requesting a link.

Ukatonen had linked with the new creature, and given it the ability to speak. It was deep work, and he had done it without a monitor, on a creature that had already killed two highly skilled elders.

"Not good," Anito told the new creature. "Ukatonen get sick. I fix."

When Ukatonen returned a few minutes later, Anito seized his arm. "Linking with the new creature is dangerous! You should have let me monitor you! Do you want to die like Kirito and Ilto?"

Ukatonen drew himself up and turned red. "I am an enkar! I don't need a monitor!"

"And I know that creature better than anyone living. I watched Kirito die. I tasted the taint that killed Ilto. The new creature is my atwa! If you die, it is my responsibility. How could I repay the enkar for your death? My village would have to spend several generations working off that debt! I refuse to carry that burden."

"Anito," Ukatonen said gently, "Eerin asked me for allu-a. I chose to do it. Even if I died, it would not be your fault. The enkar carry the burden of responsibility for the decisions they make. Your village would owe us nothing."

"But I would blame myself. Before he died, Ilto taught me how to find and clear out the new creature's taint without hurting myself. Let me check and see if you are clean. If you died because of my inaction, I would feel indebted, and my village would carry that debt," Anito said. "Please, en, let me try. I don't want you to be sick because of my atwa. You are too important to me. If I am wrong, then I am the one who looks silly. If I am right, then you would be spared sickness and death."

Ukatonen looked at her, his skin a muddy blur of conflicting emotions. At last he held out his arms, asking for allu-a. "Thank you, kene."

The two of them settled themselves in a corner. Anito linked with him. She searched through his body, and found nothing. Apparently Ilto had successfully blocked the new creature from tainting others.

"The new creature didn't make you sick, en. Please forgive me for doubting your abilities." Anito looked down, embarrassed.

Ukatonen touched her shoulder. "It's all right, Anito. Thank you for being concerned. I will ask you before I link with Eerin again. Where is she, anyway?"

Anito looked around. The new creature was gone, along with a gathering bag and its talking stone. Anito rippled puzzlement and irritation. "I'd better go and find it."

"I'll come with you."

It was raining hard by the time they reached the coast. The new creature was huddled under the deathstone tree, talking in its noisy language to its invisible new creatures. Several deep cuts ran across one shoulder, red and angry underneath a strange, translucent foam. Those wounds needed to be taken care of, or the creature would get sick. Anito felt a flicker of irritation at its carelessness.

She beckoned the new creature into the forest and, after considerable argument, persuaded the new creature to allow her and Ukatonen to heal the cuts. When they were done, they went back out to the deathstone tree. Ukatonen questioned the creature. "What is this?" he asked, pointing to the talking box.

The creature's face tightened in thought. "I talk to my people. My people very far. This box sends talk."

"I show," it said. It began making noises at the box.

Ukatonen watched intently, ears wide, then asked if he could talk to its people. The new creature fiddled with its talking stone and then guided the enkar so that he stood in front of the talking stone. Then she nodded.

Ukatonen introduced himself, and explained that the village was angry at the new creatures for burning down their forest,

and asked them how they were going to bring everything back
into harmony.

The creature looked uncomfortable and unhappy. She glanced
from the forest to Ukatonen and back to the box that talked to
the other new creatures. Then it sat down in front of the box,
and began making noises. Anito listened carefully, but nothing
in the stream of guttural sounds made any sense at all.

The creature finished the message. Anito and Ukatonen
watched the box intently for a reply.

The creature touched Ukatonen on the shoulder. "My people
are far," it said, gesturing skyward, as though its people lived
in the clouds. "They not speak—" The creature paused,
searching for words. "It be night when they speak back to us."

"Where are your people?" Ukatonen asked. "How do they
hear you?"

The creature thought for a while, as though searching for
words. Finally it set a large round pebble on the ground,
touched it, then pointed at the sky. "Rock is," it said, pointing
again at the sky.

"Rock is clouds?" Ukatonen suggested.

The new creature shook its head, and tried again. At last
Ukatonen understood. "Rock is sun," he said, and taught the
creature how to form the word. The creature picked up a
second rock. After more discussion, it declared that rock to be
the ground they sat on. Another stone became the place where
its people were.

Anito shook her head. What the creature was saying made no
sense. It was saying that its people lived in the sky like birds.
But the new creature couldn't fly. It was even afraid to climb
trees. How could her people live in the sky?

"Not can be," Anito said, mirroring Ukatonen's words.

The discussion got even crazier after that. Not only did the
new creature claim that its people lived in the sky, it also
claimed that they traveled from star to star. It told them that the
stars were like the sun, which made no sense at all. They were
smaller and you could only see them at night. Not that Anito
was crazy enough to stick her head out of the canopy at night,
where a bael could hear her with its keen night-ears, and catch

her. The creature claimed that its people were on their way to another star, and that they couldn't turn around and come back. They would return a long time from now. It wasn't clear whether Eerin was talking months, seasons, or years, but it was a long time. By the time the sun came up tomorrow, her people would be too far away to hear her words.

The creature's story was impossible, and yet Anito had heard it talking to the box and heard the box talk back. She had heard equally impossible stories about the new creatures from the villagers. If it really was from another star, then that would explain why its body was so strange. What if the stories were true? What if the new creature's people really could travel between the stars?

The venom lines tightened along Anito's back, but she didn't let her fear color her skin. She got up and walked into the forest, leaving Ukatonen to talk to the new creature. She needed to feel the forest around her, feel the reassurance of familiar things, while she thought this out.

Anito climbed high into the branches of the biggest tree in the area. She settled herself in a crotch and thought of nothing at all, letting the gentle sway of the branches soothe her. At last she was calm. What kind of atwa had she taken on? If Eerin's people really could travel between the stars, what did that mean for the Tendu? Could they come back and burn down the rest of the forest? What could her people do to stop them? Suddenly, the harmony of Anito's world seemed very vulnerable. Even this great tree with its broad branches and massive roots seemed as fragile and easily destroyed as a bird's egg.

A rustle in the branches made Anito look around. It was Ukatonen. He settled himself next to Anito.

"Your sitik died too soon," he said after a long moment of silence. "Things are becoming very interesting. Your atwa is going to be very important to all of us, Anito."

"I am not worthy of it, en," Anito said. "Please, find someone else who knows more than I do, someone who can do a better job."

"There is no one, kene. You know more about the new creature than anyone else."

"But I know so little about anything else," Anito said, bright orange with fear. "I'm just out of werrun."

"Then you must learn, kene," Ukatonen told her. "You must learn." He swung off the branch and was soon lost in the canopy, leaving Anito alone.

T e n

JUNA TILTED HER head from side to side, stretching out the kinks in her neck as she tried to focus on what the villagers were saying. She was exhausted, physically and emotionally, after her farewell to the *Kotani Maru*, but she had to pay attention. Her life might depend on this conversation.

The villagers were discussing what should be done about the destroyed section of forest. Anito had explained to her that the villagers were very angry and wanted to punish her for the forest's destruction. Ukatonen would listen and decide what should be done.

Anito told her that the villagers were describing in detail what they had lost, and suggesting suitable punishments. Most wanted to keep Juna as some kind of slave, but a few of the suggestions involved pain, injury, and even death.

At last the villagers were done speaking.

Ukatonen looked at her, ears raised. "You speak now?" he asked.

Juna stood, feeling very alone. "I understand your anger. I apologize for my people. We came to learn about the things living here. We gathered plants and animals and looked at them to see what we could learn. We afraid that we might make the forest sick, so when we go we burned the forest to kill any sickness. If we had known you were here, we not do. We look for people, but we not find you. When my people come back, we try to make right what we hurt. It easier if I am alive to help you talk to my people." Her arguments seemed very insubstantial in the face of their anger. She wished she knew more skin speech.

The aliens regarded her with their cold, inhuman eyes, skins still and neutral, watching her speak. If she thought that her arguments sounded inadequate and silly, what were they thinking?

Ukatonen waited till she was done. He turned to the assembled villagers. "What do you say to that?"

The stocky alien that Juna thought was the village chief moved to the small mound that the villagers spoke from. It glared at her, flushing red with anger.

"How many anang till your people come?" the chief asked.

Juna looked at Anito. "I don't understand. What is *anang*?"

Anito looked at Ukatonen, a flicker of lavender uncertainty rippling over her skin. "*Anang* is time. There are three seasons per *anang*."

Juna frowned. *Anang* seemed to be their word for year. She consulted her computer, which agreed with her.

"My people return in five to seven anang," Juna told the alien.

The chief elder said something, which Anito translated. "Too long to wait. Need help now."

"I help until my people return," Juna offered.

Anito laid a hand on Juna. "No. I need to go back to Narmolom. She comes with me."

The chief spoke rapidly to Ukatonen in angry hues. He replied in soothing blue tones. The rest of the village began speaking. The room was a rippling rainbow of argument and comment. Ukatonen held up his hands and the colors died away to a neutral "silent" green.

"I have heard enough. I go think. I tell you my decision *elog*," Ukatonen announced.

The gathering broke up. Anito beckoned to Juna to follow her, and they returned to their room. Ukatonen joined them. Anito and Ukatonen talked together for an hour. Juna couldn't follow their conversation, but her name sign kept appearing. They were discussing her. Juna watched anxiously, knowing that her future, and possibly her life, were at stake. Eventually Ukatonen broke off the discussion. Anito left, dark red flickers of subdued anger breaking out on her skin. The discussion must not have gone the way Anito wanted it to. Ukatonen watched Anito leave, then sat facing the wall, a sign that he didn't want to be disturbed.

Juna took out her computer and tried to work with her linguistic programs, but she was too worried to concentrate.

Ukatonen got up and squatted in front of her. Juna put down the computer.

"What is it?" Juna asked.

"All others tell me what they want," Ukatonen said. "What do you want?"

Juna thought for a minute. "I want to live. I want to return to my people. I want to go—" She paused, unsure of what the correct word for home was. At last she used *narmolom,* the word Anito used to refer to her village, unsure whether it was the word for home, or a place name.

"You not want to stay here?" Ukatonen asked.

Juna shrugged. She didn't want to live in a village full of hostile aliens. However, she needed to come back every six months or so to radio new discoveries or observations to the Survey satellites orbiting overhead.

"I not want to stay here, but I must come back to this place two times every three seasons to talk to my people."

Ukatonen's ears widened. "I thought your people not hear you."

"I leave words for my people to find if I get sick and—" She paused, not knowing the word for death. "If I no longer here, the way that Ilto is no longer here, then my people know what I learn."

Ukatonen thought over Juna's words. "I understand. You leave talk for your people, so if you *nurrun,* they know what you do." Ukatonen turned a reassuring dark blue, "Don't be scared. Anito and I take care of you. You listen to us, you not *nurrun.* Understand?"

"Villagers not *nurrun* me?" Juna asked. She was certain enough that *nurrun* had to do with dying to use it in a sentence.

"No. I not let villagers hurt you. However, your people hurt villagers. Something must be done to bring harmony. *You* must do something to help bring harmony to village."

"What can I do to help?"

Ukatonen shook his head, a human habit he used when talking to her. "I don't know. You, villagers, Anito, me, your people; all must be brought into harmony. I must find way for this to happen. I not know how. This very difficult."

Juna nodded and flickered agreement. "I understand. Not do all now. Wait. My people come. Talk to them. I help now, but cannot speak for my people. What can I do to help bring harmony to this village until my people come?"

"I go think. I tell my decision after dinner."

Juna sat back against the wall with a sigh of relief. There were still many unanswered questions, but at least she knew that Ukatonen would not let them hurt her. She picked up her computer and called up the linguistic program. She felt a lot better after talking to Ukatonen.

About an hour after dinner, a deep, booming noise reverberated through the tree.

Ukatonen stood. "It is time for the meeting."

Juna followed the two aliens into the great central meeting area by the pool at the bottom of the tree. The villagers were already assembled. They rose at their approach, ears stretched wide, necks craning for a better view. Flickers of comment, shaded in tones between pink and lavender, showed the curious, anticipatory mood of the village. They were, Juna thought moodily, looking forward to the sentencing.

She stood, letting the aliens have a good look at her before Ukatonen announced his decision. She refused to let her inner nervousness show. At last a formal pattern flared on Ukatonen's chest. The villagers' skin speech stopped, and they sat down, waiting attentively for the proceedings to begin. Anito put a hand on Juna's shoulder, guiding her to sit down as well. The head of the village stood and spoke. Its words were too complex and formal for Juna to understand.

She touched Anito's shoulder. "What say?"

Anito glanced at Juna, then turned to look at the chief. "Not much," Anito said, in small patterns on her shoulder, which Juna recognized as the skin-speech equivalent of a whisper. "Glad Ukatonen is here. Says many nice things about Ukatonen, talks about how bad things are since forest destroyed. Many words, not much said."

Anito's summation made the chief's address sound so much like human political speech that Juna smiled. Some things seemed to be universal.

At last the chief's address came to an end. Green ripples of approval flickered across the villagers. Ukatonen and Anito joined in briefly.

Ukatonen waited until the villagers' approval died away. Then he stood and moved onto the raised mound that the chief had spoken from. He waited until all eyes were on him, then launched into a formal speech. Anito provided Juna with a "whispered" translation on her shoulder.

"Greetings. Thanks for letting us stay in village, and many good things done for us." That sentence summarized the first ten minutes of the speech.

"You ask me to *tengarra* to bring harmony. The new people have destroyed part of your forest. You want me to find a way to make Juna give your forest back. I say she cannot do this thing. She says that her people would not have done this if they had known that you were here. Also, she was not there when the forest was destroyed. Yet you want bad things done to her because your forest was destroyed in ignorance. When a fire destroys forest, or a big wind destroys forest, do you do bad things to the fire or the wind? No. In this case the new people were acting like the wind, ignorant of the harm that they caused. Your talk of harming the new creature comes from being out of harmony with the world. You must restore that harmony, but not at the cost of other people."

Dark red ripples ran over the villagers' skin. They were not pleased by this. A few villagers looked away, expressing their unhappiness with Ukatonen's words. Ukatonen made a loud, shimmering sound, and the villagers' skins became still.

"Your forest is destroyed. You must get back what you lost. I know this. Anito, whose atwa the new people are, knows this.

Eerin knows this and her people know this. Eerin's people told me that they would try to make the forest better, but we must begin to repair the forest before the flood season comes. Eerin must help. Anito must help, because the new people are her atwa. I help too. But Anito belongs to Narmolom and she wishes to return there. It would be wrong to make her stay. Here is how I have said things should be:

"Anito, Eerin, and I will come back twice each year. We will work one *pida* at repairing the forest each time we come back. I will ask other enkar to come and help as well. All obligations to the enkar will be owed by the new people. When they come back, we will talk to them about repayment."

Ukatonen stepped off the mound, and sat down beside Juna and Anito. Juna looked around. The village was a wash of patterns and colors, some red, a few blue and green, many lavenders and purples. A mixed response, but that was an improvement over the uniform anger and hostility that she had seen before.

The head of the village got up and moved to the speaker's mound. It stood there surveying the people of its village for a moment before speaking.

"We thank the enkar for his *tengarra*. We hope that it will bring harmony," the chief said, and then turned and climbed up the tree.

That seemed to be a signal. The assembly began breaking up.

Ukatonen touched Anito on the shoulder. "You go upstairs," he said, gesturing at Juna. "I come later."

Juna followed Anito up the tree to their room. She began checking the computer's record of Ukatonen's speech to see if it had learned any new words. There were over a dozen new terms. Only eight of them had word-equivalents in any of the Terran languages she knew, but the computer had what appeared to be reliable definitions for almost all but one. Juna smiled. Her computer was finally beginning to put the language together. She wished she could speak the aliens' language as well as it did.

Ukatonen came in as Juna was putting the computer away. He motioned her to sit down. Anito joined them.

"Did you understand what I said?" Ukatonen asked.

"I think so. I must work for this village twice each year one *pida* each time. You and Anito will help me. When my people come back, then they will talk to the village about how to make things better. I do not understand how long a *pida* is."

"A *pida* is between twelve and thirty-two days long. There are eighteen *pida* a year."

So a *pida* was a variable unit of time, roughly equivalent to a month. She would work no more than sixty-four days a year. That seemed extremely reasonable to her.

"When will we do this thing?" Anito asked. "I cannot stay too long. I must return to Narmolom before flood season."

Ukatonen flickered agreement. "The month of Wuri is just beginning. We will work for the rest of this month. If we hurry, we can make it back to Narmolom before flood season."

Anito flickered agreement, but Juna could tell that she was not happy about this decision. Anito's behavior was puzzling. She didn't seem to like Juna very much, yet she had accompanied her on this trip, and was remaining here with her. Why did Anito stay, even though she would rather be back at her village? Ukatonen seemed to think that Anito was somehow responsible for what Juna and other humans did. Why?

She touched Anito on the shoulder. "You want to go to Narmolom. Why you stay here?"

"I must stay and work," Anito told her.

"You not destroy the forest. My people do. Why you work?"

"I must work because you are my atwa."

Atwa was a common word, but one that Juna still didn't have a good definition for. The computer indicated that it was either a relationship or a thing, but that was as far as it had gotten. Juna was no closer to a definition than the computer. It seemed to be an important term, and one that somehow applied to her relationship with Anito.

"What is an atwa?" Juna asked.

At that point, the conversation became very complicated, and difficult to understand. Every Tendu had an atwa, Anito said. Ukatonen corrected her. Only some kinds of Tendu did. Then there was a complex discussion between the two aliens. Afterwards Ukatonen agreed that all the Tendu did have an atwa for a while. Juna and the other humans were Anito's atwa.

Somehow Anito was responsible for what Juna and the other humans did.

Did Anito "own" her and the other humans? Was this more like a parent-child, or a master-apprentice, relationship? Juna shook her head. She wasn't ready to ask such complex questions yet. She wanted to know a lot more about ownership and relationship terms before getting any further into this discussion. She didn't want to agree to enslavement because of her own ignorance. Still, if Anito was responsible for her behavior, it would be wise to let Anito know that she would try to behave well, without agreeing to any kind of ownership on Anito's part.

"I do what you say. I not make things bad for you, but I not your atwa. I am my own atwa. Understand?"

"I not understand. Everyone is someone's atwa."

"Whose atwa are you?" Juna asked.

"I am the atwa of Narmolom."

"And whose atwa is Narmolom?" Juna asked.

"It is mine, and that of the other enkar," Ukatonen told her.

"And the enkar?"

"The enkar are the atwa of the other enkar."

"The enkar are their own atwa," Juna said. "I am the atwa of my own people. I am not your atwa."

"But the new people are Anito's atwa. You are Anito's atwa."

"No!" Juna insisted. "I am not. I not want!"

"You not understand," Ukatonen broke in. "You do what Anito say. We talk later, when you understand more."

This seemed to be a reasonable compromise, for now. Juna hoped that it was clear that she was not willing to belong to Anito. She flickered unwilling agreement, then added, "I not say yes to being Anito's atwa. Understand?"

Anito was about to say something, but Ukatonen laid a hand on her shoulder.

"Understand," Ukatonen said. "You go to sleep now. Next day, we work hard."

Juna wadded up her computer, washed, and crawled into her leafy bed, but she remained awake for a long time, worrying about what would become of her.

Next morning Anito woke her early. They ate a hurried

breakfast, and set out with two of the villagers, scrambling along dripping wet branches through the heavy morning fog. Ukatonen stopped them, and they climbed down to the forest floor. He gestured to Anito and the two of them picked up something heavy. Juna looked closer. They were holding a ground limpet, a large sluglike creature with a thick, mottled shell the color of the forest floor. Their anomalous physiology had been the talk of the biology lab. The limpet's skin and organs were normal enough, but the bulk of the creature was made up of enormous undifferentiated multinucleated cells with no apparent function.

"It's a huge mass of cytoplasm, waiting to be told what to do," Hernandez had remarked.

They carried four of the ground limpets back to the village tree, leaving them with Ukatonen. Then Anito led Juna to the bottom of the tree. The small green workers that the aliens called tinka were hauling huge dripping gourds of stinking mud from the bottom of the pool. Juna was put to work digging out giant tadpoles from the mud and tossing them back into the pool. The mud was then put into leaf-lined baskets, on ledges near the pool while the rest of the water drained out of it. It was unpleasant, backbreaking labor, and it took most of the rest of the day.

When they were done, Anito took Juna to a clear stream to bathe, after which they returned to their room. All that remained of the ground limpets was a wooden trough full of jelly and a row of empty shells lined up against the wall like discarded shields.

Juna ate dinner and crawled into bed, too exhausted to work on the aliens' language. Her last thought as she fell asleep was that Ukatonen had been right—they had worked hard today.

The days quickly fell into a routine. They woke, ate a hurried breakfast, and set to work. Juna found herself working with the tinka, cleaning the seeds from a vat of vile-smelling rotten fruit, rolling seeds in poorly composted dung, or hauling heavy loads of mud or seaweed. Even the smallest task was subject to correction and criticism. The compost was not properly mixed, or it smelled wrong, though Juna was unable to detect any

difference. Then the thickness of the seed coating was wrong,
or they weren't drying properly.

It was horrible, frustrating work, and the villagers seemed to
delight in making it as disagreeable as possible. Juna bore it as
best she could, although the petty harassment sometimes made
her want to scream with rage. She had no choice. Complaining
would show weakness, anger was too dangerous. At night she
was so worn out that she could barely finish dinner before
she fell asleep. Her computer sat in a corner, gathering dust.
She had no time for it now. Her entire existence consisted of
meals, work, and sleep.

One day, near the end of the second week, Juna was carrying
a heavy basket of compost and seaweed up a steep embank-
ment, when she slipped and fell. Someone helped her up. Juna
found herself looking into the pale green eyes of a tinka.

"Thank you," Juna said in skin speech, touching the tinka's
shoulder.

The tinka fanned its ears open and closed in acknowledgment. The juveniles were incapable of skin speech, something
that furthered Juna's theory that they were really a different
species. The Tendu treated the tinka almost as if they weren't
there at all. She doubted that any intelligent species would treat
its young so callously. Were the aliens sexually dimorphic? She
knew nothing about how they reproduced. She had never seen
anything that could be clearly identified as courting or mating
behavior. The tinka could be one of the two sexes. Perhaps they
were some form of slave race or species.

Juna shouldered her load, and they started out again as
though nothing had happened, but she felt that a connection
had been made. She turned to help the tinka up over the
crumbling remains of a fallen tree. It steadied her the next time
she stumbled, saving her from another fall. She had earned a
friend.

Acceptance by one tinka soon led to acceptance by all. She
found herself surrounded by helping hands. They competed for
her attention when the elders weren't around. Sometimes she
felt like a teacher with a class of enthusiastic ten-year-olds. If
she sat down to rest, eager hands would reach out to help her
take off her basket. They were constantly bringing her things:

choice fruits, flowers, once even an enormous live butterfly. Its wings were a brilliant, shiny orange, edged with intense, iridescent blue, and it had a wingspan of at least thirty-five centimeters. She admired the insect's vivid colors for a moment, wishing that she had brought her computer along to catalogue it, then let it go. The butterfly soared off into the canopy, occasional shafts of sunlight making it glow like a piece of living flame.

Just then, Anito and some of the village elders came up the trail. The tinka quickly scattered, picking up their loads. Juna, struggling to shoulder the heavy, dripping basket she was carrying, slipped and fell. None of the tinka moved to help her. Anito helped her up and tried to lift her basket. She could barely budge it.

"Why you carry so much?" Anito asked.

"They tell me to," Juna said, gesturing toward the village elders. "So I do."

Anito turned and said something to the elders. Juna couldn't follow her words, but she could tell that Anito was angry. Was she sticking up for her? Whatever it was about, Anito didn't like the outcome. She helped Juna lift the heavy basket onto her back.

"I talk to Ukatonen," Anito said in small patterns meant only for Juna. "We find other things for you to do."

Anito had to admit that the new creature worked hard. The village elders gave it the most difficult and unpleasant tasks, scolding her for the least mistake. The new creature toiled steadily, without a flicker of complaint. She kept up with the tinka, and sometimes even worked faster than they did. That was exactly the right thing to do. The new creature's patience and restraint had earned Anito's grudging respect. She had even started thinking of it as Eerin.

At last, after watching Eerin struggle under a load that would strain two Tendu to lift, Anito could bear it no longer. She turned to Lalito, who was standing by watching.

"You are mistreating my atwa," Anito told her. "That load is much too heavy for her."

Lalito regarded Anito calmly for a long time. Anito squirmed under that cold gaze, feeling every bit of her own youth and inexperience.

"Are you saying that the creature is backing out of her promise?" Lalito asked. "Do you want to renegotiate the terms that the enkar has decided?"

"No, but—" The last thing Anito wanted to do was to lose face by implying that Ukatonen's judgment had been wrong. "The creature is suffering," Anito said. "She is my atwa and I am responsible for her welfare."

"Your atwa destroyed part of our forest," Lalito retorted. "Two elders decided to die because there wasn't enough food. Bami must wait longer to become elders because of the new creatures. Why should we care about the suffering of one creature, when so many of our own people are suffering?" Lalito's words were bright red with rage. "Go!" she told Anito. "I will see no more of your words, unless you wish to renegotiate the enkar's decision." The chief elder turned her back on Anito.

Chastened and furious, Anito turned and walked away.

Ukatonen was busy checking the plant seeds developing in the jeetho when Anito came in, fuming at Lalito.

"What's the matter, kene?" Ukatonen asked.

"It's Lalito. She's letting the village mistreat Eerin. They're working her too hard, making her carry too much, giving her tasks she's not equipped to do. I talked to Lalito about this, and she says that I would have to renegotiate your decision."

"Do you want to?"

"No!" Anito said, realizing how close she was coming to making the enkar lose face. It was so easy to forget that Ukatonen was an enkar, and that would be a terrible mistake.

"No, en," she went on. "You were very generous to me, but Eerin is my atwa, and I am responsible for the new creature's welfare. I worry that she might get hurt. I must speak out about this."

"Next time, do not bother the elders with such things. Come directly to me," Ukatonen told her, suddenly becoming a stiff, formal enkar. "I will see to it that Eerin receives better treatment."

"Thank you, en."

"Good. That's solved." Ukatonen dropped his formal manner as quickly as he had assumed it. "I found a late-fruiting tumbi tree. Come and eat."

Eerin came in while they were eating, still dripping from a bath. She sat and ate, as wordless as a tinka, then crawled into bed.

Ukatonen gave the creature a long look of concern. "It's good you spoke of this to me," he said to Anito. "She will get sick if the villagers keep working her this hard."

"What are you going to do?" Anito asked.

Ukatonen turned a conspiratorial shade of brownish-green. "Wait and see."

The next day they stopped to watch Eerin as she struggled to wrap jumba seeds. The villagers scolded the new creature constantly, sometimes when she was doing nothing wrong. Anito had wrapped jumba seeds before. The thickness of the coating was not that critical. What mattered was that the mix of compost and ground seaweed smelled right, indicating that the ratio of nutrients would favor the jumba seedling over weedy intruders. The new creature couldn't smell well enough to tell the difference between good compost and bad. There were dozens of other useful things that Eerin could do, but the villagers kept her here, where they could watch her struggle and fail.

Anito kept waiting for Ukatonen to speak, but the enkar merely stood and watched silently for a long while, then left. Anito followed him, fighting back her anger and curiosity until they were alone in the jungle.

"You saw how badly they're treating her. Aren't you going to do anything about it?"

"I just did. Tumbi fruit doesn't ripen overnight. Wait and see."

The next day Ukatonen joined Eerin when she went to receive her work assignment.

Laying a possessive hand on Eerin's shoulder, he addressed the elder in charge. "I watched the new creature yesterday," Ukatonen told him. "She is completely incompetent. I will work beside her and teach her."

The elder, a short, thin Tendu named Nuito, looked as if he

had just swallowed a fire beetle. A trickle of laughter rippled down Anito's back.

"I must consult with the chief elder, en. I believe she had a special task for the new creature today. I was just on my way to talk to her."

"Good," Ukatonen said. "We'll wait."

Lalito arrived a short while later, with Nuito scurrying behind her.

"Good morning, en. I understand that you wanted to work with the new creature today."

"Yes, kene. She's incompetent, and needs someone to teach her properly. I realize that your people have tried, but she's so stupid that it requires special skills. I am familiar with the new creature, and so I have decided to work with her until she understands what she's supposed to do."

"Thank you, en. I hope you do not mind that we were going to give her a new job today. She was so clumsy that we have given up on trying to teach her. We thought we'd send her out to work at planting."

"That was a wise choice, kene," Ukatonen said. "Please, I want you to treat me the same as the new creature. If she fails, scold me too. After all, the failure of those who learn is also the failure of those who teach."

Lalito's ears twitched as Ukatonen's veiled reproof sank home. "Of course, en."

"Thank you for giving this incompetent new creature a second chance, kene. Anito and I will see to it that she doesn't fail again."

With that, Ukatonen beckoned imperiously to the new creature.

"You work with me today," he told Eerin.

Eerin flushed a shade of blue denoting pleasure and nodded. Ukatonen beckoned and the three of them set off.

Juna took the cultivator that Ukatonen handed her, and waited for his instructions.

"You dig like this," he explained, pounding on the hardened ground with the cultivator until it broke through the seared crust. Then the alien began breaking up the hard clods of dirt, and fluffing up the newly exposed soil.

Relief washed over Juna. This was just like tilling the vegetable garden back home. At last, a job that she could do! She seized a cultivator and began digging away, happy to be doing something she understood.

After the grinding toil she had endured for the last week and a half, working for Ukatonen and Anito was a great relief. They only cultivated or planted when it was heavily overcast or raining, so there were frequent breaks. During clear spells, they oversaw the gathering of leaves from the forest floor, and sometimes seaweed from the beaches along the coast. The loads that they asked her to carry were no heavier than theirs, and they let her rest when they did. The seaweed and leaves were piled into great, steaming heaps of compost, or laid out over the newly cultivated ground to prevent heavy rains from damaging the barren areas. She was surprised at the progress the villagers had made. Already a mist of bright green shoots covered the planted areas. Juna smiled at the tender new plants and bent to her work.

Anito paused to take a drink. She watched the new creature turning the dirt over at a steady pace.

"You're good at that," she told Eerin.

"I do before," she replied. "My—" The new creature paused, looking for words. "People who gave me life, they do this often."

They worked wordlessly until they had dug up another body-length of dirt. "You rest," Ukatonen told them. "I go get compost and leaves."

They squatted beside their digging.

"I not work for village now?" Eerin asked.

Anito shook her head. "You work for village, but we teach you."

"How long you teach me?"

"Until Ukatonen say you know enough."

"I not like working for village. I learn slow."

"That is good," Anito said. "You learn slow, but you work hard."

"I try. It good I know digging. I like being good."

"You good before, teachers bad. You can't do work they give you. You not smell good."

Eerin's mouth widened into a grimace, and it smelled its arm. "I smell fine," it said, then broke out in that strange choking noise that it made when it was amused. Ripples of laughter ran down her back.

Anito stared at her for a moment, perplexed, and then realized that the new creature had made a joke. It wasn't a very good joke, but Anito was impressed that she could do it at all. She joined in Eerin's laughter. It was at that moment, Anito later realized, that she began thinking of Eerin as a person.

Just then Ukatonen came up, followed by a tinka. The two of them were carrying baskets of compost. Eerin jumped up and helped the tinka lower its basket.

Surprise and irritation flickered over Ukatonen's body. Clearly, he had been expecting the new creature to help him, not the tinka. Anito was surprised too. After all, Ukatonen was an enkar, and the tinka was merely a tinka, there to be ordered around.

Anito got up. "I apologize for Eerin, en," she told him. "She isn't very smart."

A shrug rippled down his long body. "I keep thinking of her as though she were a bami. She learns so quickly and well that it's easy to forget that she's not a Tendu."

The new creature and the tinka had emptied their basket. Eerin thanked the tinka, then picked up her digger and began turning in the compost.

Ukatonen's ears fanned wide in surprise. "Is she letting the tinka know that she's willing to be courted? That makes no sense!"

The gesture had surprised Anito as well. "I don't know what she's doing, en. I don't think she knows either."

Anito chittered to get Eerin's attention. When the new creature looked up, Anito said, "No talk to tinka. Understand?"

"Why?" the new creature asked. She seemed surprised.

"Because it not good. Makes trouble."

"I not understand. Why not talk to tinka?"

"Tinka not for talk. Tinka for work. You talk to tinka

they—" Anito paused. There were no words for explaining about tinka in the limited language that the new creature understood. Explaining what an atwa meant had already proved impossible. "It hard to explain. You talk to tinka, you make trouble. Not do. Understand?"

A brief flare of anger reddened the new creature's skin.

"I understand," she said. She thrust her digger into the soil as though it were a spear, and began digging.

The next evening Lalito and some of the other village elders gathered to celebrate how quickly the work was getting done. More than half of the burnt-over area had been planted, and the elders were extremely pleased with themselves. The first saplings had shouldered their way through the dirt and mulch and begun to shoot upward. In some places they were as high as Anito's chest.

It would be a lifetime before the forest was truly back in harmony with its surroundings. It would be another lifetime before it would be impossible to tell where the forest had been burned. But the plants were coming up, holding the soil and the nutrients in place, and the elders felt the need to celebrate the rebirth of their destroyed forest. Someone brought out a box of halrin, and passed it around. The elders stuffed wads of the tart fermented leaves in their mouths and chewed. The talk became brightly colored and carefree as the halrin took effect. They praised the strength of their bami, the generosity of their neighbors, the intelligence of their elders, and of course, Ukatonen's wise decision. They began to boast about how hard they had worked.

Anito's mouth was numb and her head buzzed from the halrin, but despite the drug, she felt rather irritated. She and the new creature between them had done three times as much as anyone else in the village. She sat and brooded, growing steadily more angry and morose as the boasting continued.

Then one of Lalito's younger cronies began making fun of Eerin, imitating the way she coated the seeds. The villagers rippled wildly in amusement, slapping their hands loudly against their thighs.

"And you should see the way it digs!" one of the villagers remarked. She got up and pretended to scoop up tiny bits of dirt with a limp leaf. The villagers' ripples speeded up until it seemed that the whole room was dancing with blue and green laughter.

Anito stood somewhat unsteadily. "Eerin is very good at digging," she asserted. Ignoring Ukatonen's flicker of warning, Anito continued. "She could outdig any two of you."

Another wave of hilarity passed over the villagers at this remark. Ukatonen stood, and was about to speak, when another villager commented that a three-legged koola could dig faster than the new creature.

Anito turned bright red with rage. "That might be true, but since you can't outrun a mantu, the new creature wouldn't have much trouble beating you."

Lalito rose. "Perhaps we should see who is faster. I suggest two of the village's strongest bami race against your new creature, and see if she can dig more ground than they can."

"But it would not be a fair competition," Ukatonen protested. "When your bami get tired, their sitik give them energy through allu-a. The new creature doesn't accept that kind of help. If we are to match the new creature against the bami of this village, then it should be a fair test of her strength and ability. I'm sure that two of your bami can outdig Eerin, even without linking. Agreed?"

Lalito looked rather disappointed to have the bami's major advantage stripped away, but the enkar had trapped her. She had to agree to Ukatonen's conditions. He was, after all, an enkar.

"Agreed," she said.

They decided that the match would take place two days from now. They linked spurs to seal the agreement, and then Ukatonen and Anito went up to their room.

"That was foolish," Ukatonen told Anito when they reached the privacy of their room. The new creature slept soundly in her pile of leaves.

"I know," Anito said, brown as a dead leaf with shame. "I was angry at how badly they treat Eerin. She is clumsy and stupid, but she tries hard. Please excuse my disgraceful behavior, en."

Ukatonen touched her shoulder. "I was angry too, kene. The

villagers are out of harmony, and not thinking very clearly. What will happen when Eerin's people return and find out how badly she has been treated? What if the villagers treat the other new creatures like this? Harmony must be reached with these creatures. They are too dangerous otherwise."

"Dangerous?" Anito said, pale pink with surprise. "The new creatures are too stupid to be dangerous."

"Stupidity can be dangerous. Eerin said that the new creatures burned the forest because they didn't know about the village. They cut open animals because they didn't know what was inside. They killed an entire tree and everything living in it because they wanted to know what lived there. These new creatures destroy everything they touch in order to learn. They destroyed that patch of forest the way you or I would wave away an insect. What if they decided that they didn't like us?"

Anito's skin turned orange, deepening in tone as she contemplated the possibility of the new creatures' hostility. She had seen Eerin defend herself. Her strength and the depth of her anger were impressive. The villagers' stories of the power of the half-alive stones that did the new creatures' bidding were terrifying. The new creatures were her atwa. She was responsible for bringing them into harmony with the rest of the world. The enormity of what was expected of her began to sink in, in a new and terrifying way.

"How can I bring this atwa into harmony, en? The task is too big. I can't do it. Find someone who can."

Ukatonen rested a hand on her knee. "Who, kene? Who knows more than you do? One of the villagers here? Lalito, perhaps? Would you trust Eerin to her?"

Anito thought about the villagers, and how they would treat Eerin. "No, en. No one here."

"Someone in your village, then? Who in your village knows more about the new creature?"

Anito thought it over. There was Ninto. Ninto knew the new creature well, and she was wiser and more experienced than Anito. She would take good care of the creature, but Anito couldn't bring herself to name her tareena. Ninto had an atwa of her own and a bami to teach. It would be wrong to ask her to take on this additional burden. The only other Tendu that Anito could think of was Ukatonen.

"You, en. You could do it. You are wise enough for the task."

"But I already have an atwa, Anito. You are my atwa. This village is my atwa, every Tendu in the world is my atwa. That is what it means to be an enkar. As an enkar, I look after the interests of the Tendu. You must look after the interests of the new creatures. I will help you, but there will be times when the interests of your atwa are different from the interests of the Tendu. Then we will have to work together to find a compromise. I'm sorry, Anito, but there is no one else who can take over your atwa."

"I understand, en. I don't like it, but I understand." Anito stood and said, in high, formal patterns, "I accept this atwa, en."

Ukatonen rose and touched her shoulder. "Thank you, kene."

They stood a moment, wordless and awkward. Then Ukatonen said, "I think that this match can be turned to your atwa's advantage, kene."

"How?"

"Before you bring your atwa into harmony with the rest of the world, you must bring this village into harmony with the new creature. This way, when Eerin's people return, they will be treated well. The villagers think the new creature is stupid and lazy. We know that isn't true, but the villagers must learn to see Eerin with respect. If she wins this digging race, they will come to respect her strength."

"But what if she loses, en?"

"Then she must not lose by much. If she makes their diggers work hard to win, the villagers will still respect her."

Eleven

JUNA HAD BARELY settled into a comfortable routine when Ukatonen and Anito informed her that she would take part in a digging race against two of the village's strongest bami.

Juna leaned back against the wall of their room. She had been working hard for the last eighteen days. Even though Anito and Ukatonen didn't expect the same level of grinding toil from her that the villagers did, she still labored hard for them. She was tired.

"No," she said. "I won't do it."

"You must do it," Anito insisted. "Ukatonen and I have agreed with Lalito that this would happen."

Juna shook her head. They had entered her into this race as though she were a dumb animal. She couldn't allow them to continue treating her like this.

"This is your agreement. Not mine. I not do. I not—" She paused, searching for the right word. "I not tinka. I not yours. Understand?" She felt a red flush of anger flare on her skin.

Ukatonen touched Juna's shoulder. "The villagers treat you badly, don't they?"

Juna nodded, her skin deepened to brick red frustration.

"If you win this race, they like you more. They not treat you so badly. Understand?"

Juna thought it over. She needed to gain the respect of the villagers before the Survey returned. If they knew and respected one human, perhaps the rest would be easier to forgive. This race might help her earn some respect, but only if she could win it. Unfortunately, she wasn't physically capable of finishing, much less winning, any kind of race in her current condition. Just getting through the day was hard enough.

"I can't do it. I work for eighteen days with no rest. I'm tired. I need rest."

Ukatonen ducked his chin, thinking.

"You must work all this month. That is the agreement," he reminded her.

Anito touched Ukatonen's shoulder. "We do different work. Not hard and not where villagers can see," the alien suggested. Anito turned to Juna. "Understand?"

Juna thought it over. A chance to rest. It sounded tempting.

"Maybe can do race, if rest," she told them.

A lavender ripple of intense relief rolled over the two aliens. This was important to them as well, Juna realized. She had better win.

The next day, Ukatonen took them deep into the forest to gather seeds. They did that for about an hour, then made themselves a nest in the branches of a tree. Anito went off to hunt, while Ukatonen plied Juna with honey and fruit. He made her eat until her stomach felt as if it were about to burst. Then she fell asleep, and did not wake until late afternoon. Anito and Ukatonen fed her another meal, of honey, meat, and fruit. Then they walked home, arriving shortly after dark, and fed her another big meal. She became sleepy soon afterwards, with a suddenness that made her wonder if they were spiking her food, but she was too tired to ask. She was asleep before she had finished covering herself over with leaves.

She slept late the next day, well into midmorning, and awoke to find another huge meal awaiting her. She ate as much of it as she could. As she was finishing, Anito came in with an armful of thick bamboolike reeds.

Juna stretched, taking inventory of her physical condition. She felt better. Her muscles were still sore, but they lacked the deep bone-ache of true fatigue. She felt more energetic today than she had in weeks, despite the big meal she had just consumed.

"How you feel?" Anito asked, as Juna leaned against a wall, stretching her Achilles tendons.

"Better. Not so tired."

"Can do race?"

"Maybe."

"Want link? Link make you feel better."

Juna thought about it. It was tempting. If she accepted the link, then she would begin the race in good condition, but she had to win through her own power and skill. Only that would count toward the greater goal of winning respect from the villagers.

"No," she said. "I not link. It not good. I win by myself. Understand?"

"I understand," Anito said.

Ukatonen came in carrying several skeins of rope and strong twine, and began sorting through the reeds, lifting them up and eyeing them carefully for straightness. Anito squatted down nearby, beckoning to Juna to join them.

"We make cultivator for race," Anito told her.

Juna picked up the cultivator that she had been using to churn up the burnt-over fields. It was well made, but the design was extremely primitive, little more than a forked stick. She remembered the U-bar cultivator she had used in her father's garden. It could turn up three times as much soil as one of these, with half the effort.

"Does my cultivator have to be the same as this?" Juna asked, an idea beginning to form. "Can I use a different kind of cultivator?"

It was a dangerous idea, risky because it might backfire, and because it broke Contact regulations. If it worked, she could gain the respect of the people the Survey had harmed. If it failed, well, they didn't like her anyway. Besides, she broke Contact regulations every day. By the time the Survey returned to pick her up, this infringement would be only one of many that she would have committed in order to survive.

"No one has said you couldn't," Ukatonen told her, after thinking it over.

"If we made it wider and added another handle, and put some bracing here and here, and changed the— What do you call this?" she asked, pointing to the tines of the existing cultivator.

"✳✳✳" Anito supplied the word in skin speech. Juna's computer, sitting close by, recorded the new word and began generating a phonetic equivalent for it.

"—changed the tines like so," Juna said, using the skin-speech word that Anito had given her. "The cultivator would work better." She depicted, on her stomach, a crude picture of what she planned to build.

"It would be too tall, and the handles would be too close together," Ukatonen argued.

"Not for me," Juna replied, drawing herself up to her full height and stretching out her arms, reminding the aliens that she was taller than they were and had shorter arms.

"All right. We will build it the way you say," Ukatonen agreed.

The rest of the day was spent fashioning the cultivator, with frequent breaks to stop and eat. The aliens were continuing to ply her with food. Juna was amazed at how much she had eaten lately. Still, she needed all the help she could get to win tomorrow's race.

They finished the cultivator a couple of hours before sunset, took it to the bank of a nearby river, and tried it out in the soft mud by the water's edge. Anito and Ukatonen were impressed by how much dirt it could turn up, and how easy it was to use. Juna began to feel confident. They rinsed the cultivator off and carried it back to the village. She ate another big meal, mostly honey, seaweed, and a starchy mush made from the tubers of a wide-leafed plant that grew in the river. Juna finished her meal, spent a little time fussing with her computer, then burrowed into the compost-generated warmth of her wet, leafy bed.

She was beginning to get used to this, she realized as she composed her mind for sleep. According to her computer, it rarely fell below seventy, but it was cool enough to make her glad of the warmth of her bed. Dry, clean sheets and blankets were a distant dream, as was a good hot meal. She longed for cooked food. She drifted off to sleep, dreaming of hot couscous topped with succulent chunks of lamb, the way her mother used to make it.

Anito woke her a little after dawn. A steady, light rain was falling; they could begin the race early. They walked out to the burnt-over area. The villagers, already assembling, looked on curiously as Juna unwrapped and assembled the new implement. Then the crowd of villagers parted as Lalito led out the two bami that she was going to compete against. Juna stared at them in dismay. Muscles bulged and rippled on their shoulders. They looked like no bami she had ever seen before. A deep ochre cloud of worry passed over Anito. Ukatonen touched Anito's shoulder and the two aliens conferred. Anito came over to Juna.

"They've enhanced the muscles on those bami. Do you still want to go on with this?"

Juna eyed the two powerful-looking young bami, surrounded by the other villagers. One of the villagers glanced at her. A ripple of open derision flared on its body. Then it turned back to encourage and congratulate the bami she was to race against. A sudden surge of anger crowded out any doubts. Juna gripped the handles of her cultivator. She was tired of the aliens' scorn. She would win today. She had to. Muscles or no, the bami could accept no help from their elders until after the race. So, it was her strength and endurance against theirs. Their muscles may have been enhanced, but she had her cultivator. It was a matter of strength versus invention. Juna flickered assent.

"Good," Anito said. "Let's go."

Juna picked up her cultivator and headed over to where the villagers were gathered in a knot around their champions. They stopped before the village chief, Lalito. Ukatonen stepped forward and addressed Lalito in formal patterns. From what little Juna could understand, plus the gestures he made toward her cultivator, Juna knew he was talking about the new tool. Lalito listened, and asked a couple of questions. Then she flickered assent.

Juna looked to Anito for a translation.

"Lalito has said that you may use your cultivator."

The speech was much longer than that. Juna wondered what they had said to each other. Although her vocabulary was still

poor, she had a very good grasp of the shades of meaning
conveyed by the aliens' use of color. She was sure she detected
some fairly pointed sarcasm on both their parts.

"Thank you, kene," she told Lalito. "How is the race to be
run?"

"You will start here, where the unbroken ground begins, and
you will dig until either the sky clears or the sun sets. Your
opponents will go one at a time. When one gets tired, the other
will take over. Do you understand?" Lalito asked.

Juna replied with the most formal assent she knew. Lalito's
ears lifted in surprise. Juna picked up her implement with a
small, secret smile, and strode over to the starting place.

"Do well," Anito said. Her skin patterns were a gentle,
encouraging blue.

"I will try."

Anito handed her a gourd full of sweet honey-water. Juna
drank from it, then slung it over her shoulder. She stood
waiting, her cultivator at the ready.

The two bami were receiving last-minute instructions from
their elders. At last one of them picked up a cultivator and
stood beside her.

Lalito and Ukatonen stood on either side of the contestants.
They raised their arms. "Begin," they said in unison.

Juna plunged the tines into the loose dirt at the starting line,
placed her foot on the crossbar, and pulled back on the two
handles. The tines lifted and broke the seared crust of dirt from
below. A quick shake broke down the larger clods. She lifted
the cultivator and plunged it in again.

A ripple of concern washed over the villagers like an ochre
dust cloud as they saw how fast Juna could turn over the dirt.
The bami glanced over its shoulder and darkened with worry as
it saw how much dirt she turned. It began to dig faster. Juna
smiled and kept on digging.

The steady lift-and-pull motion loosened her muscles. She
fell into a work trance, as she did back home, working in her
father's garden. She glanced up after a while and realized that
she was several meters ahead of her rival. A short time later, the
second bami took over from the first. The gap between them
narrowed until the bami was digging beside her. After a while

it pulled ahead, a meter, then another. Juna continued the steady pace of her digging. She had once cleared half a hectare of ground in a single afternoon, on a bet with her brother, Toivo. Experience had taught her that a steady, unvarying pace always won.

Sure enough, she pulled even with the second bami, and then ahead. A while later, it dropped out. Juna stopped for a couple of minutes to drink a gourd of honey-water, and to gulp down a couple of handfuls of sweet, sticky mush. Then she rinsed off her hands and started digging again.

The afternoon wore on. It began to rain, a heavy downpour that slowed to a steady, unrelenting drizzle. Where the ground had been worked, the mud was knee-deep. Juna found herself pushing just to keep ahead of the mud. Her arms ached. Her back was a solid sheet of pain, and the skin on her hands was chafed and blistered. She concentrated on maintaining a steady rhythm of dig, pull, lift. She was slowly pulling ahead; now she was consistently more than a meter ahead. The sun, only a bright spot of glare behind the thick grey clouds, was sinking toward the horizon. She might win after all. She looked back at the trees where the villagers were sheltering. There was no sign of them, save an occasional rustling of the branches. No wonder the Survey had missed these people.

Then the second bami came out of the forest. Instead of relieving its partner, the two began to dig together. Juna groaned inwardly as she saw her hard-earned lead shrinking. Holding her hand up between the tree line and the sun, she estimated the amount of daylight left. Less than an hour. If she could hold her lead that long, the race would be over. She bent to her digging, feeling the drag of the handles against her hands as she dug, pulled, and lifted. A blister burst with a warm trickle of fluid. It greased the handles of the cultivator. Dig, pull, lift. The bami were even with her. She continued, ignoring pain, ignoring exhaustion, refusing even to spare a glance at her rivals. She must win. She would win. Dig, pull, lift. The shadows grew long and the villagers came out of the forest, their skins a whirl of bright colors as they encouraged their bami. There was a chirring noise and Lalito lifted her arm, signaling the end of the race. Juna fell to her hands and knees, then collapsed into the churned red mud, gasping for breath. She was having trouble breathing, her throat was sore. Hands turned her over. She felt a pinprick on her arm, a brief presence inside her. Then a wave of darkness rolled over her.

Anito craned her neck anxiously, straining to see what kind of progress Eerin was making. Once the sun touched the trees, the race would be over. Eerin glanced up and increased the pace of her digging. When the sun finally touched the treetops, Eerin and the bami appeared to be just about even.

Lalito chirred loudly, signaling the end of the race. Eerin fell to her knees. The two bami leaned against each other, exhausted. The village streamed out onto the path between the two expanses of dirt that each side had cultivated, eager to see who had won. Anito pushed through the crowd to the front. Ukatonen crouched beside Eerin. She was sprawled on the ground, chest heaving as she struggled to breathe. Her palms were bleeding.

"How is she?" Anito asked.

"Completely exhausted," Ukatonen replied. "She won by three and a half hand-spans."

Anito examined Eerin's palms. The protective layer of skin was worn completely through in spots, oozing blood. Glancing up at the handles of Eerin's cultivator, Anito saw that they were slick with blood, almost black in the last, dying rays of the sun.

She linked with Eerin long enough to stabilize her. When she emerged from the link, a cluster of tinka looked on anxiously. They helped carry Eerin back to the tree and placed her on the bed.

"I'll need to do some deep work, en," Anito told Ukatonen. "Will you monitor me?"

"Of course, kene."

They linked and entered the new creature's body. The depth of Eerin's exhaustion amazed Anito. Her blood was sour with fatigue. She had used up her body's reserves of energy, and had begun to consume her own muscles. Anito was surprised at this. No Tendu would work that hard except over a life or death matter. Why had Eerin done it? It was only a race. She didn't even need to win it in order to gain the respect of the village.

Anito broke down the proteins that Eerin's strange body reacted to so strongly, and filtered out the accumulated poisons. Then she turned to rebuilding Eerin's muscles and replenishing her energy reserves.

Ukatonen broke the link.

"You were giving too much of yourself, kene," Ukatonen told Anito. "Let the creature's body repair itself."

"But she won't be able to work tomorrow," Anito argued.

"She's earned a day off," Ukatonen said. "If Lalito protests, then I will call her leadership into question. I may do it anyway. She lacks harmony."

Anito's ears spread wide in surprise. She had never heard of an enkar actually questioning a village chief's leadership, except in ancient tales.

"Would you really do that, en?" she asked.

Ukatonen gestured with his chin at Eerin, lying unconscious on her bed. "Lalito nearly killed Eerin with this foolish race."

"But, en, it was I who spoke first. I goaded the villagers into it. This race is my fault."

"Lalito allowed her villagers to make fun of Eerin; she even encouraged it," Ukatonen said. "It is one thing to be angry before restitution is agreed on. It is another to maintain a grudge this way after a judgment has been made. It shows no respect for you, and no respect for Eerin. It shows even less respect for the enkar whose judgment Lalito agreed to abide by. If this agreement doesn't work out I will be obliged to die. She is putting my life at risk with her lack of harmony."

"No, en!" Anito said.

"It won't go that far," Ukatonen assured her. "Lalito lost a lot of face today. She would lose even more if she refused to grant a favor to Eerin after such a heroic performance. It will take several days for the villagers to prepare the soil that Eerin and the bami cultivated today."

A soft, chirring call interrupted their conversation. They looked up. The two bami who had raced against Eerin were standing in the doorway, with their sitiks.

"Please excuse us, en, kene," one of the bami said in simple, humble speech. "My name is Ini, my sitik is Arato, and this is Sarito and his bami, Ehna," he said, gesturing at the other bami and her sitik. "We didn't mean to interrupt, but we wanted to see if the new creature was all right."

"Please come in," Ukatonen said. "Eerin worked so hard that she made herself sick. She's asleep now. She'll be fine in a couple of days."

"I'm glad to know that," Sarito said as they entered the room and sat down. "If there's anything we can do—"

"Thank you," Anito said. "It's very kind of you to be concerned."

"Why—" Ehna said, then stopped, embarrassed.

"What is it, Ehna?" Ukatonen asked in soft, gentle hues. "It's all right."

"Why did the new creature work so hard that she threw her body out of harmony?"

Ukatonen looked at Anito, ears raised questioningly.

"That's a good question, Ehna," Anito replied. "We still don't understand the new creature very well. I think that she thought it was very important to win the race. I know she wanted the people in the village to treat her better. Perhaps she thought that winning the race would help."

"She's very strong," Ini conceded. "But—"

"Yes?" Ukatonen prompted.

"But maybe not very smart, to work that hard, and selfish, to ask you to repair her."

"There are many things that Eerin doesn't understand yet. She is like a new bami, still half-wild," Ukatonen explained. "It will take time to bring her into harmony with us."

"Eerin may not be very wise, but she is not stupid," Anito said. "She learns quickly, and well, when she is given a task that she can perform."

Ini held out the basket he was carrying. "We brought you a couple of ooloo, and some arika roots from the storeroom. Perhaps they will help Eerin recover more quickly."

It was clearly a peace offering, and a generous one. Arika roots were a great delicacy this time of year. They would not be ready for harvest for another six months. These must have been the last of their supply. Anito was equally happy to see the ooloo; they had been under protection in Narmolom for the last several years, and it was her favorite kind of game.

"Thank you very much," Ukatonen said as he accepted the gifts. "We were about to eat. Will you join us?"

It was not often that one got to eat with an enkar in private. Usually that privilege was reserved for the village chief and a few special cronies. The visitors accepted eagerly. Anito was worried that there wouldn't be enough, but Ukatonen pulled out some preserved delicacies from the bottom of his pack, and Sarito and the others fetched honey, fruit, and fish. They ate well, and the party became quite cheerful.

"It will be hard," Ukatonen said in rueful shades, "telling Lalito that Eerin will be unable to work tomorrow. She will not be pleased. I hope she doesn't make us stay longer because of it. Anito needs to return to her village before the floods. We will have to hurry back as it is. Their village doesn't have a chief, and Anito has asked me to help them decide who the new chief should be."

Sympathy flared on the visitors' chests.

"I don't think that Lalito will protest," Arato said. "Your new creature did four days' worth of work today, and so did our bami. It's a good thing that we have enough netting and leaves to protect the soil from the rains."

"Some of the other elders are unhappy about the race," Sarito told them. "The village lost much face today. They think Lalito is not acting wisely."

"Has she been chief long?" Ukatonen asked as he finished off the last bite of fish.

"Only five seasons," Sarito replied.

"It must have been hard for her," Anito mused, "having all of this happen so soon after she became chief. My sitik was the chief elder of Narmolom. It isn't an easy task, bringing so many conflicts into harmony."

"She will learn, I'm sure," Ukatonen said. "Batonen chose Lalito, and he makes good choices. This disaster would be difficult even for the best chief. Lalito cannot bring harmony to Lyanan by herself. The elders must disagree with her when she's wrong, as well as support her when she's right."

Arato and Sarito flickered agreement. "We will try, en," Sarito added.

"Thank you, kene," Ukatonen said. He stood. "Your bami

must be very tired." He gestured with his chin at Ini, whose head kept dropping onto his chest as he dozed off.

The elders and their bami said their farewells and left. As soon as they were gone, Ukatonen leaned back against the wall, and shut his eyes. Anito was surprised at how exhausted and worn he looked.

"Good," he said. "That was a good evening's work. I think tomorrow will be easier."

"You look tired, en. Is there anything I can do?"

Ukatonen flickered negation. "It's been a long month, for me as well as for Eerin. I'll be glad when it's over." He got up slowly, "I need a good night's sleep."

He burrowed into his bed. Anito sat up a little longer, looking at the sleeping forms of Eerin and Ukatonen. She was tired too. It would be good to be going home again. *Narmolom,* she thought to herself, picturing the village's name-symbol in her mind. Once everything she knew and loved was there. Now she had traveled and the village seemed smaller, but it still held everything she loved. *Almost everything.* There was Ukatonen, who reminded her so much of Ilto. It was good having someone to teach her things. It gave her something familiar to cling to during the difficult transition to adulthood.

Anito crawled into bed. She fell asleep thinking of home.

Juna awoke in a bed of leaves. She shifted slightly, wincing at the pain in her back and shoulders, remembering the race. Had she won? Slowly, painfully, she sat up. She was alone. She hobbled over to the night-soil basket and used it, grateful for the chance to move her bowels in privacy for once. She picked up the water jug and drank deeply, then washed herself off. Checking her computer for the time, she saw that she'd slept for more than sixteen hours. No wonder her stomach ached with hunger; she had eaten nothing but some kayu mush yesterday.

Anito and Ukatonen returned with full gathering bags.

"How are you feeling today?" Anito asked, setting down her bags and squatting to examine Juna.

"I hurt. Did I win?"

A gentle ripple of amusement crossed the alien's skin. "Yes, by three hand-spans of length. You dug twice as much as they did, but they only measured length."

"What do the villagers think?"

"They wonder why you work so hard. None of them would do such a thing to win a race. You nearly died last night."

Ukatonen touched Juna's arm. "Anito almost made herself sick trying to heal you."

Juna looked at Anito in surprise. "I didn't know you get sick from healing. I am sorry. Please forgive my ignorance."

Anito turned magenta in puzzlement and surprise. "You not know?"

"My people not link. How I understand linking? I not do before."

"One elder died saving your life," Anito told her. "My sitik, Ilto, got sick from saving your life."

Juna looked from Anito to Ukatonen and back, shocked at how much her life had cost these people. She remembered how thin and frail Ilto had been. She had been responsible for his illness, and the death of another elder. Yet the villagers had treated her with kindness. Anito had saved her life several times.

"Why?" she asked, fighting back tears of shame and regret. "Why are you so good to me after all the trouble that I have caused?"

Anito laid a gentle hand on her arm. "You were new, different. My sitik knew that saving you could kill him. It was time for him to die. He chose to save you even though it made him sick. He wanted to do a big thing before he died. Understand?"

"Not all, but I understand some. Are you angry with me?" Juna asked.

"I was," Anito said, then looked away, suddenly dark grey, as sadness washed over her.

Juna touched Anito on the arm. The alien looked at her. "I understand. If it was me, I be angry too. Please tell me how I can make all this better?"

Anito shook her head. "You didn't understand then. Is done. I not angry now."

"I understand now. I not forget," Juna replied. "Thank you."

Ukatonen touched her arm and handed her a large red jellyfruit. "You need to eat now," he said.

Juna tore a hole in the peel and sucked out the soft jellylike interior, straining the seeds out with her teeth. Juice rolled down her chin. She sucked the last of the sweetness from the seeds, and licked the inside of the inedible peel. With a ripple of amusement, Ukatonen tossed her another.

"You eat. You work too hard yesterday," Anito said, handing her a leafy cone containing small pieces of raw meat mixed with some sort of gluey mush. Despite its daunting texture, it was delicious. They gave her a basket full of leathery brown globes, about three centimeters across. Eggs. Ukatonen picked one up, slit it open with a deft claw, and sucked out the contents, then handed an egg to Juna.

"Lalito brought these for you," Ukatonen told her. "They'll make you well more quickly. She said that you don't have to work today."

"Good," Juna said, lavender with relief.

Juna regarded the raw egg in her hand. She couldn't refuse to eat it, not without offending Lalito. She nipped a hole in the egg and sucked out its contents. There was a disturbing solidity to the yolk. Her teeth closed on something that crunched like gristle, and there was the sudden taste of blood in her mouth as she swallowed. There had been an embryo inside the egg, she realized, repressing the urge to gag.

Her revulsion must have appeared on her skin, because Anito leaned forward, skin ochre with concern. "Are you all right?"

Juna nodded. "We don't—" She paused, searching for the right word. "We don't eat eggs with young inside."

Anito's ears spread wide. "You don't? That's the best kind!"

"How you find eggs so new?" Ukatonen wanted to know.

"We don't find them. We grow them," she said, using a verb form for "grow" that applied to raising plants. She didn't know if the aliens had any terms for raising food animals.

Ukatonen looked puzzled. "I don't understand. Eggs are not from plants."

"Eggs from birds," Juna agreed. "We grow birds. Gather eggs."

"How grow birds?" Anito asked.

Juna remembered the chicken farm on the satellite, the thick-legged birds, awkward and slow in the heavy gravity that they were kept in to make the shells thicker, the muscles meatier. Each bird in its own wire cage, looking ugly and vulnerable in the harsh glare of the sun tubes. She had gone there once, as part of a school trip. She had had nightmares about those chickens for almost a month afterward.

How could she explain the chicken farm to these aliens? Did they even understand the concept of a cage?

"It's like narey. You grow narey in pool. We grow birds in boxes. You feed narey, we feed birds. You eat narey, we eat birds, and birds' eggs. Understand?"

"How birds breathe in box?" Ukatonen wanted to know. "Air get bad."

"We put holes in box. Box is open like this," Juna explained, holding up a gathering bag and sticking her fingers through the mesh and wriggling them.

"Why you not hunt birds?" Anito.

"Growing them is easier than hunting," Juna replied. "My people not have time to hunt."

The ears of both aliens spread wide and they turned a deep, incredulous purple. They looked completely and suddenly absurd, like a matched pair of toy monsters. Juna fought back a smile and a ripple of amusement. It wouldn't do to laugh at them.

"What your people do? Why not hunt?"

"We make things. Learn things," she replied. "We play."

She remembered a moment shared with Padraig, laughing at some joke, their eyes meeting in understanding and delight. She looked away, fighting back a sudden surge of loneliness. *Oh God*, she realized, *five years without another human being. . . .*

A gentle hand touched her shoulder. Juna looked into Anito's alien eyes. The Tendu was concerned about her. She fought back another rush of tears.

"I miss my people," Juna said.

"I understand. It's a long time since I see Narmolom. I miss my people also."

Ukatonen touched her shoulder. "We not talk about your

people anymore today. You rest. You eat. We go back to Narmolom soon."

To Anito's relief, their remaining time at Lyanan passed quickly and without incident. Some Tendu from the surrounding villages had come to watch the race, and they stayed to help finish preparing and planting the last bits of the burnt-over area.

The villagers' manner toward Eerin had changed after the race. The cultivator had impressed them, even though her dogged persistence to win had not. Contempt and anger had changed to curiosity. They watched her, ears wide, flickering comments among themselves. Ini and Ehna congratulated her on winning. After that, some of the boldest bami came up and began to ask her questions.

Eerin spent her free time sitting with the bami, showing them her talking stone and learning new words. The elders watched in fascination, but hung back from the new creature, afraid of losing face.

Indeed, the last few days in Lyanan were so pleasant that Anito was almost sorry when it came time for the farewell banquet. Despite the devastation of its land, the village of Lyanan was able to produce a very creditable feast. There was a great deal of fresh ocean fish, honey, fruit, and a variety of pickled greens and fruit served over sprouting namman seeds, as well as bibbi and kiltani greens. There were several fruits that Anito had never seen before. Lalito made her a present of the seeds, to take back to Narmolom, with instructions on how to grow them.

Once the banquet was over, there was a long round of speeches. Lalito praised Ukatonen and Anito. She even had a few kind words for Eerin. Then other elders got up and made similarly complimentary speeches. Arato and Sarito were the only elders who had anything to say about Eerin, praising her strength and hard work. The eldest of the bami got up and presented finely woven carrying baskets to Anito and Ukatonen. Anito flushed a nostalgic blue-grey, remembering all the times that she had done this for guests visiting Narmolom.

From the elders Anito received a thick sheaf of yarram, a

finely woven net, two large sealed gourds full of sea salt, and several smaller gourds containing salt-pickled fruit. Ukatonen received several new blowgun reeds, neatly coiled inside a large bamboo container, another container full of blowgun darts tipped with bird down, and a gourd of neatly packaged seeds, the product, Anito was sure, of the village's finest trees.

Even Eerin received some gifts. Ini and Ehna gave her a large gathering bag, Arato gave her a small gourd of sea salt. Sarito came forward with a small hunting net. Then a tinka slipped out from the crowd, handed Eerin a coil of rope, and vanished before Anito could prevent Eerin from accepting it. It was a courting gift, something made by the tinka. By accepting it, Eerin had signaled her willingness to be courted by the tinka who had given it to her.

Irritation forked down Anito's back. She would have to speak to Eerin about taking gifts from tinka. She should have done it sooner, but she was only now beginning to realize how dangerous Eerin's ignorance could be. It was good that they were leaving tomorrow. She doubted that the tinka would leave the safety of the village and follow them through the jungle. A ripple of turquoise joy passed over her. Tomorrow they would be going home!

Twelve

JUNA FOLLOWED ANITO and Ukatonen through the trees, her heart light with relief. Her first term of service at Lyanan was over, and she had managed to improve her standing in the eyes of the villagers. Her next visit would be easier. In spite of her difficulties, she was glad to have helped restore the forest.

Around midmorning, they stopped to rest in a heavily loaded fruit tree. Juna helped them fill a gathering bag, and then they settled themselves against the trunk for a snack. This was another fruit new to Juna. It was long and green, with a thick inedible rind. Inside, the fruit was soft and mushy and tasted like chocolate-covered bananas with a hint of lemon.

The aliens had a dizzying variety of different food plants. She ate some new species of fruit or green at almost every meal. Given the diversity of the rain forest, it made sense. It also made for some interesting meals. Juna leaned forward to ask Anito what they called this new fruit, but to her surprise, the alien bounded past her into a thick clump of branches.

There was a brief flurry, and a loud squalling noise, like two cats fighting. Then Anito emerged from the clump of vegetation with a struggling tinka. Once it realized that it was caught, the tinka stopped fighting and followed Anito meekly over to where Ukatonen and Juna were sitting. As it approached Juna it reached into its gathering bag and pulled out a tightly rolled up net. It started to hand the net to Juna, but Anito grabbed the tinka's arm and pulled it away from Juna's outstretched hand.

"No!" Anito told it, bright red with anger. Anito launched into a long angry tirade to the tinka, but she spoke so quickly that Juna couldn't follow what she was saying. She seemed to be telling the tinka that it shouldn't do something, but Juna couldn't understand what. Then Anito gestured in the direction of Lyanan and ordered it to return. The tinka turned and looked pleadingly at Juna. Clearly it wanted something from her.

"Wait," Juna said. "What does it want?"

"It wants to be your bami. This cannot be," Ukatonen told her.

Juna looked at the tinka, amazed. *Bami* was the term used by elders for their apprentices. Her theory that the tinka were a related species was wrong. And now this tinka wanted her to adopt it. It was clearly impossible.

"No," Juna told the tinka. "You cannot be my bami. Go back to Lyanan. I'm sorry."

The tinka's ears widened at her apology, but then Anito once again ordered the tinka to go, in bright, angry tones. The tinka stuffed the net into its gathering bag, and with a last backward look at Juna, it set off toward Lyanan.

"What will happen to it?" Juna asked Anito when the tinka had vanished into the trees.

"It will go back to the village. Unless someone takes it as one of their bami, it will die." Seeing Juna color in alarm, Anito added, "Not soon. In a few years. This is what happens to tinka."

"Will someone accept it for their bami?" Juna asked, wishing her language skills were better.

"Probably not. The elders of Lyanan aren't going to be able to have any new bami for many years. It followed you because it knows this and is desperate. Younger tinka may try to win a place in another village. I think that one is too old to do that."

Juna looked after the tinka. Guilt knifed through her. "So the tinka will die?" she asked sadly.

Ukatonen touched her shoulder. "Most tinka do not become bami. If all tinka were made bami, then there would be no room for anything else. The jungle would be eaten bare. Only the best tinka become bami. Understand?"

Juna nodded, flickering acknowledgment.

"Good," said Ukatonen. "Now finish eating. We must travel far today."

Juna finished the last of her fruit, no longer caring what the Tendu called it. Her ebullient mood was gone. She was alone on a planet full of aliens who let their children die if they weren't good enough.

It was wrong to judge the Tendu like this, she told herself as they traveled through the jungle. Still, it seemed deeply wrong to her that the aliens would let their children die. Surely there was another way? Could the Survey help them? She shook her head, trying to drive the thought out of her mind. It was against Survey regulations to interfere with an alien culture.

Still, she was pleased when, at lunch, Ukatonen discovered that the tinka was still following them. Ukatonen ordered the young alien off, chasing it through several trees to make sure that it was on its way. Anito and Ukatonen joked with each other about the tinka's determination. Juna looked away, angered that they could joke about what was a matter of life or death to the tinka.

Anito touched her shoulder. "What's wrong?"

"The tinka will die, and you laugh at it," Juna told her. "It's not funny to the tinka."

"We all die eventually, and besides, it's only a tinka," Anito told her. "It isn't a person. It was lucky, for a tinka. It had a safe place in the village. Some other tinka will take its place if it doesn't return soon. Then it will have to live out in the jungle, where some animal will kill it. It's a stupid tinka, not fit to become a bami. Stop worrying about it. It isn't worth it."

"But it's wrong!" Juna said, unable to contain her anger any longer. "Why let tinka die? Why not have fewer offspring? Then the tinka wouldn't have to die!"

"But what would we eat?" Anito asked her. "If we had fewer young, then our villages would have to be smaller. We could not support so many people without eating our young."

Juna went beige with disgust. "You eat your young?" she asked, incredulous.

"Of course," Anito replied. "You've eaten narey too."

Juna remembered helping butcher the giant tadpoles that the aliens raised in the base of the tree, remembered the faintly cheesy taste of their raw flesh, and then realized what she had been eating.

"Oh, my God," she moaned. A sudden, horribly vivid image of a baby hung like a butchered goat rose to her mind. She remembered her little brother, his fingers clasped around one of hers, as she helped her mother change his diaper. The Tendu ate babies. Her gorge rose and she vomited her lunch over the side of the branch.

Ukatonen touched her shoulder. "Are you all right?" he asked solicitously.

"I've been eating babies," Juna said aloud. "What kind of people are you?" She turned and fled blindly through the canopy.

She scrambled through the trees until her foot slipped on a rain-slick branch and she found herself clinging one-handed over a forty-meter drop. She pulled herself back up onto the branch and looked around. Off in the distance, a few animals called. A leaf fluttered down through the canopy toward the distant ground. She was alone.

Now what? she wondered to herself. She had no idea where she was, or how to get back to Anito and Ukatonen. She looked around at the wet, dripping canopy, and felt vaguely ashamed of her sudden visceral reaction. Then the image of the butchered baby sprang unbidden to her mind, and she shuddered. How could the Tendu do such a thing?

She shook her head. She had let herself forget that the Tendu were aliens, with an alien culture. She was a biologist; she could name dozens of examples of cannibalism occurring in nature. She had to accept that this was the way they did things, even if it seemed like a great and terrible wrong to her.

The tadpoles weren't like human children, she reminded herself. They seemed no more aware or intelligent than any other tadpole. From a biological standpoint, the aliens were fascinating. No one would ever have predicted a sentient alien species whose reproductive habits were as profligate and impersonal as those of oysters. The Alien Contact people back home would have to tear up all their existing theories of cultural development and start over again.

When did intelligence begin for these aliens? She would have to ask Anito and Ukatonen what their earliest memories were. First though, they would have to find her.

Juna scanned the canopy for her alien caretakers, but there was no sign of them. She considered trying to find her way back on her own, but decided that it would only make things worse. Anito and Ukatonen were much more likely to find her than she was to find them. She hefted her gathering sack. She had food, enough for today and tomorrow, and she had her computer. She would wait here until tomorrow, and if they hadn't turned up by then, she would head back to the coast and throw herself on the dubious mercy of the villagers of Lyanan. It wasn't a pleasant prospect, but it was better than being lost in the forest.

She found a suitable spot, and built a crude nest of branches. Then she took out her computer and began to work. She was busy working with the linguistic expert system, resolving some inconsistencies in grammar, when a rustling noise above her head made her look up.

It was the tinka again. It clung to a branch, watching her work.

"Go away!" she told it in skin speech, making shooing motions with her hands. The tinka swung off into the canopy, leaving her alone again.

Juna sighed, rubbed the rain out of her eyes, and looked around. Nearby, a pooo-eet bird was calling, insects hummed, and some unidentifiable creature periodically let loose with a bloodcurdling shriek. A group of lizards fed on leaves in a nearby tree and there was the constant patter of rain. She sighed again, feeling small and alone in the immensity of the forest.

"Damn," she muttered, wishing that Anito and Ukatonen would hurry up and find her. She was in no mood to work anymore. She shut down the linguistic program, and summoned up a selection of her favorite songs. She sang along. Her voice was thick and rusty from disuse. The aliens found her voice either disturbing or hugely amusing, so she had fallen into the habit of silence. She closed her eyes and gave herself over to the music.

The song ended. She paused the music and drank some water to ease her scratchy throat. She hadn't sung since the night the *Kotani* had jumped into hyperspace. She hadn't been alone since then either. Every single moment, waking and sleeping, had been spent in the company of the Tendu.

Juna summoned up another song, one of her favorites, an ancient blues tune. She wasn't a particularly talented singer. Mostly she sang in the cleanser, or along with a recorded vocalist, but she did love to sing, especially when she was alone. At the end of the song, she opened her eyes and looked up. The tinka was watching her again, ears spread wide, head cocked in an attitude of amazement. Juna laughed aloud at the tinka's expression of surprise, and laughed again as it fled from the sound of her laughter. She wondered if she should chase it away, but decided to let Anito and Ukatonen worry about the tinka.

She started the music again, and sang along with several more songs, then paused for another sip of water. When she looked up, she saw that Anito and Ukatonen were sitting on the branch where the tinka had been. They were watching her, ears spread wide, magenta with surprise and puzzlement.

Juna switched off the music and sat up regretfully. It had been a pleasant interlude, but now it was time to get back to work. It would probably be a long time before she was alone again, and free to indulge herself in her humanity.

"Are you in pain?" Anito asked her. "Do you need healing?"

"I'm fine," Juna reassured the alien.

"Why did you run?" Ukatonen asked.

Juna shook her head again. "It's hard to explain, en," she said formally. "My people do not eat their young. We believe that it is wrong. I was—" She hesitated, uncertain how to proceed, not knowing the words to express her feelings. "I think I know how you felt, looking out at the forest my people destroyed. It is hard for me to accept that you eat your young." Juna felt faintly queasy again, thinking about it.

Anito and Ukatonen swung down to join her on the branch.

"I think we do not understand each other," Ukatonen said.

"We eat only our tadpoles, and only those without front legs. Once the front legs emerge, they aren't eaten."

"What happens to them after that?" Juna asked.

"During the flood season they swim off into the jungle. Those that survive come back to us as tinka. The smartest and best of the tinka are chosen by elders to raise as bami. Then the bami become elders. Understand?"

"I think so. It is very different from how my people treat their young. It is unusual for us to have more than one child at a time. Each child is very important to us, which is why it is hard for me to accept that you"—Juna paused, fighting back another surge of disgust—"eat them."

"We eat only the tadpoles," Ukatonen reminded her. "The tinka are free to fend for themselves."

"That too, seems wrong to me. We look after our children until they are able to look after themselves."

"But you have fewer children. It is simply not possible to look after every tinka, even those living in the villages. It wouldn't be fair to the other tinka, waiting in the forest for a place in the village."

Juna sighed. This conversation was getting way out of her depth. "Our people are very different."

"Yes," Ukatonen agreed. "We are."

Anito reached out and touched Ukatonen's arm. "We should be going, en."

Ukatonen flickered agreement. "We will talk more about this later."

They waited while Juna gathered her things, and then the three of them proceeded on their way.

The tinka continued to follow them. The next morning, Juna awoke to find a freshly killed lizard lying at her feet. Anito stopped her before she could pick it up.

"It's from the tinka," Anito told her. "Accepting the lizard will only encourage it." She picked up the lizard and tossed it over the side of the nest. They breakfasted on leftover game and fresh fruit, then set out for the day.

Anito caught the tinka about an hour later. Ukatonen again ordered it to return to the village, sending it on its way with a hard slap.

The tinka still followed them. Anito and Ukatonen began
pelting it with rotten fruit and even fresh dung. The tinka hung
farther back, out of range, but did not go away. Blows and
curses did nothing to discourage it. Finally they settled into
grimly ignoring it.

The battle of wills between the tinka and the elders would
have been funny if it hadn't been a life-and-death struggle for
the youngster. Whenever the young alien disappeared for a day
or so, Juna began to worry that it had been killed and eaten by
some predator. She stopped wishing that the tinka would go
back to Lyanan, and began hoping that it would somehow
manage to find a place in Anito's village. Surely someone
would take pity on this grimly determined youngster, and
accept it as an apprentice.

Once, while Anito was butchering a large feathered animal
with the face of a deerlike herbivore and the feet of a bird, Juna
asked if she would accept the youngster as an apprentice.

"No. I'm too young for an apprentice. It would be wrong.
Besides, I should choose one from my own village."

"What about the other elders in your village? Would one of
them take the tinka?"

Anito shook her head. "Probably it won't even get a place on
the rafts. It'll be left behind when we head downriver."

"But it's so brave and determined!" Juna protested. "Surely
that must count for something!"

"It knew its chances when it decided to follow us," Anito
said. "It was foolish to take such a risk. If it dies, it will be its
own fault, and yours, for encouraging it to follow you."

Stung by Anito's words, Juna turned away. She had been
kind to the tinka at Lyanan, and made the fatal mistake of
accepting their small gifts, thinking them no more than
kindness. Ignorance could be as harmful as active malice.

"What should I do now?" she asked Anito.

"Ignore the tinka, as you have been doing. There is nothing
else that can be done."

"What about Ukatonen?" Juna asked. "Could he accept the
tinka as his apprentice?"

Anito's ears lifted in surprise. A flicker of irritation forked down her chest. "It would be very rude to suggest such a thing to Ukatonen. Don't do it. Understand?"

Juna nodded. "I understand."

"Good."

Two days later, as they were moving through the canopy, the tinka was attacked by a large lizard. When they heard the squalling of the struggling tinka, Ukatonen and Anito glanced back briefly and continued on their way. Juna stopped. The young alien fought fiercely, biting and clawing, but it was unable to pierce the lizard's thick hide. Unless something was done, the tinka was doomed.

Anito and Ukatonen went on as though nothing at all had happened. Anito glanced back and gestured to Juna to hurry. The tinka's struggles were growing weaker. It looked at her, its pale green eyes pleading. She remembered how the tinka had gathered around her at Lyanan, like so many eager children. . . .

Juna broke off a dead branch, and rushed the lizard, shouting and yelling. It dropped the tinka and leaped into the next tree.

Juna caught the little alien just before it slipped off the branch. It was covered with blood. Claw marks scored its chest, and there were deep bite marks on its shoulders and neck. She could see a major blood vessel pulsing beneath a thin layer of connective tissue. She was fumbling out her medical kit when she felt a hand on her shoulder. It was Anito.

"Leave it. Let the lizard have its prey," Anito told her.

Juna looked at the pathetic, bleeding tinka, its eyes slitted open. It was watching her decide its fate. Saving its life would constitute a major breach of regulations; she would be directly interfering with an alien culture. This wasn't a human child, she shouldn't apply human values to it. The tinka's eyes slid closed, and its head rolled sideways.

She remembered the lengths her mother had gone to in order to keep Juna and her brother, Toivo, alive in the howling hell of the refugee camps. She had heard from her father and her aunt Anetta about everything they had done to find them. Without their love and determination, she and Toivo would be dead now. She remembered stealing food for Toivo, stolen from others needier than herself, so that her brother could live. She closed her eyes, tears pricking her eyelids, remembering how her mother had fought for their lives. How could she condemn this little alien to die?

"No."

"You must," Ukatonen told her.

"I can't," Juna said. "Not after all it's done to follow me. It's too brave for me to let it die."

Ukatonen ducked his chin, looking thoughtfully at the tinka.

"If it lives, you must accept it as your apprentice. Are you willing to accept that burden?"

Juna looked up, meeting the alien's eyes. How could she take on responsibility for another creature? She was barely managing as it was. It was also a flagrant breach of protocol regulations. Every other regulation she had broken was justifiable. She had had to do it in order to survive. But this? She shook her head. No AC specialist in their right mind would do something like this. It was completely and totally wrong. But she couldn't let the young alien die, no matter what happened as a result of her decision. The tinka had fought too hard for a chance to live. Juna had already decided, and no amount of rational thought could change her mind. This touched her in a place where Survey regulations had no hold on her. Somehow she would manage. "Yes, en. I accept this burden."

"You understand that Anito or I will do nothing to heal the tinka? If it slows us down too much, then we must leave it. Do you accept this?"

"Yes, en."

"All right, then. Hurry. We have a long way to go today."

Thirteen

Aɴɪᴛᴏ ᴡᴀᴛᴄʜᴇᴅ ɪɴ disbelief as Eerin turned back to rescue the tinka from the jaws of the golano. Her concern deepened as Eerin bargained with Ukatonen for the tinka's worthless life. The new creature's actions felt deeply wrong to Anito. Nothing good would come of this. Anito longed to step in and put the poor tinka out of its misery, but Ukatonen had spoken, and she could not dispute his decision. She could only wait and hope that the tinka would die from its wounds.

The new creature poured a clear liquid that bubbled in the tinka's wounds. Curious, Anito caught a drop of the stuff on her palm. It burned like the sting of a fire beetle. Then Eerin took a small, curved needle and a complex deathstone tool and began to *sew* the tinka's wounds together. It was horrible beyond anything Anito had thought possible. The tinka stiffened in pain. Eerin made a low, crooning noise in the back of her throat.

"Be still now. It's going to be all right," Eerin told the tinka. The tinka's struggles ceased, but occasional shivers of pain racked its tiny frame as Eerin's needle dug into its flesh. A small, creaking sound leaked out of the tinka. "I'm sorry," Eerin said, ochre with concern. "I know it hurts, but I have to do it or you'll bleed to death. It will be over soon."

Anito looked away, unable to watch. Ukatonen was leaning forward, observing. His skin was a curious shade of purple curiosity mixed with muddy patches of beige disgust and orange roils of horror.

Anito touched his arm. "Can't you stop this?" she pleaded. "She's torturing the tinka."

"Eerin has accepted responsibility for the tinka. What she does with it now is up to her."

"But it's wrong!" Anito protested. "She is my atwa, and I cannot accept this. Please, en, stop this abomination. Kill the tinka before it's too late."

"Are you asking me for a judgment, kene?" Ukatonen said. "What will you pay me with?"

Anito looked down at the tinka. Its eyes were tightly shut, its mouth open in a soundless cry of agony. She looked away again; the sight of its suffering was unbearable.

It would be a terrible mistake for Eerin to accept this tinka as her bami. How could she provide for a bami when she couldn't even provide for herself? How could Eerin teach a bami to be a wise elder when she was so ignorant? It was deeply wrong. The new creature was Anito's atwa, and it was her responsibility to stop her, no matter the price.

"Yes, en. I ask for judgment. What do you want as payment?"

Ukatonen looked at her, his eyes cold and calculating. "Are you sure that this is what you want? The payment will be very high."

"Yes, en. You may ask what you will."

"Very well, then. I ask for you. I want you to become an enkar. Do you still wish for me to deliver judgment?"

If Anito agreed to this, it meant leaving Narmolom and everything that she knew and loved, to follow the lonely path of the enkar. It was a very high price, and for a moment she almost backed down. Then she glanced down at the tinka. Its hands were curved in tight claws of pain. Eerin had finished sewing up the first deep wound and was now drawing the skin together over the pulsing vein in the tinka's neck. Anito couldn't allow someone capable of such cruelty to become a sitik. It was an abomination.

"Yes, en," Anito said without taking her eyes from the tinka's pain-wracked body.

"Very well. I will decide when we stop for the night."

"But, en—"

Ukatonen looked at her, his eyes those of a stranger. "Yes, kene?"

It took all of Anito's courage to reply. "The tinka is hurting *now!*"

Ukatonen glanced down at the tinka, then he reached out, and sank a spur into its upper leg. Instantly the tinka slumped into unconsciousness.

"Not anymore."

Eerin looked up. "I was afraid that the things that stop pain for my people might kill it. Thank you for your kindness." Then the new creature turned back to her grisly work.

Anito got up and climbed through the canopy, unable to watch any more of this obscene butchery. Ukatonen came for her when Eerin was through.

They continued on their way, covering a fair distance. Eerin rigged a sling from a pair of gathering bags, and tied the tinka to her body, leaving her hands free for climbing. The tinka hardly slowed her down. The new creature's climbing had improved dramatically since they had set out from Narmolom, and she maintained the fast pace that Ukatonen set. Even so, her fatigue was obvious by the time they stopped for the evening.

Despite her exhaustion, Eerin made sure that the tinka was bedded down comfortably before seeing to her own needs, squelching Anito's hopes that she might tire of her burden and abandon it. They ate in stillness, a quick meal of dried provisions and hastily gathered greens and fruit. Eerin tried to feed the tinka some honey and fruit juice, but it was too deeply unconscious to do more than swallow a tiny bit that Eerin spread on its tongue with her fingers. At last Ukatonen touched Eerin on the shoulder and motioned to her to come and sit down near the glow fungus.

"Anito has asked me to make a judgment about whether you should be allowed to adopt the tinka," Ukatonen said, suddenly stiff and formal.

Eerin sat up, her face working the way it did when she was startled. She turned ochre with concern, orange and red highlights of fear and anger appearing here and there. "No, en, please—"

Ukatonen held his hand up to stop her. "Be still. I have not yet decided. There is much to discuss before a decision is made. Anito, please state your objections to this adoption."

"En, Eerin is not a Tendu. She cannot raise a tinka properly. She can't perform the physical transformations necessary for the tinka to become a bami. How will the tinka be transformed? What will happen to the tinka when Eerin's people return? Will she abandon her own bami? That would be much worse than allowing the tinka to die now. Eerin is being frivolous and cruel, agreeing to a commitment that she cannot possibly keep. It is, after all, only a tinka, en."

"These are important points, kene. What do you say about this, Eerin?"

"I say that they are important also, and I do not have answers for many of these questions, en. I know that this tinka is very brave, and very determined, and I think that one with such courage deserves to live, even if you and Anito and all of the other Tendu don't. My people value such characteristics, and they have carried us very far. I believe that these other problems can be solved if the desire exists to solve them. It depends on you, en, and on Anito. I will need your help to raise this tinka well. Most of my people are raised by more than one person; often several people work together to help raise our young. It is a long task for us, en, and a great responsibility. Our young are helpless at birth, and remain so for several years. A tinka is far more capable than one of our young. I cannot teach this tinka all the things a Tendu needs to know, but I can care for it and protect it while others help it to become a good Tendu."

Ukatonen tucked his chin, thinking deeply for a while, then looked at Anito. "Well, kene, what do you say to that?"

"I still think it's wrong, en."

"If it lives, what would you do?"

Anito shook her head. "I don't know, en. It would be wrong

to abandon it then. It will have a claim on Eerin. We should have left it to die. That would have been more merciful than what Eerin did to it today." She paused. "Perhaps it's not too late to leave it behind," she went on. "Some animal will find it and put it out of its misery."

Eerin turned bright orange and moved protectively between Anito and the tinka. "No!"

"The new creature has said that she cannot raise this tinka without help," Anito argued. "Why should we allow her to raise it? How can the tinka learn to be a proper Tendu, learn to raise a bami of its own? If the new creature adopts this tinka, it will always be out of harmony with the other Tendu."

"There is no way to know that for certain," Eerin pointed out. "And there is another thing to consider, en. My people and your people are just starting to get to know each other. There will be a need for Tendu who understand my people. If I have a part in raising this tinka, then it will understand my people very well. This tinka can be a bridge between our people."

Anito looked at Ukatonen, whose ears were lifted in surprise. "That is something I hadn't thought of, but is it fair to lay out such a fate without asking what the tinka wants?"

"No, en," Eerin agreed. "But surely we can ask it what it wants when it recovers."

"Tinka become intelligent when they become bami," Anito said. "The tinka isn't smart enough to understand what we are asking it to decide."

"But it isn't fair to abandon it here, not after it has come so far at such a risk!" Eerin protested.

"It isn't fair to let it live to be poorly raised!" Anito shot back.

Ukatonen held up a hand to still the argument. "I have heard enough. You have given me much to think about. I will tell you what I think tomorrow morning."

Anito's ears spread in surprise. She had expected this judgment discussion to take longer. Often, Ilto had talked for most of a night before he retired to think. She felt uneasy. Perhaps asking for this judgment had been a bad mistake. The price was painfully high. A misty ripple of sadness clouded her skin as she thought of Narmolom. She longed to wake up to its familiar sounds and smells; she wanted to see the people she had known for almost her entire life, certainly all of the life that mattered to her.

She looked at the wounded tinka. It was impossible to tell its condition without linking, but it looked pale and its skin was dry and tight. She doubted that it would live through the night, and the thought saddened her. She had made a great sacrifice for one with no future. Why had she done it? How had this little tinka inspired such interest? Was Eerin right? Was this tinka somehow special? Anito rippled uncertainty, and began fluffing up the leaves in the nest in preparation for sleep.

As she crawled beneath the damp leaves, she saw Eerin moistening the tinka, and the bedding around it. She remembered Eerin's patient, gentle care when she had been sick. The tinka might survive.

The tinka lived through the night. It was still pale and unconscious, but its skin was more moist and yielding than it had been, a testament to Eerin's care. Anito approved. At least the new creature knew how to make her charge comfortable, despite yesterday's butchery.

Ukatonen awoke, bathed, and relieved himself over the side of the nest. Then he settled himself against the edge of the nest and assumed the stiff, formal posture of an enkar.

"I have made the judgment," he announced. "If the tinka is strong enough to recover from its wounds, then Eerin may adopt it as her bami. Anito and I will teach Eerin how to raise a bami properly, and we will teach it the things that Eerin can't. When the time comes for Eerin to return to her people, then the tinka will become my bami. If the tinka recovers, we will ask if this is acceptable to it. If it decides not to accept Eerin as its sitik, then my price for helping to select the new chief elder of Narmolom is that they make a place there for this tinka. That way the tinka will not have to fight for a place in the village. It is to be hoped that one of your elders will adopt it, Anito. Are there any questions?"

Anito shook her head. It seemed like a mistake to her, but she had asked for the judgment, and couldn't question it. "No, en. I have no questions."

"Thank you, en," Eerin said. "It seems a fair judgment to me. I have no questions either."

"Good. Then let's eat and get started. The lowlands are already flooding. We'll have to hurry to get to Narmolom before the migration starts, and the tinka will slow us down."

F o u r t e e n

JUNA LIFTED THE tinka and put it in the improvised carrying sling. It was as limp as a freshly killed animal; its eyelids didn't even twitch as she lifted it. Had saving the tinka's life been a mistake? She thought about the little alien, tense and shivering with pain, but so silent, emitting only one small noise despite its agony. The tinka's ear was crumpled against the mesh of the sling. Juna gently smoothed it out. This one deserved to live, if it could. Saving its life might be a bad idea, diplomatically speaking, but she didn't regret her decision.

Anito beckoned to her. It was time to go. She picked up her gathering bag and followed the aliens through the canopy. The tinka remained unconscious all that day, responding only reflexively to the pre-chewed fruit pulp and honey that Juna trickled into its mouth when they stopped. The Tendu watched her curiously as she did this.

Juna suppressed a surge of anger at the aliens for not helping her with the tinka. Anger wasn't useful here. She was pushing things pretty far with the Tendu already. They were very upset with her interference in the fate of the tinka. As for the Survey— Juna shook her head, trying not to think about all of the Survey regulations she had broken by adopting the tinka. Interference to such an extent could result in some serious penalties, possibly even a dishonorable discharge.

Two days went by with no response from the tinka. The exertion of carrying it began to tell on Juna, slowing her down and making her clumsy. On the evening of the second day, Ukatonen touched her shoulder.

"The tinka is slowing us down too much," he said. "If it isn't better by tomorrow, you must leave it behind."

"No," Juna protested. "I won't abandon it. Not until it dies."

"Then we will leave you behind. Anito must get back to her village. Already the lowlands are starting to flood. Her village will be leaving soon. I have promised that she will be there in time to go with them. She has endured much for you. It isn't right that she should be forced to spend the flood season alone. You have been selfish and difficult. It is time to think of others beyond yourself."

His ultimatum delivered, Ukatonen turned away.

Juna looked at the tinka. Should she leave it behind? It seemed no better than it had after she stitched it up. She had done everything that she could for it and it showed no signs of recovering. The choice was clear—either she could abandon the tinka, or be abandoned by the two Tendu. She couldn't survive alone in the jungle without the aliens' help. She had to go with them. The choice was heartbreaking.

Juna slept only a little that night, agonizing over leaving the tinka behind. She arose the next morning tired and anxious. She began bathing the tinka. When she inadvertently splashed a droplet of water in its nose, it flinched and snuffled in response. It opened its eyes.

"Good!" Juna exclaimed, both aloud and in skin speech. Anito and Ukatonen looked up at the sound of her voice.

The tinka reached for the water gourd. Juna supported its head as it drank. When it was done, she fed it one of the soft yellow fruits that Anito had gathered the night before. The tinka bit into it hungrily, devouring it in three or four bites.

There was a touch on her shoulder. It was Anito. She handed Juna a gourd of honey.

"Mix this with water and a little salt. It will give the tinka strength," Anito said.

Juna stared in surprise at the alien, weighing the round, smooth gourd of honey in her hand.

"You wanted to leave the tinka behind three days ago. Why are you helping it now?"

"Because it will live. It has proved itself strong enough to become a Tendu. Let me help you prepare the mixture. It has to be done right for it to work."

Anito blended the honey and water, adding salt and tasting the mixture with a wrist spur until it was just right.

The tinka gulped the nourishing drink greedily, then devoured more fruit. Ukatonen returned from hunting with two medium-sized tree lizards and a large, sloppy pooo-eet bird. He slit the throat of the lizard and let the tinka drink the blood while he cut out the livers from the bird and the other lizard for it to eat.

After that, the tinka improved rapidly. Juna carried it in the sling all morning, but it fed itself lunch, and was able to cling to her without the sling for the rest of the day.

That night, as soon as they had built a nest to sleep in, Ukatonen touched the tinka on the arm, asking it to watch what they had to tell it. Then Ukatonen explained his judgment concerning its fate.

"The new creature may adopt you, but she cannot teach you as well as a regular sitik. Anito and I will help her teach you. In addition, she will leave in about five years. I will become your sitik then."

The tinka looked at Juna, its ears wide with surprise.

"I must go back to my people. I have no choice," she told it.

The tinka's ears flattened against the side of its head and it looked away, clearly unhappy with Juna's statement. Ukatonen touched it and it turned and looked at him.

"You have another choice," he told the youngster. "You can go with us to Anito's village and see if another elder will choose to adopt you. Anito will make sure that you have a place among the village tinka."

The tinka looked at Anito, ears wide.

Anito flickered acknowledgment. "I will tell the other elders how brave and strong you are. Perhaps that will encourage one of them to choose you."

"This isn't fair to you," Juna told the tinka. "You deserve a better sitik than me, but I couldn't leave you to die."

"Do you understand the choice?" Ukatonen asked.

The little alien's ears flicked up and back, something Juna had seen the tinka do before, when they acknowledged a direct command.

"Do you understand that if you agree to be adopted by the new creature, that she will leave, and that I will become your new sitik?"

The tinka's ears flattened, and it looked away for a moment, then looked back at them, flicking its ears up and back in agreement.

"Do you understand that you must obey Ukatonen and Anito as though they were your sitik, and listen to them as you would listen to me?" Juna asked.

The tinka's ears flicked up and back several times.

"What do you choose, the village or the new creature?" Ukatonen asked.

The tinka looked from Juna to Anito and back again, and then pointed at Juna with its chin. It held its spurless wrists out, as though asking to link with her.

Ukatonen looked at Juna. "I ask you one last time: are you willing to adopt this tinka as your bami?" His words were displayed in such formal patterns that Juna had to look at Anito for a translation.

Juna nodded. "Yes, I accept this tinka as my bami," she replied in the most formal speech she knew.

Ukatonen turned to the tinka. "I ask you one last time: will you accept this new creature as your sitik?"

The tinka's ears flicked up and back as it agreed to accept Juna as its sitik.

"It is decided. The formal ceremony will take place after we arrive at Narmolom," Ukatonen said. He dropped back into casual language and posture. "I saw a tree with some ripe trangin on it back that way. Please go and gather some of them while Anito and I hunt."

Juna and the tinka returned with a bulging sack of the spiny orange fruit. The tinka also found some edible fern shoots and stuffed a leaf packet with fat, wriggling grubs. Anito and Ukatonen had killed a large ground lizard with a long, flexible snout, black in color with beautiful golden stripes across its hindquarters. Juna had seen them before; they ranged over the jungle floor in herds of up to a dozen, scavenging fallen fruit from the forest floor.

The evening meal was a feast. Ukatonen and Anito took turns pressing delicacies on the tinka. It ate until its stomach was hugely distended. The two older aliens gorged themselves as well. Juna was a bit more hesitant, especially about the wriggling grubs, which proved to be surprisingly rich and tasty. The trangin, which smelled vile when broken open, also proved delicious.

By the next day, the tinka was able to travel on its own, clinging to Juna only when it was too tired to keep up the pace. That afternoon, in the midst of a heavy rain, they crossed the flooded stream that marked the southwest boundary of the territory encompassed by Anito's village. Anito flushed a joyous turquoise, and let out a booming call. They paused while she listened intently. At last came a distant reply. Anito looked back inquiringly at Ukatonen.

"Go on ahead. We'll follow you," Ukatonen said, rippling mild amusement at Anito's eagerness. Anito leaped through the canopy, and was soon lost to sight, although her loud cries were clearly audible. Juna thought that she saw a faint cloud of regret pass briefly over Ukatonen.

"What's the matter, en?" she asked.

"Nothing," Ukatonen replied, his words yellow-edged with irritation. "It's been a long trip. It will be good to rest."

They continued through the treetops in the pouring rain. Wide areas of the lowlands were already flooded. Near the river, the lower branches of the canopy were barely out of the water. They had to move carefully there, for the branches were crowded with stinging insects and poisonous snakes which had climbed up into the canopy to escape the rising water.

"They will be leaving very soon for the coast," Ukatonen reflected. "It is good that we got here when we did."

About an hour later, a crashing of branches heralded Anito's return. "I've spoken with Hinato. She will let the village know that we're on our way. We should be there by tomorrow night, if we hurry."

Laughter flickered over Ukatonen at Anito's desire to be off. "We'll do our best. Please go on ahead of us if you wish."

Thanks flashed over Anito's back as she swung off in the direction of Narmolom.

Ukatonen shouldered his bag. "Let's go," he said. They set off after Anito and traveled until dark. They ate a simple meal of fruit, dried meat, honey, and seaweed, along with some pickled greens. Ukatonen gave the tinka extra-large portions. It tore into the food as though it was starving, despite a large breakfast and lunch, as well as several snacks during the day.

"You'd think that it hadn't eaten for days!" Juna remarked.

"It's healing, and it's getting ready to become a bami. Both of those are good reasons to eat," Ukatonen remarked.

"How does it become a bami, en?"

"Normally, an elder links with the tinka and transforms it, but you don't know how. I will perform the transformation for you."

"Thank you, en."

The enkar looked down and then back up at Juna. "I will become the tinka's sitik when you leave. It is right that I should be the one to transform it."

"I hope—" Juna started to say something, then stopped.

"What?" Ukatonen prompted.

"I was concerned that I had caused trouble for you. If I were a Tendu, then I wouldn't have gone back to save the tinka's life. I wouldn't have caused so much trouble."

"Living is trouble, death is easy," Ukatonen replied. "The tinka was brave and determined. If you had been a Tendu, there would have been no trouble."

"Won't caring for the tinka after I'm gone be a burden?"

Amusement flowed over Ukatonen's body, glowing in the darkness. "Only a light one. Enkar sometimes adopt a bami. This tinka will lighten my loneliness when you go. For that I thank you."

"What is an enkar? What do you do that sets you apart from other Tendu?" Juna asked.

"We travel from village to village and help with difficult problems, ones that the villagers cannot solve themselves. Sometimes an outsider is needed to make difficult decisions.

Because of this, the enkar do not belong to any village. We are always alone." Ukatonen looked away, out into the velvety darkness of the jungle. The constant clamor of the forest sounded suddenly loud. "It is late, and we have done much today. It is time to sleep," Ukatonen said. "We will start early tomorrow."

With that, the subject was closed. Juna got up and settled herself beside the tinka, under a pile of fresh leaves. For a while she listened to the noise of the jungle. Then the weight of her day's travel descended upon her, and she fell asleep.

Ukatonen woke them before dawn. They ate a scant and hurried breakfast, and were on their way as the first pale fingers of light cut through the dense, wet morning fog. As they drew near the village, Juna began to recognize subtle indications of heavy use in this area of the jungle: tree limbs whose bark was worn smooth from the passage of many hands and feet, patches of tree ferns that showed signs of heavy foraging. A couple of months ago, she would never have noticed these things. This patch of jungle would have seemed the same as any other.

Several elders came to greet the travelers, and escorted them the last couple of kilometers. When they reached the village tree, everyone hailed them enthusiastically, draping Ukatonen and Juna with garlands of flowers and greenery. A few garlands were even draped around the neck of the tinka. They were washed and led to a large, ceremonious feast of welcome in the bowl of the great tree crotch. Anito's skin was alive with chatter as she caught up with the news of the village. It was clear that she was extremely pleased to be among her own people again.

"IT IS TIME to begin the tinka's transformation," Ukatonen declared, the evening following their arrival in Narmolom.

Anito straightened, ears wide. She hadn't expected the transformation to take place so soon.

The tinka held out its arms, ears wide and quivering with excitement.

Ukatonen held his arms out to Eerin and lifted his ears inquisitively. "Eerin?" he offered.

Eerin flared orange when she realized what he was asking. "Please," she pleaded. "Is it absolutely necessary?"

Ukatonen nodded. "Do you wish to change your mind about the adoption?"

The tinka looked anxiously at Eerin. Anito suppressed a flash of hope. Perhaps the new creature would back out now. It would be tragic for the tinka, of course, but it would be the new creature's fault for encouraging it in the first place.

The adoption still felt terribly wrong to Anito, but she couldn't prevent it without the support of the other villagers. Protesting a decision made by the enkar who was to choose Narmolon's new chief was unthinkable, especially for those elders who wanted to be chief. Besides, everyone was busy preparing for the journey downriver. They didn't have time for this.

Anito hesitated for another reason. If an enkar's formal decision was wrong, he or she paid for it with their life. If Anito managed to prove that Ukatonen's decision was wrong, then he would be forced to take his own life. There had been too much death already. Anito couldn't bring herself to initiate a fight that might lead to Ukatonen's death.

"No," Eerin said. "I don't want to change my mind about adopting the tinka, but I don't wish to link unless I have to."

"I understand," Ukatonen told her. "Do you understand that if you adopt this tinka, you will need to link with it?"

"Yes," Eerin replied, "but I don't want to link unless it's necessary. Is it necessary for me to link now?"

"Yes, it is. Will you join the link?"

"Yes, en."

"All right then," he said holding out his arms. "Anito, will you join us?"

Anito flickered acknowledgment and joined spurs with them. Fear sang through Eerin, like the vibrations in a tightrope that has been plucked. The tinka grasped Ukatonen's arm eagerly, and reached for Eerin. The new creature suppressed her fear and grasped the tinka's arm. They descended into the link. Ukatonen reached out to soothe Eerin. When she was calm, his presence moved through the tinka, exploring its immature body. Anito noticed the beginnings of deterioration in the joints, in the immune system, and in its vital organs. Had the tinka stayed in Lyanan, it would almost certainly have lost its place in the village to a younger, stronger tinka in less than a year.

Ukatonen's presence hovered momentarily around the tinka's tiny, undeveloped sexual organs, exploring. The tinka was male, another strike against it, particularly in a village where food would be in short supply for the next few years. Unripe eggs laid by female bami were a source of critical nutrients for the developing tadpoles. As a result, female tinka were more sought after as bami than male tinka. Clearly the tinka's desperation had made him stake his life on Eerin's acceptance.

Ukatonen continued his exploration of the tinka's body. It was healing well. Ukatonen worked on the almost-healed wounds, breaking up bits of scar tissue and clearing away the last bits of the fine thread that Juna used to close the tinka's wounds. It was only a formality. The tinka didn't need healing. His own body was strong enough to mend well. That was a good sign.

Ukatonen reached out to Eerin, joining her with the tinka, binding the tinka's presence to Eerin's, so that his body would recognize her as his sitik. Eerin let it happen, though Anito could still feel the flutter of suppressed fear. Anito felt the tinka reach out, enfolding Eerin, calming her, merging with her.

A tart wave of satisfaction indicated that Ukatonen was ready to begin the transformation. He released a bright, sweet flood of transformation hormones. It was the flavor of life, of hope. A wave of powerful nostalgia swept over Anito. She remembered awakening from her own transformation with that taste in her mouth. She half-expected to open her eyes and find Ilto hovering solicitously over her.

She remembered how her first real thoughts had bubbled up from her brain. They were clear and sharp, unlike the hazy, frightened memories she had of being a tinka, and the muddy sensations of a narey. At first she had thought that an elder was somehow speaking to her inside her head, but then she felt her own awe and fear and wonder and realized that she was the source of that voice.

Ukatonen triggered the changes that would cause the neurons in the tinka's brain to replicate and branch, make the small body begin to grow. He also made the tinka capable of skin speech.

With that, Ukatonen was done; a new bami was created, a new future begun. Ukatonen released the sweetness of his own joy into the link between the four of them. Anito responded in kind, her doubts about the tinka's adoption swept away in the joy of the moment. Together they soared higher and higher, each feeding off the other's joy. Eerin was carried along, her fear washed away by their shared exultation. Then Ukatonen broke the link. Eerin was so drained by the experience that she hardly noticed when they eased her into bed. Then Anito slid gratefully into her own bed and fell asleep.

When she arose the next morning, Anito ate, drank, and washed, then went over to the bed where the new bami lay, and sank a spur into his arm to check his progress. He was doing well. If everything proceeded smoothly, he would be ready to awaken in another couple of days. She left the bami to sleep, and went to see what was happening outside. It was raining hard, streams of rain pouring down the inside of the trunk. The village bustled with preparations for the annual migration to the coast. Tinka and bami hurried up and down the tree, ferrying gourds and baskets to the upper storerooms where they would be safe from the coming flood.

Anito followed the stream to the broad beach where the villagers were making the final preparations for the long, hard trip downriver. Ukatonen and Eerin were helping Ninto and Baha tighten the lashings on their raft. With a faint ripple of regret Anito took the braided rope that Ukatonen handed her. She owed a considerable number of obligations to Ninto and the other villagers who helped gather the materials for this raft while she was traveling back from Lyanan. Without their help, she would have been stuck here alone during flood season, unable to trade downriver. That would have left her with nothing to trade to the mountain people during the dry season. She needed to trade well this trip so that she could settle her debts before Ukatonen took her away to become an enkar.

They had very little time. In another couple of days this beach would be under water, and the villagers would be setting out on migration. Fortunately, Eerin was clever with her hands and had rigged up a device that enabled them to tighten the lashings more quickly and tightly than they could have managed by hand. With Eerin's help they finished the raft before nightfall. That gave Anito an extra day to gather some much-needed trade goods.

Most of her trading stock came from Ilto's stores, plus a few small things that she had made or picked up while traveling. There were several large rolls of waxed sinew thread, enough to make some fish nets while they rafted downriver. She also had several stonewood fish traps, and a box full of carved bone fishhooks. Ilto's supplies yielded several large gourds of preserved fruit, two dozen pots of honey from his na trees, and eight gourds of beeswax. There was a large waterproof basket filled with dried grass, and several bundles of cured reeds. It wasn't much, but if she traded carefully, it might be enough to pay off the obligations she'd incurred.

Late the next afternoon, Anito and the others finished securing their trade goods on the raft. When they were done, they went back to check on the new bami. His mottled skin had faded to the even pale green of a healthy bami, and he slept peacefully, his breathing even and deep. Ukatonen linked briefly with the bami.

"He's ready to wake," the enkar announced, rippling with satisfaction.

"I'll go tell the rest of the villagers to prepare. We can introduce him at the leavetaking banquet tonight," Ninto said.

Ukatonen flickered agreement, and Ninto left. Eerin was sitting off in a corner, playing with her talking stone. Ukatonen regarded the sleeping bami pensively. "How should the bami be awakened?" he asked. "Eerin will need our help to do it properly."

"I don't know, en," Anito said feeling angry at him for asking. It was his decision that brought them to this impasse; he was the one who should come up with a solution. "Why are you asking me? I've never wakened a bami before."

Ukatonen looked at her. "You're going to become an enkar, kene. You will have to answer harder questions than this one. It is time you started learning how."

Anito looked down at the floor. Sadness washed over her as she thought of leaving Narmolom for the isolated life of an enkar.

"Yes, en," she said. She wanted to ask how long she had before he took her away from Narmolom, but she was afraid of the answer.

Irritation forked across Ukatonen's chest. "You are a young elder now, learning to make important decisions. There are good reasons for me to ask you how to do this. This is your village; you know the people here better than I do. This also affects your atwa. Now, I ask you again, how should we waken the bami?"

"I think," Anito said, "that we should ask Eerin about this. It is her bami. She should help decide."

Ukatonen flickered agreement. He chittered to draw Eerin's attention, then beckoned her over to join the conversation.

She looked puzzled when Anito asked her about waking the bami. "I don't understand. Is there something special about this?"

Anito restrained a flash of impatience at Eerin's ignorance.

"Wakening a bami for the first time is important," Ukatonen explained. "It is when you bond with each other. It is the best memory most of us have. There is nothing else like that moment."

"How is it done?" Eerin asked.

"The bami will not awaken until you link with him. That first link is very important. It is then that the bond forms between a bami and its sitik. They learn to know each other in that link. The bond created by that link remains until the sitik dies or leaves the village," Ukatonen said.

"I don't know how to do that," Eerin said.

Ukatonen held out his arms, spurs up. "We will show you what you need to know."

Anito clasped one hand to Ukatonen's arm, so that their spurs were lined up. Then she held out her free arm to Eerin.

Eerin hesitated a moment, then reached out to join the link. Despite her outward show of determination, Eerin's blood sang hot with fear. Anito wondered why Eerin tried to hide how afraid she was. They could taste the fear in her blood as soon as they linked.

Anito expected Ukatonen to act, but he waited until Eerin's fear began to ebb. Slowly, so slowly that Anito didn't realize what was happening until several minutes had passed, Ukatonen began to feed calmness into Eerin's body. Eerin remained completely unaware of what Ukatonen was doing.

At last Eerin was deeply entranced. Ukatonen began sliding more mood-altering chemicals into her system, stimulating feelings of harmony, awe, and wonder. Anito's own mood shifted with the changes in Eerin's mood. Ukatonen filtered most of Anito's feelings out of the link, letting Eerin's mood build with only subtle nudging from him. Anito breathed deeply, and focused on creating a well of calmness in herself, damping down her emotional resonance.

Doing so went against all of her instincts. The harmony created by linking was based on the interplay and gradual building of shared emotions into a whole that was greater and more profound than individual experience. This was much more difficult. It took a tremendous amount of control to work like this. Eerin's mood built slowly into ecstasy. Slowly Ukatonen released his control, letting his emotions melt into Eerin's. Anito matched Ukatonen's release, gently letting her emotions leak into the link until the three of them achieved emotional unison.

They rested in harmony for a while, letting Eerin get used to the feeling. Then Ukatonen's presence nudged Anito toward Eerin. He wanted her to do something. She flavored the link with a mild interrogative. Ukatonen sent back the flavor of first awakening. Anito acknowledged Ukatonen's request, and let Ukatonen guide her and Eerin together, into the deep harmony that preceded an awakening. Eerin's alien flavor grew strong in her allu-a. Anito felt it color her presence, felt her own presence merging with Eerin's, found herself sensing alien flavors, smells, and feelings. She realized that the new creature was sexually receptive. The link aroused Eerin. Anito instinctively matched Eerin's sexual arousal, and felt Eerin pull back in sudden fear. Caught up in the link, Anito mirrored that fear. Ukatonen, monitoring, broke the link before the resonances of fear and arousal built further.

Ukatonen's skin blazed a brilliant, erotic gold as he emerged from the link. Anito felt a strange urgency. The skin along the small of her back tingled and itched. Looking down, she realized that she was glowing gold as well. The new creature had brought them into heat, months out of the proper season. Eerin's skin shaded from gold to an alarmed orange. Anito looked away, shamed by her own lack of control.

Ukatonen touched Anito's shoulder. She glanced up. He held his arms out, spurs upward. His nearness made her head swim. She turned her back to him and presented herself. Her skin felt hot and dry. A mating croon escaped from her throat.

"Not now, little one," Ukatonen said, the words nearly unreadable in the brilliant blaze of his skin. "Link with me. I will make this stop."

She held out her wrists. Her skin was covered with tiny raised bumps. The touch of his hands as they closed around her arms was so intense that another croon escaped her lips. Then they linked, and coolness flooded her body like water from a mountain stream. The urgency ceased as suddenly as it began; her skin relaxed into smoothness, and she no longer felt the urge to croon.

Ukatonen broke the link. Anito opened her eyes, turning lavender with relief as she realized that she was no longer in heat. She looked up at Ukatonen. His skin was back to normal as well. A slow ripple of amusement flowed over him.

"That was remarkable," the enkar said. "What did you think of it?"

Anito looked away. "Please excuse me, en. I did not mean to behave so—"

Ukatonen gently turned her head toward him. "Don't be ashamed, kene. My control hasn't been broken like that since long before I became an enkar. Unless there is something wrong with Eerin, the new creatures are always in heat. It wasn't your fault. You behaved with admirable control, especially for one so young." A faint ripple of regret passed over him, quickly subdued. "It was good, in some ways. Now you'll know what to expect during mating season, and perhaps you won't be as frightened and ashamed by your lack of control when it happens to you at the proper time."

Juna felt the link break apart, but remained seated, eyes closed. It was good to be alone inside her skin again. The link made her feel incredibly vulnerable, as though there were no boundaries between herself and the aliens. Even the intense pleasure frightened her. It would be too easy to lose herself in it. Her loins throbbed with sexual heat. Her skin felt warm, as though a lover had been stroking her. She opened her eyes. Her skin was a brilliant, metallic gold. Was this the color of sexual arousal? The aliens were the same shade of gold. Juna fought back a wave of panic. Did this mean they wanted to have sex with her?

Anito looked at her, then back at Ukatonen. Her skin flickered, but the angle was bad and Juna couldn't see what she was saying. Then Anito turned away from Ukatonen and squatted, back arched tensely. It looked disturbingly reflexive and animalistic, not like something an intelligent alien might do. Juna backed away from the aliens, but they were too caught up with each other to notice. Ukatonen touched Anito's arm. Anito made a low, crooning noise and turned to look at him. Then they linked, and their skins faded to their usual pale green.

Juna relaxed. Whatever had happened, she sensed that it was over. She remembered her own sympathetic arousal, and colored deeply with shame.

Anito touched her on the arm. "Are you always like that, or is something wrong with you?"

"Like what?"

A patch of bright gold flared briefly on Ukatonen's shoulder. "Like that," he said, pointing to the patch of gold.

Juna flushed brown as she realized what they meant. "My people are always a little—" She concentrated and a square of gold appeared on one breast in a sudden flare of warmth. "When we meet someone we like a great deal, we can become very—" A patch of gold flared again; then, remembering Ali, she turned gold all over.

The aliens' ears spread wide, and they looked at each other, coloring deep fuchsia with amazement. They leaned forward, watching as the gold faded from her skin.

"How is it among the Tendu?" Juna asked.

"We are receptive once a year, although there are times when we mate out of season," Ukatonen told her. "Nothing gets done at that time, except for mating. If you are receptive all the time, how do your people ever accomplish anything?"

Juna smiled, remembering Padraig and his endless flirtations; the way she had felt during the good times of her marriage; how she had felt kissing Ali. Her skin grew warm, and she knew that she was turning gold again. "Sometimes it is hard, but we manage. I think it's different for my people, perhaps not so intense and more controllable. Most animals on our planet are like your people, very receptive for a short period, then not at all. My people are different."

"Is it hard for you to be receptive all the time, when your people are so far away?" Anito asked.

Juna turned a deep grey. "Sometimes." She looked away, fighting back the sudden tears that welled up in her eyes.

Anito touched her shoulder. "Can we do anything?"

Juna shook her head.

"Are you sure?" Ukatonen asked. "We could make you not receptive."

Juna shook her head, her skin flaring orange. "No, I can manage."

"Very well," Ukatonen said, "but it is improper to be receptive out of season. You must learn to control yourself."

Juna nodded. "I understand."

"Good," Ukatonen said. "Now we must awaken your bami."

"Will it—will it be like this last link?" Juna asked hesitantly. "I didn't like being made receptive."

Ukatonen shook his head. "No, that would be inappropriate. Now that we know you are receptive, we can help you block that out of the link. We have learned enough to guide you through what you must do to awaken your bami. This link will be easier and more pleasant, but it will help if you aren't frightened."

Juna gave them a wry smile. "It's an easy thing to ask for, but not an easy thing to do."

"I know," Ukatonen agreed, "but you must remember that whatever you feel in the link, your bami will feel also. Give him fear, and he will be afraid; give him happiness, and a heartfelt welcome, and he will share that with you."

"When will we start?" Juna asked.

"We must start soon," Anito said. "Already they are preparing a banquet to welcome your new bami."

After a quick meal of fruit, honey, and dried meat, they seated themselves beside the bami's leaf bed. The bami lay there, still and unmoving as a corpse. Only the slightest expansion and contraction of his nostrils told Juna that he was still alive.

She had interfered deeply in the Tendu's culture in order to save this creature's life. She might face severe penalties, even the loss of her career. Had she made the right choice? It was too late now to reconsider. She could only live with the consequences of her decision.

She stood up and held her arms out, spurs upward. "I'm ready," she said. "Let's wake my bami."

They formed a circle around the sleeping bami, clasping arms just below the elbow, ready to link.

"The first link with your bami made your bodies familiar with each other," Ukatonen said. "This link is when you get to know each other emotionally. Try to feel things that will create a strong bond. If you show fear, it will weaken that bond. Avoid feelings of sexual arousal. They will only confuse your bami, and make it hard for us to guide you. Do you understand?"

Juna nodded. She closed her eyes and breathed deeply, seeking calmness. She must not let her fear interfere with the awakening of her alien child.

"I'm ready," she said at last.

She felt herself slip into the link. The bami slept beside her. Ukatonen's powerful presence supported and reassured her. She could feel Anito looking on, watching over them. Ukatonen guided her presence into the bami. There was a faint sense of tension and then release, like sliding through the surface of a soap bubble, and she found herself inside the sleeping bami. He felt closed and remote, curled in on himself like a tight knot. Juna hovered in that dark, silent world of touch, taste, and smell, wondering what to do next.

"Welcome him," Ukatonen had told her, but how?

Juna felt Ukatonen's presence nudge her. He wanted her to act. She reached out to the sleeping bami, enfolding his inwardly focused presence, sending him feelings of warmth, memories of lying in the sun, feeling the bright sunlight on her skin, seeing its light glow redly through closed eyelids; warmth, security, pleasure. The compact knot of the bami's consciousness loosened. A wave of approval washed over her from Ukatonen. She was doing the right thing. Encouraged, Juna allowed herself to remember more: lying warm and snug in bed, feeling safe, enclosed; her mother's voice singing her to sleep; the candle by the bedside that lit her mother's dark brown face with a warm glow, the only safety in the terrifying world of the refugee camps.

The loosening knot that was the bami tightened as she remembered the camps.

No, she reminded herself. *No fear. Think safety, think welcoming thoughts. . . .*

She returned again to the warmth of the sun; her father finding her and her brother in the refugee camp. How solid his arms around her had been. He had taken them home again, where there was always enough to eat, and someone strong to protect them from harm. Juna felt the bami's presence relax. She remembered the grape harvest on their farm; how the patient horses stood in the milky, filtered sunlight, tails twitching from habit, not from flies. There were no flies on the satellite. She remembered cutting the heavy clusters of grapes, feeling them fall into her basket, smelling their rich, sweet fragrance as she emptied her basket into the cart. Harvesting grapes had always been immensely satisfying. Her work in the vineyard helped provide for her family. It made her feel strong and capable. She remembered leading the horses into the barn, smelling their good warm horse smell, and the smell of the hay. She trusted the horses. They were big and strong and placid. They trusted her in return.

The remembered barn smell triggered memories of her first lover, Paul, a neighbor's son, with pale skin, green eyes, and black raven's-wing hair. They had first lain together in the barn. . . .

No sex, she reminded herself sternly, as she sensed the sharp taste of Ukatonen's concern.

It was hard, though—so many of her happiest memories were with lovers. She thought back to her wedding, joining the group marriage, how good it had felt to be part of this big, strong family. She remembered the love she had felt then, as though her heart were about to burst. She felt that love fill her now. How good, how safe it had been to be welcomed by so many people. She took that love and enfolded the bami in it.

"*Welcome, little one,*" she thought to the bami. "*Welcome and love.*"

She remembered the birth of her brother, Toivo. Her mother had held him out to her. He had been so little. She reached out to touch his tiny, perfect hand, and his fingers closed around her finger. There had been so much strength in that small hand. His eyes opened, he looked blurrily at her, and she felt a sudden wave of love for the amazing creature that was her new brother.

She remembered the tinka's courage. He had been so small and helpless and so determined to follow them. She remembered the grip of her brother's hand again, so tiny, and so strong.

"Welcome, little one," she thought again to the bami. She felt the bami uncoil and reach out toward her. She tasted his curiosity, his joy, his amazement. Underneath that she felt the strength and determination that had carried him so far.

"How brave you are," she thought to the bami, sharing the surge of admiration and pride that accompanied her thoughts. *"You're so strong."*

In the background, she was aware of Ukatonen and Anito's approval. She moved closer to the bami. Their presences merged like the clasping of hands. She felt the bami's amazement at his own awareness. Juna had never felt anything like this contact; even the clasp of her brother's hand, her mother's love, her father's strength, the welcoming joy of her marriage, all seemed pale and distant in the midst of this overwhelming rapport.

The bami reached out to her. He felt her love, then reached beyond that, and felt her isolation. She felt his surprise, and then she felt him directing inquisitiveness at her. He was asking her for something.

In reply, Juna allowed her presence to merge even more strongly with her bami's, trusting him in this moment of bonding.

Feeling his gentle, trusting presence intertwined with hers, she realized that she was no longer alone. She still wanted to be among humans, she longed for a hot bath and a cooked meal, but the sadness and grief she felt because of her isolation was gone. She finally was a part of something on this world.

Anito slid out of the link. She sat for a minute, recovering from the intensity of the allu-a. Then she opened her eyes. Eerin grasped her bami's arm, not linked, but touching. The bami opened his eyes, and looked at Eerin, turning a brilliant, happy blue. Eerin reached out with her free hand and touched her bami gently on the shoulder.

"Welcome," Eerin said in skin speech.

Her bami's color intensified. His eyes narrowed with concentration; then, slowly, three fuzzy black bars appeared on his chest. He was trying to say "yes." He tried again.

"Yes. Glad," he said, the patterns appearing more distinct this time. "Eerin," he said. "My sitik."

"Yes," Eerin told him. "I am your sitik, you are my bami."

"Good," he said closing his eyes again.

Eerin looked at Ukatonen and Anito, faintly alarmed. "Is he all right?"

"Yes," Ukatonen assured her. "Just tired. All bami are like that at first. He needs food. So do we. That was a very intense link. You did well."

Anito stood. "I'll go ask Ninto to bring us some food."

She was glad to have some time to herself to get a little perspective on what had just happened. She had never been part of an awakening, except for her own, but she was sure that this awakening was unusual. She had never been in a link that intense before, even with her own sitik. The new creature had such strange, strong emotions. Their intensity and power frightened Anito.

She paused to rest. Looking around the trunk, she noticed the other villagers watching her, flickering amongst themselves in shades of curiosity and excitement. She continued climbing, not wanting them to know how deeply the awakening had drained her.

Her blood thrummed in her ears by the time she reached Ninto's room. She made it through the door, and then leaned against the wall, exhausted. Ninto was butchering a huge kuyan carcass with the help of her bami and a couple of tinka. She was covered with blood. Ninto's ears lifted in alarm as she looked at Anito. She handed her a large gourd of honey and fruit juice.

"Drink," Ninto told her. "You need it."

Anito accepted the gourd with a grateful flicker of thanks. She drank greedily, juice dribbling out of the edges of the gourd.

"It was difficult?" Ninto asked. "There was trouble with the bami?"

Anito began to shake her head, then stopped herself. "No, not difficult, just very strange and intense. The bami is fine. He's already speaking."

"That's good," Ninto said, coloring with relief. "I have food ready. Rest a bit and eat. Then I'll help you carry it up."

Anito flickered assent and gratitude.

"Besides," Ninto added, "I can hardly wait to see the new bami."

Anito rippled amusement. "Neither can the rest of the village. I hope they didn't notice how tired I was."

"You looked fine until you came in. Here." Ninto tossed her a ripe green and yellow banya fruit and a leaf-wrapped package of kayu. "Eat. Rest."

Anito squatted against the wall, and bit into the banya, tasting first the tart, almost-bitter peel and then the intensely sweet inner pulp. It was wonderful. She finished the banya, spitting the seeds into her hand to scatter later along their voyage. There were never enough banya vines. She felt the sweetness of the juice and the fruit rushing into her blood, giving her energy. She peeled open the packet of kayu. The starchy seeds had been plumped with taira blood and flavored with crumbles of seaweed and chopped meat. Anito turned turquoise with pleasure at its delicious taste. She finished it quickly, licking up a few stray grains from the leaf wrapper, wishing there was more.

Ninto rippled with amusement. "There's more kayu in the food basket, greedy one. You can have some when we take it up to feed the others."

Anito picked up a basket of food and slung it over her shoulder. "In that case, let's go. They must be very hungry."

As Anito, Ninto, and several tinka descended to Anito's room, the villagers began hauling out baskets of food and leaves in preparation for the feast of welcoming and leavetaking. By the time they were ready, the banquet would be too.

One of the villagers' bami, noticing Anito's gaze, flickered "Congratulations" at her in big, exuberant patterns. She looked more closely. It was Pani. Pani's happiness was understandable. It meant that she would no longer be the youngest bami in the village. Someone would be her junior in status. Anito felt a flash of anger. She wasn't the one who should be congratulated. Eerin and Ukatonen were responsible for the new bami. She would have to make that clear to the other villagers.

Ukatonen and Eerin eagerly greeted the arrival of the food. They woke the sleeping bami. He ate and drank greedily. Anito rippled with amusement at his eagerness.

"I remember how good that first food tasted," she remarked. The other Tendu flickered agreement tinged with nostalgia, remembering their own transformations.

"I was hungry all the time," Ninto said. "My sitik was always complaining about how much hunting we had to do."

"I grew almost a full hand-span in the first month," Ukatonen said, biting into a banya fruit. "But it was a week before I made any words. I was afraid to try."

"I thought that the transformation was complete," Eerin said, interrupting the flow of nostalgia. "Is he going to change any more?"

The bami, whose eyes had never left Eerin, turned a pale, worried orangeish-pink, and looked from Ukatonen to Anito.

Anito's ears tightened, and she suppressed a surge of impatience at Eerin's ignorance. "The transformation is complete," she explained, "but your bami will grow three or four-hand spans in the next year. He'll be hungry all the time. You'll be busy keeping him fed."

"But I don't know enough!" Eerin exclaimed. "I can't hunt, and I don't know what to eat."

"It's time that you learned," Ukatonen told her. "I'll help you when I can, and Anito will too. You are her atwa, and she must care for you. But," he added, noting Anito's flare of protest, "you must also learn to take care of your own responsibilities, Eerin. You are no ordinary atwa. You are like the Tendu. You can think for yourself. There is a limit to what Anito should do for you."

"I understand most of what you say, en, but I still don't understand what an atwa is. I cannot agree to something I don't understand."

Ukatonen ducked his chin in thought. Both he and Anito had

tried to explain it to her, and had failed. "What do you know about atwas?" he asked.

"I know that every Tendu has one or belongs to one. I know that many plants and animals are part of an atwa. I know that there are many rules about them, that plants and animals can't be harvested sometimes because of these rules."

Ukatonen nodded. "Every elder chooses a part of the world to look after. That part of the world is their atwa. They make sure that their part of the world is in harmony and balance with all of the other parts. Your people are a new part of the world. Anito has been chosen to look after your new atwa. She must bring your people into balance with the world. Do you understand?"

"I think I understand more, en, but not all. I'm not a plant, or animal. I'm a person. What I want, what my people want, must be listened to."

Anito spread her ears in amazement. "What you say is impossible! You eat, you drink, you shit. How can you say that you're not an animal?"

"Yes," Eerin told her, "I am an animal, my people are animals, but we are different from other animals. We change the world we live in. We make things."

Anito's ears spread even wider. The new creature seemed to believe that it was separate from the world it lived in.

"Other animals change the world too," Ukatonen said. "Even plants make changes in their world."

"But your people and my people are different from other animals. We decide *how* to change the world. Besides, your world is no longer alone. Your world and my world will touch, will change each other. Our two worlds are very different."

"All the more reason that someone should watch over you, to guide the changes."

Eerin shook her head. "It isn't that simple. It isn't something that one person can do alone."

"Anito will be the first of many. I hope that your bami will choose your people as his atwa when he becomes an elder."

Anito leaned forward. "How do your people keep the world in balance?"

Eerin shook her head again. "I'm not sure that I can explain. My people and yours are very, very different."

Just then a booming beat was sounded on the buttress of the tree, announcing the beginning of the banquet. Ninto came in with an armload of headdresses. Anito helped her drape them over Eerin and the new bami. Taking a headdress of flowers with trailing streamers of iridescent blue beetles, she arranged it on the new creature's head. The poison stripes on Anito's back tightened as she looked into Eerin's strange, deep-set eyes, with their small brown irises and round pupils. She remembered the odd emotions Eerin made her feel during the awakening. Could she ever bring such a creature as this into harmony with the world? She glanced down at Eerin's new bami. Everywhere the creature went, wrongness happened. Perhaps it would be best if the new creature died before her people came back. Maybe then her people would leave Anito's alone, and she could go back to being a simple village elder.

"Thank you," Eerin said as Anito finished adjusting her headdress.

Anito looked away. Eerin had torn her life apart, but in spite of that, there was something about the new creature that made Anito care about her. It would all be so much easier if she didn't.

Juna followed Ukatonen and Anito up the tree toward the banquet. It was raining hard. Her headdress was already heavy and soggy. She tried not to think about the strings of insects brushing the back of her neck. She thought she could feel one of them moving, and she shuddered, making the headdress slip backward slightly. It took all her self-control to keep from ripping the thing off.

Bugs had never been Juna's strong suit. As a biologist, she preferred the larger animals, especially mammals. Juna sighed. She was on the wrong planet. The closest things to mammals on this planet were the warm-blooded marsupial birds on the northern continent. She smiled, remembering the big, stupid grazers covered with spotted fluffy down. Except for their nasty habit of vomiting all over anything that threatened them, they were silly and adorable, especially when the baby stuck its head out of the mother's backward-facing pouch and peered between its mother's hind legs.

She really should catalogue the insects on her headdress when she had a moment. Survival had taken precedence over research for the last few months, but she owed it to her colleagues to start doing some work. It would help to have a large and impressive body of research behind her when the Survey discovered that she had adopted an alien child.

She glanced back at her bami, climbing up the trunk after her. He needed a name. How did the Tendu name their bami? She would have to ask Ukatonen or Anito when they were settled at the banquet. All of the Tendu's names were composed of a basic name sign. A bami's name sign was repeated only once. An elder's name sign was made up of the same pattern repeated twice. Ukatonen's name pattern was repeated three times. Juna was fairly certain that this was an indicator of rank or status. Her own name sign was repeated only once. She wondered what this meant in terms of status. Was she only an adopted child of Anito's? Or did it mean nothing because she wasn't a Tendu?

They reached the top of the trunk. As they emerged into the pouring rain, the assembled villagers set up a loud, celebratory trilling. Juna looked around her: the elders and bami were rippling in glowing colors. For a moment it resembled some weird bioluminescent seascape peopled by troglodytes. She smiled at the image, and flickered thanks back at the villagers.

Anito and Ukatonen sat down. Juna paused, uncertain where she was supposed to sit. Her bami took her hand and led her to a high spot next to them, and sat beside her.

"I help you learn," he told her, in small patterns on the back of his hand. "You are my sitik." His words were a bit blurry, but readable. He was learning to control his skin very quickly.

Juna realized that her bami wasn't a child. He had survived for years, alone and unprotected in the jungle. He had fought to earn his place among the tinka of Lyanan. He had risked everything in a desperate, impossible gamble that had nearly cost him his life. He knew the forest and his people better than she ever would. What could she possibly teach this young alien?

She put her hand next to his, and concentrated to make her words appear there. "I will try to be a good sitik."

The tinka serving the food looked closely at the new bami, as though trying to learn how he had managed to be chosen. Despite their recent meal, the bami ate a great deal. Juna was also hungry. Linking always made her ravenous, especially for sweet, starchy food. Clearly, linking had its metabolic costs.

The rain let up a little as they finished eating. The prepared food was served in covered baskets, though the fruit was left exposed to the rain. Juna picked at the last soggy bits of bloody meat and greens on her leaf, hoping the banquet would not go on much longer. She was tired. It had been a long and eventful day.

Anito nudged her. When she looked up, she realized that the villagers were watching her expectantly.

"They're waiting for you to speak," Anito told her.

"What should I say?"

"Thank them for the banquet, introduce your bami. Make your words big and try to be as formal as you can. Don't worry, they aren't expecting much. Anything you do will impress them."

"Thanks a lot," Juna muttered aloud as she rose to speak.

She adjusted her dripping headdress and looked around at the waiting aliens, lit by the pale light of glow baskets and the more diffuse wash of light escaping from the trunk of the tree. The aliens regarded her impassively.

"Thank you," she said, in the most elaborate and formal patterns that she could manage. "Never have I seen such a good banquet. The village of Narmolom has welcomed my bami with great kindness. I think you will find that he is brave and determined; and I hope that you will help him learn."

Juna sat down. It was a terrible speech, sounding woefully inadequate even to her own inexperienced ears, but the Tendu greeted it with ripples of applause. Ukatonen motioned her new bami to rise and be acknowledged.

"That was a good speech," he told Juna in small, private patterns.

Juna shook her head. "It was terrible, but they weren't expecting much."

"It was good enough," Ukatonen assured her.

Juna sat back and watched her bami speak.

"My name is **xxx**," her bami told them in large, simple patterns. "I thank my sitik, Eerin, for giving me life. I will try to be a good bami, and learn to be in harmony with the village of Narmolom."

He sat back down. Juna consulted her computer for a verbal analogue of her bami's name sign. His name was Moki. He had named himself after an antlike insect with a painful bite. Juna smiled. She liked the name. It was easy to say aloud. That might be helpful when the Survey returned. She would need all the help she could get to resolve the problems she had created for herself. She rubbed her forehead. She shouldn't have adopted him.

Moki touched her shoulder. She looked down at him and smiled. She was no longer alone. Despite everything, she was glad that she had adopted him. Five years was a long time. Perhaps a solution would present itself before the Survey returned. For now, she would try to learn to be a good sitik.

Sixteen

ANITO SCULLED HARD with the steering paddle, pushing the raft into the faster current of the main channel. The first five days on the river had been quiet and peaceful, with much feasting and trading with other villages on migration. Tomorrow they would reach the first major rapids. The land around them was getting steeper, sloping toward the sea. The river moved faster too; riffles of white water were forming on the upriver edges of islands.

Anito glanced at Moki and Eerin, sitting together in the bow of the raft. New bami needed almost constant attention and contact. Sometimes it was hard on their sitiks. Anito had expected Eerin to tire of Moki's constant need for company, but Eerin seemed to enjoy the attention.

Eerin was a model sitik in every way but one: she still shrank from allu-a. Eerin's refusal to link with Moki left him hurt and confused.

Eerin must learn how to link properly, Anito thought with a flicker of impatience. Ukatonen was going to have to help her teach Eerin to overcome her fear. Moki needed to link with his sitik in order to remain in harmony with himself and others. He needed allu-a every bit as much as he needed food, water, and air.

Moki reached into his net bag and pulled out a waterproof pouch made of a waxed fish bladder, the kind usually used to hold fishing equipment.

"Let's catch some fish," he suggested to Eerin.

Eerin turned dark green with approval. "Maybe we'll catch some more sweet-fish," she said. "They're delicious."

Anito rippled negation. "You probably won't. The river's too fast here. Sweet-fish like slower water."

Moki and Eerin settled themselves on the stern of the raft. Moki pulled out the fishing line and watched intently as Eerin tied on a bone fishhook. When she was done, he examined the knot and then darkened with approval.

"Very good," he told his sitik. "You've tied it nice and tight this time."

Amusement rippled along Anito's back at the sight of the small bami instructing the tall, angular new creature. Ukatonen had asked Moki to teach Eerin to fish. He took his task very seriously.

She looked at Ninto, who watched the new creature and her bami with quiet amusement.

"They're good together. If only Eerin would link with him. He needs her so much," Ninto said, her words greyed with sadness.

Anito flickered agreement. "Especially with Ukatonen so busy choosing a new chief."

Ukatonen had spent most of the last five days swimming from raft to raft, talking with the other villagers, getting to know the most likely candidates for chief elder. He hadn't been able to spend much time with Moki and Eerin. The burden of helping Eerin bond with her new bami had fallen mostly onto Anito's shoulders. Fortunately, Ninto and Baha were understanding and helpful. Still, Anito needed Ukatonen's help with the new creature. She couldn't make Eerin understand how much Moki needed allu-a.

Anito touched Eerin on the shoulder. "I'm going to visit Ukatonen. The river's calm here, there shouldn't be any problems."

Anito dove into the cool water, feeling the taste of the river on her skin. It was a taste as distinctive as the smell of the jungle, full of subtle, ever-changing flavors. Every stream and tributary altered the taste of the river. Now, during flood season, it tasted of mud and drowning vegetation, with a faint hint of rotting fruit. The shadow of a large fish swirled away from her into the murky depths. Anito flinched involuntarily, then relaxed. There were no large predators in this stretch of the river. Below the cataracts, however, it was a different story. She shuddered, remembering a narrow escape from the jaws of a giant kulai. Ilto had pulled her to safety just in time. The kulai had tried to leap into the raft after her. Two elders clubbed the kulai and it fell back into the rushing river.

She hoped no one would die this trip. There had been too many deaths in the village this year. Anito surfaced beside the raft Ukatonen was visiting. She greeted the other elders on the raft, and one of them, Iketo, extended a hand and pulled her aboard.

"Thank you for giving Moki the fishing tackle," Anito remarked to Ukatonen after making the expected polite greetings to her hosts on the raft.

Ukatonen rippled a shrug. "He's my responsibility too."

"It's funny, watching him teach Eerin how to fish," Anito said with a ripple of amusement. "Sometimes Moki acts like he's the sitik and Eerin's the bami."

"Good," Ukatonen said. "Eerin needs a lot of looking after. You've had to work much too hard. Let Moki help. It will make the bond between them stronger."

"Moki needs to link with his sitik," Anito reminded the enkar. "I need your help to convince Eerin to link with him."

Ukatonen flickered negation. "I can't help you. No one can. Eerin must decide to link with Moki on her own."

Anito rippled a grey, rueful acknowledgment. "But it's hard, watching Moki suffer. What happens if Eerin never learns to link with Moki?"

Ukatonen looked away, his skin misted a greyish-purple with doubt. "I don't know," he said, looking back at her. "If Eerin doesn't learn to link, it will kill Moki, but if their bonding is successful, then we will have a Tendu who understands these new creatures better than you or I will ever be able to. We need someone like that. The risk is great, but the rewards could be even greater."

"And if Moki dies?" Anito asked.

"Then I will follow him into death."

Anito looked away. Death followed the new creature like a second shadow. She wished that Eerin had died before she had been found. It would have prevented so much pain.

She turned back to the enkar, so that he could see her words. "I'm sorry, en. I shouldn't speak of such things."

Ukatonen touched her shoulder. "You're beginning to ask difficult questions. That's good. You're starting to think like an enkar."

Anito looked down at the dark-green water swirling past the raft. She didn't want to think about leaving the village.

"We'll need to watch out for them once we reach the cataracts. Neither of them has made the trip before," Anito said, changing the subject.

Ukatonen flickered agreement. "It will be especially hard for Moki. Without the reassurance of a link, he might panic."

"I wish I understood why Eerin fears linking so much."

"Why?" Ukatonen asked. He was fond of that word. He liked to make her explain everything she said. He said it taught her to think about thinking.

"If I knew why she was afraid, then maybe I could find some way to help Eerin past her fear." A faint grey mist passed over Anito's body like a sigh. "It's so hard. Every time I think I understand Eerin, she does something strange and I realize I know nothing at all about her or her people. How can I manage an atwa I don't understand, en?"

Ukatonen brushed her shoulder. "I know it's difficult, kene, but I don't think anyone could handle this situation any better than you have."

Anito looked away; she could feel pride and embarrassment flaring on her skin. "Thank you, en."

Ukatonen touched her shoulder. "Look," he said, rippling with laughter. "Eerin's caught a fish."

Anito looked up as Eerin pulled a large fish from the water. She held it up, azure with pride. Anito turned deep green with approval. The other elders on the raft laughed at the new creature's delight. Just then the fish gave a great heave, nearly slipping from Eerin's grasp. Moki tried to help and the two of them fell back onto the deck of the raft, grappling with the thrashing fish, their bodies rippling with laughter. Anito could hear the loud choking cries that Eerin made when she was amused. Moki and Eerin got control of the fish and put it into a large openwork basket. They tied the basket to the raft and tossed it into the river to keep until dinner.

"A good teacher and a quick student are a fortunate combination," Ukatonen said. "We'll eat well tonight! Let's go congratulate our fishermen."

Ukatonen dove into the river, and Anito followed him. Together they swam for their raft. As they reached it, there was a cry from the one in the lead. A line of rafts had appeared ahead of them. Eager for a chance to trade, the rafts from Narmolom began sculling to catch up to them. Ninto seized the steering oar, seeking the fastest water to push them along. Anito grabbed an oar and added her strength to Ninto's. Eerin and the others followed suit.

The two villages' rafts merged into one large fleet. There was much cheerful shuttling back and forth as elders from the two villages began to dicker and trade. A large knot of curious strangers formed around Eerin, exclaiming in amazement at this flat-faced, small-eared giant. Moki intervened protectively between the strangers and his sitik, provoking waves of amusement from the strange elders. They began to tease Moki. Anito moved to stop them, but Ukatonen held her back.

"Wait, let's see how Eerin handles this."

Eerin stepped forward. "It's all right, Moki. They're only curious. My name is Eerin, and this is my bami, Moki. I come from very far away. The people of Narmolom found me and sheltered me when I was lost in the jungle. You may look at me all you want, but please don't link with me."

Anito's ears lifted. Eerin was doing very well.

Eerin motioned Moki back and stepped into the knot of curious strangers. She let them examine her hands and feet, gently but firmly removing their hands when she didn't like what they were doing. Moki stood by, looking on anxiously.

At last Eerin looked at Anito and Ukatonen. They moved

forward to fend off the curious strangers, diverting attention away from Eerin. Soon the talk changed from the new creature to trading.

Eerin and Moki went off to one of the outer rafts to recover from the onslaught of curiosity. When Anito glanced up from her dickering she saw Moki requesting allu-a, his skin dull blue-grey with longing. Eerin shook her head, flickering negation, and reached out to hold Moki. He shrugged away from her touch and dove into the river.

Concern flowed across Anito's back. Something must be done, and soon, about Eerin's fear of linking. She left off her trading, and went over to Eerin and touched her on the shoulder.

"Your bami needs you," Anito said when Eerin looked up. "His need goes deeper than skin hunger."

"I'm doing the best I can," Eerin replied.

Anito shook her head and walked back to her trade goods. Clearly Eerin didn't understand what she was trying to tell her; she would have to find some other way to explain it to her.

That night, after the feasting and trading was done, Anito wandered back to their nest site. The strangers' curiosity about the new creature had proved profitable. She had made some good trades. Moki was sitting up, watching Eerin sleep. Anito brushed her knuckles across his shoulder as she sat down beside him. He leaned against her for a moment, seeking comfort, then shifted so that they could talk.

"Why won't Eerin link with me?" he asked, his words glowing orange with anxiety in the darkness. "Am I bad?"

"No, little one. I've watched you with Eerin. You're a good bami. It isn't you, Moki. Eerin's afraid of linking—with you, with me, with anyone."

Moki's skin flared pink in surprise, then dimmed into wordlessness. The fireflies flashing in the surrounding trees reminded Anito of half-formed words.

"Why?" Moki asked, after a long stillness.

Anito rippled a weary shade of uncertainty. "If I knew, perhaps we could teach her not to be afraid. Eerin's not a Tendu, Moki. It will be hard for you, being her bami. That's why Ukatonen is helping her with you. Link with him, Moki, let him teach you. He is of your people, Eerin is not."

"I understand. I do link with him, but he's not . . ." Moki shook his head. He was already picking up many of Eerin's gestures. "He's not Eerin. She is my sitik, not Ukatonen. I need her."

Anito put her arm around him, knowing that the gesture would do little to soothe him. Moki's need went deeper than skin hunger. Anito remembered the time that Ilto had gotten hurt while hunting. It had taken him three days to get home. She was frantic with need by the time he returned. She had been his bami for several years, long enough that the urgent need for linking had passed. Moki had gone for nine days without linking. This little one was as tough as stonewood to endure such isolation for so long. Eerin had chosen better than any of them knew.

"I'll talk to her, Moki. I'll try to explain how important it is, but it might not help."

Moki looked away for long moment. "Thank you, kene," he said, his words dim and muddied by emotional turmoil.

The next morning they arose before dawn in order to be on the water at first light. It was important to reach the cataracts early in the day so that they could make it through before night fell. Anito checked the lashings on the raft, making sure they were tight. She didn't want her raft coming apart in the middle of the cataracts.

A touch on her shoulder startled her. It was Ninto and Baha.

"Are they ready for this?" Ninto asked, gesturing with her chin at Moki and Eerin.

"I hope so. We've shown them what to do. Whether they can remember it when we pass through the cataracts is another thing entirely. It is kind of you to accept two such inexperienced people as your crew."

"We could hardly split up a newly joined pair like that, could we? Besides, I also have you and Ukatonen with me, and that makes up for a great deal."

"Yes, but—"

"You are also my tareena. Our sitik asked that I look out for you."

Anito looked away for a moment, a brilliant, wordless flare of emotions playing over her skin.

When she looked back, Ninto offered her wrists. They linked, mingling their feelings—pride, shame, their love for their shared sitik, and their grief at his death.

When they emerged from the link, Ninto gave Anito's shoulder a squeeze and turned to see to the raft. No words were necessary between them after such a sharing.

Anito glanced up at the brightening sky. It was time to be going. She helped Ninto push the raft off into the river, then hauled herself aboard. Ninto swung up on the other side as Anito picked up a pole and began to push. Moki and Eerin fended the raft off from the flooded treetops with long poles as they made their way into the main channel.

A flock of brilliant red gwais burst from a treetop ahead of them, honking loudly. Anito looked after the birds wistfully. One of them would have made a nice breakfast, but there was no time for hunting today. They would have to make do with dried provisions and fruit. She pulled several ripe ooroo pods from a vine as they passed by, and consoled herself by popping a couple of their hot, peppery seeds into her mouth.

The current grew swifter as the morning wore on and the banks of the river drew closer together. Anito nervously checked and rechecked their cargo, making sure it was lashed down tight. The channel through the cataracts was narrow and unforgiving. A mistimed move by a crew member could flip the raft, or pull it down into a whirlpool. She glanced at Eerin. Would she make it through the cataracts without panicking?

They neared the rapids shortly after noon. Yiato, their best river pilot, signaled that they would stop to take a look at the rapids before going on. Anito was glad that she was leading them through the cataracts. Yiato was one of the oldest remaining villagers, and would have been a prime contender for chief elder if she hadn't removed herself from consideration. It was a shame; she would have been an excellent leader. Ukatonen had asked Yiato to reconsider, a sign that he thought very highly of her.

Yiato and her bami, Dalo, hiked along the sheer cliffs along the river's edge, vanishing around the curve of a rock wall. The villagers waited tensely for her return. The first cataract was always the hardest. There were rougher stretches of the river, but this cataract was the first test of the rafts and their crews. Would the rafts hold together? Were the crews ready?

Yiato returned sooner than expected. The villagers crowded around her, purple shadows of curiosity boiling over their skin.

"There was a rock slide about ten li down the path," she told them. "I couldn't get around it. The water is high and very fast and most of the worst rocks are hidden, so you must watch the water carefully. From what I remember, it's best if you stay to the right around the big rock with the lovi tree on it."

Yiato held out her arms. It was traditional for the entire village to link together before the major rapids. Linking bound the village into a cohesive, harmonious unit. Out on the river, where lives depended on split-second timing, it was essential that the villagers knew what each member would do and when. That feeling of being part of a larger whole always gave Anito confidence and courage. She would need it now. She glanced anxiously at Eerin and Moki. Would they panic in the midst of the raging river, endangering them all?

Anito reached to include Eerin in the link, but the new creature shook her head and slid out of the forming circle. Moki looked after Eerin, his skin blue-grey with longing. For a moment it seemed as though he would slip away and follow Eerin, but Ukatonen took his hand and they joined the link.

Anito entered the link, feeling the familiar presence of the other villagers. United, Anito knew that they would be stronger than any river. The powerful presence of Ukatonen joined the link, making their united strength even greater. Then she felt the new, uncertain presence of Moki, aching with bitter, salty need and longing. The protective warmth of the village surged to enfold him, to dissolve his pain in the comfort of their presence. Moki's pain eased, but never vanished. It tainted the link, an irritant, like a piece of grit in a bowl of seaweed, or a buzzing fly, keeping the village from achieving total unity.

Slowly the group link separated into subgroups and affinities, then separate crews, and finally family units of bami and sitik. Anito found herself linked with Ukatonen and Moki. Moki's pain flared again with painful intensity. They attempted to reassure him, but he remained inconsolable. At last, defeated, they broke the link.

Eerin stood waiting by the raft. Anito repressed a sudden surge of anger at the new creature. If only she could make Eerin understand how much pain she caused Moki, and through Moki, the entire village. If only— A flicker of irritation flared on her spine. "If only" never accomplished anything. As soon as they were settled for the night, she would speak to Eerin. Her refusal to link with Moki affected the balance of the whole village. It could no longer be tolerated.

Anito used her anger to help push the raft off the beach. She swung aboard, grasping her oar, rowing the boat into the swift, powerful current. The river banks rushed by as the river sped up. She heard the rapids ahead, a steady, rising whisper. Moki stared apathetically at the deck in front of him, his oar ignored. She nudged him with a foot.

"Wake up!" she told him. "It's rough ahead."

Anito hauled on her oar, holding the raft straight as they shot through a narrow passage between two rocks. The river rounded a sharp bend and a roaring stretch of white water surged toward them. They shot into it, and Anito's attention was taken up with steering between huge waves and fangs of black rock. A huge boulder appeared suddenly behind a standing wave. They pulled left, just missing it, then banged into a hidden rock that turned them crossways to the current.

Moki stared at the wall of water rushing toward him. The oar was torn from his grasp and he was swept up against the bow railing. Anito watched helplessly, straining her oar against the full might of the river to turn the raft off the rock. If she tried to help him, they would all be lost. Finally, the raft turned with a huge, grinding shudder and was swept off the rock and into the rapids. Eerin managed to grasp Moki's arm, when another wave crashed across the bow, tearing Moki from her grasp and sending the bami sliding back across the deck, crashing into the stern. The raft banged into another rock. A sudden surge of water swept Moki into the raging rapids.

Eerin cried out, and reached after him as the raft slewed against another submerged rock.

Anito nudged Eerin with her foot. "No!" she said in bold

red-orange patterns, outlined in black. "Row now, or we all die!"

Eerin grasped her oar and pulled hard. The raft heaved off the rock. Moki's head bobbed up in a sudden surge ahead of them and then vanished. They shot forward around a cluster of boulders. Moki appeared again, to the right of the main channel, sheltering from the force of the current on the downstream side of a large rock. They pulled hard on the oars, trying to get close to him, but the river had them in its grasp and it swept them on past Moki and over the short, broad waterfall that marked the end of the rapids.

The raft struck the pool with jarring force. As soon as they got control of it in the quiet water below the falls, they pulled into an eddy beside the waterfall. Ukatonen grasped an overhanging branch, and pulled himself up into the trees beside the river. Eerin and Anito followed, leaving Ninto and Baha to steady the raft.

Moki huddled on top of a rock, a flaming orange spot of terror in the midst of the foaming white and green river. They watched from the treetops as a raft tried to steer toward him, but was pushed away by the force of the river. The remaining five rafts also tried to rescue the bami and failed; one nearly capsized in the attempt.

"He's going to have to swim for it," Ukatonen said.

Moki clung to the rock, small and helpless in the midst of the raging torrent.

"He'll never make it! He'll drown!" Eerin exclaimed.

Anito looked startled by this. The least of Moki's problems was breathing the oxygen-rich white water.

Then she realized that Eerin didn't understand. She didn't know that Moki was in more danger of being crushed against a rock, or getting eaten by one of the giant fish that waited below the rapids, than he was of being drowned.

"He won't drown, Eerin," Anito said. "He can't drown. He can breathe the water through his skin."

"But how can we get him out of there? He can't get out by himself!"

"He may have to," Ukatonen told her. "We can't get a raft to him, and he's too far out to reach by rope."

Moki saw them and waved. He looked up expectantly, ears wide, asking for help and guidance.

Ukatonen shook his head. "You must swim," he said in large patterns. "Try for the bank, just above the waterfall. We will be there to catch you."

"Be careful!" Eerin added.

Moki nodded. "I go," he said, his words barely visible against the intense orange of his fear.

He leaped into the river. They stared anxiously at the churning white water, waiting for him to emerge. Then Ukatonen grabbed Eerin's arm, pointing with his chin.

"There!"

Moki's limp form surged to the surface. They scrambled down to the bank, and reached for his body as it floated by. One arm trailed in the water, obviously broken. He was either unconscious or dead. Ukatonen's fingers closed around one limp ankle and pulled him in.

They laid Moki gently down on the soft sand. His skin was torn and bruised; in places it resembled chopped meat. His arm was broken in a dozen places, but he still breathed. Eerin knelt by his head, making crooning noises.

Ukatonen looked at Anito. "Monitor me."

Anito flickered acknowledgment. They linked and entered Moki's body.

The damage was not as bad as it looked. Moki had a mild concussion and had lost a fair amount of blood. Several internal organs were bruised. The broken bone in his arm had pierced his allu. That would be the trickiest thing to repair.

Ukatonen closed hemorrhaging blood vessels, and eased the building pressure in Moki's skull. Anito was dimly aware of someone outside the link straightening and splinting Moki's broken arm. The most urgent injuries attended to, Ukatonen tried to reassure Moki, but the bami's presence remained huddled and unresponsive, walled off by the depth of his grief. A wave of bitter sadness welled up from Ukatonen as he broke the link.

"Well?" Eerin asked, as they emerged from the link. "Will he live?"

Ukatonen gave a dubious, muddy ripple of affirmation.

"He's not seriously injured, but I don't think he wants to recover. He's lost the will to live. He wants you, Eerin. He needs to link with you. You're his sitik. No one else will do. You must link with him every day. Without your strength, your presence, he will die."

Eerin turned pale orange and looked away for a moment. Her jaw worked, and then suddenly, as she reached some inner decision, her skin deepened into a sudden resolve. "Show me what I must do." A flicker of fear, quickly suppressed, ran across her torso.

Anito laid a hand on Eerin's shoulder. "First you must remember that Moki is your bami, and would never do anything to hurt you. You must not be afraid. Linking is natural. Moki needs it. Even when he's healthy he needs to link with you every day. Now he needs it more than ever."

Eerin touched Moki's uninjured arm, near his allu. She looked up at Anito and Ukatonen. "Should I—can I link with him now? It won't hurt him?"

Ukatonen nodded and looked at Anito. "Will you help her, kene? I'm too tired."

Anito held out her arms. She guided Eerin's arm to Moki's uninjured spur, and then linked with Eerin. Together they entered Moki. Anito watched as Eerin enfolded Moki, flooding him with reassurance and encouragement, and some other thing that was wholly alien, wholly part of the new creature. Moki uncoiled from his knot of despair, returning the alien flood of feeling. As the two of them mingled, Anito helped Eerin's body give Moki strength. Then she broke the link between them.

Several other villagers helped carry Moki to the raft. They needed to keep going. Fortunately they were through the worst of the white water. The river was smooth except for a few small patches of rough water. Even so, Anito doubted that she could do much to help steer.

Ninto touched her shoulder. "Yiato wants you and Ukatonen to ride with her. Dalo and Kadato will take your place."

Anito agreed numbly, hardly noticing the packet of food that Baha handed her. Death's silvery sheen seemed to dance on every sunlit ripple. She was so tired. If Moki died, she would follow him and Ukatonen into death.

• • •

Juna stared down at Moki's unconscious form. His splinted arm was bound up in a fishnet sling. His uninjured arm lay outstretched. Golden sun dapples of early morning light lay across his bruised body like fallen petals. Yiato had declared a day off to give the other villagers a chance to repair rafts battered by yesterday's trip through the cataracts.

Anito and Ukatonen were clearly exhausted. Juna gathered fruit and caught fish to feed them. Fortunately the fishing was good; she pulled in half a dozen good-sized fish from small, quiet pools underneath the trees. One of them was a new species, which she duly recorded, before knocking it on the head to kill it.

Anito flickered approvingly at her catch, helping her skin, gut, and fillet the fish. Juna smiled briefly to herself. At last she was doing something right. Ever since Lyanan, life had been one mistake after another. She shook her head in frustration, drained and tired by all that had happened.

She heard a rustling in the treetops, and looked up. Ukatonen was climbing down from the nest. He squatted beside her, and linked briefly with Moki.

"How is he?" Juna asked when he emerged from the link.

"See for yourself," Ukatonen said, holding out his arm for a link. "He needs you."

Juna swallowed her fear, remembering how Moki had reached for her in the link. He had been like a starving child. He clung to her as she soothed him, vaguely aware that Anito was manipulating them through the link. Strength had flowed from her to him, and he relaxed, contented at last. Juna continued to enfold him, deeply moved by the strength of his need for her. His need for a link with her was a deeply physical one, as profound and absolute as a human infant's need to be held.

But what about her own needs? Every time she linked, Juna felt as if another layer of her humanity had been stripped away. Worst of all, she enjoyed it. Each link made her want more. Would she become addicted to allu-a? Would she still be human when the Survey found her?

Juna's spurs linked with Moki's and Ukatonen's. She was

plunged into the touch-taste-smell inner world of the aliens. Her old panic threatened to overwhelm her. Then Moki greeted her with the joyful abandon of an overeager puppy. A surge of fondness rose in her. Moki echoed that fondness, amplifying and returning it to her. The two of them spiraled higher, each cresting off the other's emotional peaks until Ukatonen gently but firmly stopped the emotional upsurge. He let them rest in their sea of emotions, then guided them gently apart.

When she was calm again, Ukatonen showed Juna the beating of her own heart pumping steadily away in her chest with a steady one-two, one-two rhythm. Ukatonen nudged her heartbeat briefly faster, then slowed it. Then he showed her how to control her own heartbeat. Juna felt her heart race and slow like some small animal inside her chest. She held her life in her hands like some fine thread made of electricity, pulsing with the beat of her heart. It was simultaneously exhilarating and scary.

Then Ukatonen guided her inside himself, showing her the steady one-two-THREE beat of his three-chambered heart. When he was through, Juna understood his heartbeat and her own in an intuitive, sensory way that went beyond anything she could have learned from dissections and observations using instrumentation. Ukatonen showed her Moki's heartbeat; it was thin and thready, not beating as strongly as his own, but it was already stronger than yesterday.

They emerged from the link.

"Well?" Ukatonen asked her. "How is Moki doing?"

"He's improving," Juna replied.

Ukatonen nodded. "It will be at least ten days before his arm is out of that splint." He paused and touched Juna's shoulder. "But it was your linking that gave him the will to live."

"Thank you, en." Juna looked away, trying to hide her fear.

"Linking still frightens you. Why?" Ukatonen asked.

"It's too—" She looked away, searching for words. "I feel overwhelmed, en. It's like I'm drowning. It's too much for me. I'm afraid I won't be able to stop, that I'll forget who and what I am."

Ukatonen ducked his chin in thought. "I don't understand. How could you forget who you are?"

"Because your presence is so overwhelming, en. I can't control what is happening to me."

"When you swim, do you control the water you swim in?" Ukatonen asked.

"No."

"You swim by being in balance with the water, by understanding its flows and shifts. You learn to move with it. You must learn to do this in allu-a."

"How?"

"You are already starting. Today I showed you the life-rhythm of the heart. You learned to change the balance of your heartbeat. Each life-rhythm you learn will teach you more balance in allu-a. You must be patient. It's as hard for Anito and me to teach you as it is for you to learn. We do such things instinctively. Thinking about them is like trying to follow the course of one bird in a large flock."

"I hope it works," Juna said.

"So do I. Now, let's go and eat. You must be hungry."

They spent the next day on the beach beside the river, resting and repairing their rafts and checking their cargo. The following day they loaded up and set off again.

Two days later they encountered the next rapids. Yiato surveyed the rapids, and reported that the water was high and the channels were clear. The safest passage was to the left. Then the villagers formed a circle for another group link. Juna shook her head when Anito invited her to join. She could barely tolerate a link with Moki. The thought of exposing herself to the entire village was too much.

Juna leaned against a beached raft, watching the villagers join together. The noisy silence of the jungle deepened, heavy with the calls of insects and birds, the rush of wind through the trees, and the occasional rustle of some unseen animal moving through the trees. She was alone for the first time in weeks. She turned on her computer and watched a comedy. The show was one of her favorites, but the jokes and laughter flowed past without touching her. It all seemed so far away and improbable. Juna paid more attention to the hot food on the table than the words of the actors.

Frustrated, she shut the program off. A soft rain began to fall as the villagers sat like a ring of green stones, totally lost in their silent communion. Humanity seemed so remote, here among these alien creatures. Juna felt a terrible gulf separating her from both her own people and the Tendu.

Eventually the villagers unlinked and pushed off onto the river. Juna sat in the stern of the raft, struggling to match their tightly coordinated rhythm. Then they were in the rapids, pulling hard around large rocks and snags. They were nearly through when someone on the raft ahead of them got swept off into the river. Ninto pulled hard on the steering oar, and they drew near the swimming alien. As Anito grasped his arm, there was a sudden tug that nearly yanked her off the raft. Baha and Ukatonen grabbed Anito and helped her pull. The Tendu shot out of the water and into the raft. It was the elder Miato. Blood gushed from his leg. His left foot was gone. It had been severed just above the ankle.

The flow of blood from Miato's stump slowed to a trickle as the river swept them into the slow water below the rapids. They beached their raft beside Miato's. Miato's bami and his crewmates lifted him from the raft and stretched him out on the smooth sand, their skins ochre with concern.

They linked with Miato, and the raw flesh at the end of his stump healed into new, tender skin. Juna recorded everything she saw, watching in amazement through the viewfinder of her computer. Even though she had seen healings like this before, they still seemed miraculous. The aliens unlinked and bandaged Miato's stump with moss and fresh leaves.

Juna got out her fishing gear and began to fish from the end of the raft. She caught several medium-sized fish, all of them familiar species. Anito emerged from the jungle with a gathering sack full of oblong spiny fruit.

"For Miato, and the Tendu helping him," Juna said, holding up her catch. Anito colored approvingly and squatted beside Juna to help prepare it.

"How terrible for Miato, to lose his foot like that!" Juna said.

Anito flickered agreement. "If only I had been a little faster. I could see the kulai coming for him, but I wasn't able to reach him in time." She sliced open the fish and neatly removed the guts, still in their translucent sac. "That almost happened to me, when I was a bami. My sitik pulled me out just before the kulai got me. It followed me onto the raft. The other elders had to club it back into the river."

"How will Miato manage with only one foot?" Juna asked. In all her months among the Tendu, she had never seen a single maimed or crippled individual.

"It will grow back."

"Grow back?" Juna asked incredulously. "His foot will grow back?"

"Of course," Anito said. "He couldn't get around very well with only one foot."

"How does it grow back?"

Anito rippled a wavy multicolored pattern that seemed to be the Tendu equivalent of a shrug. "He tells it to. He'll put mantu jelly on the stump. It will become part of his leg. His foot would grow back without the mantu jelly, but it would be a lot more work and take much longer."

"Can other animals grow back missing limbs?" Juna asked.

"Some lizards can grow back their tails, but other than that, nothing with a backbone can grow back a limb. Sometimes we will heal an injured animal to maintain the balance of the forest. That's why we healed that taira you hurt. We needed more taira to keep the puyu from killing too many young trees. We rarely heal any animal as badly injured as Miato. It's too much trouble, and it's too hard on the animal."

"It's different for my people," Juna said. "We can't grow back an arm or a foot if we lose one."

Anito's ears lifted in surprise. "What do you do instead?"

"We make them a replacement limb, if we can."

"What kind of animal do you use to grow a replacement limb?" Anito asked, looking puzzled.

Juna shook her head, startled by the question. "The replacement limb isn't alive. It's made out of dead things, like wood or stone. It doesn't work as well as the real limb, but it's the best that we can do." She couldn't explain further; the Tendu had no word for plastic or metal in their language, and she had no idea how to explain mechanical objects to them. They thought her computer was some strange kind of half-alive stone animal.

Yet the Tendu were capable of prodigies of biotechnology. Her transformation and the amazing feats of healing she had seen proved that. She shook her head. It was hard to square their primitive lifestyle with their incredible abilities. She wondered how much of their biological skill was instinctive, and how much of it was learned.

"How much training do you need in order to heal someone?" she asked Anito. "Could Moki heal someone now, or would he have to be trained?"

"He is helping to heal himself. All bami know how to do that."

"What will Moki have to learn in order to become a sitik?"

Anito shook her head and spread her hands and ears wide. "Many things. He must learn something of the balance of the atwas, he must learn the history and customs of the village, and he must learn to heal himself and others well enough to be worthy of a place among the elders. Even then he will not be ready. He must be able to make the difficult decisions required of elders. He must be responsible. When he becomes an elder, he will share in deciding what the fate of the villagers will be."

"How many years does that take?"

"It varies. I was with my sitik for many years."

"How many years?"

Anito shook her head. "I don't know. It was a long time. Long enough for a sapling like that one"—she pointed with her chin at a seedling that was little more than a slender twig with a handful of pale, shiny leaves—"to become a tree like that." She pointed at a mature canopy tree.

Juna looked at the tree and turned bright pink in amazement. It was at least fifty or sixty Standard years old. If her ears had been mobile like a Tendu's, they would have been spread wide. Anito was older than she was and she was barely an adult.

"How long do your people live?" Juna asked. "How old was Ilto when he died?"

Anito laid a hand on Juna's arm. "It is not polite to call the dead by their names," she informed her. "My sitik was the oldest Tendu in the village. He grew up in the tree our village lived in before this one. Ninto was his bami. When an elder died without a bami, Ninto was chosen to fill her place.

Because of this, my sitik lived longer than most Tendu. He did not have to die or be exiled when Ninto became an elder."

"I don't understand," Juna said. "Are you saying that an elder must leave the village or die before their bami can become an elder?"

"Of course, except when an elder dies without a bami, or if the bami dies before it can become an elder."

"Why?" Juna asked. The implications of this were beginning to sink in.

"There are only so many elders in a village. It depends on the size of the tree, and the fertility of their jungle."

"How big are most villages?" Juna asked.

Anito shook her head. "Ask Ukatonen. He knows more about what things are like in other villages." She picked up a leaf full of neatly sliced fish. "We should take this over to Miato and the others. They will be hungry."

The conversation was over, but Juna was full of questions. If her estimates were right, the Tendu lived at least 120 years, despite their primitive technology. Was this due to some intrinsic genetic characteristic, or was it due to their healing abilities? How would she be able to tell the difference?

Juna set a generous portion of the sliced fish and a basket of fruit beside the villagers who were working on healing Miato. They accepted it with a flicker of acknowledgment and thanks. She took a smaller portion of fish and some fruit over to Moki. He picked it up awkwardly with his uninjured arm, and fed himself. She peeled back the spiny rind of the fruit, exposing the translucent white inner pulp, and handed that to him.

A bami could not become an adult until its elder died or became an exile. What did this mean for her and Moki, and for Ukatonen? Could Moki become an elder after she left? Would Ukatonen have to die to make way for Moki? Where would Moki become an elder? She didn't belong to any village. She had no place for Moki to fill. Juna sighed, and offered Moki another peeled fruit. Had she made a mistake?

"What's the matter?" Moki asked, in shades of concern. "You seem sad. Is there anything I can do?"

"I'm just worried about what's to become of you, with a strange sitik like me. What village will accept you?"

Moki rippled reassuringly. "Ukatonen would not have let you adopt me if he didn't think it could work."

Juna sucked out the gelatinous pulp of a fruit. "Perhaps you're right, Moki. I'll talk to him," she said with a confidence that she didn't feel.

Ukatonen came up as they finished eating. He helped himself to a bite of fish.

"How is Miato?" Juna asked.

"He'll heal nicely," Ukatonen said in skin speech as he chewed.

"How long before his foot grows back?"

"That depends. If everything goes well, he should have enough of a foot to swim with when we reach the sea. It should be completely healed by the time we return." He brushed her shoulder affectionately. "Thank you for catching those fish. It was very helpful."

"Thank you, en. I was glad to help. The village has done so much for me."

"We should link with Moki while we're stopped here," Ukatonen said.

Juna nodded, and held out her arms. Linking still bothered her, but it was necessary in order to be a good sitik to Moki. Besides, linking with Moki wasn't nearly as overwhelming as linking with Anito or Ukatonen. The enkar let her set the pace of the link, and the level of intensity.

Moki and Ukatonen gripped her arms; she felt the pricking of their spurs, and then the link enfolded her.

She followed Ukatonen as he examined Moki's broken arm. Juna could feel the ends knitting together, though the joins were still fragile. His internal organs showed no signs of their bruising, and his injured allu appeared to be healing. Ukatonen radiated pleasure at Moki's progress.

When he was done checking on Moki, Ukatonen took Juna on a tour of her digestive system. She tasted the processes of digestion, felt her food get broken down in her stomach, and then further broken down and absorbed in her large and small intestine, until the remaining wastes were excreted. It was an amazingly intricate transformation—food into energy, raw materials, and waste.

They emerged from the link to find that the rain clouds had given way to brilliant sunlight. Juna lifted her face to the sun. The sky had been blanketed with thick, rain-swollen clouds for most of the trip. These rare sun breaks were something to treasure. She laid her computers out to top up their batteries. The villagers began unloading cargo, spreading it out on the beach to dry in the sun, checking the waxed gourds for signs of rot and water damage. Juna helped Ninto and Anito spread out their things. Two gourds of honey had small soft black spots of rot on them. Anito left them out in the sun. When the honey inside was warm and fluid, she poured it into empty gourds. Then they split open the old gourds and licked up the remaining honey from the insides.

"How old are you?" Juna asked Ukatonen as they sucked the last bits of sweetness from their gourds.

Ukatonen ducked his chin and thought for a while. "I don't know," he said. "I've lived a long time." He turned a faint, nostalgic blue-grey. "It's been a good life."

"Are you older than Anito's sitik was?" she asked.

Ukatonen flickered yes. "Much older."

"How much older?" Juna asked. The Tendu vagueness about time was extremely frustrating.

"When I became an enkar, Anito's sitik's sitik would not have been born yet. Before I was an enkar, I was chief elder of my village. I have seen trees like that one"—he pointed at a gnarled and ancient forest giant, heavily bearded with moss— "sprout and grow and die at least six times over."

Juna turned bright pink with surprise. That would make Ukatonen well over 700 years old.

"You must be one of the oldest of your people."

Negation flickered across Ukatonen's chest. "There are many enkar much older than I am. There are some who have lived ten times as long as I have, and even they are not the oldest of my people."

"Don't you"—Juna paused, searching for the word for aging—"grow weaker as you get older?"

Ukatonen's ears spread wide and his head went back in surprise. "Why should we?" he asked.

"My people only live for about one hundred of your years.

When we get to be about eighty years old, our bodies start to fail. We get sick easily, our bones become brittle. We sometimes get forgetful. Eventually we get old and die."

"You can't control your bodies well enough to stop this? How do you manage to raise the next generation if you live such short lives?"

"We have children early in our lives. Most people have children in their twenties or thirties. And children become adults much faster among our people. We are considered adults when we are about twenty years old."

Ukatonen's amazement deepened. "How can you be ready to raise children at so young an age?"

"It's the way we have always done things. A thousand years ago most people were lucky to live past forty. People started having children when they were only fourteen or fifteen. Half their children died while they were still babies, so they had six or eight children."

"All at once?" Ukatonen asked, vividly pink with surprise. "How selfish of them."

"They needed their children to take care of them when they got old," Juna explained. "In those days, children were our wealth."

"But so many young? How could you teach each one properly in so little time? How could you feed them?"

"We worked very hard. We—" Juna searched for words to describe planting crops and raising animals. "We grew big areas of food plants; we kept animals for food, the way you keep narey."

"Your people are very strange," Ukatonen said.

"My people are very different," Juna agreed. She wondered how she could explain war and famine to Ukatonen. Had the Tendu ever fought a war? Had they ever starved? She looked away. The thought of asking such questions of these peaceful people shamed her. She remembered the refugee camp, remembered her stomach cramping with hunger. She darkened with shame as she recalled stealing food from others for herself and Toivo after their mother died. She had done it to survive, but that didn't excuse the terrible things she had done.

Juna looked up as the sun momentarily dimmed. A heavy

bank of clouds was closing in. The villagers began gathering up and reloading their cargo. She helped Anito and the others load their raft. She looked at the Tendu, their moist skins gleaming in the pearly light that heralded the coming rain. Their lives were so different from hers. How could she ever explain humans to them?

The next day they stopped and portaged around a large waterfall. It took the rest of that day and the next to disassemble the rafts and carry them and their cargo around the waterfall, and then reassemble and reload them. Once past the waterfall, the character of the river changed, becoming wider, slower, and more placid. The few stretches of white water they encountered were relatively easy and safe.

Anito and Ukatonen continued teaching Juna about linking. By the time the river broadened and separated into marshy channels near the delta, she had learned to heal small cuts and abrasions on her own body. When they entered the tidal mangrove swamps near the coast, they were set upon by millions of tiny black biting insects. Anito showed Juna how to synthesize an insect repellent in her allu-a, and to adjust her skin so that the saltier water of the ocean would not burn her. At last, after several days of rowing through placid channels, they heard the sound of surf. The trees opened out and they found themselves in a wide bay.

Ukatonen dove off the raft, and vanished beneath the waves. The villagers waited, watching the water intently. All was quiet except for the water lapping against the rafts, and the distant sound of surf. Suddenly the water ahead began to boil. A sleek green shape leaped from the water, followed by several others. As they approached, the rafts drew closer together, and there was a rising flicker of excitement among the villagers. Then the creatures surrounded the rafts. To Juna's surprise, Ninto reached down and helped one of them climb aboard. It stood with difficulty on its short, stumpy legs.

"My name is Munato. I will escort you to our island," the creature said in skin speech. "Do you have any honey?"

Seventeen.

A QUIET RIPPLE of amusement flowed over Anito at the new creature's surprise when the lyali-Tendu spoke.

"What kind of creature is that?" Eerin asked as Ninto greeted the sea person, giving him a generous chunk of honeycomb.

"He's a lyali-Tendu, a sea person," Anito explained. "They are Tendu who live in the sea."

"But he looks so different!"

Anito studied the lyali-Tendu. True, Munato had prominent gill flaps and short arms with long, heavily webbed fingers and wide, flipper-like feet, but he had the red stinging stripes of a Tendu. His face was elongated, streamlined for swimming, but his eyes were the same as hers. His blood tasted saltier, but the life-rhythms were the same. He sang aloud to communicate with the other lyali-Tendu far off in the sea, but he also spoke skin speech. How could Eerin doubt that he was another Tendu?

Munato glanced curiously at Eerin. "Who is that?" he asked.

"This is Eerin," Anito told her. "She is a new creature. Her people live far away. They left her behind by mistake."

A compassionate cloud of dark ochre passed over Munato's skin. "It's hard to be away from your people."

"They'll come back for her," Anito reassured him.

"There have been a lot of strange things happening lately. The sea people saw a great stone strike the water. It rose up and floated like a giant piece of driftwood. Then it moved through the water with a lot of noise. I heard that it beached near Lyanan, and the creatures inside it caused a lot of damage."

Eerin darkened with shame. "Those were my people," she said. "They didn't know that the forest belonged to somebody. They'll repair the damage."

"Eerin is already helping the people of Lyanan replant the forest," Anito added, feeling a bit defensive and worried. She had enough problems without hostility from the sea people.

"I heard that there was some kind of digging race," Munato said. "Were you there when it happened?"

"Eerin was in the race. She won it."

Munato's ears lifted and he flushed pink in surprise. "Can you swim as well as you dig?"

Eerin darkened again. "I doubt that I can swim as well as you can."

"She can swim well enough," Anito told him.

A ripple of amusement danced across Munato's chest. "It's easy for you ruwe-Tendu to say that. You spend all your time in the trees. Come swim with me, five-fingers," he said to Eerin. He dove cleanly into the water. Eerin looked inquisitively at Anito.

"Go ahead," she said. "It's safe."

Eerin dove in after Munato. He swam in playful circles around her, then dove deep. Eerin plunged in after him, but popped back up to the surface much sooner than the lyali-Tendu. Munato surfaced, looking disappointed.

"She's not much of a diver, but she can swim well enough," he admitted, lying on his back in the water so they could see his words. "I'll go get the rest of my people."

He dove again. A few minutes later, six other sea people joined him. Ninto, Baha, and Anito threw tow ropes over the side. Then they picked up their oars and began rowing while the lyali-Tendu pulled the raft through the water.

It was well past sunset when they reached the island, a black bulk against the deep blue, star-studded night sky. Anito heard the crash of the waves well before she saw the white gleam of the beach and the faint phosphorescence of the breakers. They shipped their oars, and allowed the sea people to pull them ashore, riding a big wave that pushed them high up onto the beach, where several other rafts already waited.

Trading started early the next morning. Anito laid her trade goods out on the beach with the other villagers. The lyali-Tendu squatted in the sand and haggled. Anito drove the hardest bargains she could, but they had arrived late this year, and it was difficult to make a decent trade.

Ukatonen came by late in the day, and squatted beside her as she argued over the worth of a fishnet. She finally let it go for sixteen sheets of yarram and a string of dried fish. She gave the lyali-Tendu the net and he gave her a stack of tallies.

"You traded well," the enkar told her when the sea person left. "I saw Miato trade a net like that for only twelve sheets and a small container of preserved fish eggs."

"Yes, but it's not enough!" Anito said. "Even with all the honey I brought, I've only got a hundred and sixty sheets of yarram, two cakes of dried su ink, a string of dried fish, two gourds of salt, and a hollow reed full of guano. Last year Ilto brought home five hundred sheets of yarram, five bladders full of fish paste, eight strings of dried fish, and ten gourds of salt. And we could have brought even more if we had found a way to carry it."

"The others aren't doing much better," Ukatonen soothed.

Anito looked away, deep brown with shame. "I know. It's my fault. If they hadn't waited for me to come back from the coast, then they would have arrived earlier and made better trades."

"Every village has bad years," Ukatonen told her. "Your village is very prosperous. One bad year won't hurt."

"But it's my fault," Anito insisted.

"You could arrange a mating with the lyali-Tendu."

"A mating? But it's not mating season!"

"So? Other villages do it all the time, and you'll get a lot of trade goods," Ukatonen pointed out. "You hold the eggs inside you until the time is right. You're young, low status, and Narmolom is short on males. You'll have a better choice of mates here. Besides, it will bring new genes into your area. It's good to mate with the Iyali-Tendu. It keeps the sea people and the land people from drifting too far apart."

"What do I lose?" Anito asked.

"You won't be able to mate during the usual mating season."

"How much would I be able to get in trade goods for a mating?"

"If you act quickly, and drive a hard bargain, you could bring back at least another four hundred sheets of yarram plus other trade goods. With both Eerin and Moki, you can carry back more than Ilto did, enough to repay Ninto and the other villagers for waiting for you."

"Why are you encouraging me to do this?" Anito asked suspiciously.

"There are many reasons," Ukatonen said. "You are going to be an enkar. I want you to take this opportunity to learn more about the Iyali-Tendu. A mating will give you a connection with this band, one that you can use when you are an enkar. Also, I don't want you deeply indebted to the other villagers. It will be easier when it's time to leave Narmolom."

Anito looked away. Ukatonen brushed her shoulder with his knuckles.

"You would have had to leave, even if you hadn't asked for that judgment for Moki. The new creatures are very important, Anito. When Eerin's people return, things will change. We must be ready for that. You must be ready for it." A cloud of regret misted his skin. "I wish there was more time. I wish you could stay longer with your village. It would be better if you could be more experienced as an elder before you become an enkar, but that won't be possible. I promise that I won't take you away from Narmolom until I have to."

"How long will I have?"

"A year, perhaps two. I want to take you away this year during mating season to meet other enkar. If you mate now, you won't miss your chance this year. It's your first year as an elder, and I don't want to deprive you of a first mating, even if it isn't with your own villagers." He touched her shoulder. "I'm sorry, Anito."

Anito looked away for a long moment. Her skin was deep grey with grief. She had looked forward to mating with others

in her village. It was one of the few things that made becoming
an elder acceptable. Now Ukatonen was taking even that away.
She could tell, by the gentle, soft edges of his words, that he
truly regretted what he was asking her to do. A sudden surge of
anger rose in her. Her life was being taken away from her, and
she was helpless to stop it.

She looked over at Eerin, who sat with Moki among a crowd
of inquisitive lyali-Tendu. This was all her fault. If Ilto hadn't
found Eerin, then none of this would have happened. She might
still be Ilto's bami, preparing to take her place as an elder of
Narmolom. How far away and remote her life as a bami
seemed now.

Ukatonen must have followed her gaze, and seen her flare of
anger and resentment. He touched her on the shoulder. "I had
as much to do with your becoming an enkar as she did," he told
her. "It's not such a bad life, really."

Anito looked away from Eerin. "I'll arrange a mating with
the lyali-Tendu, en," she said, shifting the conversation back to
safer ground, "but I ask that you not take me away from
Narmolom until I have a chance to mate with my own people."

"I'll try, kene," Ukatonen told her, "but I can't promise
anything."

Anito went to the chief of the band of lyali-Tendu and
negotiated with her for a mating. She bargained shrewdly,
receiving four hundred twenty sheets of yarram, six large
bladders of fish paste, three gourds of salt, four strings of dried
fish, and a pouch full of fish hooks made from the spines of a
deep sea fish.

Once the arrangements for the mating were concluded, the
rest of Anito's trading went much better. Not surprisingly, most
of her trades were concluded with males, who almost gave
away their goods in hopes that she might favor them during the
mating. Anito enjoyed the attention but promised nothing.

They would travel home with heavy packs. Fortunately
Eerin could carry more than a Tendu. Anito planned on giving
a lot of what she had gotten to the other villagers, canceling
most of the obligations acquired on this trip.

The villagers and the lyali-Tendu finished their trading by
mid-afternoon of the next day, and began preparing a huge

feast of celebration. They gathered in a semicircle on the beach. Large flat shells were piled high with traditional dishes, symbolizing the unity of the land and sea Tendu. There was fish and seaweed, flavored with honey thinned and seasoned with seawater, and soaked grain mixed with salty fish roe. In addition to the traditional dishes, there were baskets brimming with live crustaceans, platters of sliced fruit from trees on the island, and a huge female intasti, neatly butchered and arranged in its large shell, with its freshly laid eggs heaped around the meat.

They ate until their stomachs bulged. Then baskets of glows were laid out in a circle on the sand. Drums, flutes, and shell horns were taken out. The performers strapped on rattles made from gourds and seashells, and donned headdresses and masks. When the bustle of preparation was over, there was a moment of silence; then Ukatonen blew a long, deep, haunting note on a shell horn. It made the red stinging stripes tighten on Anito's back.

The performers from the village of Narmolom shuffled in and began a rhythmic high-pitched chattering, backed up by the shimmer of the rattles on their ankles and arms. Anito glanced over at Miato. He was watching the dancers intently. Usually he led them, but this year his injury prevented him from dancing. Miato's leg was healing well—already his ankle and foot had grown long enough to reach the ground—but he still needed a crutch. It would be half a month before the bones and tendons were strong enough for normal use.

The dancers began slapping their hands against their thighs, welcoming the lyali-Tendu performers as they waddled in. They knelt in the sand, their wet skin gleaming in the faint light of the glows. A wash of brilliant blue flared on their bodies in perfect unison. The Narmolom performers turned completely black. Green splashes exploded all over their bodies as they chattered and rocked back and forth, nearly invisible except for the splashes of color. The lyali-Tendu performers responded with green and pink flares of approval and excitement. The dancers from Narmolom picked up the sea people's patterns and echoed them. This began a long improvisational call and response between the two groups which built slowly into a crescendo of movement, music, and color. The performance glided slowly to a gentle rising and falling flare accompanied only by the mournful piping of shell horns. Then it faded away to silent stillness.

The watching audience rippled wildly azure and deep green in approval. "The story, the story, tell us the story," they said over and over again, in big bold patterns. Ukatonen stood up and walked to the center of the ring formed by the performers and the audience. Narito, the chief of the lyali-Tendu, waddled up to join him. The assembled land and sea people exploded in applause.

Anito looked away, overcome by memories. Almost as long as she had been coming here, her sitik had played the part of the ruwe-Tendu in this quarbirri. Even after all this time, it was hard to see someone else in Ilto's place.

Ukatonen blew another long, mournful note on the shell horn, and Narito responded with a run of notes on her flute. The drummer beat out a deep thundering rumble on the log-drum, and the quarbirri was formally begun. The familiar story unfolded again, in music, dance, and pattern. The first land Tendu's attempts to live in the sea were simultaneously acted out and narrated in stylized skin speech by Ukatonen. His style was very old, very traditional, in keeping with his status as enkar, but within the ancient framework Anito could see movements, patterns, and turns of phrase that were startlingly new and original. Clearly Ukatonen was a master of the quarbirri.

Narito responded to the challenge of Ukatonen's impressive performance with grace and power. She acted out the role of the sea and its creatures, testing the Tendu's ability to live in the sea. Anito glanced at Eerin and Moki. They were completely absorbed in the quarbirri. Eerin had her talking stone out and was making a picture of the entire performance.

She had seen Eerin do this before, making pictures of conversations, and then watching them over and over again. Eerin claimed that this helped her learn the language, and that these recordings would help her people understand what the Tendu were saying. What would her people make of this quarbirri? How much of this stylized skin speech did Eerin understand?

A ripple of regret ran down Anito's back. She felt sorry for the new creature. She was blind to the nuances of style and technique that made this quarbirri so wonderful.

The performance reached its conclusion, the establishment of trading between the lyali-Tendu and the ruwe-Tendu. Ukatonen and Narito grasped each other's arms and danced in a circle, a movement symbolic of linking and harmony. Then each of them drew someone else into their dance. The circle grew until everyone on the beach was a part of it, even Eerin. They drew together, crooning rhythmically, and knelt in the sand. Dancing merged into a giant linking. Anito could taste the saltier blood of the lyali-Tendu merging with the sweet familiarity of Narmolom.

Juna watched in amazement as the dancers exploded with color and motion. She fumbled for her computer, configuring it into a video recorder. The Alien Contact people were going to love this. Once the recorder was set up, she sat back and enjoyed the show. It seemed to be a meaningless display of color and motion. Occasionally she saw a wordlike pattern, but by and large this appeared to be the visual equivalent of scat singing, largely improvisational and abstract. The performance faded slowly to an end, and the Tendu audience exploded in ripples of visual applause that was nearly as beautiful as the performance they had just witnessed. The applause became a rhythmic pattern of words. They were asking for a story.

Ukatonen and one of the sea Tendu moved to the center of the circle. The audience and performers rippled with approval. Juna was struck by their silence. The only sounds were the faint noises of wind and surf, and the occasional click of a rattle as a dancer shifted position. She could hear the faint whirring of her computer's recording lenses as they adjusted their focus.

Ukatonen blew a long, haunting note on a horn made from a spiraled shell. There was a deep rumbling from the big hollow log that served as a drum. One of the sea Tendu joined him. Then they began to dance, a stiff, stylized dance emphasizing the complex formal skin-speech patterns of the story.

The formal skin speech was hard for Juna to understand, but she recognized certain recurring words. They were echoed by the sea Tendu. The thread of the narrative passed back and forth between them in a visual call and response. The story was about the sea and the Tendu. Juna leaned forward, watching intently as the story unfolded. Was this some kind of origin myth? If this was about how the Tendu came out of the sea, it was being told backwards. As the narrative progressed, she realized that it was a story of the Tendu learning about the sea.

The story concluded with Ukatonen and the sea Tendu linking arms and dancing together. They began drawing others into the dance, forming a huge circle. Cool, moist hands swept her and Moki into the dance. It felt good to move after sitting for so long. Juna shrugged her shoulders, loosening her spine, and imitated their movements, crooning rhythmically. They knelt in the sand, swaying from side to side. Juna knelt with them, feeling their cool, clammy bodies brushing against hers. She felt a pinprick, and was swept into a link before she could do more than feel startled. She struggled in sudden panic. Then Moki was there with her, shielding her from the others in the link, giving her time to adjust. Once she was composed, Moki let more of the link filter through his shields, stopping as soon as Juna began to be concerned. She felt Ukatonen's presence alongside Moki's, guiding him and reassuring her.

Gradually, she began to feel the presence of the others outside Moki and Ukatonen. The spiky, salty taste of curiosity dominated the link. They wanted Juna to open herself to the villagers and the sea people.

Juna cringed against Moki and Ukatonen, terrified at the thought of strangers climbing through her most intimate feelings. They folded protectively around her. When she was calm they lifted their shields a bit, letting some of the group link filter through. When Juna began to panic, they tightened their shields again. Gradually, she relaxed into the link, letting more and more of it seep through the protective presences enfolding her. The link surrounded her like a warm sea. Moki, Anito, and Ukatonen buoyed her up, helping her learn to float in it. The link dissolved and she awoke on the beach, feeling tranquil and at peace with the world around her.

She got up and walked into the sea to wash away the sand sticking to her skin. The sea was phosphorescent tonight, glowing green as it washed around her. A green streak flashed by her. Juna drew her breath in, preparing to scream, when a lyali-Tendu surfaced beside her. She let out a shaky laugh as the sea Tendu flickered a greeting. She acknowledged its greeting and it dove beneath the surface with a flicker of amusement and swam away, leaving a glowing green streak of disturbed luminous plankton in its wake.

She took a deep breath, dove under the waves, and opened her eyes to a veil of luminous green. She drifted in the night sea, letting the green fire of the sea burn coldly on her skin. The link hadn't been that bad, not with Moki and the others protecting her. It had felt good, once she had managed to relax. The allu-a had made her feel like a part of something larger, as endless and alive as the sea or the forest. It hadn't been a violation at all. She uncurled and reached for the surface, breathing in the sweet air. It wasn't her world, and these were not her people, but still, the link had felt like coming home.

Juna swam back to shore, and rose from the sea, dripping green fire. She washed the salt and the phosphorescence from her body in a nearby stream of sweet water. Then she curled up beside Anito and the others and fell asleep.

Anito woke early the next morning. She drank and bathed in the stream, then stood on the beach looking out at the ocean, waves washing past her ankles. Today was her first mating. She was grateful for last night's group linking, but although the lyali-Tendu were familiar to her as a group, they remained strangers as individuals. Mating season had always frightened her. Ilto became preoccupied and short-tempered. Once, when she was very young, Ilto mistook her for a competing male and snapped at her. He had immediately apologized, but memories of that moment still hurt. Would she be like that? She remembered the intensity of her accidental arousal and her failure to control herself.

She heard splashing footsteps behind her. It was Ukatonen. He brushed her shoulder with his knuckles.

"You are worried?" he asked her.

She flickered agreement.

"It's always a little frightening before you become aroused. Once you're in heat though, nothing else matters. You'll be fine." He held out a basket full of freshly caught fish. "A gift from one of your admirers. You need to eat well this morning. Mating is exhausting, and you won't get a chance to eat later."

Anito followed Ukatonen back to the nest. Eerin and Moki were busy helping Ninto prepare a huge breakfast.

"You have a lot of admirers, it seems," Ukatonen told her. "All of this came from lyali-Tendu males."

Anito ate until her stomach was stretched and tight. Ninto bundled up the least perishable leftovers in leaf wrappers and put them in a bag for Anito. She slung it over her shoulder with a flicker of thanks. The others escorted her to the beach, where Narito waited for the Narmolom females who were going to mate with the lyali-Tendu males.

Ninto gave her shoulder a reassuring squeeze as Anito joined the others. "Don't worry," she said. "You'll enjoy it."

Anito flickered acknowledgment. She swallowed; her throat was dry with nervousness. Ukatonen stepped forward and touched her shoulder.

"Since Narmolom does not yet have a chief elder, I will oversee the mating on behalf of the village," he said.

Anito relaxed. Ukatonen would be there to look after her. It wouldn't be so bad.

The lyali-Tendu males came out onto the beach and sat in a clump around Narito. The Narmolom females sat with Ukatonen. Each group linked. Anito could feel Ukatonen's powerful presence among them, initiating their heat. She felt a sudden warmth flaring in her reproductive organs. It radiated outward to her skin as Ukatonen released them from the link.

Anito looked down. Her skin was a dull bronze, becoming brighter and more golden on her lower belly, flanks, and back. She glanced around her. The other females were the same color. The males were still caught up in their linking. There were at least three males for every female.

"We should invite them upriver to visit during mating season. Then we wouldn't have to fight over the good males," one of the other females remarked. It was Hanto. She had mated with Ilto last season.

The other females flickered agreement.

"It's too bad that the sea is so far away," Yanito said. "It must be nice, having enough males to go around."

"Then you should choose more male tinka for your bami," Ukatonen told her.

"But female bami are so much more useful," Barito remarked. "Their infertile eggs are such good food for the narey."

"Besides," Hanto put in, "it wouldn't help us much. By the time any new bami are mature enough to mate, I'll be long gone."

"We always need enkar," Ukatonen said. "Perhaps some of your elders with older male bami might consider leaving the village to become enkar."

The others looked away, disturbed by the thought of leaving Narmolom, but unwilling to say anything that might upset the enkar. Anito brushed Ukatonen's shoulder in sympathy. He was right, there were too few males in the village. It was something that the new chief elder would have to address.

"The lyali-Tendu are out of their link," Hanto said.

The males had turned bronze too. Anito found her gaze resting on the golden patches on their lower belly and backs. The warmth inside her spread and intensified. She felt a sudden urge to get closer to the males. The intensity of it was a little frightening. She wanted to run, dive into the sea, feel it surround her as she plunged deep. . . .

Narito beckoned them into the ocean. Anito restrained herself from running ahead, and followed Ukatonen and the others into the waves. The cool water felt good on her skin. Yellow and black fish scattered before her like a flock of frightened birds as she drove herself through the water. She dove deep, down to the rippled sandy bottom. Two sleek, powerful forms dove before her, displaying their brilliant gold patches. Anito shot toward the surface, emerging in a high, spectacular leap. The males flanked her. Two more joined them, and she found herself surrounded by brilliantly glowing males. She could taste their arousal on the water, sweet and peppery. It made her skin tingle. She looked down. Her skin was almost entirely gold now. Soon her eggs would be ready, and it would be time to mate. She sped up, diving deep, drawing the males down with her, feeling the water pressure against her ears, glorying in her strength and speed. Ripples of blue coursed briefly across her golden skin as she outdistanced them. She exhaled and followed the silvery bubbles up, letting the males overtake her, teasing them with the nearness of her presence. The males twined around her. They leaped high out of the water, celebrating their excitement in a silvery shower of spray.

The males were all gold, and her skin tingled in response. One of them brushed up against her body. She dove again, a mating croon issuing from her throat. The water vibrated with the males' response, and her arousal became a sudden flood of sexual heat. It overwhelmed her; she was helpless to stop it. She crooned again, glowing with the intensity of her desire. For a moment she understood the fear Eerin had felt about linking. Another body brushed hers, making her skin tighten at the base of her spine. She headed for the surface again. The males leaped around her, their golden skins brilliant in the sunlight. Her fear was drowned by a sudden eagerness. She let herself drift, back arched in readiness.

One of them clasped her, and she felt her back arch further in response. She everted her cloaca, felt the male's cloaca touch hers, and the sudden warmth of his sperm flooding into her, clouding the water around them with a chalky, bitter, musky flavor, heightening her excitement. Strange new muscles she had never felt before began to contract, drawing the sperm further inside her, toward the cluster of waiting eggs. The male released her and she felt another one clasp her. Thought deserted her; she was consumed by instinct and arousal.

She mated again and again, not knowing how many males grasped her. It was dark when she emerged from the ocean, drained, hungry, and exhausted. Her back was sore from arching it. Her belly felt heavy, full of eggs and sperm. Her cloaca throbbed with a pleasurable ache. Some part of her still wanted to arch, and be clasped again, but the feeling receded as the cool night air chilled her darkening skin.

Ninto was waiting for her on the beach. She put her arm

around Anito as she emerged from the ocean, supporting her all the way to the nest.

"I'm sorry I left your food behind," Anito said as they passed the patch of churned sand where the females had waited.

Ninto rippled in amusement. "It would have only gotten in the way," she said, "but you looked like you needed something to hold onto this morning."

"Where are Ukatonen and the others?" Anito asked.

"They're sleeping somewhere else tonight. I thought you might like some time alone."

Anito flickered her thanks. She did want to be alone to let the last remnants of her heat dissipate in sleep. So much had happened. She wasn't ready for company, not until she had slept. Ninto unwrapped a package of fish eggs and seaweed and handed it to her. Anito took a huge bite.

"Did you enjoy yourself?" Ninto asked.

"Ask me tomorrow," Anito said, chewing her food. "I'm too tired and hungry now to think straight."

Laughter rippled across Ninto's chest. "I know how you feel," she said. "I once did a sea-mating, when I was young. It's much more tiring than mating among the villagers, but it is a lot more intense." Blue-grey nostalgia rippled briefly over her. "I enjoyed it, but I like mating with my own people better."

A mist of regret clouded Anito's skin. "I wish that I could have mated at Narmolom this time."

Ninto brushed Anito's shoulder with her knuckles. "Don't worry, you'll have many years to do that."

Anito looked away, grey with sadness.

"What is it?" Ninto asked. "What's wrong?"

"I don't have that much time left in Narmolom. Ukatonen is going to take me away to become an enkar. I'll have to leave Narmolom in a year or two."

Ninto laid a hand on Anito's arm. Her skin was still for a long moment, dulled with sadness.

"Would he— Would Ukatonen take me in your place?" she asked at last.

"No, Ninto," Anito said, deeply moved by her tareena's offer. "I couldn't ask that of you. Besides, he wants me."

"Why?" Ninto asked. "Is it the new creature?"

Anito flickered agreement. She looked away, overcome with sorrow and anger at her fate. "He thinks the new creatures are too important for me to remain in the village," she said, turning back to Ninto.

"But it isn't right. You've only just become an elder. If he took me, it would make more sense. Baha is ready to become an elder. Let me ask Ukatonen to take me instead."

"No," Anito said. "I promised myself in exchange for a judgment on whether Eerin could adopt Moki. Besides, I think he's right. The new creatures are important. If you could have seen what they did at Lyanan—" Anito shook her head and looked away. "They need someone to bring them into harmony, before they cause more harm. No one else knows Eerin like I do, like Ukatonen does. But—" she added, looking back at Ninto, "I don't want to. I want to stay in Narmolom. If I had a choice, that's what I would do, but it would be a selfish choice."

Ninto turned away for a long moment. "I admire your courage," she said at last, "and your devotion to duty. If there's ever anything that I can do to help you with this, just ask me."

Anito flickered acknowledgment and thanks. They clasped hands and Ninto slipped off into the darkness. Anito settled herself in the nest, piling leaves over her tired, aching body and fell asleep thinking of her tareena.

Juna watched Ukatonen lead a small group of land-Tendu males down to the ocean to mate with the females of the sea people. Yesterday Anito had mated with the sea people for trade goods. Today she lay in exhausted slumber. This sudden flowering of alien sexuality disconcerted Juna. They had seemed so sexless. Now they were suddenly bartering sex for trade goods.

She shook her head. The theoretical xeno-anthropology text on her computer had told her that alien contact was a continual process of discovery and reevaluation, but she hadn't realized how often she would be reevaluating everything. She was tired of surprises. She picked up her gathering basket and digger and motioned to Moki. They needed breakfast, and there was no one but themselves to gather it. Fresh seafood was a pleasant change from raw fowl and reptile, but she missed the fruit, honey, and greens that made up so much of the land-Tendu diet. Their honey had been traded away for seaweed, salt, and other trade goods. Fruit was scarce on this small island. They could only have one piece a day.

They reached the beach, and walked along, the waves washing past their ankles. Moki was watching the sand intently. Finally he nodded. Juna set the basket down, and followed his gaze.

He touched her hand and she turned to look at him. "See all the bubbles coming up from the sand?" he said. "That's where the shellfish are." He stood over a cluster of small holes in the sand. "They can hear you coming. You have to stand very still and wait for them to forget about you."

They waited while several waves came and went. At last he said, "Get the sieve ready." Juna nodded and held the sieve out.

When the next wave began to recede, Moki exploded into motion, digging furiously, throwing sand into Juna's high-walled sieve until the next wave came flooding in. Juna submerged the sieve in the wave and shook it, letting the sand wash out, leaving behind a collection of small beach stones, and whatever was living in the sand. Moki came over and helped her sort through the contents of the strainer.

"Good," he said, holding up an odd-looking shell segmented into eight parts. "This one's delicious, and we got four or five of them. Do you want to show it to your talking stone?"

"That's all right, Moki. I think it's seen that kind already. I found a dead one on the beach the day after we got here. Thanks, though."

It took only five digging sessions to gather enough shellfish for a decent breakfast. They gathered and washed some seaweed, and carried their food back to the nest, where Anito was still sleeping.

They had the food all ready when she woke. She stretched slowly and painfully. Moki handed her a gourd full of fresh, clear water. Anito poured it over herself with a slow, vivid flush of intense turquoise.

"Thank you. That feels wonderful!"

"We got breakfast for you," Juna said, holding out a leaf piled high with shellfish and seaweed.

Anito flickered thanks. "You're a good teacher, Moki," she said.

Moki looked away, darkening with embarrassed pride.

Anito touched Juna's hand. "And you learn quickly. Thank you."

Juna looked down, pleased and surprised by the compliment.

"Thank you, kene. Eat. You must be hungry after all you did yesterday."

Amused agreement flickered over Anito's skin as she popped a tentacled sand-squid into her mouth, sucking in the squirming tentacles. Juna smiled at the sight.

They finished breakfast in companionable stillness. Then Anito sent Juna and Moki off, instructing them to enjoy themselves for the rest of the day.

"Tomorrow the hard work begins. We have to process all of the seaweed that the lyali-Tendu harvest for us."

Juna and Moki spent the morning exploring the small, rocky island. They sat in the trees and watched the mating Tendu leap and dive, explored the sea caves where the sea Tendu stored their trade goods, and went swimming in a freshwater inland pool.

In the afternoon, Juna recorded some of the endemic island wildlife and updated her linguistic and ecological notes. There was so much to write about. The two or three free hours she had each day were not enough to adequately document everything. Now she was going to have to help dry seaweed. She sighed, wishing there were more hours in the day.

"What's wrong?" Moki asked.

"Nothing. There's just so much to do, and never enough time to get it all done."

"Let me help," Moki offered.

Juna shook her head, brushing her knuckles affectionately across his shoulder. "Thank you, Moki, but there's nothing more you can do. I have to teach these talking rocks so that they can remember what I learn and tell it to my people."

"Show me how to teach them. I'll help you," Moki said, blazing with eagerness.

Juna shook her head, thinking of the Contact Protocols. "There's so much to learn. It could take years."

"But I'll be your bami for many years. Teach me," he urged "You need help. The Tendu need help. Teach me. I am your bami. I learn from you and help both our people."

Juna stared at Moki. Time and again he surprised her with the depth of his understanding. Her bami was not a child. Furthermore, he was right. The Tendu were facing a major change, and they needed all the help they could get. Moki could be extremely useful as a translator. Still, it would involve a further breach of protocol, but— She looked at Moki. She had already broken and bent so many of the rules, adopting him. What would one more matter?

"All right, Moki. I'll teach you."

Moki sat in front of her, ears wide and ready to learn. Juna realized that she didn't know where to start.

"We'll start tomorrow. I need to think about *how* to teach you."

Moki nodded, and took her hand. Juna wadded up her computer, and the two of them went swimming.

The next day, the sea Tendu began hauling nets full of seaweed up to the beach. The land Tendu washed the seaweed first in salt water, then fresh water. Then they ground the seaweed coarsely between two flat rocks and tossed it into a pool of fresh water. They screened the ground seaweed out of the pool with special sieves that left a paperlike sheet of seaweed behind. The damp sheets were laid out on drying racks made from raft poles and mats. It was a long, laborious process, interrupted by frequent afternoon rains. When rain threatened, the villagers gathered the drying sheets of seaweed and carried them into the sea caves. As soon as the weather cleared, they brought the seaweed back out again.

Moki sat with Juna during the mid-afternoon break. While the rain poured down around them, Juna tried to teach him Standard. It quickly became apparent that Moki couldn't make most of the necessary sounds. Juna wiped the rain from her face and climbed out to the end of the branch, staring out at the steady hard drizzle.

"It's no use, Moki. It's just not possible. I can't teach you my language. Your mouth won't make the right sounds."

"You show me words," Moki insisted. "I learn."

"I've been trying, Moki," Juna said. "It doesn't work."

"I see you look at words on your talking stone. Show me those words. I learn them."

"Reading," Juna said aloud. "Of course!"

"All right, Moki," she said in skin speech. "Make this shape."

Moki learned the alphabet before the rain stopped. As they carried out the mats of drying seaweed, he practiced making the letters over and over again. The other bami stopped and stared at him in puzzlement.

"I'm learning new-creature talk," he told them proudly.

"What does it mean?" one of them asked. It was Pani, one of the youngest bami in the village.

"I don't know," he admitted.

"How can you learn something if you don't know what it means?" Pani wondered.

"I'm just beginning," Moki said. "Eerin will teach me more tomorrow."

The next day, several bami sat and watched Juna's lessons with Moki. Today she was teaching him numbers. He quickly grasped numbers, and simple addition and subtraction, though he had trouble with the base 10 numerical system used by ten-fingered humans instead of the Tendu's eight-fingered counting. The bami looking on learned almost as quickly. When the lesson was over, they ran off, numbers coursing over their bodies like moving tattoos. Eerin smiled at them as she returned to work.

The next day Ukatonen watched as she began showing Moki and the other bami how to take letters and combine them into words.

"What are you teaching them?" Ukatonen asked, after she sent her pupils back to work.

"I'm teaching them the skin speech of the new creatures."

"But you don't have skin speech," Ukatonen said. "I thought you talked with your voice."

"We have a way of putting our words down so that we can

see them. Moki wanted to learn how to speak like a new creature. He can't learn to talk the way we talk, with sounds, but he can learn this. He wanted to learn, so I am teaching him."

"Anito and I should learn this too. Will you teach us?"

So Ukatonen and Anito joined the lessons as well. Then other elders joined. Soon all the Narmolom villagers began flashing simple phrases in written Standard back and forth at each other.

At first Juna became concerned that her teaching might be harmful to the aliens. Then she realized that it was a game for the Tendu. They were delighted by the shapes of the letters, and the alien grammar. Even the lyali-Tendu came up out of the ocean and sat on the beach, learning written Standard from the villagers. By the time the seaweed harvest was completed, a full-blown pidgin of Tendu skin speech and written Standard was developing. The lyali-Tendu leaped and swam alongside the rafts on the journey back to the coast, their skin a brilliant jumble of letters, words, and phrases, chosen for the Tendu's delight in their appearance rather than their meaning.

They reached the coast, landing their rafts on a shelving beach in a calm bay. The lyali-Tendu waddled ashore and bid the village a formal farewell. Then they slipped into the water, and towed the rafts back to their island. The lyali-Tendu who were not busy towing rafts leaped high. Brilliant, distorted letters appeared on their chests, like something out of a typographer's nightmare.

"Goodbye!" "Farewell!" "Eat fish" "Jump high" appeared on the sea Tendu's bodies in a sudden burst of coherence. Then the letters became abstract word-salad again.

Juna waved farewell to them, saying goodbye in both skin speech and written Standard. The lyali-Tendu disappeared beneath the waves, the empty rafts moving like a ghost fleet through the gloom of a gathering rainstorm.

Anito hefted her pack onto her shoulders, tying the waist straps that kept her pack from slipping off her back as they climbed. Juna picked up her own pack. Heaving it onto her shoulders, she followed the villagers into the familiar gloom of the jungle.

Eighteen

THE BRANCHES OF the giant na tree seemed to stretch out in welcome. They were home. Anito flushed turquoise with happiness as she swung across the final gap onto the branches of Narmolom's home tree. It was good to be back, good to empty her heavy pack into a storeroom. Her happiness faded as she surveyed her new room. It looked terrible. The floor and walls were coated with black mud from flood season.

"Look at this mess!" Eerin said.

Anito flickered agreement. "We'll just have to clean it up," she said, pale with weariness. She was tired. It had been a hard trip with a heavy load, and they had been in a hurry to get home. She wanted a big meal and a long sleep in a fresh bed of leaves.

Ninto stuck her head in the room. "What a mess!" she said. "Stay with me tonight. My room wasn't flooded. You can clean this up tomorrow, when you're rested."

"But we've imposed too much on you already!" Anito protested.

"Well, if you feel bad, you can go catch us some dinner," Ninto remarked with a ripple of amusement.

"All right," Anito agreed. "Eerin, you and Moki go pick some fruit, and gather leaves for bedding. I'll go hunting and get some fresh honeycomb from one of my na trees."

Anito paused in the doorway watching Moki and Eerin as they left, taking in the familiar shape of the village tree. The flood waters had climbed almost a third of the way up the trunk, leaving everything in their wake covered with mud. As the bami of a chief elder, she had lived high enough up in the tree that their rooms were never flooded.

"It's good to be back," Ninto said as she came up beside Anito to look out at the tree trunk.

Anito touched her tareena's arm affectionately, her worries about housekeeping forgotten. "Yes it is," she agreed. "It certainly is."

That night Anito lay awake in her fresh nest of leaves listening to the tree creak as it shifted in the gentle night breeze. There was the quiet hum of the tilan bees, fanning the cool night air through their hives and into the hollow heart of the great tree. She took a deep breath, savoring the familiar smells of home: ancient wood, mud, glow-fungus, a faint hint of honey, and the green, moist smell of fresh bedding. A ripple of pleasure flowed across her skin as she slipped into sleep. She was home.

Juna tied a rope to a basket full of dripping, smelly mud and tugged on it, signaling to the villagers at the top of the tree that it was ready to haul up. She watched for a moment as the basket rose into the air, then squelched through the mud at the bottom of the tree to fill another basket.

It was spring-cleaning time in Narmolom. The villagers cleaned their rooms, drained the reservoir at the bottom of the tree, and were busy hauling out the accumulated mud and refuse from the reservoir. It was hot, stinking work, but Juna felt strangely happy. She hefted another basket of mud and looked up. The massive trunk of the na tree rose around her, tier on tier of balconies dimming into the distance. From here, the opening of the trunk was a bright spot just a little bigger than her outspread hand. Baskets rose and fell as the villagers pulled them up, or lowered them to be filled again. The tree was alive with the sounds of hard work. Even the brilliant tilan bees buzzed about with extra urgency as they foraged in the rich muck.

Yesterday Anito had put a few drops of something from her allu-a into a gourd full of water. They sprinkled it on the floors, walls, and ceiling, and the room began to fill with bees. By the time the gourd was empty, the room was covered with a seething mass of insects. When they returned an hour later with armloads of fresh bedding, the room was immaculate. The floors gleamed like fine furniture, and the fungus on the walls glowed brightly. Juna smiled, remembering a fairy tale from her childhood about a princess tended by invisible servants. Life among the Tendu had its rewards.

A long, low roll of thunder and a pattering of rain on the muck roused her from her reverie. She carried her basket over to a dangling rope, tied it on, and tugged at the rope. It remained slack. She peered up and saw that the workers were coming down. They would be stopping to avoid the thunderstorm. The rains came less frequently now. The dry season was beginning. This storm was the first in three days. She climbed up to the top of the tree, and let the rain wash the muck from her skin. Moki and Ukatonen joined her. They had been carrying baskets of compost out to the platforms in the canopy that supported the village's dry season tree farms.

"They're just getting ripe," Moki said as he handed her a couple of spicy-sweet ati fruit and a gourd of water.

Juna flickered her thanks.

Another roll of thunder sounded, and a stiff breeze made the tree sway.

"We should go inside," Ukatonen said. "This is going to be a big storm. They usually are after a dry spell like this."

Juna smiled. Even after eight Standard months among the Tendu she still found it odd to think of three days of pleasant weather as a dry spell. They swung down into the trunk of the tree. Juna looked around her as she climbed. She had spent six months among the Tendu, most of that on the move. She was tired of traveling. It was good to be home.

Anito was waiting for them with a leaf-plate of honeycomb and a bowl of sliced meat marinated in a tart, salted fruit juice. After dinner, Anito took out a half finished basket, and Ukatonen began gluing tufts of down onto a handful of blowgun darts.

Juna held out her arms to Moki, and the two of them linked. She was getting better at allu-a. She could now control many previously involuntary reactions like pupil dilation, heartbeat, and her blood pressure. She could read many simple body functions in others, and was beginning to learn to monitor another person's link.

She entered into the link. Her fear and lack of control was a thing of the past. She had learned to put up barriers to slow the flood of sensation, learned to cope with the fluid medium of allu-a and enjoy it. Now she looked forward to linking as much as Moki did. Moki's body felt almost as familiar as her own. Sometimes she worried about what would happen when the humans came back. What would they think of her now, swinging through the trees, eating raw meat, engaging in strange practices with the aliens? Would they think that she had "gone native"?

Moki sensed her anxiety, and enfolded her with reassurance. Juna let her worries slide. Let tomorrow take care of tomorrow. She was too busy living through today. She let herself float in the communion of the link.

"It's time for me to choose a new chief elder," Ukatonen said. "Who do you think it should it be?"

Anito's ears spread in surprise. Why was he asking her? It was his decision.

"You know the village better than I do," Ukatonen went on, before Anito could think of a reply. "I want to know what you think."

Anito ducked her chin in thought. It was a difficult question. Only ten elders had enough seniority for serious consideration. Yiato and two others refused to be considered. Telito and Johito were clearly unfit for the job. One was too shy, the other too involved with her atwa to be impartial.

"There are only five worth considering, en." She ticked them off on her fingers. "Marito, Enato, Miato, Renito, and Ninto."

"Not Enato," Ukatonen said. "He can't make decisions, and Marito's too young. She needs another five years before she'd be ready."

"That leaves three. Miato, Renito, and Ninto," Anito said.

"They're all qualified, but which one's best?"

"Renito's the oldest," Anito said, "but her bami, Kina, is nearly as old as I am. If we pick Renito, Kina will have to wait even longer before he can become an elder."

"And Kina's male. Narmolom needs more male elders. That leaves Miato and Ninto. Which one would you pick?"

"Ninto is my tareena. I can't pick fairly."

"But you will be an enkar someday, kene. You must learn to decide things like this. Tell me what you know about Ninto and Miato."

"They're both about the same age, en. Miato's sitik was almost picked for chief elder, and Miato is on the village council. My sitik thought highly of Miato, en. He usually took Miato's advice. He's known for his fairness and wisdom. I would trust him to make good decisions."

"And Ninto?"

"Ninto was raised by Ilto. He relied on her counsel a lot. She understands people very well, and often can see a problem before it starts. You've seen how much she has helped me with Eerin. She's really interested in the new creature. She's wise, observant, and good with people. Ninto and Miato would both be good chief elders, en. It would be hard to decide between the two. I know I can't."

A greyish-yellow mist passed over Ukatonen's skin. "I know, kene. That is my problem as well. I must decide between the two of them." A ripple of ironic amusement crossed his skin. "I had hoped that your advice would help. I guess I'll just have to talk to Ninto and Miato."

They found Ninto first. She was in her room, busy making rope. She set her work aside as they came in, and offered them some fruit juice.

"Kene, I wanted to talk with you about what you would do if you became chief elder."

Ninto's ears spread wide and she turned pink in surprise. She looked from Ukatonen to Anito and back again. "Why are you considering me? There are older, more experienced elders to choose from."

"Because I think you're qualified," Ukatonen told her. "Do you want to be chief elder?"

Anito saw shadows of indecision pass over Ninto.

"It would be an honor to follow in the footsteps of my sitik, en. I love Narmolom greatly but—"

"But what?"

"Is it true that you will be taking Anito with you to become an enkar?"

"Yes, kene, I must. She needs the training and status of an enkar in order to deal with the new creatures when they return."

"Then I will go with her and become an enkar. I withdraw my name from consideration for chief elder. I would have withdrawn it earlier, had I known you were considering me."

"No!" Anito protested. "Ninto, you mustn't. Please don't leave Narmolom because of me."

A ripple of fond amusement flowed across Ninto's body. "It's my life, Anito. I want to go with you and learn about the new creatures." She looked at Ukatonen. "You need more people who are familiar with the new creatures. I know Eerin better than anyone in the village except for Anito."

"But what about Narmolom?" Anito asked. "What about Baha?"

"Baha is ready to become an elder, and he can take over my atwa. I'll miss Narmolom, but without you, without our sitik, it's an empty place for me. Ukatonen and Eerin have shown me that there is more to life than Narmolom. It's time to move on, if the enkar will accept me."

"They'll be pleased," Ukatonen said. "We need more elders like you."

"Who else were you considering for chief elder?" Ninto asked.

"Miato."

"He's a good choice. Narmolom will be well cared for."

"Thank you," Ukatonen said. "Ninto, I want you to understand that you haven't committed yourself to becoming an enkar yet. If you want to change your mind, you can."

Ninto shook her head. "I've decided."

Ukatonen flickered acknowledgment and thanks. "I need to tell Miato that he is my choice for chief."

After the usual arguments and protestations about not being qualified, Miato agreed to become chief elder. The villagers were surprised but pleased with Ukatonen's choice. The skill and speed with which Miato had grown back his missing foot had impressed them. They were also surprised by Ukatonen's fee. Instead of requesting that one of the villagers become an enkar, which was customary, he asked that the next five bami chosen to become elders should be male, and that the next seven tinka chosen as bami should also be male.

There were flickers of subdued protest from the males. They were in such high demand during mating that the female villagers gave them many fine gifts for their favors. The females, however, looked pleased.

The banquet celebrating Miato's selection as chief elder was exceptionally lavish. Grateful villagers presented Ukatonen with preserved delicacies and other gifts, which he graciously accepted. The villagers performed a quarbirri telling the history of Narmolom. To Anito's surprise, the last act told of Ilto's discovery of the new creature, and Ilto's death, a new chapter added to the official history of the village. The part of Ilto was danced by Ninto. Ukatonen played the part of the new creature, to the villagers' intense amusement. He performed the part very well, although he'd only had a day to practice. Even Eerin understood what Ukatonen was doing, and rippled laughter along with the rest of the village. She joined the rest of the village in wild ripples of appreciation at the end of the performance.

At last the party broke up and Anito headed back to her room, leaving Eerin and Moki to help clean up the remains of the banquet. Ukatonen was there, loading his pack.

"You're going?" Anito asked when he looked up.

He flickered acknowledgment.

"But— Why?"

"I've been here a long time. You've got a new chief elder now. If I stay, I'll only get in his way."

"Where will you go?"

"I'll visit some of the neighboring villages, then spend some time talking to the other enkar. They need to know about Eerin."

"But you'll be all alone!" Anito said.

A shrug flickered across Ukatonen's chest. "I'm an enkar.

I'm used to it." He thrust a few more things in his pack and tied it shut.

"I'm leaving the gifts that I can't carry with me," he said. "Will you keep them for me until I return?"

Anito flickered agreement, fighting back a mist of sadness. "When will you be back?"

He shouldered his pack. "Look for me near the end of Menano." He peered out the door. "Good, almost everyone is asleep. I wanted to leave quietly." He stepped out on the balcony. "Come with me to the top of the tree, kene?" he asked.

Anito flickered acknowledgment and followed him up the trunk. They came out into the cool, misty darkness. Eerin and Moki were busy supervising the tinka as they bundled up the food-soiled leaves left over from the banquet. They glanced up as Anito and Ukatonen emerged from the trunk. Moki's ears lifted when he saw the enkar's pack.

"I came to say goodbye," Ukatonen told them.

"You're leaving?" Eerin and Moki asked almost simultaneously, the brilliant pink flare of their surprise fading to grey sadness.

"Why?" Eerin asked.

"Because it's time," Ukatonen said. "But I'll be back in a couple of months."

"But how will I manage Moki on my own?" Eerin asked.

"You and Moki are good for each other. You don't need me to interfere. If you need help, there's Anito and a whole village of Tendu to give you advice."

Moki was the color of wet clay. He touched Ukatonen on the leg. Ukatonen knelt. "Will you take care of Eerin for me?"

Moki nodded, his grey fading. "Yes, en."

"That's good," he told him. "I'm sure you'll do very well."

Moki's skin turned azure with pride, though a faint misting of sadness still overlaid it. Ukatonen brushed his knuckles across the bami's shoulder affectionately. Then he stood, and did the same to Eerin.

"Take care of Moki."

Eerin nodded and brushed his shoulder back, her eyes watering.

Then he touched Anito on the shoulder. Anito felt a great

wave of fondness sweep over her. "I'll miss you," she said in small, private patterns.

"I'll miss you too," he said. "Take care of yourself while I'm gone."

Then he turned and swung off through the trees.

Anito looked at the others, deep grey with sadness as she was herself. She touched the other two on the shoulder. "Let's go," she said. "It's late. We should get some sleep."

N i n e t e e n

THE NEXT THREE months passed quietly. Juna got caught up on her research, documenting dozens of new species and filling in many linguistic details. Every day brought new discoveries. It was a busy and productive time.

Moki learned to read and type with surprising speed, and soon began entering data on her spare computer. Although Moki's written Standard was still rough and ungrammatical, he had an excellent eye for detail, often describing features of a plant or animal that Juna missed. She began having him check over her descriptions before entering them in the catalogue.

Anito settled into village life, filling the role of junior elder, which involved doing the work scorned by more senior elders. Since she had been the bami of a chief, much of it was familiar. Juna helped out by gathering fruit, harvesting honey from Anito's na trees, and netting fish out of the shrinking pools left behind by the floods.

Ukatonen returned about three days before the end of the month of Menano. The villagers clustered around him in eager welcome. He greeted them with his usual dignified reserve, graciously accepting Miato's offer of hospitality and a feast in his quarters. He greeted Anito, Moki, and Eerin with the same formal reserve as the other villagers. Anito was sent off to organize the banquet. She took Eerin, Moki, and several tinka with her to gather food and supplies.

They came back with full gathering bags. Anito set the tinka to laying out the leaf-plates and cleaning the serving dishes. Eerin and Moki helped prepare and arrange the food. Set out before the waiting elders, it was a magnificent feast.

Miato eyed it critically. "I'm sorry that we have nothing better to offer you than this, en," he said in formal patterns. "Please do us the honor of accepting this meager meal."

Ilto had used the same polite formula with honored guests, Anito recalled. She still missed her sitik terribly.

Ukatonen looked up at Anito, his expression carefully neutral. "Thank you, kene," he said to Miato. "It will do."

The ritual formulas of politeness completed, the elders commenced eating. Anito stood by, motioning to the tinka when a dish needed to be replenished or carried away.

At last the elders sat back and belched politely.

"I'm sorry that we don't have more food to offer you, en," Miato said, as though the leaf plates around them weren't still half full.

"It's all right," Ukatonen replied, as though his stomach didn't form a visible bulge in his long, lean body. "I shouldn't burden you with my hunger, kene; not when I've come to ask a favor of you and your village."

"Narmolom is in your debt, en, after all you've done for us. If there is anything at all we can do for you, we will."

Anito repressed a flicker of amusement. It was clear that Miato had not been chief elder for very long. Her sitik would never have made such a blanket promise, especially not to an enkar.

"I would like to take Anito, Eerin, and Moki away with me for a month to a month and a half."

"She will miss our mating," Miato pointed out.

"She mated with the lyali-Tendu. I will bring her back in time to lay her eggs, so that Narmolom will not be deprived of her narey. It's important, or I wouldn't ask. The other enkar want to see the new creature and talk to Anito about Eerin."

Miato was still for a moment, his chin ducked, as though he

were pondering a decision that everyone in the room knew had already been made.

"When will you be going?"

"Tomorrow, if you will permit it, kene."

Miato flickered agreement.

"Thank you, kene," Ukatonen said. "The enkar are in debt to you for your sacrifice."

The talk turned to trivialities. Ukatonen asked about the villagers, displaying a deep knowledge of things that had happened in his absence. The other villagers were very impressed, but Anito knew that Ukatonen would have spent the last few days spying on the village.

Anito motioned to the tinka to clear away the food. When the feast dishes were cleaned and put away, she climbed down the trunk, slid into her warm, moist bed, and fell asleep instantly.

Ukatonen woke Juna and Moki early the next morning. Juna sat up groggily.

"What is it?" she said, yawning.

"Start packing, we're going on a trip. The enkar want to see you."

Juna looked over at Anito, still sleeping in her bed of leaves.

"Let her sleep," Ukatonen said. "She was up very late last night."

They filled traveling packs with the gifts the villagers had given Ukatonen. When they were done, Moki laid out a quick breakfast of fruit and honeycomb and woke Anito.

The villagers escorted them out of the tree and followed them with farewells until they reached the border of Narmo-lom's territory. Ninto was the last to see them off. She touched Anito on the shoulder.

"Have a safe journey," Ninto said. "Come back soon."

Juna saw Anito return Ninto's affectionate touch. "I will," she said, and turned to go.

They went north and inland, toward the distant green-shouldered mountains. After a week of hard traveling, they crossed the low range of ancient, rounded mountains and the jungle around them changed. The trees were taller and wider than what Juna was used to. The canopy was denser, the branches thick with epiphytes, and heavy with fruit.

"This is the forest of the enkar," Ukatonen said when Juna remarked on the change. "Typhoons don't come in this far. They're deflected by those mountains we crossed."

"It's like village land, only more so," Anito said.

"We gather seed from the strongest and most fruitful trees from villages up and down the coast," Ukatonen told them. "We've spent thousands of generations selecting and improving them. Guano from the lyali-Tendu, and greenstone from the mountain people make the land fertile. The enkar carry it in from all over. We have to support more people on less land than the villagers do, and we can't shift our boundaries when the forest wears out the way you na-Tendu can."

"But I thought the enkar traveled alone," Anito said in surprise.

"We do, but sometimes we need a place to rest and take counsel with other enkar. We come here, or to one of our other valleys up and down the coast, to rest, to learn, and to train new enkar." Ukatonen paused, then said, "You wait here. I'll let the others know that we've arrived."

He climbed to the top of the tree, and let out a deep, booming call. After listening for a moment, he repeated it. In the distance, they heard a reply. Ukatonen responded.

Half an hour later, four enkar came swinging through the trees. They greeted Ukatonen with affectionate shoulder brushings and embraces.

"Anito, Eerin, Moki," Ukatonen said, "these are Opantonen, Besatonen, Garitonen, and Hutatonen."

Each enkar lifted his chin in acknowledgment. They were taller than the village Tendu, with long, solemn muzzles. They moved with the same easy grace as Ukatonen. Even if Juna had known nothing at all about the Tendu, it would have been obvious that these four and Ukatonen were somehow related.

Their tall, elegant guides led them through the leafy, sun-dappled cathedral of the forest until they came to a circle of six immense na trees. They followed the guides to a low mound in the center of the circle of trees. Hutatonen let out a loud, booming call, and dozens of Tendu appeared, climbing down the trees or walking from out of the understory that moments before seemed completely empty.

The enkar gathered around the mound, waiting expectantly.

Anito touched Ukatonen's arm. "Are they all enkar?" she asked in tiny, awestruck patterns.

Ukatonen rippled quiet amusement. "Yes, they are."

"I've never seen so many Tendu in one place before," Anito said.

"This is only one group. There are others scattered throughout the Tendu lands."

"How many enkar are there?" Juna inquired.

"Less than there once were," Ukatonen replied. "Most of these trees are half-empty."

Hutatonen touched Ukatonen on the arm and motioned for him to speak.

He stepped to the top of the speaker's mound. "Many of you know me. I am Ukatonen, of the Three Rivers Council. I was headed to Lyanan on the coast, when I met Anito of Narmolom, with this new creature, who is called Eerin, also heading for Lyanan."

Ukatonen called Anito forward to tell the enkar about her discovery of the new creature, and how her sitik had transformed it. Ukatonen stepped in and talked about his judgment for the elders of Lyanan, and his judgment to allow Juna to adopt Moki. Then he called Juna forward.

Juna stood on the mound, with the intent, impassive eyes of the enkar watching her, their ears spread wide with curiosity. Her stomach was heavy with nervousness. She didn't entirely understand the role the enkar played in Tendu society, but she knew they were important. She swallowed, her throat dry despite the humidity.

"I greet you for my people," she said in the most formal patterns she could manage. "We come seeking friendship and knowledge. Our destruction of the forest near Lyanan was a mistake. My people will do what they can to heal the damage. The Tendu have shown me great kindness and patience, and I am extremely grateful. Thank you."

She stepped back behind Ukatonen, who gestured to Hutatonen, and they stepped from the speaker's mound. Juna expected the enkar to mill around her like the other villagers, but instead they treated her with polite but remote curiosity. Moki clung to her hand, subdued by the presence of so many enkar. Anito also seemed out of her depth. They followed Ukatonen through the crowd, pausing as he stopped to greet old friends and to exchange news from distant gatherings and councils of enkar.

At last someone took charge of the visitors and led them to an empty room near the top of one of the trees. Anito and Moki shrugged off their packs and slumped against the wall, worn out by all the excitement.

"You two rest here. Eerin and I will go and get food, water, and bedding," Ukatonen told them.

Juna followed him down to a storeroom, where they found some empty water gourds and rolled-up floor mats. They left the mats by the door for Anito and Moki to arrange, and went out to gather bedding. It was startlingly menial labor for an elder of a highly respected social caste.

"Don't the tinka and bami usually do this sort of thing?" Juna asked.

"We don't have tinka," Ukatonen said. "When one comes to us, we send it over the hills to one of the na-Tendu villages."

"Why?"

"It is very rare for us to adopt a bami. It wouldn't be right to have tinka here, where they wouldn't be adopted. We don't mate here."

"You don't?" Juna said, surprised. "But I saw you mate with the sea people."

"We breed elsewhere; with the sea people, or out among the villages. Not here. This isn't a village, merely a gathering place for the enkar. Most of us stay a while and then move on."

"It sounds lonely," Juna observed, beginning to understand some of the villagers' dread of becoming enkar.

"We avoid forming bonds with others. It impairs our ability to render judgment. It can be a difficult discipline," Ukatonen admitted.

"What about Anito? She doesn't seem to be very happy about the idea of becoming an enkar."

A sad grey mist clouded Ukatonen's skin. "It is her fate to

become an enkar. I wish she could stay with her village and become the wise elder that she shows such great promise of being, but the enkar need her now."

"Why?"

"Because of you," he told her. "No one among us knows you as well as she does."

"But what about you? You know me almost as well."

"I am not enough," Ukatonen said. "Anito isn't enough. Even Moki, who will surely understand you better than any of us, won't be enough. That is why we are here, among the enkar, where no villager usually comes. The enkar need to know you, Eerin. We need to know you, and through you, your people. I have seen only a few of the things that your people can do, and it is enough to make me realize your power. I watch you with your talking stone, and my blood turns to water in fear."

"I'm sorry," Juna said. "I don't want you to be afraid. How can I reassure you?"

"You can't. You shouldn't. I need to see you as you are."

"I want you to be my friend," Juna told him.

"I am an enkar, Eerin. I am no one's friend." Ukatonen handed her a pair of water gourds. "Let's go, we have work to do."

Anito helped Moki unroll the mats. This amazing, fertile, ancient forest, peopled only by enkar, terrified her. It was so different from village life, cold somehow, and sterile. There were no bami, no tinka, none of the ordinary bustle and routine of village life. The forest was too well-managed, too tame. It went beyond harmony into perfection, and it grated on her. She longed for the familiar chaos of Narmolom, where they strove to keep their forests as close to the balance of the wild lands as possible while still supporting their village.

Here, with so many living so densely, useless plants and destructive animals had to be weeded out. Anito understood that, but she hated it nonetheless. If this was her future, she wasn't sure that she wanted it. She understood now why Ilto had chosen death rather than exile.

There was a rustling and a hesitant, interrogative chirp at the door. Anito looked up. An enkar was standing outside with an armload of bedding. It was one of the four who had escorted them through the forest.

"I thought you might need some of this," he said. "And I also brought some water, in case you were thirsty."

"Thank you, en," she said.

"You're welcome. My name is Garitonen."

"I'm Anito."

"I know. I saw Ukatonen say that you were going to become his apprentice. I only finished my training last year."

"Was it hard?" Anito asked, wondering how he could stand to be so far away from home.

"It was at first. I missed my village all the time, and it was frightening being here with all these enkar; but the work is interesting. Once I started learning how the enkar do things, I stopped being scared and lonely. There's too much to learn, too much to do."

A ripple of amusement ran over Anito's skin as she remembered the way Ukatonen appeared to know everything about the village because he had watched it for several days. "I think I know what you mean," she said. "Are you lonely?"

"Sometimes," he admitted. He looked down at the floor for a moment, his skin faintly clouded with grey. "So tell me what the new creature is like."

"Eerin? She didn't know much at first. She couldn't talk and she could hardly even climb a tree. She learned quickly, though. She still can't hunt or weave baskets, but she's getting better."

"I heard about the digging race at Lyanan. Is it true that she wore out two of the village's strongest bami?"

"Yes, but she made herself sick doing it." Anito glanced away, ashamed. "It was my fault. I got angry when the villagers made fun of her, and I said she could dig faster than they could. It wasn't something I'm proud of."

"But it turned out well, and you learned something, didn't you?"

Anito flickered agreement.

"Then don't be ashamed of it. Ukatonen thinks very highly of you, you know. He taught me more about allu-a than I thought there was to learn. He's one of the best in the whole Three Rivers Council."

"I thought all enkar were like that," Anito said, recalling the smooth, subtle power of his presence.

"We are better at linking than most villagers, but Ukatonen has made it his specialty." Garitonen held out his arms. "Link with me?"

Anito could feel Ukatonen's influence as soon as she entered the link. Garitonen had Ukatonen's power and his deftness of touch, though he lacked Ukatonen's utter surety. There was a sense of contentment, of happiness, even mischievousness, that Ukatonen lacked. Feeling it, Anito realized how long Ukatonen had lived, and how lonely he felt.

"He needs you, you know," Garitonen said when they emerged from the link. "When he came through a month and a half ago, he was less restless than I've ever seen him. You and the new creature you call Eerin have given him something to keep him occupied. Eerin is new and different, and you're young and eager to learn. It's a potent combination."

Anito looked away, embarrassed and moved by the compliment. "Thank you," she said at last, looking back at Garitonen. "I've learned a lot from Ukatonen."

"I know," Garitonen said. "I could feel that when we linked."

There was a clicking sound from the corner. Moki had taken out a talking stone and was playing with it.

"What's he doing?" Garitonen asked.

"That's one of Eerin's talking stones. She's shown Moki how to play with it."

"But what's it *for*?"

"Eerin says that she keeps her memories on it, so that she can tell her people what happened without forgetting anything."

Garitonen squatted next to Moki.

"What are you doing?" he asked when the bami looked up.

"I'm telling the talking stone about the enkar."

"How does it work?"

Moki tilted the talking surface so that the enkar could see what he was working on.

"What is that?" Garitonen asked, pointing at the screen.

"It's the new creature's skin speech."

"I thought they couldn't speak skin speech."

"They don't. They paint it on things instead, or they store it in talking stones like this one. Eerin told me that they use something like sheets of yarram, only white, to speak on."

"What's the point to that?" Garitonen said. "They'd only get in the way and rot."

"Eerin says that they don't rot, and that they tie the sheets together so they don't get in the way. Most of their really important skin speech is put on these talking stones anyway. Also the talking stones can talk to each other over very long distances, so lots of people can see the same words."

Garitonen ducked his chin and ran a hand over his scalp. "It seems very strange to me."

Moki nodded, and flickered agreement. "It is, but it makes more sense when you can understand their skin speech. They have a lot of different kinds of stones: some that talk, some that move things, some that cut time up into little pieces, and some that make noises. They have different names for all of the different kinds of stones, but I don't understand what most of the stones do. This one is called a *computer*," Moki said, using the new creature's skin-speech term for her talking stone.

"Can you teach me the new creatures' skin-speech?" Garitonen asked.

"Of course, en. It's very easy. Everything's made up of a group of the same basic shapes. Anito knows a little of it and so does Ukatonen, but I work with it every day, so I know it very well. If you ask Eerin, she will probably teach it to you herself."

"I will, thanks," Garitonen said.

Ukatonen and Eerin returned bearing net bags crammed with fresh leaf-bedding. "Hello, Gari," Ukatonen said as they came in. "Garitonen was my student for a while," he explained to Anito. "I helped him learn more about allu-a."

"I know. He has your touch in the link, en. Even if he hadn't told me about being your student, I would have known."

Both Garitonen and Ukatonen glanced away, glowing with embarrassed pride. Ukatonen picked up a bundle of bedding and carried it over to the mats spread on the floor. Moki started showing Eerin how to shred the leaves. In Narmolom, the tinka usually performed this task; here, it was left to them.

The others settled down and helped shred leaves for the bedding, carefully pulling out any twigs and undesirable foreign matter. Drawn by the smell of torn leaves, a line of small insects emerged from the walls. They explored the steadily growing pile, emerging with choice bits of leaf matter and small insects, and laying down chemicals and bacteria which encouraged decomposition. They were called yerowe. They lived in every village tree, and kept the bedding fresh and free of unpleasant insects.

A couple of other enkar came in with some more food and water. The enkar took over the bedmaking while the visitors ate. Uncomfortable, Anito looked questioningly at Ukatonen.

"It's all right, Anito. You're our guests. We're not as formal and worried about rank as they are in the villages. There's no one else to do the work here except the enkar."

The patter and hiss of the afternoon rain falling into the center of the tree could be heard as they finished making up the beds. The pressure of the falling water sent a moist, refreshing breeze through the room. The enkar began romping in the column of falling water. Ukatonen and Garitonen went outside to frolic with them. Anito stood in the doorway and watched, amazed at the sight of these dignified, ancient elders playing like bami in the rain. After a moment's hesitation, Eerin and Moki joined them. Anito hesitated, unsure whether they were being rude, but Garitonen swung past and splashed her.

"Don't just stand there!" he said. "Come play!"

Anito swung into the column of water, letting it wash her clean. Ukatonen leapt onto the vine that Anito was clinging to, rippling brilliant laughter. She splashed him, and he laughed again and splashed her back. Soon she forgot her dignity, her fears, and her position as an elder of Narmolom, and played the way she had as a bami.

There was a feast that evening, out on the leafy forest floor within the circle of trees. It was extremely informal; everyone brought baskets of food which were placed in a circle around the speaker's mound. There was no rank or precedence order;

the enkar and their guests served themselves and sat wherever they wanted.

Eerin and Moki were the focus of a large interested group, as were Anito and Ukatonen. Everyone was eager to learn as much as they could about Eerin and the new creatures, but to most of their questions, Anito had no answers. She didn't know how the talking stone worked, or how the new creatures lived on their world, or even what they ate. Eerin's altered metabolism let her digest Tendu food. She ate almost everything they did, although she disliked eating grubs and insects. Listening to their questions, Anito realized how much she still had to learn about her atwa.

The enkar finished eating and cleared away the remains of the feast. Hutatonen stood on top of the speaker's mound and chittered to get everyone's attention. Then he held out his arms, requesting a link.

The others joined hands. Anito turned to Eerin, ears raised inquisitively. After a moment's hesitation, Eerin nodded, and clasped hands. Ukatonen colored in approval and encouragement, and took Anito's other hand. Together, they plunged into the link.

It was like no allu-a Anito had ever been in. Once, as a bami, she had a pet snake. She remembered the strength of its body, coiling around her arm. The enkar reminded her of that, a sensation of immense power, held in check. The enkar's presences nosed at her like curious fish. She opened herself to them, and their presences flowed through her like a strong wind. She wove herself into their powerful harmony, feeling her own strength grow as the others buoyed her up and carried her along.

Eerin was too frightened by the power of the link to let herself relax. Anito enfolded her, giving her a chance to adjust.

The enkar, sensing trouble, drew back. The link calmed, changing from a maelstrom of excitement to a quiet pool of immense depth and clarity. The enkar waited while Eerin relaxed and, slowly as a flower, opened herself to the link.

It was late when they emerged from the link. Eerin seemed pale and tired. Moki and Ukatonen fed her a little leftover fruit and helped her up the tree. She seemed to recover a bit as they climbed. Garitonen hovered anxiously until they reached their room.

"Is she going to be all right?" he asked Anito. "Is there anything I can do to help?"

Anito shook her head. "She needs some privacy and a good night's sleep. Linking is hard for her."

"Good night, then," Garitonen said.

They stayed with this group of enkar for another three or four days, then moved on to another gathering of enkar. Garitonen and Hutatonen went with them. Moki and Eerin began teaching them the new creatures' skin speech.

They visited four enkar gatherings. Other enkar joined them as they traveled. By the time they headed back to Narmolom, there were over two dozen enkar traveling with them. It was like being part of a small floating village. They parted company with their escort a day outside the boundaries of Narmolom. As the last of the enkar vanished into the thick foliage of the canopy, Anito felt a pang of sadness. She would miss the enkar's gentle humor and deep wisdom.

"Now that you've spent some time among us, how do you feel about becoming an enkar?" Ukatonen asked as they wove branches into a nest for the night.

"I know now that the villagers see only a small part of what it is to be an enkar. It's very interesting, but—" Anito rippled a shrug. "If I had a choice, I would stay in Narmolom," she said after a long, thoughtful stillness. "But it won't be such a bad life. I like the enkar."

"I missed my village at first, but the work is interesting," Ukatonen told her. "It keeps me involved in the world. There are so many older village elders who can't see beyond the boundaries of their own village. It makes me glad of the choice I made. As an enkar, I see everything. Every village is different. I've lived up in the mists with the mountain people, and in the sea with the lyali-Tendu. I'm never bored. Lonely sometimes, but never bored."

Anito squeezed Ukatonen's shoulder, and held out her wrists for allu-a. "Please, en, let me help with the loneliness."

A ripple of gentle fondness flowed over Ukatonen's body. "You already have, kene."

Twenty

JUNA SLID ALONG the branch toward the ooloo, adjusting her skin coloration to match the changing shadow patterns. Her nostrils flared, taking in the lizards' musky, vaguely sweet scent. She had asked Anito and Ukatonen to improve her sense of smell. The world had acquired a new dimension as a result. Traces of other creatures clung to every surface of the forest like invisible footprints.

Preoccupied by a fight for dominance, the ooloo never noticed her gradual approach. The two largest males squawked at each other, neck ruffs extended. When Juna was close enough for a clear shot, she slowly slid her blowpipe up along her body, then extracted a poison-tipped dart from a bamboo container and stuffed it into the flared end of the pipe.

Bringing the loaded blowpipe up to her mouth, she considered her possible targets. At this distance, the dart would glance off the scales of the squabbling males. Of the four remaining lizards, two were females carrying young, and one was an immature male, half-screened by a leafy branch. Juna's best target was the fourth lizard, another young female, who sat facing her, engrossed in the fight between the males. Juna put the blowgun to her lips and took aim. The ooloo stretched out a foreleg to draw a fruit-laden branch close, exposing the soft, vulnerable skin of her chest. Juna puffed hard through the blowgun. The dart buried itself in the ooloo's underarm, exactly where she had aimed it. The ooloo jumped, whistling in alarm. It pulled out the dart and turned to follow the others as they fled through the trees.

Juna watched, sure something had gone wrong. The dart hadn't been tipped with enough poison, or hadn't struck deeply enough to drive the poison into the bloodstream. Then in midstride, the lizard crumpled and fell.

Moki leapt out into space, caught the lizard as it fell, grabbed a branch with his free hand and swung around, letting the momentum of his swing carry him back to the tree where Juna waited. He handed her the dead ooloo.

She hefted the limp weight of it in her hand and smiled, flushing turquoise with pleasure. It was her first kill. She had never thought a dead animal could please her this much, but then, this meant much more than a meal to her. It meant she was no longer as dependent on the goodwill of the villagers for food. She could provide meat for herself and Moki, and contribute more than just fruit to the village feasts. This dead lizard symbolized her own self-sufficiency. She slit its throat and let the blood patter down onto the distant forest floor, her nostrils flaring at the smell of fresh blood.

"Don't forget to cut out the scent glands before they taint the meat," Moki reminded her.

He helped her slice the glands out from under the base of the tail and the forelegs. The rest of the butchering could wait until they got back to the village.

"Let's go home and show Anito," Moki said. "She really likes ooloo meat. She'll be so pleased."

Juna rippled agreement. "I wish Ukatonen were here to see this as well."

"He'll be back by the end of the month," Moki said. "We can catch another ooloo for him then, or maybe something even more difficult."

They swung into the village tree, bearing the lizard aloft.

"Her first kill," Moki bragged to the villagers, as proud as if he had done it.

A wave of disquiet passed over the elders.

"What's the matter?" Juna asked Moki. "They don't seem pleased."

"I'm not sure, but I think maybe we weren't supposed to be hunting ooloo."

"Why didn't you tell me?"

"I didn't know. You're my sitik; you're supposed to be telling me these things," Moki reminded her. "Besides, people ate ooloo all the time in Lyanan."

Anito pushed her way past the elders to Juna. "Baha came and got me. What's the matter?"

"I made my first kill," Juna said, holding out the dead ooloo. "It seems to have upset the elders. What have I done wrong?"

A grey mist of regret, shot through with yellow flickers of irritation, passed over Anito's skin. "Ooloo are protected. We'll have to make restitution to whoever is responsible for that atwa," Anito said.

"I don't understand. We ate them all the time in Lyanan, and when we were traveling."

"Ooloo aren't protected in the wild lands and in Lyanan. They are here in Narmolom."

Another elder pushed through the crowd. It was Johito, a senior elder, but not one Juna knew well. She saw a small flicker of concern fork down Anito's back. That was probably not a good sign.

"Kene, I understand that your atwa is in conflict with mine," Johito said. "I ask for resolution to this."

"Eerin killed an ooloo. It was her first kill. She didn't realize that it was protected. I will help her make restitution, kene."

Johito looked at Eerin for a long moment, disapproval flaring on her skin. "The new creature must learn what can be hunted and when. It is disrupting the harmony of Narmolom. We should hold a council about this," she said. "I'll speak to Miato. He'll help us bring the village into harmony, and decide on the restitution to be made."

"That would be best," Anito agreed. She turned and motioned for Juna and Moki to follow her to their room.

"I'm sorry, Anito," Juna said when they got there. "I didn't know."

Anito touched her shoulder. "It's all right. You'll learn." She flickered briefly grey. "You'll have to, and so will Moki."

Juna held up the ooloo she had killed. "What should we do about this?" she asked, deep brown with shame.

"We eat it. It is your first kill, after all. I'm proud of you, even if it was a protected animal."

Juna looked away, suddenly fighting back tears. Anito's praise pleased her more than she could adequately express.

"Thank you," she said, whispering the words aloud as she said them in skin speech. "Thank you."

Anito brushed her shoulder affectionately. "Will you finish butchering it while Moki and I get the rest of the meal ready?"

The ooloo was really too small to be shared among three people, but somehow they managed to make it enough.

That night Miato came by to see them.

"Johito was very unhappy about the ooloo," Miato began. "She wants some form of restitution. What would you suggest?"

"We could have Eerin and Moki help Johito for a while," Anito offered. "She could teach them her atwa so that they can learn how not to interfere with it."

"I will suggest that, but she may want more than that."

"Then we will discuss that in the council, kene," Anito replied.

Miato flickered agreement. "We must also find some way to teach Eerin what she can and cannot hunt."

Juna touched Miato on the shoulder to get his attention. "Excuse me, kene, but I can speak for myself in this matter."

Miato's ears widened in surprise, and Juna was briefly afraid that she had somehow insulted the chief elder. "Well, then," Miato said, lowering his ears. "What do you have to say?"

"I am sorry about killing the ooloo, and interfering with Johito's atwa. It was done out of ignorance. I want to be responsible for repaying Johito myself, since it was my own mistake, not Anito's."

Miato's ears lifted again and he glanced at Anito. "How do you feel about this, kene?" he asked her.

"I am willing to let her repay Johito, but I must bargain on Eerin's behalf to make sure that the arrangement is fair."

Miato looked at Juna.

"That's fine with me, kene," Juna told the chief elder. "I trust Anito to bargain well for me, but I also need to learn what I can hunt and what I can't hunt. I don't want to make another mistake like this."

"We'll need the help of the entire village," Anito added. "It's just like training a bami. She and Moki can learn at the same time. I'll help them both."

"I'll need to consult with the other elders before I can agree to this," Miato said. "Some of them are complaining about the new creature. They think she's interfering with the harmony of the village." Frustration flared on his skin. "If someone's bami had killed a protected animal, this would be a small problem, quickly resolved. It's because Eerin is an outsider and a new creature that Johito is making such a big issue of it."

Juna felt her stomach tighten, remembering the hostility of the villagers of Lyanan. Was that going to happen here?

"I am sorry, kene. I did not mean to interfere with the harmony of Narmolom. Please tell me how I can restore it."

Miato rippled a mild negation. "For some, the only cure will be time and familiarity. For others, nothing would be enough." He turned to Anito. "You were not the only one who blamed your sitik's death on Eerin. Others did as well; some of them are senior members of the village council. They are also angry about the death of Kihato's sitik, even though she knew what she was doing was dangerous."

"And you," Juna asked him. "How do you feel about me?"

Miato looked at her a long time. Juna was suddenly aware of the vast, yawning gulf between herself and the Tendu. "Anito's sitik was healed of your taint before he died. I was one of the elders who helped heal him. He died because he had finished your transformation, and his life was complete. It was time for him to die. His death was not your fault, Eerin, and I don't blame you for it. Most of the village doesn't either, but some still do. It causes a rift in the harmony of the village, one that will not be cured until either you or they leave." Regret flowed over his body like a grey mist.

"I spoke to Ukatonen about these concerns," Miato told Anito. "He told me that you will be leaving to become an enkar soon. I am willing to endure the disharmony until then, but you must try very hard not to disrupt things."

"I'll try, kene," Anito told the chief elder. "I'll try."

Anito sat back against the smooth, curved wall of her room, her hands covering her face, her ears clamped tightly to the side of her head. She could feel her skin darkening with grief, more grief than she had felt since Ilto's death. The village's disharmony was a wound deep inside her, one she could not heal. She wanted to hide her shame, flee to the wild lands, and become a hermit.

Yet she was angry too. Despite her strangeness and ignorance, Eerin was trustworthy, useful, and even possessed a strange wisdom. Anito had come to like the new creature, and to trust her, within the limits of her knowledge. Eerin had become like a bami to her. Anito wanted to protect her from the anger and hatred of the other villagers.

Someone touched her on the shoulder. It was Eerin, ochre with concern.

"Anito?" she asked. She held her arms out. "Would linking help?"

Anito shook her head. She didn't want to link with the new creature right now. She was too angry at her.

"Is there anything else I can do?" Juna asked.

Anito shook her head again.

"Is it the other villagers? We managed to win them over in Lyanan. We can do the same here."

Anito looked away for a moment, searching for words. "This is different. This is Narmolom. I belong to this village. It . . ." She trailed off, not knowing how to express the wordless pain she felt at being responsible for the disharmony in the village. "If only Ukatonen were here. He could help. I can't—I'm part of the village."

"But the village isn't you. I know that you don't hate me," Eerin said.

Anito got up and paced across the room. "You don't understand. The village is me, I am the village. When we are in harmony, that is how it should be. Now—" She paused again, searching for words. "Now, the village is out of harmony because of me. I feel— It hurts. I-I don't have balance."

"Please let me help," Eerin implored. "This is partly my fault."

Anito looked into Eerin's small, deep-set alien eyes. "There is nothing that you can do. I am responsible for you."

"No, kene," Eerin disagreed. "I am responsible for myself. You help me. You keep me from causing trouble, but I am responsible for my own actions."

"You are my atwa," Anito insisted. "I am responsible for you. If you cause problems, they are my fault. The village blames me. I blame myself."

"But I don't blame you. I want to undo the damage I have caused. It is my responsibility, but I need your help."

"You are still my atwa. The village holds me responsible. It is my fault."

"I wish Ukatonen was here," Eerin said. "He would know what to do."

"Maybe we should be glad he isn't here," Anito said. "He might be called upon to render a judgment, and we might not like his decision. This is better decided among ourselves."

"What should I do?" Eerin said.

"Go to the council meeting," Anito told her. "Apologize. Offer to make restitution, ask to be taught properly about atwas. Then let me bargain for you. I'll try to work out the most lenient punishment I can." Her skin clouded momentarily, the skin-speech equivalent of a sigh. "It's all we can do."

Juna took a deep breath, reaching inward to ease her nervousness as she stood before the village council. "Kene, I am here to acknowledge the wrong that I have done, and to offer to do what I can to repair the damage to Johito's atwa. I acted in ignorance, and I apologize. I wish to be taught enough to avoid such mistakes in the future. Because I am new to these councils, I ask Anito to speak further on my behalf."

Miato flickered acknowledgment, and Anito rose to speak. "I ask for understanding. Eerin is new among our people and does not know our ways. Teach her, and she will not trespass again. Teach her, and she can teach her people when they return. They will cause less harm, and will behave better if we teach Eerin our ways. This will help all Tendu."

An elder rose to speak. It was Omito, one of the senior elders who was passed over when Ukatonen chose Miato to be chief. "Why should we care about what is good for all Tendu? We are Narmolom. Here in this council, we must decide what is good for Narmolom alone. Our previous chief elder saved the new creature's life. It killed him. It has adopted a bami, even though it does not know how to raise him properly. Our bami have learned strange skin speech and stranger ideas from the new creature. Who knows what will happen if this goes on?"

Moki darkened in anger and shame. Juna gathered him into her arms, but she couldn't shield him from the pain of Omito's cruel words. Because she had adopted him, Moki would always be different from other Tendu, but at least he was still alive. Only time would tell whether she had acted wisely.

"This strange animal is violating the structure of our atwa," Omito continued. "This is wrong, and we should exile the new creature from Narmolom before it causes more harm."

Omito sat down amid scattered ripples of applause. Most of the villagers looked surprised, but some were looking at Juna closely, their skins ochre with concern.

Hanto rose to speak. Miato flickered acknowledgment at her.

"You claim that Anito's sitik was killed by the new creature. However, I was there, linked with him, as he purged the taint of the new creature's blood from his body. He chose to die because he felt that it was time for Anito to become an elder. Saving Eerin's life was his last and most impressive feat. He did it because he saw something in the new creature that was worth his life. I think we should be patient with her, out of respect for our former chief elder's sacrifice."

Anito stood.

"It is true that in this council, we decide what is good for Narmolom. But sheltered as we are, the wider world affects us. Exiling Eerin would only tell the world that Narmolom is afraid. I know Eerin well, I have seen what her people can do. They are powerful and intelligent people, with much to teach us. They travel between the stars in the sky the way we float down a river. I say that it is not wise for Narmolom to turn its back on such people. They can teach us a great deal, if we are willing to learn."

Juna rose to speak. Out of the corner of her eye, she saw alarm flare on Anito's skin.

"I wish to speak about my bami, Moki. Ukatonen formally approved of my adopting him. I am learning how to be a good sitik to him. With the help of the people of Narmolom, I will learn more quickly. I am learning the ways of Narmolom as fast as I can; I beg for your patience and help."

Another elder rose to speak. "What can the new creatures do to help us? What can they do for Narmolom? There is nothing that we need from them!"

Juna rose again, and Miato acknowledged her. "I believe that there is a great deal that the Tendu and my people can do for each other. I cannot say exactly what that will mean. I hope that Narmolom will not turn away from me and my people before we fully know each other."

Other elders rose to speak, arguing for and against Juna. The weight of village opinion was on her side, but the opposition was determined. She noted which elders opposed her. If she could prove to them that she was not a threat, then her acceptance in Narmolom would be assured.

At last Miato rose to speak. "Thank you, elders of Narmolom. It is time for the council to deliberate. We will let you know our decision tomorrow night."

The elders filed out, except for the village council. Juna recognized several of them as having spoken against her, but there seemed to be as many who had supported her right to remain. Ninto, their strongest ally on the council, flicked an ear at them as they left.

"What do you think?" Juna asked Anito when they were settled in their room.

"I don't know what will happen," Anito told her. "I expected more discussion about repaying Johito. That could be very bad, or it could be good. We'll have to wait and see." She touched Juna's knee. "Get some sleep. It will make the time pass."

Anito walked into Miato's room with Eerin and Moki behind her. The village council waited for them, seated in a semicircle around the raised edge of the sleeping platform. As she sat down, Anito's eyes were drawn to a familiar irregularity in the bark of the tree. It reminded her of a face. She had spent many hours staring at it when she lived in this room with Ilto; daydreaming while Ilto dealt with the boring minutiae that made up much of a chief elder's day. It reminded Anito of how much her life had changed. She felt a sudden longing for the simplicity of those earlier times, when Ilto took care of the difficulties and she took care of Ilto. Now Eerin and Moki were under her care. She was responsible for whatever trouble they caused. She hoped that the village council's decision wouldn't be too harsh.

She looked at the council, hoping for some clue to Miato's decision. Johito looked pleased. Her concern deepened. If Johito was happy with the decision, it probably wasn't good for her. She glanced at Ninto, ears wide. A deep blue shadow of reassurance passed over her tareena's body, like the shadow of a cloud on the ocean.

"We have discussed the problem of the new creature," Miato said, once the preliminary courtesies were dispensed with.

"I have decided that Eerin and Moki must work with Johito to learn about her atwa for the rest of the month. If Johito believes that they have learned enough by the end of the month, then they may remain in Narmolom. If they remain in Narmolom, then Eerin and Moki must spend time learning each atwa. They may not hunt until Johito has approved them. Once they have completed their time with Johito, they may hunt, if Anito or some other elder is present."

Anito looked down at the ground, trying to hide her disappointment. No wonder Johito looked pleased. Everything depended on her approval.

"Thank you for your decision, kene," Anito said, her skin feeling tight and dry as she depicted the intricate patterns of the polite formula.

Perhaps it would be better to just go ahead and leave now, before Johito forced them out, Anito reflected as they left the council. It might be better to accept exile and dishonor, and begin her training as an enkar half a year early. Narmolom was only one village out of many. As an enkar, her ties with

Narmolom would be severed anyway. Several generations might pass before she saw the village again. If she visited them, it would be as a stranger.

Still, she wanted very much to leave Narmolom with her self-respect intact. It was the only home she had ever known. If only Ukatonen were here to advise her. She was too close to the situation to see it clearly.

They returned to their own room. Moki served them honeycomb and gourds of fruit juice.

"Well," Eerin said. "At least we get to stay for another month."

Anito rippled agreement tinged with doubt and caution. "If we decide to stay."

Eerin's brow wrinkled and she turned pink in surprise. "Why would we want to leave now?"

"It might be better to leave now instead of being exiled in a month. If Johito doesn't think you've learned her atwa well enough, we'll be forced to leave."

"Is it that hard to learn?" Eerin asked.

"It isn't whether you can learn," Anito explained. "It's whether Johito approves of you. Even if you understand her atwa as well as she does, she can still say it isn't good enough. If she doesn't want you in the village, we'll have to go."

"Then I'll have to get her to like me, as well as learn her atwa," Eerin said.

"It won't be easy," Anito told her. "She's afraid of you."

A polite chirring at their door interrupted their conversation. It was Ninto.

"Please come in!" Anito said. "I was just explaining the situation to Eerin."

"What I don't understand is why we should leave now," Eerin said to Anito. "You want to stay in Narmolom, and I want to try to convince Johito that I'm not a threat."

"Leave?" Ninto said. "Why should you leave?"

"Johito has already decided that Eerin doesn't belong here," Anito explained. "I don't think we can change her mind."

"It's no harder than what you did at Lyanan. In fact it's easier. You only have to persuade one person, not an entire village."

"I want to try," Eerin said. "Even if I fail, I will have learned more about the Tendu than I know now. At least I will know what doesn't work."

"I don't want to leave the village in dishonor," Anito protested.

"If you leave now, you will be leaving in dishonor," Ninto told her. "Stay and make the village's harmony include Eerin."

Eerin touched Anito's arm. "You've done so much for me. Let me pay back some of that obligation. I want the chance to win the right for us to stay here as long as we can. Please, Anito," she said, coloring pink with urgency. "Let me try."

Anito looked from Eerin to Ninto. She doubted that they would win this battle, but they still wanted to fight it. It would gain her an extra month at least, and she could use that time to say goodbye to Narmolom.

"All right," she said. "We'll stay."

_T w e n t y - o n e_

JUNA PEERED AT the flickering display on her computer. It was low on power. She was going to have to leave it out in the sun to recharge tomorrow. As soon as Anito agreed to stay, Juna had set to work, quizzing Anito and Ninto about atwas in general and Johito's atwa in particular. They were asleep now, and she was reviewing what she knew.

An atwa, to the best of her knowledge, was a clan affiliation responsible for the management of a portion of the ecosystem for the benefit of the village. Most atwas were based on location. There were clearly defined layers of the jungle: ground-based; mid-trunk level; lower, middle, and upper canopies, as well as rivers, streams, ponds, and marshlands. Other atwas were based on important food or shelter commodities: tree ferns, pollinators and pollen sources, game animals, the na tree and its dependents, and different kinds of fruit trees. Generally the species-specific atwas were coordinated by the location-based atwas. When there was a conflict between two atwas, the village elder resolved things, usually with the help of the village council.

Juna smiled. She had already been through such a conflict resolution. Her admiration for Miato, the current chief elder, had increased. It wasn't an easy job. She hoped that most of the differences that arose were easier to resolve than hers was.

Johito was responsible for eight different varieties of fruit trees. This meant that she also monitored the animals that pollinated them, as well as the animals that fed and nested in them. Since these fruit trees fed a number of important game animals, those animals also fell under her atwa, though they overlapped into several others as well. After that, Anito's explanations had gotten too complicated to follow.

The ooloo, it transpired, were an important distributor of the seeds of several different kinds of fruit trees, and a pollinator of another. Their population had fallen off due to excessive predation. Until their numbers rose to an acceptable level, hunting them was prohibited. Juna had killed a young female, just about to begin her breeding cycle. This was worse than killing a male, but not as serious as killing a pregnant female, or a mother with young.

Juna rubbed her tired eyes. Her notes on the plant and animal species in Johito's atwa were very sketchy. She could identify most of the fruit trees involved, but she knew absolutely nothing about the insects, birds, lizards, and other plants that interacted with them. She scanned through her meager notes one last time, and shut the computer down. She rested her head against the wall, and closed her eyes. Here she was, humanity's sole representative on the planet, in danger of being kicked out of the village for killing a lizard. If the implications of it weren't so serious, it would be funny.

The tree creaked faintly as it swayed in the breeze, the only sound in the late-night silence. She should get some sleep. Tomorrow was going to be difficult.

Anito woke her and Moki early. After a hurried breakfast, they met Johito at the top of the tree. Johito led them through the forest to a tree covered with ripe fruit, and alive with feeding birds and lizards. The feeding animals scattered at their approach. Johito pointed to a wide branch in the midst of the tree.

"This is a gauware tree. Sit there. Be still. Watch. I will return for you later," she told them and left.

Juna stared after her, ears wide. Then she looked at Anito, her skin purple with puzzlement.

Anito flared red. "She's not going to teach you anything!" Her patterns were jagged with anger.

Juna rippled a shrug. "It's only the first day. Let's do what she says. There's a lot that can be learned just watching."

"I'll watch with you. Maybe I can help," Anito said.

Juna hung her computer up in the sunshine at the top of the tree to recharge. Then they settled themselves in the gauware tree and waited. Soon the birds and lizards returned and began to feed. Juna watched with a trained biologist's eye, noting which species were feeding, and how they interacted. Occasionally, when something startled the feeding animals, and they fled, she turned and asked Anito for the names and habits of the animals she didn't know. By midmorning, when the animals faded into the brush, Juna had identified twenty-five species. Some had only stopped to perch for a moment in the tree or to display and court in the top branches. Some had come to feed, and others to prey on them.

Juna fetched her computer from the treetop. She and Moki set to work cataloguing all they had observed. She had Moki depict the animals on his skin so that she had a visual record of what they looked like. The pictures were recognizable, though lacking in fine detail. Still, they would do for a beginning. She had a feeling that she would have lots of chances to get pictures of the actual animals over the next month. The cataloguing took until well past noon. Anito went and gathered lunch for them.

After lunch, they climbed down to the forest floor and observed what came by to feed on the fallen fruit. This time of day it was mostly insects. Now that her computer was recharged, Juna could catalogue directly as she watched, with the computer in helmet configuration, subvocalizing into a throat mike. She recorded almost forty species of insects, everything from fruit flies to a large, many-legged arthropod with claws that clearly filled much the same ecological niche as a land crab. There were half a dozen different butterflies feeding on rotting fruit.

Several amphibians came by, including a tiny jewel-like frog that sat in a shaft of sunlight, bobbing up and down, flickering through a range of brilliant colors. Juna watched, intrigued, as a larger, red frog responded to the other frog's courtship ritual. The tiny frog clasped the larger female and they scuttled off into the leaves to mate. Juna smiled. If she hadn't seen them pairing off, she would have catalogued the two as completely different species.

As the sun began to sink toward the horizon, the larger animals came out into the treetops to feed. Juna and her two assistants climbed back up to watch them.

It was almost sunset when Johito returned. She led them back to her room, where her bami had laid out a good-sized meal.

"What did you learn today?" Johito asked Juna when they were seated.

As she ate, Juna reeled off a list of the animals that had visited the gauware tree and what they had done there. She speculated on how their visits affected the tree, identifying possible seed dispersers, and noting animals that she knew were desirable game. She worked from memory as much as possible, consulting Moki or Anito only when she was uncertain about something. She wanted Johito to know that she had a good memory for the kinds of details that might be useful for learning an atwa. If Johito was impressed by how much she could learn on her own, she might be more willing to teach her. Juna knew that there was no way that she could master such a complex ecosystem by herself in less than a month. Unless she understood how the Tendu used the atwas to guide their interactions with the forest, all of the natural history in the world wouldn't help. For that she needed Johito's cooperation.

Johito watched her recital of the day's events impassively. Her skin remained neutral, with no hint of emotion. At last Juna ran out of things to say. There was a long moment of stillness. Johito sat as though she were carved from a huge block of pale green jade, her chin tucked in thought.

"I want you to go back to the same tree and watch again tomorrow," Johito said, breaking her stillness at last. She looked away. They were clearly dismissed.

Juna's shoulders slumped. She followed Anito and Moki out the door, feeling defeated.

Anito touched her on the shoulder when they reached their room. "You did well today. Don't let Johito bother you. You were up late last night. Get some sleep."

Juna nodded.

Moki touched her arm. "We learned a lot today. We'll learn more tomorrow. Good night, siti."

"Sleep well, bai," Juna said, giving her bami a quick hug. They hadn't linked today. She missed the closeness they shared through linking.

She held out her arms, suppressing a jaw-cracking yawn. Just a quick link, to quiet her conscience, then off to bed.

Moki linked with her, and they shared the familiar closeness and peace. It felt so good, like a warm bath or a hug from her mother. Drowsily she broke the link and burrowed into her warm, moist, leafy bed. She felt rosy and peaceful and connected with Moki, and through Moki, with all of the Tendu. She yawned, covering her mouth with her hand to keep the leaves out. She wondered now at her previous fear of allu-a. She would surely have gone mad from sheer loneliness without it. Sleep claimed her, as deep and profound as the dark, eternal forest around them.

The next few days were much like the first. She watched the tree, noting everything that interacted with it—animal, insect, or plant. Every night Johito listened to her describe what happened in the gauware tree, and then sent her back to watch some more. By the end of the seventh day she felt that she had learned everything there was to know about the tree. When Johito sent her back for an eighth day of tree-watching, she began to protest. Anito touched her arm. A small, private glyph of negation flickered on the back of her hand. Juna stilled her skin speech with an effort.

"Yes, kene, I will go back to the tree tomorrow," she said after Anito apologized for her. "Only please tell me what I am supposed to be looking for that I have not yet noticed."

Johito said nothing for a long time. Juna sat perfectly still, determined not to move until Johito said something helpful.

"You have more to learn. Look more carefully," Johito said at last. Then she got up and crawled into bed, as though they had already left the room.

Juna turned bright red with anger. Anito plucked nervously at her arm.

Juna took a deep breath. Anger would do nothing to help her. Johito was trying to see how far she could be pushed. If she lost her temper, she would lose everything.

"I'm all right," she told Anito. "Let's go."

Juna lay awake, shifting uncomfortably in her bed. Was she missing something, or was Johito being difficult? Tomorrow she would go over every inch of the tree. If she didn't turn up something new, then she would tell Anito that she was giving up.

The next morning Juna arose early. She woke Moki and they slipped out of the tree while the forest was still dim and thick with mist. The first shafts of light were gilding the treetops when they reached the gauware tree. Juna stationed herself on the branch of a nearby tree, and considered her next move.

Everything depended on whether Johito was playing fair with her. After seven days spent cataloguing everything that happened on that damned tree, Juna was sure that Johito wanted her to fail.

So, how would Johito try to keep her from succeeding? Johito had to play fair according to Tendu custom. To do otherwise would make her lose face if it was discovered. Johito was testing her. If she passed the test, then she was worthy to take on as a student. There was still some hidden fact about this tree that Juna needed to discover, something that was the key to the gauware tree's survival.

Whatever it was that Juna needed to find out, it was not something that Moki, Anito, or Ninto knew about the tree. They had given her what information they had. The rest she had to figure out for herself.

She turned to her bami. "Moki, go ask Anito and Ninto if they know of any other gauware trees nearby."

Moki nodded and swung off through the trees. Juna climbed down to the ground, and began examining the tree minutely, starting at the wide buttress roots. She knocked on the roots. They resonated like a drum. Were they hollow? She climbed, pausing from time to time to knock on the trunk. It too resonated. It was hollow. About midmorning Juna pushed aside a bromeliad and found what she was looking for, a hole in the crotch of the tree, twice the size of her fist.

So, the tree was hollow. What lived inside? She could format her computer as a camera and drop it through the hole on a rope, but she didn't want to risk losing it. Better to wait and see what Moki could find out.

She swung through the trees to a nearby stream, and washed off the accumulated grime of her morning exertions. It was amazing how dirty she got, just climbing a tree. She plunged into the stream, whooping at the feel of the cold water on her skin. She emerged shining and clean to find Anito and Moki waiting for her.

"There are several gauware trees nearby," Anito informed her. "Let's eat and then go look at them."

The second tree they looked at had a large gaping hole in its trunk, big enough for Juna to climb into. She sent Moki for a long coil of rope and a large fresh chunk of glow-fungus.

"You're going to climb down inside that gauware tree?" Anito asked, ochre flickers of concern highlighting her words.

Juna nodded.

"Be careful. You don't know what lives inside that hole. It might be dangerous."

"Yes, but I have to know what's down there."

Anito flickered resigned agreement. "You're probably right. Johito won't be satisfied until you tell her about the inside of the tree, but if you die in the process, she won't mourn. For all we know, there could be something dangerous in there. Be very careful."

It was early afternoon when Moki returned with the necessary climbing equipment. They lowered the glow-fungus down, but aside from a flock of sleepy, wide-mouthed araus, birds that looked like a cross between an archaeopteryx and a whippoorwill, they saw nothing except vague, shiny, writhing shapes in the dimness. Those shapes could have been anything from a giant snake to a colony of harmless beetles.

Moki looped one end of the rope around a branch and tied it securely. Anito tied a series of loops in the other end. "For

footholds," she explained, and then braced the rope behind her
back. Moki paid out a body length of rope into the hole. Juna
checked her gear, and swung herself into the hole. She stuck
her feet through the bottom loops in the rope and then nodded
to Anito, who began lowering her into the dark cavern of the
hollow tree. As soon as Juna was far enough down, she hooked
the glow-fungus onto a loop above her head. It cast a pallid
blue light on the rough interior of the tree. A warm current of
air blew past her, carrying the stench of death and decay. She
swallowed against her gag reflex and wished she was enclosed
in an environment suit.

Two and a half meters down, a wide shelflike projection
partially blocked the hollow. It was covered with dark brown
beetle-like insects feeding on decayed leaf litter. These bugs
were what she had seen moving in the light from the glow-
fungus. As Juna carefully eased her way past the obstruction, a
bright yellow snake with vivid red bands bordered by thin
green stripes lifted its head out of the leaf litter and regarded
her alertly. Juna froze. It was a tiakan. Its bite was extremely
poisonous. The Tendu could counteract the poison, but it took
months for all of the effects to wear off. She watched it watch
her for a very long time. At last the snake lowered its head and
crept off, backwards. The motion was odd and very unsnake-
like. Gingerly she unhooked the light from the rope and held it
closer. She let out the breath that she had been holding, and
laughed. It was a harmless giant millipede, its tail colored to
resemble a tiakan's head. Using a long bamboo probe, Juna
stirred the leaf litter around the anthropod. It lifted its tail again,
mimicking the poisonous snake. The illusion was almost
perfect.

She gave the rope two tugs, the signal to lower her farther
into the darkness. For a moment, the light from the glow-
fungus was cut off by the projection. Her pupils widened, but
the darkness was nearly absolute. Something wet and slimy
fluttered past her, chirring and squeaking. She screamed. The
sound was swallowed by the soft, rotting wood on the inside of
the tree. Then the glow-fungus slid past the projection, and
Juna saw that she had disturbed a colony of frog-bats. They

were ugly but harmless. Conditions inside the tree were perfect for them. They needed a very hot, humid environment. The temperature had to be almost 35 degrees Celsius, and the air was saturated with moisture.

As she continued her descent, she had time to survey the inner surface of the tree. It was covered with a variety of different kinds of fungi. Clouds of tiny insects swarmed around her light. The walls opened out as she continued descending. It was like being in a cave. Great plates of multicolored fungi hung down like stalactites. Several different species of frog-bats made the tree their home. They clung between the fungal stalactites, chittering uneasily at her invasion. Their guano rained down on her head. She wiped it off with a sweaty palm and continued her descent. This reeking wooden cavern was a far cry from Narmolom's comfortable, well-lit village tree.

At last the bottom of the cavity came into sight. Something fled squeaking at her approach. She jerked the rope three times, the signal to stop, and hung a couple of feet above the guano-covered floor. The fleeing animal paused at the edge of a dark hole. It was the size and shape of a large hairless rat, white with blotchy yellow patches. It was a gootara, an amphibian like the batlike creatures she had startled in her descent. The female laid its eggs in a pouch on the male's abdomen, where he fertilized them. The eggs hatched and the young lived in the male's pouch until they finished developing and were old enough to survive on their own. She pushed off from a projecting rib and grasped a woody knob on the other side of the tree to look more closely at the gootara, but the creature fled down the passageway.

Juna reached down with a bamboo probe and stirred the guano, disturbing a seething sea of insects and worms that burrowed frantically into the detritus. There was plenty of food for the gootara down here. She dug further, trying to see how deep the layer of guano was, and whether there was wood or earth underneath. She struck earth about fifteen centimeters down, densely packed with roots. The guano was evidently a major source of nutrients for the gauware tree. Sequestered inside the tree like this, it was held for the exclusive use of the gauware tree. Perhaps this was what Johito had wanted her to find.

Juna unhooked the glow-fungus and shone it down the passageway formed by the hollow root of the tree. Several other hollow roots radiated out of the central cavern. She wondered what other creatures used these underground passageways through the jungle. She put the glow-fungus back in its case of nutrient solution, and hung there in the dark, listening. There were crisp rustling and popping sounds around and below her. The hole at the top of the tree was only a dim, distant circle of light. The outside world seemed very far away from this dark, stinking, bug-infested hell.

At last her eyes grew used to the darkness and she could make out, faintly, the bulges and irregularities on the inside of the tree trunk. Something rustled behind her. The rope swayed as she turned her head to look. Peering through the darkness, she could make out only a vague shape. She pulled out the glow-fungus.

Fresh from its bath in the nutrient solution, the fungus glowed brightly, revealing a huge lobsterlike creature, twice as long as her hand. Its eyes reflected the light as it backed into a crevice, its long feelers waving. Several other land lobsters were peering out from a root cavity. Instead of claws, the lobsters had immensely long, powerful mantislike arms. She jumped like a startled mouse as one of the creatures snatched a many-legged white beetle the size of her palm from the litter on the floor, and carried it to its jaws. She heard the rustle of chitin and wings as the big beetle struggled to escape, then the implacable crunching noise as the land lobster mechanically dispatched its prey, its eyes never leaving her.

Juna shuddered. She hated bugs, and there were too many of them in this awful hole. A sudden surge of claustrophobia gripped her. It was time to go. Hopefully Johito would be satisfied by her investigation of the hidden world of the tree.

To her surprise, the sun was touching the treetops when she emerged from the tree. She felt the cool breeze on her skin and took a deep breath. Never had fresh air smelled and tasted so good. Moki embraced her with his free hand, and Anito

brushed her shoulder, relief evident on her skin. Moki coiled
the rope and slung it over his shoulder.

"Let's go," Juna said. "I want to find a stream and wash off."
She was black with filth, relieved only by splotches and streaks
of brown guano from the frog-bats.

They headed for a nearby waterfall. Juna stood underneath it
in the last golden rays of the sun, feeling the cool water blast
away the accumulation of grime on her skin. She dove into the
pool below the falls and emerged, clean and dripping. Looking
up, she noticed that night birds and bats were already beginning
to flicker through the trees overhead. Johito would be waiting
for them at the other tree.

Suddenly she was struck by an idea. Juna laughed. Let Johito
wait. She had just thought of another portion of the ecosystem
that she needed to observe.

"Anito, can we build a nest in the hollow gauware tree
tonight? I want to see what happens to the tree at night."

Anito flickered agreement. "We'd better hurry, though. It's
getting dark."

They built a nest in the gauware tree she had climbed inside
of. They took turns watching through the night, waiting for a
rustling nearby, then uncapping the glow-fungus to see what
was there. Often they were rewarded by a glimpse of some
visiting creature. They catalogued five species of larger animals new to the tree, as well as numerous insects, drawn by the
light of the glow-fungus.

Johito met them as they returned to the village, tired but
happy.

"Where were you last night?" Johito asked them, ochre
concern warring with yellow irritation on her skin.

"We were out studying your atwa," Anito said.

"We've learned a great deal," Juna added. "May we tell you
now, or would you rather wait until tonight?" She hefted a full
gathering bag, bulging with fruit and game. "We've brought
breakfast. It isn't much, but—"

"Thank you," Johito said. "I can listen now."

They followed Johito down to her room and sat down. Moki
and Johito's bami set about preparing breakfast.

"So, what did you learn about the tree?" Johito asked, ignoring the usual polite preliminaries.

Juna told Johito about her trip into the hollow gauware tree, and their night watch. She listed the species they'd found and speculated on the nutrients the tree got from the guano of the animals dwelling inside it, She ignored the breakfast set before them, though her stomach was hollow with hunger.

At last she was through. Johito regarded them for a very long moment.

"Well," she said at last. "Eat a big breakfast. Today will be long. You have a lot to learn."

Juna looked at Anito, who nodded at her. She had won the first battle. Johito was going to teach Juna about her atwa.

She ate hugely, savoring her victory. When she was finished, Johito took her out and showed her everything she had missed about the gauware tree.

To Juna's satisfaction, most of what Johito had to show her were things she couldn't have observed. Because the gauware tree was not in bloom this time of year, the network of pollinators, pollen thieves, and their predators and parasites was not there to be discovered. Also the large breeding colonies of darru beetles that filled the inside of the hollow trees wouldn't congregate until a month before the next flood season.

Still there were surprises, such as a complex symbiotic relationship between the nocturnal araus and the brilliant ngulla birds. The ngulla birds fed on a species of flying insect that laid its eggs on the arau chicks, weakening and killing them. In return, the arau provided warning of nocturnal predators to the sleeping ngulla. That relationship would have taken months of study to discover.

They spent the whole day in the gauware tree, stopping only for a brief, light lunch of fruit, greens, and honey. Juna's brain was whirling by the time the sun touched the treetops. Johito looked like she was ready to go on all night, but Anito intervened, pleading exhaustion.

"We were up all night, kene," she said. "I don't think that two nights in a row would be wise."

"Tomorrow then," Johito said. "We will meet in my room for

breakfast. Moki and Eerin will tell me what they have learned today. If it is satisfactory, then the lessons will continue."

Juna was glad that she'd had the presence of mind to record Johito's lessons. She and Moki managed to review them briefly that night, before exhaustion claimed them both.

The review the following morning was grueling and minute. Juna remembered her harrowing Ph.D. defense. Compared to Johito, her professors had been vague and undemanding. Her stomach was in knots by the time Johito finished her interrogation.

It never got any easier. Several times, Johito suspended lessons abruptly, claiming to have lost patience with them, sending them back to review what they had already learned. Always there was some simple fact that they had failed to take into consideration. Johito's skin remained expressionless. Her words were simple black patterns on neutral green skin. It was impossible to tell how they were doing until she either passed or failed them. By the end of the month their nerves were shot. They flared angrily at each other at the slightest provocation. Even linking failed to ease the tension.

Ukatonen showed up four days before Johito was due to pass judgment. He took one look at them and pulled rank, claiming he needed them for some work he was doing in the wild lands. He took them to a lovely spot in the middle of the wild lands and demanded the whole story.

"No wonder you're so tired. Rest, eat, relax, link. You need it, all of you."

"But Johito—" Juna began.

"Johito can wait until you're back in harmony. I'm sorry I wasn't here to help."

"We did all right," Anito said. "Eerin and Moki have both learned an enormous amount about Johito's atwa."

"I'm sure they have, but perhaps I could have done something. . . ."

"This was the best bargain we could get. At least I've had another month here in Narmolom."

"Johito hasn't exiled us from the village yet," Juna said. "We don't know what she's thinking. She may let us stay."

"The whole village is talking about how hard you've been working," Ukatonen said. "Johito will lose face if she can't prove that you don't know her atwa."

Anito brightened considerably at that thought. "Do you think we'll get to stay?"

"Perhaps. Everything depends on Johito, and no one knows what she thinks. However, you need to be relaxed and calm when you go in for judgment. Stay here and enjoy yourselves. We'll go back tomorrow and I'll see what I can do behind the scenes."

They returned to the village feeling rested, calmer, and more even-tempered. Johito greeted them as though they had never left. They spent the afternoon with her learning about several parasitic plants that lived on the kandar tree, another species that was part of her atwa. Several of these plants produced food; others provided crucial food sources for animals in other atwas. Ukatonen came with them, but the presence of the enkar appeared to make no difference to Johito. She continued to lecture them in the same impassive patterns she'd used all month. At sunset they returned to the village, where they ate and reviewed their lessons. The next day Ukatonen stayed behind to learn more about the situation from the other villagers.

He had dinner waiting for them when they returned.

"There's nothing I can do. Miato has told me that this is an internal matter, to be decided by the village."

Anito's ears lifted at this.

"Miato's right," Ukatonen continued. "Unless someone asks me for a judgment, I can only offer suggestions, and I have asked too much of this village already."

"I could—" Anito began, but Ukatonen rippled negation.

"Don't ask for judgment. I would refuse." He darkened with shame. "I am too close to you to be impartial. Even if I felt I could be fair, the judgment would be contested."

Juna touched Anito on the shoulder. "Ukatonen's right. Let me win this on my own. It will mean more to the villagers and to me if I can."

Anito looked at her for a long moment, then rippled the Tendu equivalent of a shrug. "All right."

Juna and Moki studied far into the night, going to bed only after Anito threatened to take the computer away from them. Anito linked with them, pushing them into a deep dreamless sleep.

The next morning Johito summoned them to the bottom of the tree. A group of elders were waiting with Johito. Juna recognized them. They either shared Johito's atwa or worked in closely related atwas.

"Tell us about my atwa," Johito directed.

For the rest of the day, Juna, and to a lesser extent, Moki, were questioned about Johito's atwa. Lunch and dinner were brought down, but the interrogation was ceaseless. Juna was tired and her skin felt sore and tight from all the talking she'd done. At last the questions came to a halt. Johito and the others huddled to confer. Juna leaned back against the side of the tree, too tired to care that the aliens could see her exhaustion. She was almost too tired to care about what Johito decided. Anito squatted beside her, and held out a piece of honeycomb. By the time the elders' conference was over, she was feeling better.

The elders sat back down, except for Johito, who moved forward. "Eerin has learned enough to please me," she announced. "Moki must learn more, but he is young. Eerin may stay."

Juna embraced Moki, weak with relief and exhaustion. They clung together for a moment; then Juna rose to speak.

"Thank you, kene. You have taught me well," she said. It was truth of a sort. Once Johito had decided that Juna was worthy of her teaching, she was a painstaking and thorough teacher, even though she had never spared either of them a word of encouragement.

Johito flickered pleased acknowledgment at the compliment. Juna swallowed her anger. She would only lose the respect that she'd worked so hard to gain.

"We must go now, kene. We are very tired." Juna motioned to Moki and the two of them climbed slowly up to their room, leaving Anito behind to make whatever polite excuses were needed. Juna was sick of excuses and politeness and face and all of these alien rituals. She wanted to sleep for a week, longer if they would let her, and wake up somewhere familiar and undemanding.

She slept until late the next afternoon, and rose to find a substantial meal laid out for her. Her skin still ached. It hurt to talk. She ate, washed, and stretched, then sat around for a while, enjoying the solitude. She thought about listening to some music or reading a book, but she'd spent so much time working with the computer lately that she didn't have the energy to turn it on. At last, she crawled back into bed and fell asleep.

She slept through the night. Anito woke her for breakfast. It was a relief to linger over breakfast without worrying over the day's lesson.

"What shall we do today?" she asked Anito.

"Ukatonen invited us to go hunting with him."

They met the enkar in the bowl of the tree's crotch, and swung off through the canopy together. They found a plump, unwary muwa hanging in a patch of sunlight, clinging to a branch with its head buried in the feathers between its forelegs. Juna dispatched it just as it woke. She and Moki settled into the wide crotch of a tree to butcher it. Ukatonen and Anito soon returned with a brace of large birds, which they gutted and hung in the shade to bleed dry. They sat in the tree, eating lunch, while the blood from their kills pattered onto the forest floor below.

"It's about time that we returned to Lyanan," Ukatonen told them.

"So soon?" Anito said.

"It's almost the end of the dry season. I don't want to wait much longer."

Anito clouded over with regret. "You're right, but I have so little time left in Narmolom."

"Why don't you stay here?" Juna suggested. "Ukatonen can look after us well enough. You deserve some time off."

Anito glanced at the enkar, ears lifted, pink with surprise.

"Why not? You've been working very hard. A rest would be good for you," he said.

"But Eerin is my atwa," Anito protested.

"And she will continue to be your atwa for many years to come. As you said, you have very little time left. Enjoy it."

They set off five days later. Anito accompanied them as far as the beginning of the wild lands. They bid her an affectionate farewell, and headed off for the coast.

Twenty-two

THE RECOVERY WAS proceeding rapidly at Lyanan. The vine-draped radio beacon rose out of a thick mat of regrowth, well over three meters high. It took Juna a moment to realize that the tilted tree trunk she'd bumped into was in fact the piling of the antenna tower. She activated her computer, and spent the rest of the afternoon downloading her field notes and observations through the radio beacon out to the waiting satellites.

Sitting there, monitoring the transmission, she realized how much she had learned in her nine months among the Tendu. She had catalogued hundreds of species. Moki and Anito had shown her details of the plants and animals' natural history that would have taken years for a Survey research team to gather. The report on Johito's atwa was an impressive piece of scholarship, the kind of thing that would be the high point of anyone's career in xenobiology, and probably in alien studies as well. Several other reports were almost as good. When she got home, she could have any job she wanted, even if the Survey disciplined her severely. Universities and research institutions would be clamoring for her to come work with them.

Juna didn't really care. Her life with the Survey felt like a dream. Soon she would push her way back through the brush to where Moki and Ukatonen waited, and they would continue on to Lyanan. The thought disturbed her. She was human. She had friends, a family, people she loved back home. Someday she would carry on a conversation aloud, take a hot bath, eat a hot meal, touch someone whose skin was warm and dry. But it felt so distant, so unreal, here in this alien world.

Warm tears stung her face, and she altered her skin so that the salt from her tears wouldn't irritate it. Activating her spare computer, she had it play one of her favorite songs. Juna tried to sing along, but her voice was rough and husky from disuse. She was forgetting who she was. She needed to spend more time alone with the computer, seeing plays, listening to music, reading books and old letters from friends and family, reminding herself of who she was and what she would be returning to.

The shadows were long when she finally finished transmitting her notes to the waiting satellites. She sighed, crumpled up the computers, and tossed them into her pack. Leaving the beacon behind was like leaving the grave of a close friend. She could feel the ties between her and humanity fraying and growing weak. She remembered Alison, and how worried she'd been by Juna's transformation. By now Alison was beginning her retirement, after forty-five years in the Survey. How was she dealing with the changes in her life?

They arrived at Lyanan just after sunset, and were welcomed by Lalito, the chief elder, who seemed genuinely pleased to see them. The village seemed more tranquil, settled into itself. It felt more like Narmolom. Juna mentioned that to Ukatonen.

"Healing the jungle has made a big difference to the villagers. When we were here before, they were like ants whose nest has been disturbed, running around, attacking anything that moved. You will be treated better now."

Ukatonen's prediction was accurate. The villagers seemed genuinely glad to see her. The tinka clustered around Moki, ears wide in surprise. Moki ignored them with regal grace and disdain. It surprised Juna. He treated the tinka of Narmolom much more kindly.

"You were rather unkind to those tinka, Moki. Don't you

remember what it was like?" Juna remarked when they were alone in their room.

"Of course I remember," he replied. "It was awful."

"Then why don't you treat them like the tinka back home?"

"Because I remember how they drove me out of the village just before you left."

"Oh," Juna said, realizing just how desperate Moki's plight must have been. No wonder sending him back to the village hadn't worked. He no longer had a place there.

"When I gave you the firewing butterfly, you thanked me. I thought maybe you were interested in me. I didn't have any place else to go. So I followed you. I knew you were different, but I didn't understand." He paused, looking away, suddenly clouded over with sadness and shame.

Juna touched his shoulder. "What is it, Moki? What's the matter?"

"You didn't want me. I forced you to take me."

"No, Moki! It's true I didn't want to adopt a bami, but you were so brave and determined that I couldn't let you die. I wasn't sure about it at first, but now—" Juna paused, searching for the right words. "Now I'm glad it happened. You've taught me so much. You're my bami, and I want you," she said, her skin intense with pride and love.

Moki looked relieved. Clearly this was a fear he had been holding in for a long time. Juna reached out and held him tightly, glad that they'd had this discussion.

"Next time something like this bothers you, you come talk to me about it. Understand?" she said, holding him out at arm's length so that he could see her words.

He nodded solemnly. They reached out to link, but just then Ukatonen came in with Lalito and several of the village council.

"Greetings, kene," Juna said to Lalito. "The village seems to be recovering."

"We are more in harmony than before," Lalito admitted, "but it will be a long time before the jungle is healed. It is good that you are helping to heal it. There is much to do, but we will worry about that tomorrow. Tonight you are our guests. I

understand that you have adopted a bami, and that he was a
tinka from our village."

Juna glanced at Ukatonen and caught a flicker of alarm. Best
to be tactful, she decided. "Yes, Moki is from here," she
replied. "He's a fine bami, very intelligent and attentive. I am
grateful to Lyanan for the opportunity to adopt him." It was
tactful, if not entirely honest.

Ukatonen gave a small flicker of relief. Juna smiled ironi-
cally, grateful that these strangers couldn't read her face. By
Tendu standards, nothing wrong had been done, but Juna still
felt angry at the incredible cruelty they had shown to Moki. She
had lived long enough among the Tendu to accept the way they
treated the tinka, and the necessity for it. But Moki was her
bami; she felt toward him the way she would feel toward a
child of her own. She couldn't be impartial about Moki.

"We are hosting a small meal in my room. The food is poor,
but it is the best we have. Please come and be welcome."

"Thank you," Juna replied. "I am sure whatever you have is
enough," she said, giving the polite, formulaic response. She
was hungry, and she had grown used to long, formal banquets.
At least the food was always plentiful and good.

Lalito kept her word, mentioning nothing about the work
they would be doing tomorrow. Juna sensed the villagers' eyes
upon her, watching her and Moki curiously. Conscious of the
attention being paid to them, they were both scrupulously
polite. Out the corner of her eye, Juna noticed the villagers
discussing her and her bami. She couldn't make out their
words, but they were colored with surprise and amazement.

"You have learned a great deal since we saw you last," one
of the elders remarked.

"Thank you, kene," Juna replied, suppressing a flicker of
pride. "I have had excellent teachers."

"And they have had an excellent student," Ukatonen said.
"She learns more every day. Before we left Narmolom, Eerin
was studying the atwas of that village. She has just finished
learning the Bramera atwa."

Surprise and amazement flickered over the villagers' skin.

"Is Eerin going to become an elder at Narmolom?" Lalito
asked.

"No. Anito will be leaving Narmolom after mating season to become an enkar. Eerin will be coming with her."

"But Anito's so young! How sad for her. What about Moki?" Lalito asked.

"Moki will come with us," Juna said, fighting back a flare of impatience.

"Won't he feel out of place among so many enkar?"

"He will be welcome among us. We see so few bami," Ukatonen said. "And we have no choice. Anito is making a great sacrifice on your behalf, and on behalf of all Tendu. The new creatures will bring great changes, and we must be ready to meet them. The enkar need Anito's experience with the new creatures."

"Why not just tell them to go away? Why should we change?"

"When the world changes, those animals who cannot adapt, die. The new creatures are coming. They bring change. We must learn what those changes may be, and try to understand them, or we will lose ourselves," Ukatonen told them.

"Most of the changes will be gradual and carefully thought out," Juna said. "My people mean no harm."

"But even when you mean no harm, you still bring new ideas, and new ideas cause change," Ukatonen pointed out.

Juna looked away, remembering the mass suicides of the beautiful, delicate Sawakirans, and all the destruction brought about when one culture contacted another. Ukatonen was right. So was the Survey, but their restrictive rules about alien contact were useless. Once two cultures came into contact with each other, change was inevitable. She wondered what change she had already caused in her time here. Already she had cost Anito a secure future, but balancing that, in her own mind at least, was the fact that she had saved Moki's life. She had taught them her alphabet, and shown them a better way to cultivate the soil. These things were mere novelties, but sooner or later something the humans did or said would cause a deep, permanent change in the Tendu. This was not the place to talk about it, however. She needed to discuss it with Ukatonen when they were alone.

"You are right, en, but my people come in friendship. We

also want these changes to take place slowly. We want to create harmony between our people," Juna said. "It is a complex problem. It will take much time and discussion to resolve."

Ukatonen leaned back with a ripple of contentment. "That was a delicious feast," he said, stretching to show his bulging belly. "You have gone to a great deal of trouble for us. We appreciate it."

"It was no trouble at all," Lalito protested. "I hope this meager meal didn't leave you unsatisfied."

Juna, recognizing the formulaic argument signaling the end of a feast, helped herself to another couple of handfuls of the fresh fish tossed with seaweed, and picked up some fruit to eat later. Moki followed her lead. Ukatonen was winding things up early; clearly he wanted to continue the conversation in private. She smiled, surveying the heaped remains of the feast. The tinka would eat well tonight.

At last, the polite words of departure completed, Ukatonen, Juna, and Moki climbed up to their guest room.

"Please explain how you think your people will change things for the Tendu," Ukatonen asked her when they were settled.

"I don't know. Meeting new people is not my atwa. I am supposed to study how living things work. It was an accident that I was lost, and luck that you found me."

"Perhaps, but you know the Tendu better than anyone among your people. I trust that knowledge. Tell me the best that you can."

Juna explained about the Sawakirans, and the Survey's rules for alien contact. She confessed to humanity's shameful history of colonialization, the extermination and enslavement of native peoples, and the gradual realization of how impoverished it left them culturally. She explained the First People's movement, and the New Tribalism of the twenty-second century, and how that led to the Survey's alien contact protocols. It was late when she finished explaining all this to Ukatonen.

"Well," said Ukatonen, "it is good that your people have thought a great deal about how not to hurt the people they meet, even though they haven't had any practice at this; but haven't they worried about what our people can do to theirs?"

Juna shook her head. "My people didn't know that the Tendu even existed. How could we worry about that?"

"I don't know. But this contact affects us both. You should think about what this means to your people. The Tendu could change you as much as you change us. Let the enkar worry about the Tendu. That is our atwa. Your atwa should be to care for your people in this meeting."

"Yes, but when my people come, things will change. I will go home."

Tears rose in Juna's eyes, as memories swept over her. She thought of her father, waiting for her on the porch of their house, the filtered sunlight milky and bright. The tears stung and she altered the skin of her face. That broke the train of memories, and she was able to get herself under control. Moki came up and clung to her.

"I'm sorry. It's just that I miss my people."

Ukatonen nodded and brushed her shoulder affectionately. She smiled, hugging Moki briefly, and then releasing him.

"What about me?" Moki said. "What will happen to me when you go?"

"Then I will take over raising you, Moki. You know that. You agreed to this arrangement when you were a tinka," Ukatonen told him.

Moki looked away, the color of a rainy sky. Juna felt torn; her need for home and her love for her adopted child warred within her. She touched Moki on the shoulder. He pulled away, red lightning bolts of rage dancing across the greyness of his sadness. He looked like a miniature storm cloud. Then he calmed himself, and turned to face her.

"It's years yet, Moki. Perhaps a solution will work itself out," Juna soothed, hiding her doubts. "There's nothing that we can do about it now."

Moki came to her, his skin a muddy whirl of conflicting emotions. She held him, taking comfort in the familiar, damp scent of his skin.

"Well, it's late, and we should get some sleep," Ukatonen said. "Lalito will have a great deal for us to do tomorrow. We'll talk more about this some other time."

Lalito did, indeed, keep them very busy. They spent the next month culling weed trees, gathering and washing seaweed to use as fertilizer, and planting new species that required shade in order to germinate. It was physically demanding, but Juna was treated more like a co-worker, and less like a slave. She and Moki worked with other elders and their bami, and socialized with them at meals and during breaks. The villagers became individuals, having status and relationships with other people in the village. Juna and Moki struck up a firm friendship with Arato and her bami, Ini. Ini had been one of the two bami in the digging race. Arato seemed to feel a debt to Juna, and helped introduce her to the other villagers. Soon she and Moki were teaching the elders and their bami written Standard. The Iyali-Tendu and the villagers of Narmolom had treated written Standard as a novelty, quickly losing interest. The people of Lyanan, however, were even more determined than the enkar to master this alien language. At first they came out of a sense of self-protection. Then their natural curiosity took over, and the villagers began peppering Juna with questions about her people.

As a result, Juna found herself thinking more often of home and the people she missed. She began spending more time alone, sitting on the edge of the cliff staring out at the ocean.

She was sitting on the cliff, watching the lizard-headed seabirds wheeling against the setting sun, and thinking of home when Ukatonen came up and squatted beside her. He picked up a handful of pebbles and began pouring them from one hand into the other.

"Moki is worried," he told her. "You spend all your free time dreaming of your home. It scares him."

Juna looked away, staring out over the alien sea for a long moment. "I'll have to go home when my people come," she said at last. "I miss talking in my own language, eating familiar foods. I miss mating. I need those things, en. I have a—" She stopped, realizing that there was no word for "family," or "home" in skin speech. "I have a sitik, a tareena, a village of my own. They need me. When my people come, I will go with them. What will happen to Moki then?"

Ukatonen shook his head, a human gesture, learned from her. "If Moki cannot live without you, then I will die."

"I don't understand," Juna said. "Why will you die if Moki can't live without me?"

"Because I have rendered judgment on this matter," he told her, tossing pebbles over the edge of the cliff one by one. "I am an enkar, and when we render a bad judgment, then we are obliged to die."

Juna looked back at the setting sun, now half sunk in the ocean. She felt as though the ground had opened up beneath her. Every time she began to feel that she knew the Tendu, something like this would happen, revealing how little she actually understood.

"I'm sorry, Ukatonen," she said, laying a hand on his arm. "I didn't know."

His skin rippled in a shrug. "It doesn't matter. If Moki cannot live without you, I will die. Your lack of understanding doesn't alter that. What we must do is try to help Moki. The more you sit here"—he flung the remaining pebbles over the cliff—"and dream of your people, the more worried your bami becomes. You are neglecting your bami, and it must stop." He stood, and offered her his hand. She took it and he pulled her up.

"But what will we do about Moki when I have to go?"

Ukatonen stared at her for a long moment, his eyes cold and distant. "I don't know. Moki is your bami. You are the one who must find a solution."

Twenty-three

MOKI ADJUSTED HIS backpack as the others waved goodbye to the villagers of Lyanan. He was glad to be leaving. Lyanan represented failure and loss to him. He had failed to be adopted here, and it was here that he would lose his sitik when her people came back to claim her. The new creatures had looked like swollen corpses in their puffy white suits. It was hard to believe that Eerin had been one of them.

Eerin had shown him pictures of the new creatures on her talking stone. It was called a *computer,* he reminded himself, spelling out the word in Eerin's skin speech on the inside of his arm. Out of their suits, the new creatures, *humans,* looked perpetually embarrassed or surprised. Eerin had told him that they didn't have skin speech, that they were always the same color.

She showed him a picture of herself, before Anito's sitik had transformed her. It was a stranger who stood there, her body concealed by finely woven wrappings in bright colors. The things they wore on their body were called *clothing*, and were made out of *cloth*. There were two people with her in the picture, her *brother*, and her *father*. A *brother* was like a tareena, only their sitik (*father*) had two bami at the same time, instead of one after the other, as was decent. And they usually had more than one sitik at a time; sometimes several adults took care of each other's bami, which they called *children*. It was a strange and confusing world. How could Eerin want to go back there?

Perhaps, he hoped, her people would forget, or their *starship* would get lost on the great sky ocean, and Eerin would be able to stay here. He liked Ukatonen, he was kind and funny and a good teacher, but Eerin was his sitik, and no one could replace her. She had been so strange at Lyanan, wanting time alone, listening to her *computer* make noises, and sometimes noises and pictures at the same time. Sometimes she would make strange noises as she listened to the *computer*. Other times she would sit on the edge of the cliff, her skin grey with sadness, staring out to sea. If he tried to distract her she would ignore him, or worse, order him to go away.

He was glad they were leaving. Once they were away from Lyanan, perhaps she would start behaving more normally. He was eager to head back to the safe familiarity of Narmolom.

But instead of heading north toward Narmolom, they turned south along the coast.

"Where are we going?" Moki asked.

"We're going to visit the enkar," Ukatonen told him.

"Why?" he asked.

"If we headed straight back to Narmolom, we'd get there less than a month before mating season. We'd only have to leave again when mating starts. I'd rather let Anito have some time alone in the village before she has to leave. Besides, you and Eerin are disrupting the harmony of Narmolom. It would be better to visit the enkar, and leave the villagers alone. It is more important that the enkar get to know you. They are the ones that Eerin's people will be dealing with."

"Won't Anito be worried?"

"She knows you're with me," Ukatonen said.

Moki's ears flattened against his head at the news. He liked Narmolom. Once they left with Anito, they could never return. Instead, they would be living among the enkar, who lived like ghosts and hermits, dead to their villages. Like the enkar, he would belong nowhere.

Eerin touched him on the shoulder. "I'll miss Narmolom too, Moki."

They headed south, away from the coast, toward the distant mountains. There was snow on the tops of the tallest mountains. Eerin told him that there was snow like that in the village of her sitik's sitik, her *grandfather*.

Moki was busy absorbing the idea that her grandfather had lived in a different village than her sitik, her father, had, when Ukatonen spoke up.

"Why didn't your sitik's sitik die?" Ukatonen asked her.

"Die? Why would he die?" Juna asked.

"The snow kills us. It's too cold. We go to sleep if it gets too cold."

"It can kill my people too, but we cover our bodies with warm coverings that keep us from getting cold."

"How do you keep the coverings warm?"

Eerin flushed purple in puzzlement for a moment. "What do you mean?"

"The covers, they keep you warm, yes? How do they make heat?"

Eerin made that funny barking cough that she sometimes made when she was amused. She called it *laughing*. "The covers don't make heat, en. They keep in the heat that our bodies make, the way a bird's feathers do. That's why there are so many birds way up north, where it gets cold and snows part of the year."

"You've been in the Cold Country?" Ukatonen asked her, his skin a brilliant, incredulous pink, his ears spread so wide that they quivered. "Tell me about it!" he demanded.

They stopped there for the rest of the afternoon and the night, eating dried food from their packs instead of hunting, while Ukatonen listened to Eerin's tales of the Cold Country. Moki built their sleeping nest by himself. The others were too engrossed to heed him.

Moki couldn't blame Ukatonen. The stories were fascinating. There were great, open spaces as wide as the sea, covered only by grass and bushes. Giant birds roamed these terrifyingly open spaces, eating grass or each other. They were as tall as

Eerin, and weighed twice as much. You could look for many yai in all directions and see only grass and animals, no trees.

Moki closed his eyes and tried to picture the Cold Country. It was cold and open and utterly terrifying. Seeing his fear, Eerin put an arm around him, and drew him close to her warm body.

Juna drew Moki close to her. Her descriptions of the northern steppes seemed to have frightened him.

"There is a quarbirri, one of the earliest, very simple, very moving, that describes death coming from out of the Cold Country like a wall of white," Ukatonen said, when she was through describing the steppes.

He took a simple wooden flute from his pack, stood, and drew himself up, becoming a performer. Placing the flute across his nostrils, he blew a haunting melody, discordant and tuned to an alien scale. It made the stinging stripes along Juna's back tighten. Compared to the elaborate quarbirri performed by the villagers and by the lyali-Tendu, this was as simple and stark as a classical butoh dance.

The enkar moved with the slow, fluid grace of a tai chi master. First he was a Tendu villager, then a sudden cold wind, blowing from the north. The jungle withered and died, and then he became a group of enkar, journeying north to see what had happened. One by one, the cold struck them down, except for the last, who was visited by the spirits, who gave her a secret power that enabled her to continue on toward the end of the world, until at last she found herself staring at a wall of whiteness streaked with earth and pieces of the sky. She turned back, her spirit power failing her just as she reached the borders of the remaining jungle. She lived long enough to tell the other enkar what she had seen, that they might prepare for the coming of the great wall of death.

The story at an end, Ukatonen sat back down, clearly tired. Moki handed him a large chunk of honeycomb. Juna fumbled for her computer. She had been so caught up in the performance that she had forgotten to record it. Some part of her was relieved that the Survey would never see it. The memories of this quarbirri were hers alone. She paged to the geologic survey record. The most recent ice age had occurred about 25,000 years ago. Her stinging stripes tightened again as she realized just how old the quarbirri had to be.

"The Tendu have a very long memory," she told Ukatonen. "According to what my people know of your world, the last wall of ice was many thousands of years old. If this story dates from that time, then it is older than any memories of my people."

"This is not a story from the last great cold," Ukatonen informed her. "It is much older than that. It has helped us survive four Great Cold times."

Juna's stinging stripes prickled as she examined the geological record. If the Survey's record was accurate, then the quarbirri was well over a hundred thousand years old. Even if the geological surveys had overestimated the time between ice ages, the story that she had heard was older than all but the most ancient prehistoric digs. It predated the disappearance of the Neanderthals, she realized, paging through a summary of human history. She shivered and crumpled up the computer, overwhelmed by what she had just learned.

"How do you know when our last Great Cold was?" Ukatonen asked her. "Your people got here only last year. How did they know what happened before they got here?"

"They went up, almost as far north as you can go into the cold country, and cut into the—" She searched for a term for glacier. "Snow mountains" was the best term she could come up with. "The snow mountains do not melt in the summer. Each year a new layer of snow falls on them. Each layer marks a year. We examined the layers, and could tell by their size what the snow was like in a certain year."

Ukatonen pondered this for a moment. "Your people are very clever, even though they are young," he said at last. "There is much that we can learn from each other."

They traveled for the next two months, visiting three gatherings of enkar. Juna answered questions and described Earth and the Survey for the enkar, teaching them the Standard alphabet and some rudiments of Standard. They stayed only a few days in each gathering, but, as before, they acquired a group of enkar who followed them to the next gathering. These were soon capable of carrying on simple conversations in Standard skin speech. Soon Juna was able to delegate most of the introductory classes to them and concentrate on her advanced students.

Finally it was time to return to Narmolom. They did not hurry, even though it was well past mating season. None of them wanted to take Anito away from Narmolom. When at last they reached the village na tree, Ninto came out to greet them. She was polite, and claimed to be glad to see them, despite the mournful color of her skin.

"Anito is out distributing the last of her narey among her na trees," Ninto told them. "She will be back at nightfall. She's already shown Yahi everything he needs to know to replace her. We can be ready to leave tomorrow, if you like."

"I want to make sure that you get a good farewell feast," Ukatonen said. "Five days should be enough time."

"As you wish, en," Ninto said. "I will go and tell Miato that we will be leaving."

Anito was returning to the village with a basket of fresh-caught fish, when she saw Ninto. The color of her tareena's skin told her what had happened.

"He's here to take me," Anito said, going grey with grief.

Ninto brushed her shoulder. "He's here for both of us, Anito. I won't let my tareena go alone."

"I wish you'd change your mind," Anito said. "You don't have to go."

Ninto shook her head, rippling a denial. "Baha is ready and I'm ready. I'll miss Narmolom, though." Her mourning colors deepened, and she looked away. "It's better than dying. Perhaps it's selfish of me to want to go on living, but I do. I like life. I never could understand those who would rather die than leave Narmolom. Even our sitik. He would have made a wonderful enkar, if he'd had the courage."

"Ilto was not a coward!" Anito blurted, forgetting to avoid her sitik's name in her eagerness to defend him.

"No, he was very brave, but he was afraid to go on living if it meant leaving the village. He told me so himself. You were not the only one who tried to talk him out of dying. It was more than fear, though. He wanted to stay here, to be buried with a na seed in his belly, to be part of Narmolom forever. If it were only a matter of fear, then Ilto would have become an enkar. He did what he wanted, and I'm doing what I want. I only wish you didn't have to go as well."

"There's no point in wishing for that. My fate is to leave Narmolom before my time. I'll just have to make the best of it."

Ninto brushed her shoulder, and the two turned back toward home.

The village bustled for five days, preparing their farewell feast. Tinka scrubbed feast dishes. Bami and adults streamed in and out of the tree with huge baskets of food. The storeroom was ransacked for preserved delicacies.

Anito wove a funeral coffin. Because she was leaving, a tinka would be sacrificed to take her place. At least, she thought, it would be a wild tinka from the forest, not one from the village. She tried not to think about Moki, but the memories of his valiant struggle to follow them kept springing to mind.

"Rot and infestations on that bami!" Anito muttered, pushing the coffin away and pacing across the room. "If it wasn't for him, killing a tinka wouldn't bother me!" She grabbed her gathering sack and headed for the forest. She swung through the trees, flying from branch to branch, fleeing the image of Moki lying in the coffin she was making. Moki was a bami now, and safe from such a sacrifice, but a tinka would be killed to take her place in the coffin.

She paused, panting, beside a waterfall on the river. Someone touched her on the shoulder. It was Ukatonen.

"What's the matter, Anito?" he asked, his skin speech pastel with gentleness.

"It's the tinka, en. The one who will be going into my coffin instead of me. It—" She paused looking for a way to explain that wouldn't make her sound stupid.

"It bothers you," Ukatonen prompted.

"Yes, en. I keep seeing Moki in that basket. I know it won't be him, but—"

"It bothers me too."

"It does?" Anito said.

Ukatonen looked away, turning brown with shame. "It's the

new creature. She's made me look at the tinka differently. It's one thing to let the tinka we can't adopt die a natural death, but this—" He paused. "I'm going to talk with the other enkar and see if we can change this."

"But that won't save the life of the tinka who will take my place in the coffin."

Ukatonen clouded over with sadness. "No."

"I could always just leave, instead of going through with the funeral feast."

"Would you leave Narmolom out of balance?"

Now it was Anito's turn to look embarrassed. "I guess I can't just leave. What can I do?"

"Try some subterfuge," Ukatonen suggested, and then leaned forward to explain what he had in mind.

Anito flickered polite thanks as one of the elders congratulated her on the unusual design of her coffin. Mounds of funeral offerings were piled over the small body of the tinka inside it. At last the speeches were over, and it was time to weave the coffin shut. After that was finished, she and Ninto, whose coffin also held the body of a tinka, shouldered the few belongings that they were taking with them, and followed the procession to the holes where the coffins would be buried. The villagers acted as though they weren't there. Once the coffins were woven shut, Ninto and Anito were dead to the village.

They stood off to one side, watching as the two coffins were buried near each other in neighboring sun breaks, the two tareenas as close in pretend death as they had been when they lived in the village.

Watching the villagers, Anito felt as though she really had died. There was an impenetrable barrier between her and Narmolom. Even if she returned as an enkar, the villagers would not recognize her. She would be a stranger to them. As far as Narmolom was concerned, she was dead.

Baha, soon to be Bahito, lingered a while after the others had gone, carefully arranging the branches piled on Ninto's grave. At last he turned to leave. He paused on the edge of the clearing, and looked for a long moment at the spot where his sitik and Anito were standing. He lifted a hand in a brief, forbidden gesture of farewell, then vanished into the forest.

Anito turned to go. Ukatonen, Moki, and Eerin would fall back from the procession and dig up the tinka in her coffin and revive it. The tinka's breathing rate was slowed so far that it wouldn't suffocate in the short time it was buried.

Ninto caught at her arm. "Anito, I have a favor to ask you." She was faintly brown with embarrassment.

"Yes?"

"Will you help me dig up my grave? I didn't kill the tinka in my coffin. I-I want to set it free."

Anito rippled laughter. "Yes, Ninto. I will help you. If you will help me dig up my coffin, and free that tinka. But if we wait, Ukatonen and the others will help us both."

"You mean you—"

"I didn't kill the tinka either. There's a makino with a na seed underneath it."

"That was clever of you. I didn't leave anything. No tree will sprout from my coffin." A mist of regret passed across Ninto. "I just couldn't leave the tinka to die."

Anito rummaged in her pack and drew out a large brown nut the size of her fist. It was a na tree seed. "It's from one of Ilto's trees," she said. "I was taking it along to remember him by, but this is a better use for it. Let's dig up the tinka and go kill something to plant the seed in."

A soft rain began pattering down as they set to work. Ukatonen and the others arrived to help just as they uncovered Ninto's coffin. Ninto stooped to undo the weaving, and lifted the tinka out. It was alive and unharmed. She set it gently at the base of a tree.

"It's getting dark," Anito said. "Let's go hunting. The others can open my coffin."

It was fully dark by the time they returned, dragging a large hikani bird between them. Moki was squatting beside the two tinka, watching over them while Ukatonen and Eerin finished piling the branches back on Anito's grave. The two of them slid the ground bird into the coffin, piling the garlands over it. Ninto rewove the coffin shut, while Anito held a glow-fungus to light what she was doing. Then they reburied the coffin.

"Well, that's done," Ukatonen said. "We'd better go. Let's take the tinka with us. We can leave them near the next village. It's not likely that anyone would recognize them, but it would be better not to take that chance."

They slung the tinka over their backs, and set off through the dark forest. Near dawn, Anito stopped.

"We're near my sitik's tree," she said. "I want to visit it."

"Go on," Ukatonen told her. "We can wait."

"I'll come with you," Ninto offered.

The young na tree rising from Ilto's grave was now a thriving young sapling, rising toward the canopy.

"It's doing well," Ninto said, indirectly praising Anito's care of the na tree.

"I hope Yahi takes good care of it," Anito said.

"I'm sure he will, Anito. He's a good bami. I've asked Baha to look after it as well."

Anito flickered thanks. "He was a good sitik," she added after a long pause.

"Yes," Ninto said, putting her palm against the slender trunk of Ilto's tree.

Anito placed her hand just below Ninto's. They reached out with their free hands and linked, their shared sadness mingling and dissipating. Underneath Ninto's sorrow there was an eagerness to find out what came next. Anito let that feeling flood into her, creating a seed of hope to carry inside her. She was glad that they were doing this together. It was good to have a tareena. Ninto echoed Anito's gratitude as they slid from the link.

Day was breaking. Long rays of dawn light were turning the mist at the top of the canopy to gold.

Ninto touched Anito's arm. "Let's go join the others."

Anito shouldered her pack, rested her palm one last time on Ilto's tree in a final gesture of farewell, and turned to follow her tareena.

T w e n t y - f o u r

"No, YOU MADE a mistake. Try again," the instructor, a tall, gaunt enkar named Naratonen, told Anito.

Juna watched as Anito repeated the last phrase of a quarbirri. Still dissatisfied, the instructor turned to Ninto, and asked her to try it. She also failed.

"Like this," Naratonen said, demonstrating a complex hand gesture. "Your color is off too, it should be lighter and more blue, and you're fading it in too late."

Juna stretched and yawned. She had been sitting for several hours while Naratonen taught them this quarbirri about the creation of the na tree. She was glad to be allowed to sit in on Ninto and Anito's enkar training, but just watching demanded great patience and stamina. They had been working through this particular piece for two hours now. Soon it would be noon, and time for her to leave for lunch and then her language lessons. She was looking forward to that.

Anito and Ninto repeated the phrase of the quarbirri again.

"Better. Try again, more slowly this time."

They did, and Naratonen flickered grudging approval. "It still needs some work, but you're improving. That's good enough for now. Go get some lunch and come back later."

Juna got up to follow them, but Naratonen put a hand on her shoulder to stop her.

"Yes, en," Juna said, afraid that he was going to complain about her watching the lessons.

"Your speaking stone," he said. "I understand that it makes pictures of things. Did it make pictures of this lesson?"

"Yes, en."

"May I see them?"

"Of course, en," she said. Was the enkar going to forbid her to record his lessons?

She replayed the last fifteen minutes of the lesson. He watched intently.

"How far back does it remember?" he asked her.

"Every lesson that I have been to, it remembers, en. I have taken some parts out of some of them, places where nothing happened, or where you repeated the same movement over and over again."

"Can I see the part of the lesson where I first showed them the movement?"

"Of course, en," she said, skipping back to the appropriate part of the lesson.

Naratonen watched the replay of the lesson intently.

"I see," he commented when the replay was finished. "I needed to slow down. No wonder they didn't understand. Thank you, Eerin. That is a very useful thing," he said, gesturing at the computer. "May I come and look at it some more when you aren't busy?"

Juna hesitated, wondering if this was a good idea. She didn't want the Tendu to begin coveting human technology. Still, she could hardly refuse an enkar.

"Of course, en. Perhaps tonight, after dinner?"

"Thank you," he said.

Juna left to join Anito and Ninto for lunch. She would have to hurry. She barely had time to eat before her pupils gathered for class.

It was a big class, by Tendu standards. There were ten pupils, seated in a semicircle, waiting for her to show up. They were impressive students, attentive, tightly focused, and retentive. She rarely had to repeat herself. They could repeat long lists of words perfectly from memory. The hard part was teaching them grammar and meaning. Time and again she had to explain that color had no emotional meaning in Standard. They kept adding color to their words to express emotional content. The idea that there were separate words for happiness, laughter, anger, and so forth was hard for them to accept.

This was her third lesson in the rudiments of diplomatic protocol. It was slow going. She had to stop and explain everything. Today she was explaining the ranking of a ship's crew.

"First there's the captain—she's like the chief elder of a village. She gives orders and is in charge of solving problems if something goes wrong. Then there's the first mate—he's in charge when the captain is asleep or resting. If the captain is sick or dies, he takes over."

"Why don't they just wake the captain up if something goes wrong?"

"Usually they do, but they need someone in charge when there isn't an emergency, so that the captain can get some sleep."

"Why don't they just stop for the night?"

"Because they can't," Juna said firmly. "A ship is very complicated and they need people to watch over it constantly. It's a bit like a raft on the river, only we're too far from land to pull the boats ashore at night. Someone needs to steer the boat and watch out for trouble.

"Now, the second mate takes over when the first mate and the captain can't. That way, there's always someone watching over the ship who is rested and ready to deal with trouble. He ranks below the captain and the first mate."

"Why? He does the same job."

The class wore on slowly, each word she explained spawning dozens of new questions. As always, her pupils left the class purple with puzzlement, arguing amongst themselves.

Ukatonen swung down from an upper branch as the class broke up.

"They're learning well," he said.

"I suppose so," Juna responded. "But I don't think they understand what they're learning."

"Neither do Moki, Anito, or myself, but what you are

teaching us now will help us understand your people more quickly."

"I hope so."

"You've been working too hard. Let's take the afternoon off and go fishing."

"But I have another class to teach!"

"Tell them to come back tomorrow."

"But—" Juna began to protest.

"You teach almost every day. None of the enkar do that. Even Anito and Ninto take more time off than you do, and they're studying to become enkar."

"All right, let me tell Moki to pass along the word to my students."

"I was planning on taking him along as well. You're working him too hard. He needs some time off too."

"But who will teach the newer classes?"

"Eerin, stop worrying. We have years before your people come back for you. I'll take over some of the new classes, and Garitonen and some of your other advanced students can take over the others. I've already told Garitonen to take over Moki's class, and he'll tell the rest to take the day off."

He tossed her a gathering sack full of fishing gear, and set off in search of Moki. Juna followed him. He was right. She had been working too hard. She didn't have to teach Standard to every single Tendu on the planet. She already had the beginnings of a solid team of translators.

Moki turned brilliant blue at the news that they were going fishing. Juna felt a pang of guilt. She really had been overworking him. He looked thin and a bit worn. They hadn't linked fully in a couple of weeks.

"This was a good idea," Juna remarked as they unrolled their nets and assembled their fishing spears. They were fishing at a wide spot in one of the placid, slow-moving jungle rivers that flowed through the enkar's territory. The surface of the water was covered with drifts of golden pollen, flower petals, and bits of fluff shed from the ika tree. Inside each bit of fluff was a small seed. Slanting beams of late afternoon sunlight illuminated streamers of lianas cascading down from the branches of the trees.

"I wish we could stay here for a while," she said wistfully.

"Why not?" Ukatonen said.

"I promised Naratonen that I would show him what I've recorded of his classes in my talking stone," Juna replied, pointing with her chin at the computer recharging in a pool of sunlight.

"Don't worry about it," Ukatonen told her. He waded over to a half-submerged log, and dripped a few drops of clear liquid on it. Several large wide-winged insects settled on the spot almost immediately. Ukatonen picked one up and set it on his spur for a couple of minutes, then waved it off his arm. It flew off in a straight line. He repeated that with several more insects before returning to Juna.

"I've invited Naratonen to bring Ninto and Anito out here for a couple of days, and told him to let the others know that you wouldn't be teaching for a while."

"Those insects carry messages?"

"Yes, it's called a meaki. I sent them back to the enkar gathering. When one of them gets there, it will start doing a special dance. Someone will catch it and read the message I have given the meaki. Then it will be passed on."

"How do you make the message?"

"I make it in my spurs, and feed it to the insect. It spreads throughout its body and sends the message-bug where I tell it to go. When it arrives, an enkar will link with the insect and read the message in its cells. Then the enkar will turn off the message, feed the meaki well, and let it go. Naratonen will get my invitation before nightfall, though we probably won't see him until tomorrow."

"I never saw the villagers do that," Juna remarked.

"Only the enkar use meaki. The chief elders use birds to let us know when we're needed. I was responding to such a message when I met you and Anito." Ukatonen picked up a spear. "Now, enough talk. Let's fish," he said.

He waded out to a submerged rock, and stood as still as a fishing bird, waiting for a fish to come within range of his spear. Moki headed downstream with the net. He was young and hungry, eager for a big catch. Juna took her spear and knelt on the log where Ukatonen had summoned the message bug.

Silence fell as they waited for the fish to forget about them. It was a silence filled with living things, resounding with the distant calls of birds and lizards, and the buzzing of the matas, strange insects with wings like leaves and bizarre, elongated heads that served as resonators. Occasionally another meaki would come and circle around, drawn by the fading scent of the attractor Ukatonen had dripped onto the log.

She had been here among the enkar for three and a half months now. Teaching the enkar was demanding work. It was good to take a break. A shadow moved beneath the log. Juna waited, poised and still, until the fish edged within range of her spear. She threw it, striking the fish. Grasping the shaft of the spear, she impaled the struggling fish against the sandy bottom until its struggles ceased.

She pulled in the spear and removed the fish. It was a pugginti, a sweet, succulent fish that fed mostly on fallen fruit. She held it up and Ukatonen flickered approval.

Naratonen arrived with Ninto and Anito in tow the next day. He sent his two students off to practice, and sat with Juna while she showed him how to work the computer. Once he knew what he was doing, she left him to study while she and Moki went swimming with Ukatonen. They floated on their backs, watching the light flicker through the trees. The river pushed them past the bank where Ninto and Anito were practicing their quarbirri.

Ukatonen rolled over and splashed over toward them.

"No, no, no!" he told them. "Like this." He grasped Ninto's arm and moved it through the gesture she was trying to perfect. "Your hand needs to be bent further back, so we can see your spurs, and your elbow stays down."

Irritation flickered across Ninto's back. Her patience was beginning to wear thin. Juna rippled amusement, rolled over and dove deep beneath the surface, then leapt up out of the water. Moki followed her, and the two of them played like otters until they were panting and out of breath.

They pulled out onto a sun-heated rock to rest. Moki held out his arms and they linked, reaffirming and strengthening the bond between them. Juna's skill at linking had increased during her time among the enkar. Sometimes in the link, she seemed to feel the presence of the forest around her, pulsing with the threads of many lives. It was impossible, of course. Linking was merely a deep awareness of another's physiology, a form of incredibly direct biofeedback that seemed to involve a greatly heightened form of chemo-reception via the allu.

Still, linking with Moki made her feel at home on this world, made her feel a part of the jungle around them. It was probably entirely subjective, but it made her happy. She lay back in the sun and closed her eyes.

Ukatonen finished working with Ninto and Anito, and wandered over to see how Naratonen was doing with the *computer*. Ukatonen shook his head. The new creatures had such strange skin speech. Eerin had explained that they used sound to communicate most of the time, but the *humans'* skin speech was easier for the Tendu to learn.

He tried to imagine a room filled with people like Eerin, only brown and pink, their skins still, their mouths producing sounds like the ones she made occasionally. They must sound like a room full of mating yirri, he thought. It was hard to believe that sensible, intelligent people could communicate in this way. How could they possibly understand each other?

Naratonen was hunched over the computer, studying the pictures of himself that Eerin had made. He looked up as Ukatonen squatted beside him.

"This is fascinating. I can see how I move, it's much clearer and sharper than skin-speech pictures. I'm learning a lot about how I teach."

Ukatonen looked over Naratonen's shoulder as the computer played and replayed a phrase from the quarbirri he was teaching. Ukatonen had dismissed Eerin's talking stones as a curiosity, but here was Naratonen, pink with excitement at seeing himself on the thing. Ukatonen looked away, uneasy at the sight.

Eerin came over and squatted on Naratonen's other side. "Well, en, what do you think of it?"

"It's wonderful!"

"I have a few full quarbirri performances in here somewhere," she said, reaching down and fiddling with the controls.

The picture changed, and she pointed at something; then the picture changed once more and she pointed again, until the screen showed her what she wanted. Ukatonen had seen her do this before, but never really paid much attention.

"Here, watch this," she said.

The screen darkened. There was the sound of a shell horn being played. A tall enkar was blowing on it. Then a lyali-Tendu responded with a run of notes on her flute. Ukatonen recognized her. It was Narito, leader of the band of lyali-Tendu that Narmolom had traded with last year. Ukatonen's stinging stripes tightened as he realized that he was watching himself performing the quarbirri of the origin of the lyali-Tendu. Frightened and intrigued, he observed himself moving through the performance, his skin alive with words. He glanced up, and saw that Naratonen was watching with a critical eye. Ukatonen was glad that he had performed well. The truth of the talking stone wouldn't shame him.

As the quarbirri proceeded, he was drawn into watching himself, evaluating his technique, for the most part pleased, but noticing certain things he wished he had done differently. When the recording drew to a close, he wanted to watch it again, as Naratonen was doing. He began to understand the fascination that the talking stone held for Naratonen. It bothered him. He scooped up his hunting gear, and swung off into the forest to think it over.

Ukatonen perched in the top of a tall ika tree, looking out over the canopy. Eerin had said that her people would bring change. He hadn't wanted to believe her, but here it was. The talking stone had fascinated both him and Naratonen. It wasn't decent, it wasn't healthy to be fascinated by a dead thing like that. This obsession with dead things could spread among the Tendu. What should be done about it? He could destroy the talking stones, or hide them, but that would anger Eerin and her people. He could ask her to hide her talking stone, but sooner or later something else would come along that would hold the same fascination.

He needed to talk this over with other enkar, with Naratonen, with Anito, and with Eerin. What should be done?

An unwary quanji landed in a nearby branch. Ukatonen

lifted his blowpipe and shot it as the bird spread its wings to fly. He caught the bird neatly as it fell. He butchered it and went swinging back through the trees to rejoin the others.

"Well, what should we do?" Ukatonen finished.

Anito sat back, rich ochre with concern. "I don't know," she said. "Change and adapt, I suppose. You're right, we can't hide from it."

"Yes you can," Eerin said. "You can ask us to leave you alone."

"Why?" Naratonen asked. "It would be wrong. There's so much we can learn from you. The Tendu have never turned away from knowledge. Why should we start now? We're enkar, not some head-in-the-mud villagers. It is our job to learn and study. It is our atwa to bring our knowledge to the other Tendu and share it with them."

"But," Ukatonen responded, "it is also our atwa to protect and guide them, to steer our people away from things that can hurt them. It is our atwa to judge for them. Our lives, our honor, rest on those judgments. Remember, we do this so that those 'head-in-the-mud' villagers can continue to live like that."

"And is it right?" Naratonen asked, getting up and pacing around, his colors bright with urgency. "Is it right that their heads remain in the mud? Is it right that the villagers stay so much to themselves? Is it right that the villagers would rather die than face exile when it is time to give their place in the village over to their bami? Is it right that we have to trap the villagers into becoming enkar through obligation? There are fewer enkar all the time, and this is not good for the Tendu."

"We've had problems like this before," Ukatonen reminded him. "We've always managed to solve them ourselves."

Anito listened to the enkar debating, and thought of her sitik, how much she wished that he had chosen to live. She thought of her time among the enkar, of all the things she had learned. She was sure that Ilto would have loved being an enkar. It would have given him the room to satisfy his curiosity. She and Ninto had been too busy learning new things to miss Narmolom.

"No," Anito said. "It isn't right that the villagers are

uninterested, but then, it isn't right that the enkar should make the villagers change. They like their lives."

"The villagers are our atwa," Naratonen argued. "Like other animals, the Tendu must either change or die out. Sometimes it seems like the Tendu are like a dying pond left behind by the flood. Our world gets smaller and smaller. How soon before we stagnate and die? I look at the new creatures, and I see them bringing things to make our world large again. Already, I am learning better ways to teach. I watched some of the new creature's *plays* and *movies*. There are ideas and techniques that we could use in our own performances. I'm tired of teaching the same traditional quarbirri over and over again. We make a new one every twenty years or so, but no one wants to learn them, because they're not traditional! It isn't enough. I want more!"

Anito sat, mesmerized by Naratonen's words, which were almost a quarbirri in themselves. He was right, but so was Ukatonen. How was she, barely even an elder, supposed to guide the Tendu through this? How could she bring harmony out of this chaos? She realized then the terrible, frightening task that the enkar had taken upon themselves. No wonder most people shrank from becoming enkar. Who would want the responsibility of determining the future of the Tendu?

Eerin stood and laid a gentle hand on Naratonen's arm. "Excuse me, en, but it isn't that simple. Knowledge is a knife with two edges. It can cut cord, or skin game, but it can also hurt and kill. Not all the things my people know are as benign as this *computer,*" she said, using the new creatures' word for her talking stone. "Even this computer contains things that might be harmful for your people to know."

"What sort of things?"

"Hunting equipment that can be used to kill another Tendu."

Anito looked at Eerin in puzzlement. What she was saying didn't make sense.

"Why would we wish to hunt ourselves?" Ukatonen asked, his skin deeply purple in puzzlement. "That would be silly."

"My people have always killed each other in anger," Eerin said, her skin deeply brown with shame. "Sometimes they have killed each other in large numbers. It is what we call a *war.*"

She looked away; water was flowing from her eyes. Her skin was a muddy turmoil of shame, anger, fear, and concern. Moki put a protective arm around her.

"My people are different from the Tendu," Eerin went on. "We don't wish to hurt you, but we do bring ideas that might cause harm." With that, she got up and walked away into the forest, shrugging off Moki's attempts to follow her.

Juna sat on a rock by the river, letting the low, constant murmur of its flow soothe her. The Tendu needed to know about her people's flaws as well as their virtues, but she felt deeply ashamed. Even now, there were wars on Earth. When she left Earth, the news net had been full of bulletins about the escalation of an ethnic conflict in Punjab.

Even before her great-great-grandfather's time, people had been working to create an end to war. They had succeeded in some ways. Little wars no longer escalated into world wars, but still people killed each other over lines drawn on the dirt. Living in space, seeing the Earth revolving below, those fights had seemed strange, but even in space, tensions between Earth and the colonies had occasionally erupted into blockades and skirmishes.

There was a rustling in the leaves behind her. Juna looked up. It was Naratonen. He squatted beside her.

"Why do your people kill each other?" he asked.

"We fight over land and water. We fight over different ideas. We fight because one people looks different from another people. We have always fought, en. Some have tried to stop the fighting, but there is always a new battle somewhere. There are very many of us, en. Too many, and there isn't enough food or water for everyone."

"There should be fewer people."

"We're trying, en. It's a long, slow struggle. There are less of us than there were in my grandfather's time, but it will be many years before there will be enough for all. Children still starve to death, en. Not as many as before, but—" Juna looked away, remembering her own hunger.

Naratonen touched her shoulder. "Once, many years ago, our people were as numerous as the leaves on the trees. There was

not enough room or food for us all. We chose, as your people
did, to let fewer of us live. The enkar decided to let sickness
loose among our people. We also began eating our narey then,
and have continued to do so to keep our numbers down. Some
of us went to live in the ocean, and became the lyali-Tendu.

"There are many sad quarbirri from that time. Half the Tendu
died from the sickness we created. Tinka, bami, elders, and
enkar died in equal numbers. Whole villages died or disbanded.
It is sad when someone dies, but their memory is held by the
people of the village. When a village dies, the memory of all
those people dies with them. It is as though they have died
twice."

"You made a sickness that you knew would kill your own
people?" Juna asked.

Naratonen flickered agreement. "The enkar who made this
judgment were among the first to die. They went from village
to village spreading sickness, then died alone in the forest.
Only one survived. He was the one who knew how to stop the
sickness when it had done its work. When it was time, he
taught the others a cure. Then he went off into the forest, and
let the sickness kill him."

"How could you do such a thing?" Juna asked, horrified at
the scale of the enkar's genocide.

"You have wars, we have sickness. Is there a difference?
Which one of us is better than the other?" Naratonen got up and
walked off into the forest, leaving her there in the darkness to
ponder his unanswerable questions.

Twenty-five

"BUT GIKITONEN SAID that the population levels of ganro in the upper Hirrani valley were more influenced by rainfall than by the levels of mikkarra," Anito said to Ninto.

"Yes, but the levels of mikkarra are dependent on rainfall. You can't separate the two factors."

Juna sighed and looked away. She was tired of these abstruse technical discussions of ecological theory. She would be glad when it was all over. The last three years had been a steady grind of tutors and training. The intense study had taken a heavy toll on Ninto and Anito. They were thin and weedy-looking, their tempers short, and they thought of nothing but their training.

A flicker of resigned agreement passed over Moki in response to Juna's sigh. Juna brushed his shoulder affectionately. The others' focus on the upcoming test had thrown the two of them together more often, strengthening their bond. It was one of the few good things to come out of all this training.

"It'll be over soon," she told him. "Ninto's test begins tomorrow, and Anito's will start four days after that. We'll be done with all of this in less than half a month."

"Can we go fishing when the testing's done?" Moki asked in plaintive hues.

Juna laughed and flickered agreement. "Yes, we can go fishing after the testing is done. Until then we need to take care of Anito and Ninto."

Ukatonen and Ninto went off to spend the night before the test in the peaceful refuge of the forest. Juna and Moki stayed in the gathering with Anito, helping her review for her test.

Ninto and Ukatonen returned the next day, and headed directly to the center of the ring of na trees for Ninto's first test. Anito joined the other two candidates waiting to be tested. Juna and Moki were sent out to gather food; Ninto would be hungry when she was done with the examination. They came back with bulging gathering sacks of fruit, game, greens, and omkina tubers. Moki peeled the tubers and pounded them into a smooth paste while Juna butchered game and laid out the fruit and greens.

Ninto came back from the questioning weak, shaky, and exhausted. She was too tired to speak more than a few words. They fed her, washed her, and helped her into bed. She was asleep when Anito came in.

"How is she?"

"Exhausted," Ukatonen told them. "It was a difficult session."

"Did she do well?" Moki asked.

"I won't know whether she passes or fails until everyone has been tested. It will depend on what the judges think," Ukatonen said.

Juna thought Ukatonen seemed worried and withdrawn. She glanced at Anito, but she couldn't tell whether she had noticed it too. She remembered her own dissertation defense. She had been an utter wreck by the time it was over. She understood what Anito and Ninto were going through.

These tests were a trial of the candidates' endurance as much as a test of their knowledge and skill. Each examination left Ninto more drained and exhausted than the last. Ukatonen, Juna, and Moki fed her, linked with her to repair her exhaustion, and helped her into bed. Anito tried to help, but Ukatonen sternly forbade her to do more than prepare and serve dinner. She had to save her own energy for the upcoming test. Flickers of rusty red frustration passed over Anito as she watched them heal Ninto.

The final examination tested the candidate's skill at quarbirri, and was open to anyone who wanted to attend. Ninto performed a solo quarbirri, and took part in a multiple quarbirri, both chosen at random by the judges. Then the judges asked her to act out scenes from the traditional quarbirri that Naratonen had taught them.

This was one of the most physically demanding tests. Even though Ukatonen had linked with her between phases of the test to give her strength, Ninto was visibly tired by the end of her final scene. Ukatonen helped her back to their room. She ate a little fruit and honeycomb, linked briefly with Ukatonen, and then fell asleep. Anito squatted protectively beside her tareena's bed.

"Worried?" Juna asked, sitting near her.

Anito looked away. "Ninto's older, more experienced than I am. If she's this tired, how will I do?"

"You've both studied very hard. You'll do all right," Juna reassured her.

"I wish we had never left Narmolom. I'm not ready for this."

Juna patted Anito on the knee. "Yes, you are. Just don't wear yourself out worrying. Eat well, sleep a lot. Let us help you through it as much as we can. That's what we're here for." Juna held out her arms.

Anito flickered her thanks, and the two of them linked, Anito sharing her fear, and Juna reassuring her. Then they unlinked and Ukatonen shooed them off to bed.

Anito woke just before dawn. Today her testing began. She stared up at the thick grey night mist, and tried to remember what she needed to know. For a terrifying moment, nothing happened. Her mind was blank. Then she remembered the pollination cycle for the ika flower, and everything else flowed into place. She was as ready as she could be. Even if she failed this time, as most of the enkar candidates did, she could test again next year. Most candidates passed on their second attempt. A few failed and went on to a third try. Those that passed became enkar; the rest no one spoke of.

She rolled over and woke Ukatonen. They got up and gathered fruit and greens for breakfast. Anito bagged a sleeping urranga, which they butchered and ate immediately. After washing off in the river, they raced each other back to the gathering. Anito won, bursting into the midst of a solemn procession of enkar heading for the testing, nearly bowling one of them over before she could stop herself. She started to apologize, but then Ukatonen hit the same branch and collided with another enkar. The entire group rippled with amused laughter, and escorted Anito to the center of the ring of na trees.

Fear descended upon her like a falling branch as she entered the crowd of assembled enkar. Ukatonen touched her shoulder in reassurance. Anito fanned her ears wide and flickered acknowledgment. She noticed Eerin and Moki in the crowd. Eerin raised a hand and turned a deep, reassuring blue.

Moki slipped through the enkar, and handed her a leaf-wrapped package of food. "For when you get hungry," he said, and slipped away again.

Anito glanced down at the neat package in her hand. She looked at Ukatonen, at Eerin, and at Moki, and felt her nervousness ease.

"You'll do fine," Ukatonen said. "I'm proud of you."

Figotonen, the eldest enkar in the gathering, held up her hand, fingers spread, and the flickering conversations stilled.

"Who sponsors this candidate?" she asked.

Ukatonen stepped to the speaker's mound. "I do, en."

"Tell us about her studies."

As Ukatonen named the enkar who had taught her, and described what she had learned from them, Anito remembered her training. They had traveled up and down the length of the land, and spent time swimming with the lyali-Tendu while Moki and Eerin worked at Lyanan.

She and Ninto had learned the name of every village between the coast and the mountains, as far north and south as the Tendu's territory extended, and the names and locations of other Tendu enclaves around the world. Ukatonen had taught them about the various councils and gatherings of enkar, what they did, and how they worked together. They had studied tracking and hunting with a thin, wiry mountain hermit who seemed as old as the mountains and as serene as a cloudless sky. Naratonen had taught them the full traditional cycle of quarbirri, and many more that were not part of the cycle. He had also coached them in the art of public speaking and formal manners.

Makitonen taught them how to link. She was the enkar who had taught Ukatonen. Linking with her had been like linking with the earth itself. She was one of the oldest Tendu now living, and had seen generations come and go like so many short-lived kika flies.

It had been a long, demanding three years. Most enkar candidates took five years to learn what Anito had learned in three. Some of the enkar doubted the wisdom of pushing her so hard, but Ukatonen wanted her to be an enkar by the time the new creatures, the *humans*, returned.

Ukatonen's recitation of her training ended, and Anito snapped out of her reverie. The testing was about to begin.

Ukatonen stepped off the speaker's mound and brushed Anito's shoulder, flickering reassurance at her.

Figotonen stepped forward. "Greetings, candidate," she said. "Tell me about the villages south of the Wainu River."

Anito suppressed a flush of relief. She was starting with an easy question. "There are only four villages south of the Wainu, en. They are Ballanari, Anakra, Frenamo, and Wallana." She went on to describe the four villages' boundaries, their population, and the names of their chief elders.

There was a long silence, as if Figotonen was waiting for something else.

"There is another village site south of the Wainu, en," Anito said at last. "It was the village of Manalim. It was abandoned after the last Cold Time, and allowed to return to the wild lands. When the next Cold Time comes, it will be started up again."

"Very good, candidate," Figotonen said. "Please describe the mating dance of the kinirri."

"Do you want me to describe the dance of the mountain kinirri or the lowland kinirri?"

"Please describe both, candidate."

The questions continued for hours. Each one contained tricks and details that required close attention and subtlety of thought

to catch. Figotonen stepped down and was replaced by Naratonen, who was replaced by another enkar, and then another
one after that. The afternoon rains began and ended as the
questions continued. Anito's skin was tired and sore when
Ukatonen stepped forward to ask a question.

"What is the name of the chief elder of Narmolom?"

A ripple of amusement ran over the assembly.

Anito stopped, examining the question carefully on all sides,
looking for the catch, the trick that would slip her up and make
her fail. She could find none. Perhaps the trick was that there
was no trick.

"Miato is the chief elder, en. You chose him yourself."

"Very good, candidate. The questioning is over. You may rest
now. Tomorrow we will test your skill at allu-a."

"Thank you, en," Anito said. Though she felt like dropping
on the spot, Anito stepped off the speaker's mound and strode
out of the central clearing as if she were fresh and ready for
more questions. Eerin and Moki followed her. Ninto met her at
the door to their room. Anito collapsed as soon as she was
inside.

"How did it go?"

"Hard," Anito said. It hurt to talk. "Hungry. Thirsty. Need
rest."

Ninto handed her a gourd of pounded omkina tubers mixed
with honey, bird blood, and arana eggs. Eerin handed her a
large gourd of water.

The sweet, starchy omkina roused her appetite. She gorged
herself with food and drink, then burrowed into the damp,
comforting warmth of her bed.

The next morning, her skin felt tight and bruised from too
much talking. She got up slowly, stiff muscles protesting, and
limped over to where a large breakfast had been laid out. She
ate, and then settled herself in a corner and turned her
awareness inward to ease her aching, overused skin and sore
muscles. She wanted to balance herself today, as a warm-up for
the test of her skill at linking. Afterwards, she ate a little more,
then went back to bed until it was time for the test.

Ukatonen woke her shortly before noon, and escorted her to
Figotonen's room for the examination. Her teacher Makitonen

was there among the senior enkar. Anito's ears lifted, surprised at Makitonen's presence.

"Are you ready for your test, candidate?" Figotonen asked her.

"Yes, en," Anito replied.

Figotonen gestured at Makitonen. The ancient enkar held her arms out, spurs up. Anito's skin stripes tightened in fear. Familiarity only intensified the fear and awe she felt when linking with Makitonen. She had been a tough, fair teacher, and Anito was sure that her testing would be as thorough as her teaching.

Anito glanced at Ukatonen. He nodded, a gesture of encouragement they had both learned from Eerin. Strengthened by Ukatonen's reassurance, Anito reached out and laid her arms on Makitonen's, grasping her teacher's forearms near the elbows. They linked, and she was plunged into the cold immensity of Makitonen's presence.

Once, during their training, Ukatonen had taken them into a cave in the mountains to show them the strange blind frogs, white lizards, and misshapen pink fish that lived in its depths. They entered a large cavern, and Ukatonen had them uncover all of the many glows they'd brought along. Eerin cried aloud in noisy, echoing wonder when the glows illuminated the glittering walls of the cavern. There were fragile crystal formations so delicate that a breath would crumble them into powder, and rippling limestone walls like waterfalls turned to stone.

Eerin had been delighted by the cave, but it frightened Anito. She had never seen a place with so few living creatures in it. The cave would still be there, unchanged, long after she had crumbled to dust. Nothing there would decay and return to life again. It would merely exist, changeless and perfect. Makitonen's presence reminded her of the cold, eternal beauty of that cave.

Makitonen moved through Anito, examining her minutely, searching for physical flaws, imperfections in the way she maintained her body. Anito looked on, worrying. Had her self-repair been adequate this morning? There were still signs of fatigue in her body, which she hadn't repaired because she was afraid it would leave her too drained for this test.

Finally Makitonen pulled back, radiating mild approval. Anito's physical body was acceptable, even with its flaws.

Then Makitonen had Anito examine her. The enkar's body seemed as ancient and strong as the hills. There was no weakness, no flaw. Makitonen's body felt as static in its cold perfection as that beautiful, lifeless cave.

Anito pulled back, radiating awe. Makitonen had her look again. Their communication was wordless, deep, but Anito understood her perfectly. She looked again, and suddenly there was a tumor growing in the enkar's liver. Anito repaired it. Another problem replaced it, this time an irregularity in Makitonen's heart valves; that too was fixed. A broken leg. A ruptured kidney. A stomach blockage. The nightmare procession of physical problems went on and on. As soon as Anito repaired one, another would spring into existence. At last, a deep, hemorrhaging wound proved too much for her. She had no strength left to heal Makitonen. She was exhausted, her reserves gone. If she healed this injury, it would kill her. She stopped, drew back, prepared to pull out of the link and summon the help of the enkar who were watching.

Makitonen stopped her, holding Anito in the link. As she watched, Makitonen arrested the bleeding and healed the ravaged flesh. Then she restored Anito's depleted reserves, and repaired the physical toll of fatigue that the test had taken.

Makitonen broke the link, and Anito emerged. To her surprise, it was only the middle of the afternoon. It seemed to her that it should be nighttime.

"We will eat and rest for a while before continuing with the rest of the examination," Makitonen announced.

Anito fought back a flicker of surprise and chagrin. She had thought the test was over. A quick ripple of amusement passed over Makitonen.

"First we tested your physical abilities in allu-a. Now we must test your emotional skills."

Anito bolted down as much food as she could hold and stretched out in a corner to sleep for as long as they would let her.

It seemed as though she had only closed her eyes when Ukatonen woke her later that afternoon. She sat up and stretched, trying to force her sleep-sodden brain into wakefulness.

Makitonen sat like a stone in the same spot she'd been in all day. Anito sat down before her, and they linked. Makitonen began testing Anito's defenses, pushing against them, probing for weaknesses, then lunging with sudden feints, and pulling back again. Each time, Anito blocked Makitonen's thrusts.

At last the ancient enkar yielded, flooding the link with her approval. Anito held her defenses tight. Only after Makitonen lowered her shields, leaving herself vulnerable, did Anito let down her own guard. She risked offending the ancient enkar, but it was better than being caught unprotected.

As soon as Anito relaxed her defenses, the next phase of the test began. They moved together, cautiously at first, then merging, blending into harmony. Each time they approached harmony, Makitonen threw the link out of balance, plunging them into emotional turmoil. Laboriously Anito drew them back into harmony. The struggle for balance was wearing her down. If the test continued, the next fall would be her last. She focused her entire being on achieving equilibrium, on blocking Makitonen's attempts to unbalance the link.

Makitonen drew Anito in. They spiraled toward equilibrium, drawing closer and closer to harmony. Anito relaxed. Makitonen was going to let things proceed to a balance point. She had passed the test.

Then Makitonen took her down again. Anito fought all the way, scrabbling against the force of Makitonen's presence, but she had been taken by surprise. Utterly exhausted, she was plunged into the maelstrom of her own pain. She felt anew her grief at Ilto's death, her anger at being forced to care for the new creature, her loss at leaving the village. It was like falling into a nest of fireworms. She writhed and struggled against her own fear and despair, but she was caught like an insect in a dinnari's silken trap. Escape was impossible. She collapsed, exhausted by pain and the effort spent fighting it, and lay there amidst her grief. She had lost control and failed the test. She let her anger and loss go, let it sweep through her and drain away, leaving her as empty as a broken gourd.

Makitonen lifted her up, filling her with joy and peace, letting her rise like a bubble toward the surface. They joined in exhausted harmony for a few moments. Beneath the cold, ageless, impassive depths of the enkar's presence, Anito felt a deep, echoing emptiness. She wondered how Makitonen could live with such emptiness inside her. Anito reached out instinctively to fill it, despite her exhaustion and failure, but Makitonen block d the attempt and broke the link.

A circle of senior enkar welcomed them as they emerged from allu-a, enfolding teacher and pupil in a gentle, healing link. They treated Makitonen's presence with profound awe, faintly tinged with pity, fear, and curiosity. They knew about the empty place inside Makitonen. Anito could feel them carefully avoiding that emptiness as they replenished the ancient teacher's depleted reserves. What must it be like to be Makitonen? Not only to live with that emptiness, but to be treated with such pity by the others.

Then the enkar enfolded Anito in their solicitude, and the puzzle of Makitonen fell into the depths as she was flooded with joy. Anito emerged from their link feeling euphoric, despite her poor performance on the test.

Ninto and Eerin had a meal waiting when Anito and Ukatonen returned to their room. The remnants of Anito's euphoria faded as she began to eat.

"I'm sorry, en," Anito said, when she was through eating. "I failed the test of my allu-a. I hope you will forgive me."

"How do you know you've failed?" Ukatonen asked.

Anito described the test, how she had given in to her anger and despair.

Ukatonen touched her shoulder. "Tomorrow is your final day of testing. Focus on tomorrow, not today."

Ninto touched her tareena's arm. "I felt bad after this test too. In some ways it's the hardest. It gets easier after this. You'll think hard, and work hard, but the emotional strain isn't as bad. Wash up and get some sleep."

Anito brushed Ninto's shoulder. "Thank you," she said, grateful for her tareena's gentle sympathy.

She fell into sleep like a koirah diving onto its prey, and slept till nearly noon. Waking, she stretched luxuriously, scattering leaves from the pile. The enkar's healing had gone deep. For the first time in days, nothing hurt. She stuck her head out of the bed of leaves and looked around.

Ukatonen was sitting beside her bed, eating a tumbi fruit. "The others are out hunting, but they'll be back in a bit. How are you feeling?"

"Very good," Anito told him.

Ukatonen nodded. "Most candidates do on the morning after the allu-a test."

Anito sat up and studied Ukatonen. He looked worn and tired, and his skin seemed stretched over his bones. He was sponsoring two candidates at once, healing them and giving them strength. It must be very draining.

"You've been giving too much of yourself to us."

Ironic amusement flickered over his chest. "I'll be all right," he told her. "Today's the last day of testing. I'll manage."

She was failing Ukatonen, after he had given so much of himself to her.

"I'm sorry," she said, looking away. "I'm going to fail, and you've done so much . . ."

Ukatonen brushed her shoulder. "Stop that," he said. "Don't fail yourself. The enkar don't always judge you the way that you think they will; I've been a judge myself, and I know. Keep going. If you stop to doubt yourself, you *will* fail."

"Thank you, en," Anito said. "I'll try not to worry about yesterday."

Ukatonen gestured toward the water gourds standing in the corner. "Get up and eat. Take the afternoon off, but don't do anything too strenuous. You'll need your strength for the quarbirri test tonight."

Anito spent the afternoon lounging in quiet solitude beside a waterfall, occasionally diving into the pool below for a leisurely swim. It was good to get away, to let the afternoon pass moment by moment, like thick drops of honey. How long had it been since she had an afternoon with nothing to do? One year? Two? Whether she passed this test or not, she was going to do as little as possible for a while. Moki and Eerin had been talking about a fishing trip. Perhaps she would go with them.

Long, golden beams of late afternoon sunlight were gilding the pool when she took her final swim and swung back to the enkar's gathering. One more examination, and then she could rest for a while.

When it was time for the quarbirri test, Ukatonen led her out to the na tree grove, where all the enkar were seated in a circle. They watched her walk to the speaker's mound, where she had stood for her first examination. Stepping to the top of the low mound, she turned toward the judges, ears spread to indicate her readiness.

Figotonen stepped forward. "Greetings, candidate. Perform the quarbirri of the river hermit Hassa."

Relief soared through Anito like a rising flight of birds. She knew this story well, and liked it.

She crouched beside the assembled musical instruments, thinking over the quarbirri. Hermit Hassa told of the hermit's life along the Hassa River. He sat on a big rock beside the river for many seasons. Generations of trees grew tall, grew old, and died while he sat there. Whatever he needed, the river provided. It was said that the river brought him fish and fruit, even honey and yarram. The river spoke to him, in patterns of light on the water, teaching him all the things that the river knew. It taught him the flavor of each stream that gave itself to the river; it taught him the art of making stones smooth, and the dance and shiver of the fish in its depths. It taught him the power of the rapids, and the gentle, patient grace of slow water.

Hermit Hassa had a friend, an enkar named Mubitonen, who would come and sit beside him. Sometimes Hassa talked to her about what the river had taught him. One day, Mubitonen asked if she could become Hassa's disciple. She wanted to learn everything that he knew about the river. Hassa refused. Several years later, Mubitonen returned and asked again. Again Hassa refused. Each time Mubitonen visited, she asked the hermit if she could become his disciple. Hassa always refused. This went on for many, many years.

Finally Mubitonen asked Hassa why he wouldn't teach her. The hermit sat still for a long while, watching the river.

"I don't know enough yet," he said. "You may become my disciple when I am a worthy teacher."

Mubitonen went away with a sorrowful heart, and she didn't visit her friend Hassa for many years.

Then one day, as she was returning from a journey by a route that took her close to the place that Hassa lived, Mubitonen decided to visit her old friend.

Hassa greeted her excitedly. The river was about to tell him its final story. Once that happened, she could become his disciple. To celebrate, they went on a long fishing trip up one of the tributaries. While they fished, Hassa told her countless stories of the river. Mubitonen drank them in, happy that Hassa was finally going to let her become his disciple. The enkar and the hermit feasted on fish and remembered the good times they had spent together.

They returned to Hassa's place by the river near sunset. Hassa was very happy. Tonight, the river would tell him its final story.

"What story is that?" his disciple asked as they sat beside the river, eating dinner.

"I want to know what happens to the river when it meets the sea," he said. "I have learned everything but this one, final secret. Now it is time for me to learn that. Then everything I have learned will be yours."

Hassa went out to the rock where he always sat to watch the river. The enkar went to bed, eager for the next day to come. In the morning Mubitonen went down to the river to see what Hassa had learned. In his place was a large upright boulder. The river had taught Hassa his final lesson and taken him away.

Anito mused over the story while she tried various flutes. One of the reasons that she liked it was that it could mean so many things. Told one way, it was a tragedy about the death of Hassa; told another, it was a teaching story about rivers. It could be the story of two old and devoted friends, or a parable about trying too hard to be perfect.

She found a flute with a tone that she liked and selected a set of wrist and ankle rattles made of shells. How should she tell this story to the enkar? What did they want to hear?

She looked up at the audience, the judges, the enkar, the

candidates. Ukatonen was sitting right in front, with Moki and Eerin beside him. She wondered what Eerin would think of the story.

Then she knew how she wanted to tell this quarbirri. It was risky, but then, after failing her allu-a test, it really didn't matter. She would tell it in a way that felt right to her, even if it defied every tradition of storytelling.

She looped the thong of a hand drum over her wrist, picked up a rainstick, and stood, flute in one hand, rainstick in the other. She spread her ears wide to let the judges know she was ready, and drew herself up proudly.

Anito inverted the rainstick, and the tiny pebbles inside pattered like falling rain as they dropped to the other end of the stick. With gentle, almost invisible motions of her heels, she began to shimmer the rattles on her ankles. She lifted the flute, and played a simple thread of melody: Hassa sitting beside his river.

She began the story, describing Hassa and his history, creating a word portrait to match her sound portrait, lulling her audience with the ancient, traditional story.

Then she introduced Mubitonen. She used human skin speech, delivering Mubitonen's lines in a mixture of human and Tendu. The enkar sat up, magenta with surprise, ears spread, but too fascinated by her storytelling to look away to talk to each other. Anito continued, using the story of Hermit Hassa as a parable of humans and Tendu, of the friendship they could have, of the things they could teach each other, and the danger of being swept away by too much change.

When she finished, the audience was still for a long moment. Anito swallowed, afraid that she had offended them. Then they erupted in ripples of excited approval. Anito bowed her head, closing her eyes in relief she dared not show on her skin. As she stepped off the speaker's mound, Naratonen came up to her.

"That was very well done," he said. "People will be talking about tonight for a very long time."

"Thank you, en. You were my teacher."

" 'The student honors the teacher by surpassing him,' " Naratonen said, quoting an ancient saying. "Ever since that argument I had with Ukatonen and Eerin about learning from the humans, I have been trying to think of a suitable way to talk about it in a quarbirri. Now you've done it for me."

Ukatonen held out a packet of omkina paste and a gourd of fruit juice.

"There isn't much time. Eat, drink. You'll need the energy."

She bolted the food, washing it down with the fruit juice and a full gourd of water as the judges finished conferring. She rinsed herself off with another gourd of water as Figotonen stepped to the speaker's mound to announce the next quarbirri.

Ukatonen squeezed her shoulder. "You did well," he said, and slipped back to his place at the front of the crowd.

The rest of the evening passed in a blur of concentration. First there was the group quarbirri; then she had to reenact scenes from a number of other quarbirri.

"Thank you, candidate. That is all for tonight," Figotonen announced.

It took Anito a moment to realize that the test was over. Her knees were weak and watery; her skin felt tight and tired. Eerin and Ukatonen were heading toward her. She longed to collapse into their arms and let them carry her back to her room, but she was going to be an enkar. She wouldn't let them see how tired she was. She drew herself up and walked out of the circle of enkar unaided, and then somehow forced her tired muscles to make the long, hard climb home.

As soon as she reached her room, her legs folded beneath her, weak as waterweed. Eerin gathered her up in her short, strong arms and set her on the bed. As Eerin piled the bedding around her, Anito remembered how patiently the new creature had cared for her when she was recovering from werrun. So much had passed between them in the four years since. She reached out and touched Eerin affectionately on the arm, flickering thanks.

"The Hermit Hassa piece was wonderful," Eerin said, taking her hand. "I'm glad I recorded it. It has a lot to say to my people, as well as yours."

Eerin slid her hand up Anito's forearm, until their spurs were lined up for allu-a, her skin darkening to the purple of inquiry.

Anito flickered Yes, and they linked briefly, feeling the human's alien strength flowing into her body, along with her

Amy Thomson

gentle, warm spirit, so different from the Tendu, yet so good to link with. Eerin had given her so much. She felt her gratitude rise and enfold Eerin, felt the human's familiar, deep affection well up and receive her thanks.

Gently, Eerin slid Anito out of the link, patted Anito's arm affectionately, and piled the rest of the bedding over her. Anito settled herself into the warmth of her bed and fell asleep.

Anito stood with Ninto, waiting for the judges to come out and announce which candidates had passed the test. The ten-day fishing trip had done a lot to restore them all. Ukatonen had lost most of the worn look he had acquired during the testing. Moki was as happy as a fat ooloo in a patch of sunlight, and for that matter, so was Eerin. Ninto was beginning to put on some weight and no longer looked like a walking skeleton.

Ten days of lazy living beside the river had improved her own spirits. Her energy level was higher, and she no longer lost her temper at the slightest provocation. She would be glad when the test results were announced and they could go back to the river for some more fishing. Anito wanted to do as little as possible for the next month or two.

The crowd of enkar parted to let Figotonen and the other judges walk to the speaker's mound. The candidates and their sponsors fell in behind them. Moki and Eerin squeezed through the crowd until they were standing just behind Ukatonen and the others.

When everyone had settled into place, Figotonen held his hand up to indicate he was about to speak. The assembled enkar settled into stillness to watch his words.

"The following candidates have passed the test: Hisatonen, Anitonen, Bikotonen, Gesatonen, and Suzatonen. Jisato, Ninto, and Konito may return to be tested next year."

It took Anito a moment to recognize her new fourfold name sign, changing her name to Anitonen. Her initial surge of joy died quickly as she realized that Ninto hadn't passed the test. She looked over at her tareena. What would they do now?

Ninto laid a gentle hand on her shoulder. "I'm sorry, Anito—I mean Anitonen. I'm sorry I didn't pass."

"You'll pass next time," Anitonen told her. "I'm sure of it."

"What should we do now?" Ninto asked Ukatonen.

"I don't know. First, I need to talk to Figotonen and the others, and find out what you need to work on to pass next year's test. Then we can worry about what to do next."

They huddled disconsolately in their room, repairing fishing gear, and picking disinterestedly at their dinners until Ukatonen returned. He looked tired and defeated.

"What happened?" Anitonen asked.

"Well, they want Ninto to choose a different sponsor. Naratonen volunteered. I think he would be a good choice; the judges said that Ninto needed to work on her quarbirri some more. It was, apparently, a very close decision. She should pass next year with no problem at all. There's one more thing, though," he said, addressing Ninto directly. "They want to separate you and Anitonen."

"What!" "Why?" Ninto and Anitonen said almost simultaneously.

"They think that the two of you are too close."

"Why?" Eerin wanted to know.

"Because Anitonen is an enkar now. She is expected to be solitary, to avoid ties that might sway her judgment."

"But you aren't solitary. We've been living in gatherings full of other enkar."

"This is a gathering, not a village, Eerin, and we are enkar. We are expected to avoid deep emotional ties to any person or place. Ninto and Anito are from the same village, and they are tareena. That is a deep tie, and if they are both to become enkar, this tie must be cut. This is why so few villagers are willing to become enkar. We have no people and no place of our own. We are expected to be complete in ourselves, even when we are among others."

"How soon will we be leaving?" Anitonen asked.

"We'll be staying here. It's the closest gathering of enkar to Lyanan. Ninto, you'll have to talk to Naratonen about when and where you two will be going."

"Isn't there anything you can do?" Eerin asked.

Irritated by Eerin's persistence, Anitonen looked away. No, there was nothing Ukatonen could do. She was an enkar now, and was not allowed to have any ties. It was probably inevitable that they would be separated like this.

Ninto touched her shoulder, and Anitonen looked up. "They can send us far away from each other, but they can never separate us where it counts," Ninto said, brushing Anitonen's head and spurs. "We will always be together inside ourselves. You are my tareena. We are linked by our sitik and our memories, no matter where we are."

"When you pass your test, and we are both enkar, then we can spend more time together," Anito responded.

Ninto flickered tentative agreement. "I hope so."

Naratonen came in then and addressed Ninto. "Ukatonen told you about the judges' decision."

Ninto flickered yes.

"Are you willing to take me as your sponsor?"

"Yes, I am," Ninto replied in formal patterns.

"Then we will be leaving early tomorrow morning."

"Yes, en. I will be ready."

"Good," he said briskly. He glanced over at Anitonen, who was the color of a heavy-bellied rain cloud. "I'll leave you to pack and make your farewells," he continued, in softer, gentler patterns.

"Thank you, en," Ninto told him.

Anitonen looked away, anger and grief boiling just beneath the surface of her skin. She was losing her last connection to her former life. Soon there would be nothing left but her memories.

Ninto touched her cheek. Anitonen looked up at her tareena. Ninto held out her arms for a link. Anitonen nodded and the two of them sat across from each other, clasped arms, and linked.

It was one of the most intense links Anitonen had ever experienced. They merged as deeply and completely as possible. It took a long time to separate and return to themselves, and perhaps the separation wasn't entirely complete. Ninto's presence clung to Anito like a lingering scent. It was very late when they emerged from the link. Ukatonen was sitting in the shadows of the darkened room.

"How are you?" he asked.

"Fine," they replied, in unison. "We're fine."

"Let me see." He reached out and linked briefly with each of them. "Yes, you're all right. Just barely, but you're all right. I've packed your things, Ninto. Get some sleep. It's late."

Naratonen had taken Ninto away when Anitonen awoke the next morning.

"Ninto wanted your linking last night to be her goodbye," Ukatonen told her.

"It doesn't feel like she's gone. She's right in here," Anito responded, gesturing at her chest with her palm.

"That will fade in time."

"Perhaps, but it's enough for now."

Twenty-six

"*THAT WILL BE all for today, class,*" Juna told her students in Standard.

"*Thank you, teacher,*" they responded before scattering back to their other work, or off to relax somewhere. Teaching Standard to the Tendu was hard, and would continue to be hard. She could give them facts, but none of them had any experience or context to put them into. Past a certain level of complexity, it was all nonsense to them. Still, she taught them as much as she could, hoping some of it would make sense as they learned more about humans. It was hard, frustrating work, and she was glad that they were leaving for Lyanan in a couple of days. Over the past four years, the villagers of Lyanan had become friends. It would be good to see them again.

Lyanan was also where she felt most connected with Earth. Juna closed her eyes for a moment, remembering the smell of clean sheets. She felt an almost sexual longing for simple human comforts, a bath, a hot meal, a bed with clean, dry linen. The thought of a conversation with another human being, or the touch of a warm human hand, made tears prick at the insides of her eyelids. Going to Lyanan reminded her of all the human things she tried so hard to forget the rest of the time. Forgetting was how she survived without going crazy.

Juna felt a touch on her arm. It was Moki. What was going to happen to him when her people came back? The question loomed larger as the time drew near. In the two months since the enkar examinations, she had encouraged Moki and Uka-tonen to spend a lot of time together. Perhaps if the bond between the two of them was strong enough, her leaving would not tear Moki apart.

Juna reached up and took Moki's hand. He knew she was thinking of her people again. She could read it on her skin. She looked away, fighting back a surge of guilt. She couldn't help longing for her own species. It was as natural as Moki's own intense need for his sitik.

She held her arms out, spurs up. They slid into a link. She tasted Moki's fear, sharp and urgent, and he tasted her longing for her own people. Nothing he could do would ease that longing more than a little. She answered his fear with all the love she felt for him, but none of that could ease his worries about the future. The link settled into an uneasy equilibrium that was not the harmony they both longed for.

It was raining when they arrived at the village tree of Lyanan. Juna's shoulders were chafed and sore, despite the padding of wet moss that lay between her skin and the pack straps. She looked forward to shedding her burden in a warm, dry room. Lalito emerged from the trunk as they descended toward the na tree's massive, bowl-shaped crotch.

"You came very quickly. I sent the message about the new creatures only yesterday. They arrived two days ago. They're staying on a great floating island off the coast."

"They're early. I didn't expect them for another year, at least," Juna said. A welter of conflicting emotions warred within her. She wanted to shuck her pack and race through the trees to see her people—and yet she also wanted to take Moki and hide in the mountains until the humans left. Juna thought of her alien skin, bald head, altered body, and she felt suddenly afraid. What would the humans think of her, looking like this? More importantly, what was she going to do to help her people and the Tendu achieve harmony? She had been so busy worrying about Moki and writing reports and field notes that she hadn't thought about what she would do when the humans arrived. She wasn't ready for this. If only she had more time!

Moki touched her arm. She reached down to embrace him, sudden tears welling in her eyes. She had longed for this day. Now, she wanted to turn back the clock. She wasn't ready, and neither was Moki.

"We need to rest and talk before we go to meet the new creatures," Ukatonen said.

They were shown to an empty guest room. Juna eased off her pack with a sigh of relief and sat down. Moki busied himself with unpacking their things, and directing the tinka who came bearing armloads of bedding and refreshments. He was trying to bury his grief in busywork. This was going to be very hard. She got up and touched her bami on the arm. They linked automatically, sliding inside each other. She was awash in Moki's fear and grief, and her own sadness and guilt. They drifted inside each other's pain for a long while, then slid out of the link.

"Oh, Moki. I—"

"There was nothing that you could do to change any of this," he told her. "It was all set in motion when you decided to save my life."

"Should I have left you to die?"

Moki looked away. "No. Yes. I—I don't know."

Ukatonen touched them both on the shoulder. "It is pointless to worry whether your decision was correct. You both must live with the consequences of your choices. We don't have time for regrets and recriminations. Your people are here, Eerin. What should we do?"

"Go and meet them. Talk to them about the Tendu."

"We need to discuss the damage they did the last time they were here," Anitonen reminded her.

Juna inclined her head in a nod, and flickered agreement. "We should bring Lalito with us."

"Yes. It's late. We're tired. It would be best to wait until tomorrow," Ukatonen suggested.

Juna looked away. "Yes. It would." She felt oddly relieved to be putting off her meeting with the Survey.

Ukatonen touched her on the knee. "I'm sorry to make you wait. I know how much you want to see your people."

Juna smiled. "It's all right, en. I want to spend one more night with my friends before I go back to my people."

It was a quiet night, full of reminiscences and bittersweet laughter. The four of them linked, sharing the nostalgia they felt. Ukatonen and Anitonen slipped out of the link first, leaving Juna alone with Moki, his sadness tempered now by the gentle peace of the evening. At last they moved together into an emotional equilibrium, lingering in the link, savoring the harmony they shared.

The Survey base rode at anchor, large and incongruous in the small bay. It was a large, flat rectangle, the color of a bereaved bami, and covered by a huge clear dome. Juna winced inwardly at the inauspicious color of the ship. She hoped it wasn't an omen.

Anitonen touched her arm. "Look, there are new creatures moving around on it."

Juna nodded. Several people were working on the deck. One, in an unsealed e-suit, stood on the observation deck with what appeared to be a pair of binoculars. She really should radio first, but the beacon was clear around the point from where they were, and she wanted to get this over with.

"I'm going down to the beach and let them know that I'm here." Juna touched Moki on the arm. Their eyes met for a moment. "I'll come back," she promised.

Juna climbed to the ground and walked down the path to the edge of the cliff. She stood where she was plainly visible from the base, turned a bright yellow and orange, and swung her arms over her head. It would look odd to the Tendu watching from the trees, but it attracted the human's attention. The lookout glanced up at the movement, startled, and put his binoculars to his face. The lenses caught the bright morning sun and flashed back at her. She waved her arms once more, and then walked down the zigzag trail to the beach. An excited crowd gathered on the observation deck, pointing at her.

Juna reached the beach, and waited while they launched a boat, bearing two people in environment suits. They landed the boat about 150 meters down the beach. One of them stepped out of the beached boat, carrying a computer collapsed into the shape of a smooth white sphere. The Alien Contact people theorized it was the least threatening shape for contact purposes since it had no sharp edges.

Juna smiled. Ukatonen had used a stone about that size and shape to bash in the head of a tiakan last week. The AC people meant well, but they were all theory and no practice.

Juna glanced up at the trees, making sure that the Tendu had a clear view, and flushed blue to reassure them. The human trudged up the beach in his baggy white e-suit. Juna smiled, remembering the thousands of hours she had logged in those hellish suits.

He stopped about ten meters away from her and slowly set the computer down in the sand, then stood, arms held out from his body, palms forward, fingers spread.

Juna recognized the pose, and fought back a sudden laugh. This was the standard Alien Contact protocol that she had learned in the Survey. He didn't recognize her. She looked down at herself, seeing her elongated hands and feet, her hairless alien skin that covered her nipples and her navel, and flickered with silent blue and green laughter.

I probably wouldn't recognize myself if I saw me in the mirror right now, she thought.

The human was standing there, in that goofy low-threat pose, looking like a large, dumpy penguin. It was too much to resist. She stepped forward hesitantly, peering at the man in front of her as though she had never seen someone in an e-suit before. She paused about three meters away, and squatted on the sand. She could see his face framed by the recording instrumentation of the suit. He looked vaguely familiar to her, but she couldn't place him.

He smoothed the sand in front of him and set down a bright, shiny gold sphere. Juna rippled in amusement. What would the Tendu have made of something shaped like a lizard egg, the color of someone in heat?

She moved forward to pick up the sphere and made a great show of examining it, smelling it, shaking it to see if it rattled, rubbing it on her skin, and tasting it. Then she put it back down on the sand in front of her.

"I believe the correct line is 'Dr. Livingstone, I presume?' " she croaked, her voice husky and hoarse from disuse. "I'm Juna Saari. The real Tendu are up there in the trees, watching us."

"Oh shit!" he exclaimed, staggering back. Even through his helmet, the look of surprise on his face was very satisfying.

"Well, that's one that won't go down in the history books," Juna said.

"I'm very sorry," he said, recovering himself. "I'm Dr. Daniel Bremen, expedition head with the *Unity Dow Maru.* I'm honored to meet you. "

"No wonder you looked familiar. I've seen your Tri-V shows."

"I'm glad you liked them. It's always a pleasure to meet a fan in an out-of-the-way place."

Actually, Juna disliked Bremen's shows. They oversimplified many important concepts, and ignored others entirely, but she wasn't about to tell him that. She needed to work with him to build bridges with the Tendu. She wondered how a Tri-V celeb had wound up heading the expedition.

"Before I did the *Universalities* series for Edu-Net, I was the head of Alien Contact Studies Department at UCLA," he explained, as if anticipating her question. "The Survey felt that my celebrity status would help make this trip more accessible to a wider audience."

It made sense. The Survey was chronically short on funding. They wanted someone along who could make the most of this historic event.

"I wasn't expecting the Survey to get here so soon," Juna said.

"The Tendu are an important discovery. They inhabit a biological treasure house. Some of the new proteins and complex organic molecules are opening up whole new possibilities in medical and chemical research. So far, we've derived two new antibiotics effective against resistant diseases and a nonaddictive painkiller more effective than morphine, from materials collected during the first mission. And then there's you."

"Me?" Juna asked, suddenly wary.

"You're the only human known to have survived continued exposure to a life-bearing alien planet. If we could find out how you survived, it might open up whole new worlds to colonization. The best doctors in the Survey are falling all over themselves to study you."

"I'm sure they are," Juna said dryly. She dreaded the prospect of being a research subject.

"After we've made contact with the aliens, we'll return to the base for a briefing. If I'd known that it was you out on the beach, I'd have brought your debriefing team. As it is, I'm sure that they'll be waiting aboard ship. They're very eager to talk to you."

Juna wondered why the debriefing team hadn't come with him anyway. Had Bremen pulled rank on them? If so, she was relieved that he'd come alone. She wasn't ready for an intense grilling.

"Can I get a decent meal and a hot bath before the debriefing? It's been four and a half years since I've had either," she said.

"I'll talk to the base commander and make sure that they're ready for you. But first, could you show me the aliens?" he asked eagerly.

"Of course, Dr. Bremen. This way."

The cool gloom of the jungle felt good after standing for so long under the brilliant sun.

"Wait here. I'll go get the Tendu," she said, then turned and scrambled up the tree. Bremen stared after her, amazed. Ukatonen, Anitonen, and Lalito met her as she reached the middle level of the canopy. Moki followed behind them hesitantly, his skin grey with grief.

"Well?" Anitonen asked her.

"They've only sent one person. *Dr. Bremen* is his name. He wants to meet you. Then I have to go out to the big raft and talk to my people."

They climbed down the tree, where Bremen waited.

"You climb like a monkey, Dr. Saari," he said.

"I've had to live in the trees for the last four years. I got a lot of practice." She gestured at the aliens. "This is Ukatonen and

Anitonen. They're enkar. You've read about them in my notes, I assume."

Bremen nodded.

"And this is Lalito, the chief elder of the village of Lyanan."

Bremen frowned. "Yes, I read about how badly treated you were by her village."

"That was a long time ago," Juna reassured him. "Since then, my relationship with the villagers has significantly improved."

"Please translate this for me," Bremen said. "'I bring peaceful greetings from all of mankind to your people. I hope our two peoples will grow and prosper together. Thank you for taking such good care of Dr. Saari for us.'"

Juna translated his message into Tendu skin speech. She made her words big, so that any villagers watching the talks from concealment could see what she was saying.

Anitonen stepped forward and shook Bremen's hand, human-style. *"Greetings, Dr. Bremen,"* Anitonen spelled out in Standard. *"We look forward to negotiating with your people."*

Dr. Bremen's eyebrows lifted inside his helmet.

"Both Anitonen and Ukatonen are reasonably fluent in written Standard," Juna explained. "I thought it might prove useful during our discussions."

Moki slipped between the two enkar, and leaned against Juna, putting an arm around her hips. Juna thought she saw a flicker of shock cross Bremen's features, quickly hidden. She laid her arm around Moki's shoulders.

"And this is Moki, my bami," she spelled out in Standard. *"He understands written Standard too."*

"Your adopted child," Bremen said, his face carefully neutral.

"Yes," Juna said. "I saved his life."

"I remember that from your journal. It was very moving. It broke every alien contact protocol in the book, though."

Juna shrugged. "I think Moki will become an important link between our two peoples. He's already more fluent in skin speech Standard than any of the other Tendu."

Ukatonen touched her shoulder. "We should set a formal time for us to begin negotiations," he said in Tendu. "Lyanan has been waiting a long time for reparations. They are obligated to many others for helping repair the damage caused by your people."

"Perhaps we could start tomorrow. That will give me time to meet the other humans and talk to them," Juna replied in skin speech.

"What are you saying?" Dr. Bremen asked her. "I only understand a little Tendu."

"Ukatonen wants to begin discussing the reparations owed to Lyanan for the damage the Survey did to their forest. I suggested that we begin preliminary talks tomorrow. That will give us time for a briefing."

Bremen radioed the ship, and received an agreement to proceed with the talks. "Very well, then. What time?"

They agreed to meet by the top of the cliff path at noon, and then it was time to go.

Moki looked at her expectantly. She embraced him. "I'll see you tomorrow," she reassured him. "Go with Ukatonen and be good."

Moki nodded and held out his arms for allu-a. Torn, Juna glanced up at Dr. Bremen. She was sure that they already suspected her of going native. Linking with Moki would only confirm that.

Juna squatted down so that she was eye to eye with him. "Moki, this isn't a good time for allu-a. I'll try to link with you tomorrow. You should link with Ukatonen while I'm gone. He's going to be your sitik when I leave. You should start to get used to that now."

Moki shook his head and looked away. "No! You are my sitik," he insisted.

"Oh, Moki." Juna rested her forehead against his and sighed. "We've known this day was coming for a long time. I'm sorry, but this is the way it has to be." She brushed his shoulder and stood, her skin deep grey with grief and anguish.

She glanced at Ukatonen. He put his hand on Moki's arm. "It's time to go," he said gently.

"*It was good to meet you Dr. Bremen*," Ukatonen said in Standard.

Moki followed Ukatonen with obvious reluctance. He gave Juna a long, pleading look, then climbed into the canopy and vanished into the forest with the enkar. Juna looked after the Tendu as they left, longing to go with them, but someone needed to bridge the gap between the Tendu and humans. Suddenly she understood some of what it must be like to be an enkar, unable to be close to anyone. This was not going to be easy.

She looked over at Dr. Bremen. He was watching her curiously. She wiped away the tears, suddenly and irrationally angry at him for his ignorant alienness.

"Let's go," she said, leading him back to the beach.

"Dr. Saari, the galley wants to know what you would like to eat. Oh, and the chef says that they have two cases of Chateau ad Astra."

Juna stumbled in surprise. Her father's wine. Somehow, they had gotten some of her father's wine.

"Do they have a bottle of the '24 Chardonnay?"

"She says there are six bottles of it in one of the cases."

Joy rose in her heart like a soaring seabird. The entire run of '24 Chardonnay, only twenty-five cases, had been bottled in a nitrogen atmosphere, aged to perfection and stored in their wine vault, reserved for the family's personal use. Somehow her father had gotten two cases of his own personal stock on board for her.

"What would the chef recommend with the Chardonnay?" Juna asked.

"She has some flash frozen Copper River king salmon, which she ordered specially to be eaten with this wine."

"Please thank the chef for me," Juna said, as if she ordered dinner like this all the time. She fought back a wave of hysterical laughter. It was suddenly all too much, a gourmet meal with her father's wine, a hot bath and clean sheets. It felt unreal; dreamlike.

"Your chef sounds rather different from the usual Survey cooks," she observed.

"The crew says they've never eaten this well during a mission," Bremen said. "She volunteered for the trip. Her credentials were excellent, so I approved her request. It's done amazing things for crew morale." He laughed. "Our mother ship, the *Kaiwo Maru,* keeps pleading with us to send her back, but the ground crew would kill me if I did."

They had reached the boat.

"Welcome back, Dr. Saari," the woman operating the boat said. She stepped out of the boat and shook Juna's hand.

"Thank you," she said. This was the first human contact she'd had in four-and-a-half years; it took her a moment to let go.

Bremen introduced the woman. "Dr. Saari, this is Dr. Guralnick, one of the Survey's top xenobotanists."

"Pleased to meet you," Juna said. Guralnick was a tall, slender woman with green eyes. Wisps of silver hair were visible around the edges of her faceplate. She moved gracefully despite her baggy e-suit.

Juna noticed a couple of sampling bags lying in the bottom of the boat, and smiled. "You've been busy, I see."

Guralnick looked embarrassed. "It's just some stuff I picked up along the beach. I hope the Tendu don't mind."

Juna shook her head. "They won't miss this. Just don't destroy any live plants or animals until we've negotiated with the villagers about what you can collect. I'll go over your samples with you later and identify as much of it as I can."

"That would be wonderful," Guralnick said. "Thank you, Dr. Saari."

"Please, call me Juna."

"Only if you'll call me Kay."

"We should be going. They're waiting for us on the base," Dr. Bremen said.

Juna climbed into the sturdy little landing craft. Kay pushed the boat off the beach, came aboard, and started the quiet little hydrogen-powered motor.

Juna looked back at the jungle as they swung away. She turned a deep, reassuring blue, and raised a hand in farewell to the Tendu. She thought she saw a flicker of color in return as the shoreline receded from view, and remembered her last sight of Moki, looking at her reproachfully as he followed Ukatonen up the tree.

She looked away, her skin cloudy with sadness. *"Oh Moki,"* she thought to herself. There was a touch on her shoulder.

Kay's gloved hand was resting there. The gesture seemed very Tendu to Juna.

"You looked sad, there," Kay told her sympathetically.

Juna nodded, but couldn't think of a reply.

"Could you—" Kay looked embarrassed. "Could you say something in Tendu?"

Juna sat up and began the chant of the birds from the quarbirri of the animal spirits. The visual nonsense rhyme was one of the prettiest pieces of skin speech that she knew.

"That's beautiful," Kay said when Juna had finished. "What did you just say?"

"It's a list of bird species from a Tendu performance piece called a quarbirri."

"I'd like to tape that sometime," Bremen said.

Juna shrugged. "You should see someone like Naratonen do the piece. He's one of the best artists the Tendu have. It probably wouldn't be hard to get permission to film it. Naratonen was always borrowing my computer to watch the quarbirri I recorded, so he understands the concept of filming something."

"You let one of the natives borrow your computer?" Bremen asked with a frown. "That's a violation of the Contact Protocols."

"Dr. Bremen, I had a choice," Juna replied, suppressing a sudden flicker of irritation. "I could have obeyed the Contact Protocols, or I could have survived. I chose to survive. It was impossible for a person in my situation to adhere to the Protocols."

"Those protocols are the result of decades of careful thought and research," Bremen replied.

"They were developed on the basis of our experience with the Sawakirans, Doctor. The Tendu are not the Sawakirans. They're much more sophisticated and outgoing. The protocols, as written, don't work here."

"We're nearly there," Kay said, touching her on the knee.

Kay slowed the boat as they swung into the looming shadow of the floating Survey base. The boat glided toward a floating dock. Juna leaped to the dock and held out her hands for the bow line. Bremen tossed her the line, his dark eyebrows arced high in surprise. She secured it to a duraplast cleat, then secured the stern line.

Bremen stepped onto the dock. "That was quite a jump!" he said.

"Was it?" Juna replied.

"We were two meters out from the dock and still moving! There's a sizable swell, too."

Juna looked from the dock to the boat. She hadn't even thought about it. They had gotten within range and she had just jumped.

"I spend most of my time thirty meters in the air, jumping from tree to tree. I make jumps harder than that every day," she said. "I have to, to keep up with the others."

"Aren't you terrified?" Kay asked.

"I was at first, but I got used to it. It wasn't like I had much choice. Besides"—she held out her hand so they could see the ridged gripping surfaces on her palm and her elongated fingers—"the Tendu modified me so it was easier to hang on." She arched her nail-less fingers, extending her claws. Bremen blanched and backed away. Kay leaned forward to take a closer look.

"We'd better go. They're waiting for us up top," Bremen said.

Kay scooped another couple of sealed specimen bags from the bottom of the boat. "Could you help me carry these, Juna?"

Juna stepped forward to take the bags from Kay. "Be careful with Bremen," the botanist said in a low, cautious whisper. "He wields a lot of power here."

Juna nodded, flickering acknowledgment out of habit. "Thanks, Kay," she whispered back, tucking the bags under her arm. "After you, Dr. Bremen," she said, as she and Kay approached the end of the dock, where the Tri-V celebrity waited impatiently for them.

They walked up the long, steep stairway from the dock to a middeck hatchway. People pressed against the plexi outer shell, craning their necks to look at her. She suddenly realized that she was completely naked. Her skin darkened to a deep, embarrassed brown, and she faltered in her climb.

Bremen waved at the staring onlookers, and looked back

expectantly at Juna. She managed a tentative wave. The crowd cheered in reply, though the sound was cut off by the plexi dome.

"I didn't expect so many people," Juna said as Bremen drew ahead.

"It's a big expedition," Kay told her. "One of the biggest ever mounted by the Survey. Every A-C spec with any kind of pull at all is up there. There's a whole team of different specialists assigned to study you. It's amazing that there's any kind of room at all for biologists, zoologists, and botanists. There's a lot of politics here. I'd bear that in mind, if I were you."

"Thanks, Kay," Juna said, grateful for the information, and wishing that she'd thought more about what to do when the Survey returned.

Kay shrugged, the motion barely visible through the suit. "*C'est rien* . . . You let me keep the samples. I just thought you should have some warning before you're thrown to the lions."

They reached the top of the stairs. Bremen was waiting for them at the airlock.

"I'm to escort you through decontamination procedures, Dr. Saari," he told her, holding open the airlock door. Juna stepped through into the airlock. She glanced back at the verdant, hilly coastline, feeling a sudden surge of longing. Bremen pulled the heavy door closed with a muffled thud, shutting out the alien world. Juna closed her eyes for a moment and breathed deeply, smelling the newly familiar scents of plastic, paint, and metal. She was among humans again.

She opened her eyes. Bremen was holding out a brand new e-suit, still in its original packaging.

"I'm afraid you're going to have to wear this when you're not in quarantine."

"I see."

Juna took the e-suit, her moist fingers clinging to the plastic, feeling oddly sad and hurt. She slit the plastic wrapper with a claw and shook out the suit. It was her size, but the gloves and boots were too small for her elongated hands and feet. Kay helped her rig temporary coverings out of specimen bags, sealing them with repair tape.

Bremen stepped through into the disinfectant shower that hosed off his e-suit, and then into the next airlock. Juna followed him through the series of washings and rinsings designed to clean off every trace of the world outside. She felt silly going through decontamination in her e-suit, but it was necessary. Bremen was waiting for her by the elevator that would take them up to the top deck. He was freshly groomed and ready for the cameras. Juna was impressed. She always emerged from decon looking like a drowned rat.

"Ready?" he asked. "The Tri-V people are waiting for us. It's a big moment."

Suddenly she was glad for the suit. It would shelter her from the cold, mechanical eyes of the Tri-V cameras.

"Shouldn't we wait for Kay?"

He shook his head. "She has all those samples to process. It'll take her a while."

Bremen pushed the button and the elevator doors opened. He motioned Juna inside with a showman's gesture, and stepped in after her. The tension mounted during the elevator's slow climb. By the time the elevator slid to a stop, Juna felt as though only the e-suit kept her from exploding. She took a deep breath and shut her eyes, reaching inside herself for the bio-manipulation skills she had learned from the Tendu. She exhaled, pushing the tension out of her body, and opened her eyes. Bremen held the elevator door open, waiting for her.

She stepped out of the elevator, fighting a returning surge of excitement. Bremen took her arm and escorted her through the open bay doors and into an enthusiastic mob. They cheered loudly as she emerged.

Bremen led her to a balcony overlooking the main deck and handed her a mike. She stared at it for a moment, then plugged it into her suit. She was crying, her nose was running, and she couldn't wipe it. The defogging fan started up, blowing air across her face plate. She sniffled and was embarrassed to hear it reverberate over the crowd.

"Thank you. I—" She paused awkwardly. "I wasn't expecting such a reception. It's good to be back among my own people again."

"Tell us about the Tendu," someone shouted from the crowd.

"What's it like out there without a suit?"

Suddenly, there was an avalanche of questions. She looked down at the crowd of faces and felt a sudden wave of panic at the sight of all these people. She looked at Bremen. He stepped forward, holding up his hands.

"Dr. Saari just got here. Give her time, and she'll answer all your questions. We've promised her a good meal and a hot shower. Since she hasn't had either for more than four years, I don't want to delay her any longer. I suggest you post your questions on the net for now. Once Dr. Saari's been debriefed, we'll arrange some kind of forum for everyone."

Juna unplugged her mike and handed it to Bremen. He led her through another door, where they were greeted by a group of people wearing unsealed e-suits. A slender, elegant, white-haired Eurasian man stepped forward. Juna's eyes widened in surprise when she recognized him. Dr. Wu had been one of the chief researchers at Sawakira. She was amazed that he was still alive, and even more amazed that a man of his age had passed the physical and made it onto a Survey mission.

"Thank you, Dr. Bremen," he said. "I'm Dr. Paul Wu, head of the Alien Contact team, and this is the rest of the preliminary debriefing team."

"I'm honored to meet you, Dr. Wu," Juna said. "I've heard so much about your work with the Sawakirans." She reached out to shake his hand, then remembered that her hands were covered in plastic bags, and stopped.

He smiled and bowed, a gesture that should have seemed archaic and stilted but was, instead, both formal and warm.

"And I am honored to meet you, Dr. Saari. We were intending to meet you with a full debriefing team, but Dr. Bremen found you instead."

Juna nodded. "Thank you, Dr. Wu. It's good to be back."

He turned to introduce her to the rest of the debriefing team. Her eyes widened as she recognized Antonio Miyata. He had been her research director on her first Survey mission, and had taken an active interest in her career.

"Tonio! It's good to see you!" Juna said, putting her hands on his arms. "How long has it been? Six years? Seven?"

"Seven," he confirmed. "A long time. I saw your log. It was impressive."

Juna smiled. "I had a good teacher." Tonio had taken her in hand on her first mission, and taught her most of what she knew about field research.

"Thank you," he said. "You were a good student. I want to hear all about your time here, when you have the chance."

"Sure, Tonio, that would be great," she replied.

"The debriefing team will meet with you at 1700 ship time. That's about four hours from now," Wu said, seeing Juna's look of confusion. She hadn't noticed what time it was. "Before we begin the debriefing though, we need to give you a thorough physical."

He left her in the care of the medics, who escorted her to quarantine. They sent her through the airlock into her new quarters with a urine cup and instructions to provide them with a specimen.

She looked around her new room. It was a hospital room, clean and sterile with hard, easy-to-disinfect surfaces. There was a tiny, economical bathroom with a shower. She sighed regretfully. A tub bath would have to wait.

Juna put on the hospital gown that had been laid out for her. She pulled the top sheet back on the bed, and ran her hand over the clean linens. A real bed. Going to sleep tonight would be something to savor. Then she picked up the urine cup and headed for the bathroom. She dutifully peed in the cup, and then flushed the toilet for the sheer pleasure of hearing working plumbing.

When she emerged from the bathroom the doctors were waiting for her. They took the urine specimen from her with a nod of approval.

"Are these the *allu* that you wrote so much about?" one doctor asked, probing the spur on her forearm. Juna winced and pulled away.

"Yes it is, Doctor, but please be careful, they're very sensitive."

"Could you show us some of its functions?" the doctor asked.

"All right," she said.

She picked up a scalpel from the tray of medical implements and made a long cut on the back of her arm.

The doctors and nurses gasped in astonishment and moved toward her.

"Wait!" she commanded, holding out her wounded arm. She focused her attention on the wound. The blood trickling down her arm and dripping to the floor slowed, then stopped. One of the doctors grabbed a petri dish and collected some of the blood as it fell. Juna held the edges of the cut together, and felt the skin knit.

"Doctor, would you please wash away the blood on my arm?"

He did so. All that was left of the cut was a pale line on her arm. The doctors crowded around to look at the healed cut.

"I've read everything you've written about those spurs," one of them remarked, "but it's different, seeing it actually work."

After examining the healed cut, the doctors gave her a painfully thorough medical examination. They took samples of everything: blood, skin, feces, saliva, vaginal fluids, bone marrow, and biopsies of her human/alien skin interface from several places in and on her body. It was grueling and humiliating, and the energy it took to repair the damage they did drained her further.

Juna's stomach growled. She was hungry and it was getting late. "Are there any more tests you need to perform? Dr. Bremen promised me a hot meal and a hot shower. I haven't had either one for a long time. Besides, healing that cut took a lot of energy. I need food to replace it."

"We'll do the rest of the tests later," they told her.

"Thank you," Juna said, turning lavender with relief.

One of the doctors picked up the phone and called out.

"I've told the kitchen you're ready for your meal," he said as he hung up. "The chef says that your dinner will be delivered in half an hour."

"How soon till the quarantine is lifted?" Juna asked.

"That will depend on the results of our tests. Soon, I hope."

The doctors gathered up their samples and instruments, and filed out, leaving her alone. She felt isolated and out of place in this sterile, empty room. The Tendu suddenly seemed very far away.

"Well," she said to the empty room. "Well."

There was a scratching sound off in one corner. It was a white mouse in a small cage. As she watched, it climbed onto its exercise wheel. The wheel turned, creaking faintly. Juna smiled. She was not entirely alone.

She lightly touched the bars of the cage and murmured reassuringly at the mouse. She hoped it would survive being in quarantine with her. It was here to test whether or not her presence would kill it.

She took a long, glorious shower, as hot as she could stand it. Unfortunately, the soap stung her sensitive alien skin, so she settled for a good hard scrub with a washcloth. After toweling off, she slipped into a clean, dry uniform. It was good to be back, she thought, smiling contentedly. Now all she needed was a solid meal under her belt and she'd be ready for anything.

As if in reply to her wish, the door buzzer sounded. When the status light on the door turned green, she opened it. Inside the airlock was a cart with a covered tray. She wheeled the cart into the room, set the tray on her table, sat down, and removed the cover.

The meal was beautifully presented on spotless linens and fine china: a fillet of salmon, steaming hot with a light covering of dill cream sauce, accompanied by fresh orange chanterelle mushrooms, pickled baby carrots, and spinach, served Nippon style, compressed into tight rolls and then sliced. All her favorites. Her eyes misted over.

The salmon was perfectly done. Juna closed her eyes, savoring its subtle aroma. Then she reached for the half-bottle of wine, cradled in a napkin to keep it from rolling off the tray. As she undid the napkin, a note fell out. She picked it up.

"Welcome back," it read. "I couldn't miss this trip, so I signed on as cook. Stop by the galley when you get a chance. I have news of your family. Alison."

Tears stung Juna's eyes, blurring the familiar handwriting. Alison was here. She was responsible for bringing her father's wine aboard.

She picked up the chardonnay and read the familiar label. Looking at it, she felt her father's rough hands on hers, showing her how and where to prune the vines, his patient voice lecturing her on the growth habits of grapes.

She opened the bottle and poured her father's wine. It tasted as clean and sharp as she remembered it, but there were a host of more subtle notes that she'd never noticed before. She took another sip, remembering the vineyard stretching out away from their tiny, formally landscaped yard. Not an inch of growing space was wasted. Even the porch posts supported wine grapes. She pictured her father, sitting in his favorite cane-bottomed rocking chair, white-haired, skin reddened and seamed from decades of working in the sun. He was nearly ninety now, getting old enough for her to worry about the possibility of his dying before she saw him again. She hoped Alison had good news.

Her stomach growled. She blinked back tears with a laugh. Her magnificent dinner was getting cold. She picked up her fork and started eating.

When she finished, she wheeled the cart over to the door and pushed it into the airlock, activating the inorganic disinfect cycle. She had another fifteen minutes to kill before her debriefing.

She went over and looked at the mouse in its cage. It stared at her. She held out her fingers. The mouse sniffed at them curiously for a moment, then went back to eating a sunflower seed. It looked healthy and active, a good sign. Usually test animals died within a few hours of exposure. If it survived till tomorrow, she would try to see if it would let her pick it up.

The phone on the wall chimed politely. Juna picked it up with a smile. She hadn't spoken over the phone to anyone for years. "Hello?"

"Dr. Saari? This is Dr. Wu. I was wondering if you were ready for the debriefing."

"As soon as I climb into my suit, sir."

"Good. I'll come by in about ten minutes to escort you."

"Thank you, sir. I'll be ready."

Juna put on her suit and went through the decontamination procedures. Then she tried to get the airlock to cycle and let her out, but it wouldn't respond to her commands. Just as she was starting to panic, the fans switched on and the lock began cycling. Wu was waiting outside for her.

"I'm sorry if I kept you waiting, Dr. Wu. I couldn't get the airlock to cycle. I'll have to notify the medical staff and let them know it isn't working properly."

"You're in quarantine, Dr. Saari. I'm afraid that the airlock won't open for you."

"Oh," Juna said. She looked down, embarrassed. In her excitement at being back among her own people, she had forgotten the Survey's quarantine procedures. "How soon will I be let out of quarantine?"

"I'm afraid that it may be some time. We need to prove conclusively that you are not a danger to others."

"I see." She swallowed, her throat suddenly tight. It was a reasonable precaution. She understood the need for the restrictions, but it hurt to have them enforced after all she had been through.

"If I'm going to do my job, I'll need access to the rest of the ship," Juna pointed out.

"Please, Dr. Saari, let us discuss this at the debriefing. Perhaps the others will be able to work out some kind of compromise."

"Very well, Dr. Wu."

The meeting was held in a standard conference room, spartan and functional, with a wide table of plasteel. Most of the department heads were already seated. Juna recognized Morale Officer Mei Mei Chang, sitting near the head of the table, and her heart sank. Chang stood and extended her hand to Juna.

"Good afternoon, Dr. Saari. Do you remember me?"

"Of course I remember you, Officer Chang. It's a pleasure to see you again," Juna lied smoothly, as she reached out to shake Chang's hand.

"Welcome back to the Survey, Dr. Saari," Chang said.

Juna looked around the table. She recognized Bremen, Miyata, Wu, and Dr. Baker, the head of the medical team that had examined her. The rest were still strangers to her. The captain of the ship was present too, a thin woman with short salt-and-pepper hair dressed in the black and silver uniform of the Space Service.

When the last chair was filled, Wu stood. "Thank you all for coming. We're here to begin your debriefing, Dr. Saari. Before we get started, I'd like to introduce you to some of the people you haven't met yet: Captain Edison." The captain inclined her head. "Dr. Agélou, head of psychology." A thin, nervous-looking man with a small fussy goatee nodded to her. "Dr. Holmes, who is in charge of biochemistry; Dr. Tanguay, who is in charge of alien linguistics, and Dr. Nazarieff, in charge of resource management."

"Thank you, Dr. Wu." Juna smiled at the team members. "I'm afraid it will take me a little while to learn all of your names. Please be patient with me."

"Welcome back, Dr. Saari," Wu said formally. "On behalf of all of us, I want to apologize for the circumstances that led to your being left behind. I also want to thank you for the copious and detailed log of your sojourn among the Tendu. We spent three months in orbit cataloguing, cross-referencing, and study-ing it. Everyone is full of questions about your observations, but the first item on our agenda is to discuss the Survey's negotiating position and to determine your role in those negotiations."

"I had expected to act as a negotiator and translator," Juna said.

"You don't have any formal training or experience in diplomatic negotiation," Bremen pointed out.

"No, but I've worked with Anitonen and Ninto as they studied to become enkar. I've gone through negotiations with the people of Lyanan and Narmolom. I understand the Tendu better than any other human. They know me and trust me. It would be foolish to throw away that kind of advantage."

"Yes, it would," Wu agreed. "And we're not planning to do so. However, we need to work out some kind of framework that utilizes the diplomatic training of our Alien Contact people as well as your irreplaceable on-the-ground experience. We want to avoid violating the Contact Protocols any further."

"I see," Juna said, relieved by Wu's reassurances.

"We have revised the protocols, based on the information in

your log. However, there are several situations whose implications must be considered. There is your adopted child, Moki. What will happen to him after you leave? Will your relationship with him affect the negotiations? Then there is the physical linking known as allu-a. How has that affected your psychology? How will that affect your ability to negotiate? Dr. Agélou wants to perform an in-depth psychological evaluation to determine this. And then there are the countless other violations, committed while you were trying to survive in that difficult and challenging environment. How have they affected the Tendu? All of these questions must be considered."

"Ukatonen has agreed to adopt Moki," Juna said, "but we are very worried that Moki will not accept him as his sitik." She sighed, a flicker of ochre concern crossing her skin. "I have been encouraging him to spend more time with Ukatonen, to ease the shock of my departure, but you arrived earlier than I expected. As it stands now, only time will tell whether Moki accepts Ukatonen as his sitik. If Moki rejects Ukatonen, then Ukatonen will commit suicide. It is what an enkar must do if he makes an unwise judgment." She looked down at the plasteel table, remembering Ilto's crushed body lying on the floor of the forest.

"As for allu-a," Juna continued, "I don't believe that it is harmful to the negotiations. In fact, it could be a considerable help, since it will reinforce the truth of what I am saying. Lying is impossible in allu-a."

"I'm not sure that is entirely an advantage, Dr. Saari," Wu told her.

"Dr. Wu," Juna said, "we must negotiate with the Tendu in good faith. We can't build a lasting agreement with the Tendu unless they trust us."

"Even so, there are times when even truth is conditional. Do you intend to share your private knowledge of the details of an agreement with the Tendu?"

"Allu-a isn't a psychic link," Juna explained. "It appears to be an exquisitely detailed reading of the participants' physiological state, imparting to each one a deep, empathic understanding of the other's emotions. I won't be giving away any state secrets, Dr. Wu. The Tendu can't get any hard information from allu-a. However, they will be able to tell how I feel about an agreement. They will know if I have any doubts about it."

"I see," Wu said, looking down at the table. Juna could tell he wasn't convinced.

"Dr. Wu," she said, rising. "I want to create an agreement that will bring our two people into harmony. To do that, both sides need to trust each other. That trust has to start somewhere. I will need to link with the Tendu in order to maintain their trust. I need to spend time with Moki, to help him get used to Ukatonen as his sitik. You will have to trust my judgment in these matters. I can't negotiate for you if you don't trust me." She paused and looked around the table at the faces watching her. "Currently I can't get out of quarantine unless someone lets me out. I am effectively a prisoner. I need access to both the Tendu and to the researchers and negotiators on board ship. I understand the need to maintain quarantine, but I can't do my job unless I have more freedom of movement."

Captain Edison stood. "Dr. Saari, would you be willing to accept a security escort when you are wandering around the ship? You would, of course, have to wear an e-suit to maintain quarantine, but you could meet with whomever you needed to."

"How long would I need a security escort, Captain?"

"Dr. Agélou will be doing a complete psych profile on you, Dr. Saari. If he feels that you aren't a security risk, I would be willing to suspend the escort." The captain turned to Dr. Agélou. "How long will it take you to complete your profile, Doctor?"

Dr. Agélou shrugged. "Perhaps as soon as a week, depending on our schedules. Maybe somewhat longer."

"Well?" the captain asked.

"Thank you, Captain Edison, I think that's a very reasonable solution," Juna responded, relieved to have solved at least one of her problems.

"I will allow you to continue linking with the Tendu, pending further developments," Wu said. "However, if there are any indications that it is interfering with the negotiations, or causing cultural damage to the Tendu, then you will have to stop."

"Thank you, Dr. Wu." Relief washed over Juna in a wave, turning her skin pale lavender. "Thank you."

Glancing up, she noticed several of the staff members staring, and realized that they could see her color changes through the helmet of the e-suit. She flushed leaf-brown with embarrassment, which only made matters worse.

Dr. Bremen rose. "I think it's time we moved on."

"My staff is eager to get some hands-on experience with the Tendu, as are all the other researchers on board ship. How soon can you get us permission to go ashore?" Wu asked.

"That may take some time," Juna said. "The Tendu are waiting to see how we handle the problem of reparations to Lyanan. We may have to deal with that first. Then we can work out the conditions under which we can conduct research in the Tendu's forests."

"Is there any way to negotiate some limited research while we work out the reparation agreement?" Bremen asked.

"I don't know, Dr. Bremen. I'll see what I can do. You must remember, all of you, that the Tendu have a very different approach to time than we do. This may take a while. Until we resolve this, I'll be happy to conduct seminars on what I have learned, whenever I can." She held up her hands in a gesture of helplessness. "I know it's not much, but it's all we can do."

"Do you have any recommendations on negotiation strategy, Dr. Saari?"

"We should definitely take a gift," Juna said. "Something that doesn't violate the protocols. A good sturdy coil of hemp rope would be ideal."

"Do we have some rope?" Bremen asked Captain Edison.

"I believe so. We included a fairly wide stock of possible trade goods, based on what we knew about the culture from the information Dr. Saari downloaded to the *Kotani Maru*."

"Good," Juna said. "The hard part will be explaining the Contact Protocols to Lalito, the chief elder of Lyali. She would be insulted to find out that we're coddling her. Does anyone have any suggestions?"

The meeting bogged down in a long and complicated wrangle over negotiating strategies. Nothing was decided, and at last Wu called a halt.

"One more thing, before we wind up the meeting, Dr. Saari," Wu said. "Your time is going to be in very high demand. I'd like to assign Dr. Tanguay to you as your assistant. She is more fluent in Tendu than anyone else on board ship, besides yourself, and she's eager to learn as much as she can."

Juna looked at the small, dark woman. Wu was right. She needed an assistant. "Thank you, Dr. Wu," she said gratefully. "I'm sure Dr. Tanguay will be a great help."

The meeting broke up, and Dr. Tanguay came over to talk Juna.

"I'm honored to be working with you, Dr. Saari," she said. "How soon can you start teaching me more skin speech?"

Juna smiled at the woman's eagerness. "Perhaps tonight, after dinner. Say 2100 hours? I'm afraid that you'll have to come to my quarters. You can't see my skin in this suit."

"That would be fine. I'll bring my computer. You can tell me whether you think the visual interface we're using will work."

"Good. I'll see you then," Juna said.

"Dr. Saari?" Captain Edison said, as they left the room. "I wanted to take this opportunity to personally welcome you back to the Survey." She shook Juna's hand admiringly. "It must have been an incredible four years," she added with a wistful note in her voice.

"It was, Captain, it was."

"I hope you can tell me more about it, sometime."

A tall, rangy red-haired woman in an ensign's uniform came up and saluted the captain.

"Dr. Saari, this is Ensign Laurie Kipp. She'll be your security escort."

Juna shook Ensign Kipp's hand. "Nice to meet you, Ensign."

"*Sano Laurie vaan,*" Ensign Kipp said, in Finnish.

"*Sa puhut suomea*?" Juna replied in Finnish.

Laurie nodded. "My mother grew up in Tampere. I think that was why Captain Edison assigned me to you."

"My father was from Mikkeli." She smiled. "But that was a long time ago. It was very kind of Captain Edison to assign you to me."

"She's a good captain."

They chatted pleasantly in Finnish while Ensign Kipp

showed Juna around the ship. They stopped often to shake hands and talk with the crew, who were eager to meet her. All this attention made her feel awkward and self-conscious, like some kind of Tri-V star. Fortunately, Laurie realized when she was getting overwhelmed, and gently ushered her on to the next lab, diplomatically shooing the crowd away.

Juna had never served on a research ship before. Because they were large and difficult to transport, the research ships were used only in very specialized circumstances. It was a shame that they weren't used more often, Juna thought as she toured the spacious, well-equipped labs, and shook hands with dozens of lab techs.

But that was one of the drawbacks of being first. The Survey sent out a lot of advance teams, but could only afford the bare minimum in terms of collection and bioanalysis tools. Other, more specialized teams were sent in their wake if the advance teams found anything useful or interesting to report. The advance teams were usually made up of bright young researchers looking for their first big break, with a few seasoned scientists along to oversee their efforts. It was never hard to staff the advance teams; the romance of being the first human to set foot on a planet was a big draw, though the reality could be very disillusioning.

Juna smiled, remembering how hard her first trip had been. Half the first-timers had resigned after that trip out, but not Juna. Despite the cramped conditions, minimal equipment, and often petty regulations, she loved her work.

"You know, I wouldn't trade being on an advance team for all the lab space on this ship," she remarked to Ensign Kipp as they settled themselves into the crew lounge just forward of the dining room.

"Why?"

Juna shrugged. "Less politics, more adventure, I guess."

Laurie rolled her eyes. "You don't know the half of it."

"Oh?"

"Too many presidents, not enough staff. Most of these people were running their own departments back home. They're not used to taking orders."

"I see."

"Everyone seems to think their own department comes first. Captain Edison has her hands full just settling interdepartmental disputes."

"Isn't that Bremen's job?" Juna asked.

Laurie rolled her eyes again. "Near as I can figure, his job is to look good in front of the cameras for the people back home. He wasn't supposed to go ashore alone like that, but he pulled rank in order to set up a good scene. The crew nearly split a gut laughing when you introduced yourself. You made a lot of friends with that."

"Coffee?" a familiar voice inquired.

Juna looked up. It was Alison.

"Alison! Thank you for the wine!" Juna stood and hugged her friend.

"Most people would have thanked me for that excellent meal!" Alison teased her fondly. "It must run in the family."

Juna held her friend out at arm's length. She looked good, a few pounds heavier, some lines a little deeper, but healthy and relaxed.

"So how did you get on board?" Juna asked. "I thought you had to retire."

"The retirement age for cooks is seventy-five. I'm only seventy, and unlike most Survey chefs, I *can* cook. I couldn't miss this trip! So I pulled a few strings and here I am."

"How did you get the wine?"

"As soon as I got the job, I went and visited your father. He gave it to me then," Alison told her. "I kept it under lock and key in my cabin so it wouldn't get requisitioned by one of the officers. Even Bremen didn't know about it until after he met you. I had the communications officer tell him."

"My father, how is he?"

"He's well, but getting on, like all of us," Alison said.

"And my brother?"

Alison's face clouded over. She took a letter out of her apron pocket. "You need to read this. It's from your father."

Juna opened the letter, blinking back tears at the familiar sight of her father's bold, sprawling handwriting.

Dear Juna,

I am well and the farm is prospering. We put up several fine vintages while you were gone. I'll be sending them along with the private stock that Alison is taking. I hope and pray daily that you will be found safe and healthy. There has been too much other sadness here. Someone may already have told you about Toivo. I hope not. I would rather you hear about family from family.

Toivo was playing spinball and fell against a support strut that broke away, carrying him and it into gravity. It was a miracle he wasn't killed. He fell directly on another strut, crushing several vertebrae in his lower back. The spinal cord was crushed beyond repair. The doctors say that he will need a wheelchair the rest of his life, but he's determined to learn to use an exoskeleton in low gravity.

Juna put the letter down. Alison sat beside her, and put an arm around her shoulder. Juna swallowed her tears and picked up the letter again.

Toivo is doing well, all things considered, but I'm concerned with his obsession to learn to use an exoskeleton and take up life in zero-gee. I hope it will pass, but you know how stubborn he is. Aunt Anetta has come to help out, and Toivo's spouses have taken turns caring for him, as have the children. He married into a good family, dear, and I'm very glad for it. The children are taking it hard, though. I try to spend a lot of time with Danan and the little ones, when the farm isn't keeping me busy. It's hard managing without Toivo. Danan is trying to help, but he's only eleven, and not yet strong enough to do the heavy work. I don't know how much longer I'm going to be able to keep the vineyard going. I'm not as tough as I once was; a full day's work takes a heavy toll at my age. Come home soon, dear. Your presence would help us all.

I love you,
Dad

There was a picture included with the letter. Toivo was sitting on the porch in his wheelchair; her father and Toivo's son, Danan, stood on either side of him. In the distance, the family's vineyards stretched up and away.

She put the letter down, and let the tears flow. Alison held her, patting her shoulder with that odd awkwardness that comes in the face of profound grief. When the first flood of anguish subsided, Juna held her arms out, spurs up.

"The Tendu could heal him," she said, her voice hoarse from crying. "They could heal him."

"Juna," her old friend said gently, "the doctors tried everything. Too much of the cord was crushed for neural repair. "

Juna shook her head. "The Tendu could grow his spine back again. They could make it just like new. I can't, not yet, but maybe if I studied hard with one of the enkar, I could learn how."

There was a clatter of pots and pans in the galley. Alison glanced nervously over her shoulder.

"I should get back before they ruin dinner." She peered at Juna. "Are you going to be all right?"

Juna nodded. "Thanks, Alison, I'll be fine. Go on. I'm so glad you're here!"

Alison gave her arm an affectionate squeeze, then headed for the galley.

"I'm sorry to hear about your brother," Laurie said.

Juna managed a brief thank-you. It had been an emotional day. She was worn out, and there was still that language session with Dr. Tanguay.

"I think I want to go back to my quarters now."

Juna felt a rush of relief as the lock door closed behind her. It was good to be alone. She stripped out of her suit and headed for the shower. The hot water felt wonderful against her tight, dry skin. Dad was right, they needed her back home—but she wouldn't be home for months, perhaps as long as a year. And the Tendu needed her too. Juna sighed, got out, dried off, and ordered dinner. That done, she poured herself a glass of water, and stood sipping it, looking around the sterile cubicle. Her gaze fell on her computer. She should read her mail.

After the first three offers for her memoirs, she switched her mail scan to personal correspondence only, and caught up with her friends while she ate another of Alison's glorious meals. Couscous this time, with fresh vegetables and chunks of lamb. The spices and the heat burned her aching throat, but it was so good to eat a hot meal again that she didn't care.

Dr. Tanguay came by for her lesson. Juna stripped down to her briefs and began testing her knowledge of skin speech. As long as Juna spoke slowly, in large, simple, informal patterns, Dr. Tanguay could understand most of what she said. The translation device proved to be a large graphic slate, crammed to the gills with linguistic software. It was slow but workable. It disturbed Juna to realize how easily she could be replaced. It was hard to get used to the idea that she was going to have to share the Tendu with people who would never understand them as well as she did.

Her voice gave out after about half an hour, and they called a halt, agreeing to get together after the staff meeting tomorrow for another lesson. Juna drank a liter of water; the air in the room sucked the moisture out of her. She found the environmental controls and turned the humidity up as high as it would go. Then she crawled into bed. It was good to sleep in a real bed again. She was so tired that she fell asleep before she could repair her tired, aching throat.

She woke in the middle of the night in agony, her skin tight and aching, her throat burning with dryness. She stumbled into the shower stall and turned on the water, then crouched there, mouth open, letting the warm water stream down her throat. The warmth and moisture eased the dryness of her skin, and she felt better, except for a tight ache in the skin over her elbows and knees. She would have to speak to the medical staff about the humidity tomorrow. Surely something could be done to make the room more comfortable.

She climbed into bed again without drying off, letting the moisture from her body seep into the sheets so that the bed would be moist and comfortable. It would be a mess in the morning, but at the moment she didn't care. She had spent years dreaming of cool, dry, clean sheets, and now all she wanted was to burrow into the rotting wet warmth of a Tendu bed.

Twenty-seven

ANITONEN WATCHED AS the humans' raft took Eerin away. Eerin waved, and Moki replied with a flash of brilliant colors, fading quickly back to deep grey. Anitonen glanced back at the floating island. New creatures moved over it like niku over a rotting log.

She missed Eerin already. Eerin had acted so differently when she was with the other new creatures. Her skin was strangely still while she made the mouth noises that passed as communication among the *humans*. Only when she translated what *Dr. Bremen* had said did her skin come alive. It felt like Eerin was gone even before she walked out of the jungle and got on the new creatures' raft.

Moki was taking this hard. A ripple of regret passed over Anitonen's skin, and she touched his shoulder reassuringly. He shrugged off her touch, his eyes never leaving the floating island. Orphaned bami his age almost never recovered from the loss of their sitik. Even with the kindest of care, they wasted away and died, or vanished into the forest, never to be seen again. Moki was exceptionally intelligent and fiercely determined, but the same determination that drove him to follow them through the jungle worked against him now as he clung to his sitik.

Anitonen laid a hand on his shoulder. He turned to look at her. "Eerin isn't dead, Moki. You'll see her tomorrow," she told him.

Moki turned to look at the ship again without responding.

Ukatonen touched Anitonen on the shoulder. "Go on, we'll sit here together for a while."

Anitonen nodded and swung off into the trees. She settled on a high branch and looked out at the humans' island, watching the new creatures come and go. How was she going to fit all of these strangers into her world?

Anitonen shook her head. First she had to deal with the problem of Lyanan. Their resentment of the humans had softened, thanks to Eerin's patience, hard work, and skill, but it could flare again if the negotiations went badly.

She needed to find some form of exchange that would satisfy both humans and Tendu. It needed to be valuable and easily divided, so that it could be used to help excuse the obligations that Lyanan had incurred while they were replanting the forest. It also had to be something that the humans were willing to trade.

Eerin had explained that there were very strict limits on what the humans would give to the Tendu. The humans couldn't give the Tendu anything that they didn't already have or use. This seemed like a strange rule to Anitonen. Why trade for something that the other person already had? Eerin had explained that the humans were afraid that the Tendu might hurt themselves with the gifts that they gave them. Too many new things might make the Tendu change too fast. Anitonen shook her head. Why should the humans worry about what the Tendu might do with their trade goods? That was the enkar's concern. If the enkar didn't like the way things were going, it was up to them to stop it.

It wasn't going to be easy to find trade goods that would settle the issue. She shook her head again, rippling frustration, and set off to find Lalito. They needed to discuss what Lyanan wanted to get out of the negotiations.

The humans arrived for the meeting shortly before noon the next day. Anitonen watched with Ukatonen and Moki as the humans headed toward the beach in their strange self-propelled rafts. As they drew closer, Anitonen saw Eerin sitting in the bow of the first raft. Her body was covered with *clothing*. How was she going to be able to talk when she was all covered up? Moki scrambled down the tree and out onto the cliffs, eager to greet his sitik. Anitonen lifted her ears inquiringly at Ukatonen.

"I told him he could escort the humans to the meeting. He'll get to see Eerin, and be quieter during the negotiations."

"Shouldn't you keep Moki away from her?"

"It would be like keeping the ocean away from the beach. Those two need each other too much."

"But you're supposed to become Moki's sitik now."

Ukatonen shook his head and looked away. "Moki won't accept me," he said, grey with sadness. "Some other solution must be found."

"What other solution is there?" Anitonen asked.

Ukatonen shook his head. "I don't know."

Anitonen looked at him. He had rendered the judgment that Juna should be allowed to adopt Moki. If Moki died, so would he. Someday she might face a similar threat. For a moment she longed to be back in Narmolom, where life was simple. But her people needed her here.

The humans reached the top of the cliff. Eerin carried Moki on her shoulders. He was radiantly turquoise with happiness. Eerin seemed pleased as well, though it was hard to tell through all that alien clothing. The other humans paused just outside the forest while Eerin stepped behind a bush. Anitonen rippled relief as Eerin emerged, naked and familiar, her clothing in a bundle under her arm.

Anitonen and Ukatonen followed the humans through the forest. A few humans glanced up as branches bowed and rustled, but none of them appeared to see the two enkar. They were too busy trying to look at everything, and as a result, they saw very little.

At last they neared the river bank, where the meeting was to take place. They hurried ahead, and were waiting with Lalito and the other Tendu on the soft, damp sand when the humans arrived.

Moki came in first, head high, obviously proud to be

entrusted with the duty of escorting his sitik and the other humans through the forest to this meeting.

"Greetings to the people of Lyanan, and to the enkar who have kindly agreed to attend this meeting," Eerin said in flawless formal skin speech. "May I present *Dr. Bremen*, the chief elder of the humans who have come here. *Dr. Wu*, whose atwa is learning about the Tendu; *Dr. Tanguay*, who has the same atwa; *Dr. Nazarieff*, whose atwa is learning about the Tendu's world; and *Captain Edison*, whose atwa is the floating island."

It was a fine introduction. Eerin's time among the enkar had not been wasted. Anitonen suppressed a flare of pride and stepped forward to reply.

"We are honored to meet you. I hope we can achieve harmony between our two peoples," Anitonen replied in equally formal skin speech. "May I present Lalito, chief elder of the village of Lyanan, and her bami, Lani. This is Sarito, who is on the village council, and his bami, Ehna. This is the enkar Ukatonen, and his bami, Moki"—Moki flinched at that—"and this is the enkar Garitonen." She felt silly introducing Ukatonen and Garitonen as enkar, when it was implicit in their names, but Eerin had said that it was a good idea. "I am the enkar Anitonen," she continued. "My atwa concerns Eerin and the other humans, so I will be guiding these talks toward harmony."

Anitonen waited while Eerin translated her speech into the noisy sound talk that the new creatures used. It took a long time. Then Dr. Bremen got up and said something.

"Greetings," Eerin translated for Dr. Bremen. "We are honored to meet you. I hope that we can achieve harmony between our people."

Lalito stepped forward and delivered a speech about the conditions at Lyanan, describing how her people had suffered from the destruction of the forest. Eerin asked her to pause several times while she translated her words into sound talk for the humans.

When the speech ended, the humans conferred noisily among themselves. It reminded Anitonen of a flock of kidala birds, and she suppressed a ripple of amusement. Then the one called Dr. Wu stood up to speak.

"Eerin has told us of the damage that we caused to your people, and we wish to make reparations. We want to meet our obligations in this matter. As a pledge for reparations, please accept this gift from us." He gestured, and one of the others brought forward a large coil of rope of very fine quality. It was a handsome gift.

"We thank you for this gift," Anitonen replied, "and we hope that these talks bring our people into harmony."

"It is our wish to keep the disruption our people cause to a minimum," Wu said. "We want to introduce the things that we make very slowly. We are afraid that certain trade goods might cause changes that you would not like, and we don't want that to happen. Though this limits the ways we can fulfill our obligations to you, I believe harmony can be achieved in this matter. It may take longer, but everyone involved will be happier with the decision. We hope that these agreements will last for many generations. Therefore we need to think everything through very carefully. I ask for your patience and understanding as we bargain."

Anitonen lifted her ears at this. He sounded like an enkar. Or was that merely Eerin's translation? She glanced at the others. The villagers seemed impressed, but it was more difficult to tell with her fellow enkar.

Ukatonen saw her inquiring look. "I like this Dr. Wu. He seems wise and reasonable," he told Anitonen in small, private signs. "Do you think he really is, or does Eerin just make him sound like he is?"

"I don't know," Anitonen replied. She turned back to Eerin and the other humans. "We will confer with Lalito and the village council and meet here again tomorrow."

"One other thing," Dr. Wu said. "Our people would like to come ashore and explore. Is that possible?"

Anitonen turned to Lalito. "Well?"

Lalito tucked her chin in thought for a few moments. "I don't want them destroying any more of our forest," she said, "or killing things like they did last time. I'd want one of the villagers along to keep an eye on them, and we'd need Eerin to come, too, and translate."

"I want some of the enkar along as well," Ukatonen said. "I

suggest that they send out no more than eight people, and that one of them must be Eerin. We will send along eight Tendu to watch over them."

The humans agreed to this, and the meeting broke up. Moki came over to Eerin and held his arms out, asking for a link. Eerin shook her head, glancing nervously at the other humans.

"I'm busy now, Moki. Perhaps later."

"Could you ask to stay a little longer?" Ukatonen proposed. "We need to talk with you about the meeting. And Moki wants to see you. Even if you don't link with him, a short visit would help him get used to your being away."

Eerin nodded, then turned and spoke to her people.

"It's all right," she told Ukatonen. "They'll send a *boat* to pick me up later on in the afternoon."

Garitonen escorted the other humans to the beach. Anitonen could see him trying his human skin speech out on the humans as they walked off through the jungle.

The Tendu waited until they could no longer hear the humans crashing through the leaf litter, and then they followed Lalito back to the village. The villagers had a beautiful meal laid out for the enkar in Lalito's room. After the ritual apologies and compliments, they sat down to eat. Eerin ate lightly, mostly fruits, greens, and a little raw fish.

"I ate a big meal just before I left," she explained when Anitonen remarked on her lack of appetite.

When they were full, Lalito signaled, and the tinka came in and removed the leftovers.

"Do your people understand the problems they have caused the village?" Lalito asked.

Eerin flickered yes.

"Then why do they restrict what we can bargain for?"

"Kene," Eerin said, "our people are very different. We wish to make restitution in a way that will best achieve harmony between my people and yours. This will take some time. Please be patient."

"We've waited four years for your people to come back."

"I know, kene, I know, and we are working hard to arrive at a solution. Tell me, what do you want from us?"

Lalito ducked her chin in thought. "Your people have many

things that we could use: computers, rafts that move themselves, deathstone tools that don't rot or break."

"What would you use to pay back the obligations incurred to the other villagers and the sea people if a fire or storm had damaged the jungle?"

"For the sea people, we would give them fresh and preserved fruits, nets, ropes, twine, and fish spears made of bone and stonewood. We usually give the land Tendu yarram, fish paste, salt, seeds from our best plants, and greenstone and guano for fertilizer."

"I see," Eerin said. "I'll talk to my people about what you have told me and see what we can do. It may take several months to bring us into harmony in this matter."

She turned to Anitonen and the other enkar. "My people also want to negotiate an agreement with all of the Tendu. How should this be accomplished?"

Ukatonen thought for a moment. "First you must reach harmony with Lyanan. Then we will talk about another agreement."

Eerin inclined her head. "I'll tell my people."

"Good," Ukatonen said. "I think we're through." He looked around inquiringly; there was no disagreement. "Eerin should have some time with Moki before she goes back to her people. Why don't you come to our room for a while?"

"Thank you. I'd like that."

Anitonen followed them back to their room. As soon as they got there, Moki held out his arms, requesting a link.

Eerin hesitated.

"Go ahead," Ukatonen urged. "It will make the separation easier if you link a bit from time to time."

A ripple of uncertainty passed over Eerin, but she held out her hands and Moki eagerly reached out to link with her.

Intense relief flowed over Ukatonen's body. "I was worried that Eerin wouldn't link with him," he told Anitonen. "Moki needs her so much, especially now, when everything is changing. I don't think this is going to work out." A ripple of regret clouded his skin for a moment.

Anitonen touched his shoulder in sympathy. "Things are just starting. I'm sure we'll find a solution to this problem."

Ukatonen shook his head. "These new people are so strange," he said. "How can we ever reach harmony with them?"

"We managed with Eerin."

"She was only one person. These others, in their suits, they seem much stranger and more remote. I don't understand them."

"Don't worry," Anitonen said. "They're new and strange, yes, but inside those suits, they're like Eerin. I already like Dr. Wu. He thinks like an enkar." It felt strange, reassuring Ukatonen, who had always reassured her, but Anitonen looked forward to getting to know these new humans. Her life with Eerin, Moki, and Ukatonen had become routine. She was ready for a new challenge.

"I just wish I could see them without their suits. I want to visit that floating island of theirs, and see how they live," Ukatonen said.

"Why don't we ask if we can visit their island? After all, if we're letting them come here, we should be able to go there," Anitonen replied.

Juna slid out of the link, feeling calm and happy. So much had happened since the Survey returned. It seemed like a whole month had passed since she had last seen Moki, instead of only a day. It was good to feel his familiar presence again. Leaving him behind would be like tearing off an arm. She loved Moki as much as she loved her father and brother. As her adopted child, he was part of her family. She felt as though she were being split in two by the people she loved the most.

"Oh, Moki," she whispered. "What am I going to do?"

Moki's ears lifted inquisitively at the sound of her voice.

"I missed you so much," Juna told him in skin speech. "I don't want to leave you behind."

"Then stay," Moki said.

"I can't. My brother's been hurt. They need me at home."

"Someone else can heal him, can't they?"

Juna shook her head. "They can't heal him. He can't walk; he needs a special machine to help him get around."

"Why hasn't he chosen to die?"

Juna closed her eyes, fighting back a sudden flash of anger.

"That's not how our people behave, Moki. There's still a lot that he can do. He wants to live." She looked away, remembering Toivo's obsession with learning to use an exoskeleton in zero-g. Perhaps Toivo didn't really want to live.

"It doesn't matter why, Moki. I need to go home."

"Then take me with you!" he pleaded. "I can help you heal your brother."

"You wouldn't like it where I live. It's too dry, and there aren't any trees to climb in. This is your home."

"But you would be there!" Moki insisted. "My home is with my sitik!"

"Ukatonen is your sitik now. You must stay with him."

Just then Juna's wrist chrono chimed.

"It's time for me to head back."

"Let me come with you to the beach!" Moki begged.

Ukatonen put a hand on Moki's shoulder. "You may come with us to the boat, Moki, but you must stop asking Eerin to take you with her. You're making things harder for all of us."

Moki subsided into stillness, turning a dull, sullen red. He trailed after them, sulky and obstinate, all the way to the edge of the jungle.

As they were about to come out into the open, Ukatonen put a hand on Juna's arm. "Could we visit the floating island where the humans live?" he asked.

"I'll ask Dr. Bremen and Captain Edison," Juna replied. "You'll have to wear an e-suit while you're there. Talking will be difficult."

"That doesn't matter. I want to see how you humans live. It will help me understand your people."

"Can I come too?" Moki asked, his sullenness forgotten.

"It will depend on what Dr. Bremen and Captain Edison say," Juna told him.

"I hope they say yes. I want to see where you live," Moki said.

They left the jungle and walked through the rain to the beach. A boat launched from the Survey ship arced toward them over the grey water. It pulled up on the beach and the crew members got out.

"Hello," Moki said in skin speech Standard. "My name is Moki. Who are you?"

"It knows Standard!" one of the crew said, a startled expression on his face.

Juna nodded. "Moki is my bami. I've been teaching him written Standard."

"So this is your adopted child," the crewman said. He bent forward and said, "Hello, Moki. My name's Bruce Bowles. Nice to meet you."

Juna translated for Moki.

"Hello, Bruce, I'm pleased to meet you too," he replied in Standard.

Bruce chuckled. "What a cute kid!" he remarked to Juna. He stuck out his hand. "Can you shake hands?"

Moki looked up at Juna, ears spread in inquiry. Juna explained handshakes to him. He nodded and extended his hand, which Bruce enfolded in his huge glove, and gently shook. Then he laughed and patted Moki on the head. Juna found herself bristling at Bruce's condescension.

Ukatonen came forward. "My name is Ukatonen," he said in Standard, holding out his hand.

The crewman shook the enkar's hand. "Pleased to meet you," he said.

Juna smiled, and translated his words.

"This is Anitonen," Ukatonen said in Standard skin speech. Bruce shook Anitonen's hand.

"Why didn't he touch us on the head?" Anitonen wanted to know.

"He's treating Moki like a human child. Sometimes people do that with children. It's a way of showing affection."

"What are they saying?" Bruce asked, intrigued.

"They wanted to know why you didn't pat them on the head, like you did with Moki."

Bruce laughed. "Oh hell, I've just made a fool of myself, haven't I?"

Juna shrugged, suddenly liking this big, stocky man. "No more than I did when I first met them. Moki is almost as old as you are, by the way."

"Really? He looks like a kid!"

Juna nodded. "He does, but he's at least thirty years old." She shook her head, remembering. "He was determined to get adopted. It was either that or die of old age while he was still a child."

"I've read some of the summaries of your notes," Bruce said. "It's hard to believe anyone could be that cruel to their young."

"It's normal for them, and it works," Juna explained. "Still, it's hard to watch it happen."

"What are you talking about?" Anitonen asked.

Juna summarized their conversation in skin speech for her, judiciously softening some of Bruce's more critical remarks.

"That's really something," Bruce commented. "Watching your skin change color like that, I mean. What does it feel like?"

Juna turned a deep, embarrassed brown, and looked away. "I don't know. How does it feel when you move your arm?"

"I'm sorry, I didn't mean to embarrass you. It's just so beautiful, and well, you know, strange. And you do it so well."

Juna looked up and met his gaze. Bruce had large brown eyes that looked both sad and earnest. He had a nice voice, too, deep and resonant. She felt a flicker of golden warmth run up her spine. Glancing around, she saw Anitonen's ears lift in inquiry. Again, she flushed with embarrassment.

"Hey, Bruce, we'd better get back," the other crew member shouted. "It's nearly dinnertime, and those mucky idiots won't leave anything for us."

Juna nodded, grateful for the interruption. Her own stomach was growling with hunger. "I'm sorry to keep you." She turned and embraced Moki. "I have to go now," she told him in skin speech.

He looked away, turning the mournful color of the rain-clouded sea.

Juna touched his chin. "I'll see you tomorrow, Moki."

His color lightened and he nodded. Reluctantly, he let her go.

"Goodbye, Moki," Bruce said. "It was nice meeting all of you."

Juna translated Bruce's words, thankful for the distraction that made this parting easier.

"Goodbye, Bruce," Moki spelled out in Standard. He reached out and shook Bruce's hand.

Juna turned and climbed into the boat. "I'll see you tomorrow," she repeated.

The Tendu watched as the boat pulled away from shore. Moki's color greyed, his figure receding into the steady rain.

"It must be hard on both of you to be separated," Bruce remarked. "He reminds me of my nephew. He's about eight years old." He shook his head. "He's the closest thing I have to a son. I miss him."

Juna nodded, remembering her own nephew, Danan, and understanding how he felt. "I love Moki very much," she said. "I'm grateful that Ukatonen is adopting him. I hope it works out." She blinked back sudden tears.

Bruce squeezed her shoulder in wordless sympathy, then turned to see to the boat. Juna looked back at the beach. She couldn't see anything but dark blurs that might be clumps of seaweed on the beach. Moki was lost in the rain.

Twenty-eight

MOKI FOUGHT THE urge to claw off the restricting suit he was wearing. He felt as if he were being smothered. *Concentrate on what's going on around you,* he told himself sternly. *This is important.* Eerin had gotten permission for half a dozen Tendu to visit the humans' *Survey* ship. It was fascinating, though the *e-suits* kept them from saying much. He had to talk to the others through the clear coverings over their faces, so it was hard to understand what they were saying.

Moki looked up at Eerin, who was also wearing an uncomfortable e-suit. Her height and her obvious ease in the confining suit made her stand out from the Tendu. He wondered how she managed it. The other humans escorted them down a long cave called a *hallway*. It was like a hollow tree trunk turned on its side, with doors opening on two sides instead of all four like the trunk of a na tree. It was lit with hot yellow globes of light, much harsher and brighter than the cool blue light of glow-fungus. Moki paid close attention, trying to memorize every detail of the humans' ship.

Humans peered out of the doorways at them. They looked like Eerin, but they had hair all over the tops of their heads, and little furry caterpillars over their eyes. Some of the male humans had hair on their chins and over their mouths. Moki wondered why some males chose to grow beards and others removed them. Did it reflect some kind of status? Was it an indication of their willingness to mate?

The humans looked either pink and excited or different shades of embarrassed-looking brown. They were hugely tall, even bigger than Eerin. One of them, a female named *Laurie*, followed Eerin everywhere. She had bright orangey-red hair that looked like it couldn't decide whether to be frightened or angry. At one point, she knelt down and let Moki touch it. He could feel almost nothing through the thick *gloves* of the e-suit, but it seemed short and bristly. She made a sound like the one Eerin made when she was happy or amused. Eerin called it a *laugh*. Moki decided that he liked Laurie, despite her funny-colored hair.

They stopped outside the doorway to Eerin's room. It was different from the other doorways, thicker, and more imposing. Laurie opened the door for them. Eerin led three of the Tendu into a small room and closed the door. A red light came on, then turned green again. When the door opened, the room was empty except for Eerin. Moki's ears rose.

"The others are inside, waiting for us. This is an *airlock*, like the door we used to enter the ship," Juna told him.

She motioned the rest of the Tendu in. The room was small, and dimly lit. It was a pleasant change from the harsh yellow light of the hallway. Eerin closed the door, and a red light came on. She took off her helmet and gloves.

"All right," she said in small patterns on her scalp. "You can take off your suits now."

Eerin removed her suit, then moved to help the others off with theirs. As soon as their suits were off, they flickered with bright bursts of relieved talk. Moki took his suit off last.

"Oh, it's wonderful to get out of that thing!" he said. "Did you see those funny lights in the corridor? And all that hair on the humans' faces. And the—" Moki stopped himself with a ripple of laughter; he was babbling too.

Then Eerin opened the inner door, and they were in her room. It was cold, dry, and too bright. All the surfaces were shiny and wet-looking. Moki reached out to touch the wall. He was surprised to find that it was dry. Ukatonen wandered into a smaller room and started playing with the silvery deathstone knobs. All of a sudden he jumped and chittered in surprise.

"Water's coming out," he said. "It's hot!"

Moki followed Eerin into the room. She twisted one of the deathstone knobs and the water stopped. The other Tendu crowded around as she turned knobs and pushed buttons and showed how the *bathroom* worked. The other Tendu took turns in the *shower*, letting the hot water spray down their backs. It felt good, although the water had something in it that stung his eyes.

Finished with his shower, Moki wandered out into the larger room and began looking around. He heard a rustling and saw a small white animal, covered with hair, inside a box made of shiny deathstone. It sniffed curiously at his wet hands, completely unafraid. He opened the door of the box. The animal sat and watched him as he slowly moved his hand toward it. It seemed neither afraid nor angry. Moki scooped it up gently and placed it over his allu. It jumped and squeaked as his spur pierced its skin, then relaxed bonelessly on his arm as he tasted its cells. It tasted like Eerin, only different. It was absolutely fascinating. He took it over to the others. They crowded around it curiously, eager to taste the small creature's cells themselves.

Eerin came over to see what they were looking at. When she saw the animal sprawled on Moki's arm, she turned a horrified shade of orange.

"What's the matter?" he asked.

"Please, Moki, put him back exactly the way you found him. If he dies, I may never get out of *quarantine!*"

Moki made sure that the animal was unchanged and unharmed; then he gently lifted it off his allu and placed it back inside the box while the other Tendu watched. In a little while it woke up, sniffed itself thoroughly, and began to walk. It was a little groggy, but otherwise it seemed fine.

A ripple of relief passed over Eerin. "Good," she said. "I'm glad it's all right. If it died, it might keep me from getting to go out into the ship without a suit."

"What does the animal have to do with your suit?" Garitonen asked.

"They put the *mouse* in here to see if I would make it sick. If it stays healthy, then I'm safe to let out among the other humans."

"Why?" Lalito wanted to know.

"When Anitonen's sitik found me, I was dying. The world was killing me. I was *allergic* to substances in pollen and in the mold and fungi spores in the air. Those strange substances made my body fight so hard that it threw itself out of harmony. My breathing passages were so swollen, I couldn't breathe. I was having convulsions. We humans are allergic to every living world but our own. The other humans are afraid that I will make them sick the same way, because I've been here so long."

"We could fix them," Moki suggested.

Eerin shook her head. "They won't let you. They're afraid of linking."

"Besides," Ukatonen said, "we should wait until we understand the humans better."

Just then there was a strange, high-pitched noise. Eerin picked up something and held it to her ear. She began to make human sound speech into the thing, pausing occasionally to listen. Moki thought he recognized the word "Tendu." Then she stopped talking and put the object down.

"That was Dr. Wu. The people who study the Tendu are waiting to meet you. We should go and see them."

Moki's ears lifted. "What do you mean? Dr. Wu is too big to fit in there."

Eerin laughed. "No, Moki. Dr. Wu is somewhere else. He has a *telephone*, just like that one, and he uses it to carry his speech to me."

"Oh, like a radio," Anitonen remarked.

"Exactly," Eerin agreed. "Now we have to put on our suits again so that we can meet more of my people."

Regretfully, they entered the small room, and put on their suits. Then they followed Eerin to another room where a crowd of humans were waiting to meet them. Moki shook hands with dozens of humans, feeling awkward and muffled in his suit. He could recognize a few of the humans' sound speech words: his name, the term they used for his people, and their words for yes and no. One of the humans took out a flat rectangular object and sat in the corner watching the assembled people. She was doing something to the surface of the rectangle. Intrigued, Moki went over to see. The human was making pictures on the white surface of the rectangle with a small stick. She held it out so he could see what she was doing.

Moki nodded, and handed the thing back. She drew on it, and as he watched, a shape emerged, a plant with a flower. She pointed to the plant and then to herself. Then she handed him the rectangle and the stick, pointing to him, and then to the rectangle.

Awkwardly he drew a rough version of his name sign. Then he drew "My name is Moki," underneath in human skin speech. She replied with, "My name is Marguerite Mee."

Soon they were drawing messages back and forth to each other. He would point at something and she would write the name for it. Underneath his uncomfortable suit, he would shape the word in human skin speech. The stick was called a *pencil*. The rectangle was called a *pad*. It was made of *paper*.

Each time the paper surface filled up, she flipped to an empty *sheet* beneath the one they had just been drawing on. It was a really interesting thing. His fingers twitched; he longed to touch and smell the paper.

"You will come visit us soon?" he asked.

Marguerite nodded.

"Bring pad?"

"We talk with pad again," she drew in reply.

Eerin came over and rested a hand on Moki's shoulder. Marguerite showed her the pad. Eerin nodded. Moki could see her skin turn deep green with approval. She picked up the pencil.

"Very good, Moki," she drew in Tendu skin speech. "You're learning a lot." Her words seemed flat and unemotional on the paper, but he knew by the color of her face that she was pleased. She turned and said something in sound speech and everyone came over to see what he and Marguerite had done. The others, both Tendu and human, were impressed. More paper and pencils were produced. Soon everyone was busy writing back and forth. This was enjoyable, but it wasn't helping Moki learn what he needed to know. He needed to get out, to see more of the ship.

"Where's Bruce?" he asked Eerin.

"I don't know, Moki," she said. "He wouldn't be here. He has a different atwa."

"Can we go find him?"

Eerin looked at the others, who were busy with pencils and paper. Another knot of Tendu and humans were clustered around a computer. "All right, Moki, I don't think they need me for a while. Let's go."

Eerin picked up a pad and pencil, then beckoned to her friend Laurie, and the three of them set off down the hall. They walked past the food place and through a door, and down a long *passageway* with steps in it. They came out in a noisier, slightly darker passageway. Eerin talked to the first person they saw. He pointed down the hall. Eerin nodded and they set off again. They entered a room full of deathstone pipes, and mysterious, big stone objects. Somewhere there was a deep throbbing noise. It sounded as if they were inside the heart of a giant beast. Eerin spoke to a woman, who nodded and went off.

"She's going to get Bruce," Eerin wrote on the pad. "We'll wait here."

At last the woman returned with Bruce. He was liberally covered with dirt, and was wiping his hands on a piece of cloth.

He said something to Eerin, then bent and shook Moki's hand.

"Hello, Moki," he said in human sound speech.

"Hello, Bruce," he wrote on the pad, pleased that he could understand the human's greeting. "It's good to see you. Will you show me the ship?"

Bruce looked at Eerin; she nodded. He took one of Moki's hands and Eerin took the other. Laurie followed them. Bruce showed them the *machine* that circulated the air through the ship, the main computer for the ship in its mesh of cables, and many more rooms full of strange machines and people. Moki paid close attention to where they were going; he didn't want to get lost the next time he visited the ship.

Then Bruce led them down some stairs and through another hallway, and opened a door into a large room. He led them over to a wide window covered with the same clear stuff that covered the top of the raft. They looked out at a water-filled cave inside the ship. Inside it were many strange human machines. Bruce pointed at one that looked like a giant deathstone insect.

"That's called a *flyer*. It flies like a big bird," Bruce wrote. "We climb inside it, and then it leaves out that big door there. Then we fly north and land at another floating island. We get on a bigger plane, called a *shuttle,* which takes us to the sky raft."

Moki looked at the flyer, trying to memorize every detail.

"Could I ride in the flyer?" Moki asked. "Could I see the shuttle place? I would like to see the shuttle climb up to the stars."

Bruce shook his head. "No," he said, then used human sound speech Moki didn't understand yet.

"You need to stay with your people, Moki," Eerin wrote. "The shuttle place is far away, in the north. It's too cold for the Tendu there."

"If you were with me it would be all right."

"No, Moki, it simply isn't possible," she wrote in Tendu skin speech. "I can't get permission to take you there."

Moki shrugged, a gesture he had learned from her, and a useful one in this suit.

"We should go back now," Eerin wrote. "It's getting late. They may need me, and Bruce has work to do."

"Goodbye, Bruce," Moki wrote. "Thank you for showing me the flyer."

Bruce shook Moki's hand. "It was fun. I hope I see you again."

Moki nodded and rippled blue, then turned and took Eerin's hand. He had learned a lot of important things today. Together with Laurie they headed back upstairs. Moki paid close attention to the way back. It was important. Under his suit, where no one could see his words, he kept repeating, "*I will go with you. I will go with you.*"

Twenty-nine

"WELL, DR. AGELOU," Dr. Bremen said. "What are the results of Dr. Saari's tests?"

Juna swallowed nervously and looked around the room. Dr. Wu, Dr. Baker, and Captain Edison also waited for the psychologist's verdict.

"I'm afraid that there were some inexplicable anomalies in her brain scan, and some significant changes in her personality tests as well."

Captain Edison leaned forward. "What sort of anomalies, Doctor?"

The psychologist glanced at Juna, his fingers plucking nervously at his fussy little goatee.

"Her abilities to smell, taste, hear, and see all appear to have been enhanced. She can see into the ultraviolet, and down into the infrared, and her color discrimination is much more subtle than normal. Her kinesthetic senses are also enhanced. The medical team reported significantly faster reflexes and increased coordination, which was corroborated by my neural and brain scans."

Juna looked down at the table, tracing the marbling in the plasteel tabletop with one gloved finger. So far he had only pointed out that she could run faster and see better. They already knew that. She wondered what it had to do with her psychological profile.

"Also, Dr. Saari's brain-wave pattern has altered in some significant and fundamental ways. She has much deeper theta and alpha waves than I have ever seen before, and she possesses a degree of physiological control documented in only a few of the most disciplined yogis and fakirs. In addition she appears able to alter her emotional state almost at will."

"You mentioned some personality changes, Doctor?" Captain Edison prompted. "Could you please elaborate on that."

"Chiefly, she exhibits a close bonding with the Tendu, a condition known as xenophilia. Consequently, her loyalties are deeply divided between her own species' interests and those of the aliens. In addition, her values profile has shifted significantly. Her respect for authority has diminished, and her willingness to identify strongly with a group has shown a remarkable increase."

Juna looked on, amazed that her fondness for the Tendu could be referred to in such pathological terms. She took a deep breath, suppressing her rising anger. This wasn't going to be good.

"What is your recommendation?" Dr. Bremen asked.

Dr. Agélou sighed and looked down at the table. "I believe that there are just too many psychological unknowns here. I have discussed these changes with Morale Officer Chang, and we agreed that changing Dr. Saari's security status poses too great a risk to the health and safety of the crew on this mission." He turned to Juna but did not quite meet her gaze. "I'm very sorry, Dr. Saari."

Captain Edison stood. "I think you're basing your recommendation a little too heavily on psychological testing, Dr. Agélou. Given the circumstances, I think that the changes in Dr. Saari are quite understandable, and even reasonable. I see nothing in your data that would lead me to believe any of these changes make Dr. Saari a security risk. The reports I have received from Ensign Kipp and others on the security detail are quite favorable. I don't believe she poses a risk to the crew. I recommend that we discontinue the security escort."

"Thank you, Captain Edison," Juna said, looking up at her. "I appreciate your trust in me."

"Just a minute, Captain," Dr. Bremen said. "I don't think you should ignore Dr. Ágélou's doubts."

"I'm not ignoring them, Dr. Bremen," the captain replied. "I've taken his recommendation into account, along with the reports from my security detail. I feel that Dr. Saari is not a risk to the crew of this ship. Besides, Dr. Saari's expertise is too valuable to keep locked up. I'm already getting complaints from some of the researchers."

"Dr. Agélou is a highly trained professional, Captain Edison. I'm not sure that it's wise to disregard his advice."

"Dr. Bremen, I have spent twenty years in the Survey, five of them as a captain. I have had to evaluate people's trustworthiness and fitness for duty many times during my career. Psychological profiles are an important part of any such decision, but there are a great many other factors to consider. I have considered those factors, and I believe that Dr. Saari does not pose a risk to my crew or my ship."

"This is the most important Survey mission in decades," Bremen responded. "I don't want to take any unnecessary risks. I'm sorry, Dr. Saari, but I'm afraid that until further notice, you will continue to have a security escort."

"I understand, Dr. Bremen," Juna said, fighting to keep her anger from showing.

She stood. "Captain Edison, thank you for taking my part in this matter. I'll try to prove that your trust in me is justified."

With that, Juna turned and walked out the door, too angry to wait for an official dismissal. Under her suit, her skin was alive with anger, hurt, and disappointment.

She flung open the airlock door, slammed it shut, started the lock cycle, and began stripping off her suit, fighting back tears. Her gloves jammed on their threads, so she fought her way out of the suit, leaving its gloves and boots attached. Then she had to wait until the lock finished cycling to get into her room.

Only when she was in the shower did she allow her tears to flow. The hot water flowed over her body, washing away the tears and soothing her tight, dry skin. She leaned her forehead against the side of the shower stall. Hot water poured around her ears and down her cheeks, trailing off the point of her chin. She knew that she should have stayed and tried to convince Bremen to change his mind, but she had been too angry to think straight. It was all too much—her cold, dry quarters, the quarantine, the constant surveillance, the way Moki clung to her, and the demands of the Tendu. Worst of all was the fear in the eyes of her fellow humans. Still, she had to bear it. The Tendu and the humans needed her to reach harmony. She wondered how the enkar managed.

She climbed out of the shower, and began to dry off. She wanted to climb into bed, pull the covers over her head, and never come out again.

The phone rang. She reached to answer it, then hesitated as it rang again, and again. She picked it up just before the messaging clicked in.

"Hey, it's Laurie. How're you doing?"

Juna sighed and rubbed her forehead with the back of her hand. "I've been better," she confessed.

"You want someone to talk to? I'll be happy to suit up and come in."

Juna glanced around the anonymous cubicle she occupied. "I think I'd rather come out."

"Okay."

Laurie opened the airlock door after it finished cycling. "Let's go sit on the landing dock. That way you can get out of that suit for a while."

"Can I do that?" Juna asked.

"Sure. You're under guard, after all. C'mon."

Laurie let Juna through the airlock to the outside first. She stood at the top of the steps, looking longingly at the low green line of forest-covered hills, inhaling the scent of the sea and the green, complex scent of the jungle. If only she could dive off the dock and vanish into the forest, leaving all her problems behind. She shook her head and stepped back from the railing.

The airlock door slid open with a hiss, and Laurie stepped out, looking even taller and more imposing in her e-suit.

"Let's go sit down by the water," Juna said. "I want to dangle my legs over the side."

Laurie nodded and followed her down the steps to the dock.

"I've heard so much about the jungle and the Tendu from you and the others who've been ashore. I wish I could see it," Laurie said when they were settled.

"Do you want me to take you over there sometime?" Juna asked. "It would be easy for me to get permission from the Tendu."

Laurie looked down at the water. "I'd like to, but there are so many people who haven't been ashore yet. It wouldn't be fair."

"Fair?" Juna smiled, thinking of her own treatment. "What's fair? You've been good to me, treated me like a human being." She looked up at Laurie. "I wish more people did."

Laurie looked away for a long moment. "You don't mind that I report to the captain about you?"

Juna shrugged. "It's part of your job. Captain Edison said that the reports she's heard have been good."

Laurie nodded, but there was still a hunched and guilty look about her.

"What is it, Laurie? What's wrong?"

"They watch you," she said after a long pause.

"I know that," Juna said.

Laurie shook her head. "You don't understand. They watch you all the time. Everywhere. There are cameras in your room, and surveillance equipment in your suit. There's a team of people trying to decode everything you say to the Tendu. They questioned Alison when they found out she was a friend of yours."

Juna put a hand on Laurie's shoulder. "You think I don't already know that they're treating me like an exotic lab rat? They have to be watching me. I'd be surprised if they weren't. They need to know how I've changed. I just wish I could explain to them that it's still me inside this skin. I'm just a little older, a little wiser, and a whole lot greener than I used to be."

Laurie smiled, and then looked away, out toward the coast. "You still shouldn't be treated like this, after all you've been through. You don't need a security escort, Juna."

"They think I do," Juna said with an ironic smile.

"I've served under Captain Edison for four years. You work that long with someone, you get to understand them pretty well. She isn't happy with this trip. There's too many interdepartmental turf wars, and Bremen isn't doing anything to stop them. When people go over his head to Captain Edison, he gets upset. I think he sided with Chang and Agélou because he wanted to assert his authority over the captain."

"Politics," Juna said. "It's politics. Most of the people on this ship are here because they've got pull. The Tendu are the most important discovery in years. Careers can be made here, especially for the AC people." She looked out toward the green hills. "I liked being on the advance teams because there was a lot of good science being done without a lot of academic politics."

Laurie patted her knee. "I don't think this situation can last very long. You're too necessary to the success of this mission. Sooner or later Chang and Agélou are going to have to cave in. Besides, you're well-liked, and everyone who's dealt with you knows you aren't a risk to the mission."

"It isn't just the humans," Juna told her. "There's Moki and the negotiations with Lyanan. There's pressure from all sides." She shook her head. "It's a lot to deal with."

"Just remember that you have friends on board."

"Thanks, Laurie," Juna said. "It helps a lot." She looked again at the forest. "You know, coming out here was a good idea. I feel a lot better."

"I'm glad it helped," Laurie said. "You ready to go in now?"

"We'd better," Juna agreed. "They're probably starting to wonder what I'm up to out here."

"Thank you for coming, Dr. Saari," Captain Edison said. "Please sit down."

The captain sat behind her desk. "I want to apologize for this mistreatment. I think you've been through enough. If I could stop it, I would." She spread her fingers in a gesture of helplessness. "But Bremen won't budge. As a researcher, you're in his chain of command. I can only advise him. There's not a lot I can do about your situation, Dr. Saari, but I wanted you to know that I'm on your side, and that I'm doing everything in my power to help."

"Thank you, Captain. I appreciate it."

"I wish I could do more," Captain Edison said. "Most people

in your situation would have fallen apart, yet you've survived and adapted. The Survey needs more people like you."

"Is there anything I can do to help change the situation?" Juna asked.

"Keep your head down, do your job, and hope that something comes along to help change things." The captain held her hands up in a gesture of helplessness. "I'm afraid that's the best advice I can give you."

Juna passed through the final airlock and stood on the landing, feeling the refreshing bite of fresh air on her moist skin. Her sleeveless shirt fluttered in the light breeze. She closed her eyes, savoring these few moments of freedom before the others emerged.

"It must feel very good to get out of that suit," Dr. Tanguay remarked as she came out of the airlock. "You're turquoise all over."

Juna flushed brown with embarrassment.

"I'm sorry," Dr. Tanguay said. "I didn't mean to make you uncomfortable."

"It's all right, Patricia," Juna said, looking away toward the coast.

"Could we— Could you talk in skin speech?" she asked. "I need to practice."

"Of course," Juna said in Tendu. "Are you ready for the negotiations?" she asked, pacing her words more quickly than Patricia was used to in order to test her progress.

"Slower, please," Dr. Tanguay replied.

Juna was repeating the question when the airlock door hissed open. It was Dr. Wu. Juna noted a look of concern on Dr. Tanguay's face as she turned to escort Wu down the long stairway to the boat, asking him about the agenda for today's negotiations. She helped Dr. Wu into the boat, and allowed him to help her step in. Juna followed them, accepting Dr. Wu's hand to assist her.

At last, the negotiation team was assembled in the boat and ready to leave. Today, the team consisted of Dr. Wu, Dr. Tanguay, Dr. Bremen, Captain Edison, and Juna. Bremen nodded to Bruce, and he cast off from the dock. As they headed for shore, Dr. Tanguay continued to work with Juna on understanding skin speech. Wu, who usually watched with interest, was looking down into the bilge of the boat. He looked a little pale, but that could just have been the reflection off the water. Juna was about to ask him, but Dr. Tanguay interrupted her with a question about skin-speech grammar. When she turned back to Dr. Wu, they were getting ready to land.

As soon as they stepped onto the beach, Dr. Tanguay took Dr. Wu's arm. The two of them plodded down the beach, chatting amicably. Patricia stopped often to pick something up and exclaim over it. They trailed the group by thirty meters by the time the others stopped to rest at the top of the cliff. Dr. Wu was sweating profusely and breathing hard when he and Tanguay reached the top of the cliff. She's covering for Wu, Juna realized.

He looked as if he needed a chance to rest before they continued on. Juna decided to make sure that he got it.

"You wait here. I'll go see if the Tendu are ready for us," she said.

Juna entered the cool forest with a sigh of relief, slipping out of her clothing as soon as she was out of sight of the other humans. Anitonen chittered at her from a branch in the lower canopy, and Moki swung down to greet her. They embraced and linked briefly.

Wu looked better when Juna returned for the team. They followed her to the stream bank where the negotiations were being held and settled down to work. There was little progress. The Tendu would not discuss anything else until the question of reparations for Lyanan was resolved. So far, Wu and the others had refused every suggestion made by Lalito, except for a set of aerial photographs and detailed topographical maps of their territory, made of indestructible plastic. Even that was pushing the letter of the law, but it was the villagers' most benign request so far, and the humans needed to give the Tendu something in order to keep the negotiations going.

But Lalito wanted more. She kept asking for things she had seen on her trip to the ship: computers, electric lights, steel tools, plastic containers, bags, and sheeting. She even wanted some mice like the one in Juna's room. Juna had suggested alternatives: more coils of hemp rope, beautifully woven baskets, flint-knapped arrowheads, and fishnets. All had been flatly refused. At least they were still negotiating, though Juna felt that was a tribute to the endurance and patience of the Tendu.

After an hour and a half, both sides took a break. Juna pulled Dr. Tanguay aside.

"What's the matter with Dr. Wu?" she asked. "He's been looking pale all morning. You've been hovering over him like an anxious mother hen."

"He said he wasn't feeling well," Patricia replied. "Perhaps it's a touch of the flu." Her tone of voice was not convincing.

"You're worried it's something serious, aren't you?"

"I'm afraid that it might be his heart," Patricia confessed. "He barely made it through the health screening, and he's been getting steadily worse the whole trip. I've been trying to keep him from getting too tired. He's too important to lose."

"Perhaps we should take him back to the ship," Juna suggested.

Patricia shook her head. "I've suggested that, but he won't go." She glanced over at Wu. "He's afraid that the doctors will bar him from the negotiations."

"I'll do what I can to help," Juna reassured her.

Juna watched Wu as the negotiations progressed. He looked distinctly unwell. She saw some of the others watching him also. Even the Tendu seemed to notice. She was about to call for another break when Wu suddenly doubled over, clutching his chest.

"My heart," he gasped.

Captain Edison was on the radio immediately, calling for assistance.

"What is it?" Anitonen asked.

"Something's wrong with his heart," Juna told her. "We're calling for medical assistance."

"He's unconscious!" Patricia exclaimed.

Anitonen pushed past the humans and squatted beside Wu. "Help me get his suit off," she told Juna. "He needs help now!"

"Let the Tendu help," Juna told the others as she began removing Wu's helmet.

"No!" Patricia said, pushing Juna's hands away. "It'll kill him!"

"The Tendu can stabilize him," Juna told her. "By the time we get him to a medical team it will be too late."

"But it will kill him!"

"No it won't!" Juna insisted. "The Tendu saved my life. They can save his." She took Dr. Tanguay's hands in hers. "Patricia, I care about Paul too. Let me help Anitonen save his life. Please!"

"They can't get a medical team to us for at least fifteen minutes," Captain Edison informed them. "Let the Tendu do what they can for him." The captain slid an arm around Patricia's shoulders. "Dr. Tanguay, I need you to come with me to help guide the medical team in."

"Thank you," Juna said as the captain turned to go. She nodded at Anitonen. "All right."

Anitonen got Dr. Wu's gloves off, and sank a spur into the palm of his hand. Wu's breathing eased immediately and color returned to his face.

"You know your own people better than I do. Monitor me," Anitonen told Juna.

Juna flickered yes. Aloud she said, "I'm going to help Anitonen with Dr. Wu. Please, don't disturb us. It might kill Dr. Wu, and could harm Anitonen or me."

She helped Anitonen remove Wu's helmet and open his suit. Juna clasped one of his arms, Anitonen took the other, and then they linked.

Juna could feel Wu's heart laboring. His oxygen-starved blood tasted flat and rusty. Anitonen dilated the blood vessels supplying the heart, increasing the blood supply. They fed all the oxygen their bodies could spare into Wu's bloodstream. Then Anitonen set about repairing the damaged tissues of his heart. It began to beat more strongly as oxygen-rich blood began reaching the starved muscle, and Anitonen continued restoring the damaged heart.

Wu regained consciousness. Juna felt him tense and begin to panic. She shielded him from the intrusion of their presences, as Moki had shielded her so long ago. Wu's panic changed to curiosity as he felt Anitonen's presence exploring his clogged arteries. The Tendu began clearing the arteries around his heart, filtering the greasy cholesterol out through her allu. It was a long job. Juna could feel Anitonen tiring, so she fed her some energy.

Wu's presence reached out tentatively, full of wonder and excitement at this strange new contact. Juna enfolded him in reassurance and calmness. Anitonen finished clearing the arteries in Wu's chest and lungs and began work on the rest of his body, but she was getting too tired to continue. Juna gently eased the link apart.

She opened her eyes. Dr. Wu was smiling, tranquil. His eyes opened, he looked at her, and his smile widened. "Thank you," he said. He sat up and reached for Anitonen, grasping her hand. "That was amazing." He stood. Juna reached to steady him, but he shook her off. "I feel better than I have for years." He took a deep breath of the alien air. "It smells green," he said. "Very green, and alive." There were tears in his eyes.

"Anitonen gave you something to help your body fight off an allergic reaction, but it won't last very long," Juna told him. "You should go before you start to react."

"There's a flyer on the beach," Bremen said. "We need to get you to the infirmary."

Wu nodded. He looked as if he were in a dream. He touched Juna on the arm, and Juna realized that she was finally touching another human being skin to skin. She took his hand.

"Please thank Anitonen for me," Wu said. "Not just for saving my life. But for the other. The allu-a—" He paused. "It was what I have wanted all my life. To touch the alien." He shook his head, wonderingly. "It was—" He spread his hands wide, his face suffused with joy. "I don't have words for it, but please, thank her for it."

"I understand," Juna told him.

"So do I, now. Thank you, Juna." He clasped her hands in his for a moment.

Juna translated Dr. Wu's thanks. Anitonen rippled amusement.

"Tell him that he has a good presence, and that it was an honor to link with him."

Juna translated, and Dr. Wu smiled in response. He clasped Anitonen's hands and turned to go.

"How did he get like that?" Anitonen asked. "So full of things wrong with him?"

"It happens to humans as they get older," Juna replied. "I should go and make sure the doctors don't do anything to reverse what you've done."

"I'll come with you," Anitonen offered. "If they have any questions, I can answer them."

The two of them caught up with Wu, and got on the flyer with him. Once they were in the air, Anitonen looked out the window, utterly fascinated as they skimmed over the ocean toward the ship. Brilliant hot pink ripples of excitement flowed over her skin. The medical techs watched her, mouths agape.

When the flyer landed, Dr. Wu was placed on a gurney and rushed to the ship's medical wing. He was put into a second, hastily set up quarantine room. Juna and Anitonen donned suits for the trip from the airlock to quarantine.

Dr. Baker came in a few minutes after they arrived. "Why isn't this man on oxygen and a drug drip?" he demanded.

"Because I don't need it, Doctor," Wu told him calmly. "Anitonen has healed me. I feel better than I have in years. No more shortness of breath, no angina."

"But—" the doctor began.

"Do I look like a man suffering from a heart problem?" Wu asked.

Dr. Baker shook his head. "Let me examine you," he said, taking out his stethoscope.

Anitonen watched alertly as the doctor examined Wu.

"Amazing," he announced. "If I didn't know better, I'd say that your heart was that of a twenty-year-old. Your pulse is strong, your blood pressure is low, your color and breathing are excellent. Are you sure it was a heart attack?"

Juna stepped forward. "Dr. Baker, I helped monitor Anitonen when she healed Dr. Wu. It was definitely a heart attack. I felt it. I tasted it."

As soon as he was sure that Wu really was stabilized, Dr. Baker questioned Juna and Anitonen minutely about what they had done. Finally Anitonen put her hand on Juna's leg.

"I'm tired and hungry. Could we talk again later?"

Juna realized that she, too, was light-headed from hunger.

"I'm sorry, Doctor, but we need to take Anitonen back. She's tired, and she needs food and rest. So do I. Healing is very draining work."

Dr. Baker nodded. "I'd like to talk further with Anitonen about this some other time. She's already suggested several interesting ideas worth researching. Perhaps you could bring her back tomorrow?"

Juna translated his question.

"I'd be glad to," Anitonen replied. "I've learned a great deal today. Tell Dr. Wu to sleep as much as he can, and to eat a lot of protein. His body is not done repairing itself. He will need to rest and eat well for another three or four days. We can resume the negotiations when he's fully recovered. Also, please thank Dr. Wu. I learned a great deal from him today."

"I should be thanking Anitonen," Wu replied with an ironic smile, when Juna translated Anitonen's words. He reached out and touched Anitonen on the shoulder, imitating the Tendu's gesture, and said, "I owe you my life, and more. Thank you."

Juna escorted Anitonen back to shore, returned to her quarters, ate a huge meal, and fell asleep.

She woke the next morning feeling better than she had in days. She lay in bed, looking up at the impersonal white ceiling of her room. The negotiations were called off until Wu was better. She should spend that time getting more of a handle on the politics aboard ship.

She called for her security escort. Laurie was subdued and awed as she let Juna out of quarantine.

"I hear you saved Dr. Wu's life," she said.

Juna shook her head. "Anitonen did that. I merely helped."

They reached Dr. Wu's room. He was lying in bed, attached to several monitors.

"Juna!" he called out as she came in. He held up a wire-festooned arm. "It's good to see you. They're still running tests on me."

She took his hand. His grip was strong and firm.

"How are you?" she asked.

"I feel better than I've felt for years," he told her. "The

doctors are amazed. I'm amazed, and I was there. It feels like a miracle. Thank you for helping save my life."

Juna looked away, feeling distanced by his awe.

One of the nurses came in. She looked at Juna as though she expected her to walk on water at any moment.

Juna looked down, even more embarrassed. "I need to go, but I'm glad you're feeling well. You haven't had any allergic reactions?"

Wu shook his head.

"Good. I'll be bringing Anitonen over around noon to give you a checkup."

"I'll see you then," Wu said.

Juna patted his hand and left. The medical techs were clustered at the door, watching her. They parted to let her through, like the sea parting for Moses.

As she was leaving the medical wing, she ran into Patricia Tanguay.

"How is he?" she asked Juna.

"He's fine. The doctors are busy running tests on him, and Anitonen will be coming in around noon to check on his progress and answer the doctors' questions."

"I'm glad to hear it. The whole ship is abuzz about your saving Dr. Wu's life."

"I've noticed," Juna said. "Anitonen is the one who saved Dr. Wu. I only watched."

"Juna, I heard about what happened. You and an alien clasped the arms of a dying man, closed your eyes, and sat still for perhaps twenty minutes. When you were through, Dr. Wu was healthier than he had been for years. The doctors are amazed. You helped perform a miracle."

"It wasn't a miracle," Juna insisted. "Anitonen and the other Tendu do this sort of thing every day. It's a little harder to work on a human because we're new and strange to them, but it's a skill that every single adult Tendu possesses."

"It's still a miraculous skill."

Juna spent the rest of the morning visiting labs, answering questions, and making suggestions to various researchers. It was nice to be able to take part once again in the work that she loved. It also reminded the researchers of how valuable a resource she was. The morning passed quickly, and Juna was sorry to have to leave the labs to go pick up Anitonen.

She entered the airlock, climbing out of her uncomfortable e-suit and into some light cotton clothing. Temporarily freed from the restrictions of quarantine, she opened the heavy outer door, and ran down the gangplank to the floating dock. Bruce was waiting for her in the boat. She smiled, and her step lightened. For once she was going to get to visit the forest without a gaggle of noisy humans trailing behind her.

"Hey there, miracle worker!" he said as he helped her into the boat.

"Oh please!" Juna said. "I've heard that all morning long!"

"It's all over the ship. The boat crew yesterday got an earful from the people they took back. So what really happened?"

Juna shrugged. "Anitonen and I performed some Tendu first aid on Dr. Wu. We saved his life, but it was not a miracle. Anitonen just did what any Tendu does. All I did was monitor Anitonen in case anything went wrong."

"Can you do what Anitonen did?"

Juna shook her head. "I'm not that good. I can only heal easy things like flesh wounds and simple fractures. I might have been able to stabilize Dr. Wu until the medics came, but I couldn't have cleared his arteries or repaired his damaged heart."

"Anitonen did all that?" Bruce asked incredulously.

"The doctors say that Dr. Wu has the heart of a twenty-year-old now," she replied.

"Well, tell him to give it back!" Bruce said with a grin.

Juna laughed, relieved that he wasn't treating her like some kind of saint. Bruce was one of the few who saw through her alien skin to her human self.

"You've got a nice laugh," he told her.

Juna turned a deep brown and looked away. "Thank you."

The boat nosed onto the beach, and Juna leaped out to help pull it ashore.

Anitonen was nowhere in sight.

"Where is she?" Bruce asked.

"I don't know," Juna said. "The Tendu have a very flexible

concept of time. Why don't we go up and see if we can find her?"

"That would be wonderful," Bruce agreed. "I've never seen the jungle."

"Then let's go."

Somewhere near the top of the cliff path, Juna took Bruce's hand to help him over a rough spot. They remained hand in hand as they strolled through the cathedral-like forest. Bruce moved quietly, Juna noted with approval. They paused in a sun break created by a recently fallen tree. The upper branches of the downed tree were covered with bromeliads. The tree's fall had carried the doomed bromeliads down into a zone that was too dark and moist for them to survive; they bloomed in a last brilliant rush to procreate before they died.

Juna leaned against the tree's massive flank. The noises of the jungle seemed very loud in the silence that hung between them. Bruce settled himself beside her, sliding one arm around her shoulder.

"It's beautiful," he said, breaking the heavy silence.

Juna nodded and looked up. "It's even more beautiful up there. It's like a whole separate world."

He followed her gaze into the canopy. "What's it like?"

"It's a lot cooler, there's more wind. Even the big branches sway in the wind." She shook her head, remembering. "I was too scared at first to notice much, but now there's so much up there to look at, I don't have time to be scared. I'll miss it when I go."

"You sound like you don't want to leave."

"I've come to love this planet. There's the forest, the Tendu, and the freedom of the life that I've found here. And then there's Moki. I wish I could tear myself in two and leave one part here with him."

"His people will look after him."

Juna's eyes welled with tears. "He won't accept another sitik. If I go, he'll probably die."

"I'm sorry," Bruce said. "I wish there was something I could do."

Juna shrugged and looked away. "The hardest part is living in that damned suit. You know," she said, looking up at Bruce through the glare of his faceplate, "Dr. Wu was the first human being I've touched in four years."

Bruce drew her closer. She leaned against him. Suddenly she was weeping, all the loneliness and isolation of the last four years pouring out of her.

Bruce held her, patting her back as she cried herself out. Her cheek stuck to the slick plastic of his e-suit. She felt a small, cool hand on her thigh. It was Moki, ochre with concern. She rippled reassurance at him and drew him close. Moki's hand clasped her arm, and he linked with her. His small, observant presence blended with the secure warmth of Bruce's arms.

At last she broke the link with Moki and pulled away from Bruce. She wiped her eyes. "Thank you," she said, feeling suddenly awkward.

"Any time," he replied with an affectionate squeeze of her shoulder.

"God, I hope not," Juna said with a shaky laugh. "If I cried like that all the time, I'd melt away like a sugar cube in a rainstorm."

She glanced down at her wrist chronometer. "We should go find Anitonen. The others will be wondering where we are."

"Anitonen's waiting at the top of the cliff path," Moki told her. "She was talking with Lalito and the village council until almost noon."

Bruce scooped Moki up and set him on his shoulder. Moki rippled with laughter. "Let's go, then," Bruce said, taking Juna's hand.

They walked together through the forest, hand in hand. Moki rested one of his long arms on Juna's head. It was a good moment, bridging the best of both worlds, and Juna was sorry to reach the edge of the forest.

Anitonen swung down from the trees, greeting them cheerfully. Bruce said hello to Anitonen, set Moki down, and then went on ahead to get the boat ready.

"Bruce makes you happy," Moki said as they were crossing the beach, hand in hand. "I'm glad. Will you be mating soon?"

Juna blushed brown. "I don't think so," she told him. "It's different with my people, Moki."

"He arouses you, though. I felt it in the link."

Juna looked out at the distant ship. "Moki, I've been away from my people for a long time," she said. "I'm easily aroused, but I don't mate with strangers. I don't know Bruce well enough. Besides, there's the quarantine."

"Anitonen says you won't make anyone sick," Moki told her.

"But they don't believe her," Juna said, gesturing at the ship with her chin.

"Do you believe her?" Moki asked.

Juna shrugged. "I'm afraid to be wrong. It could kill someone, or make them very sick. I'd lose what little trust they have in me if I broke quarantine without permission."

Moki looked out toward the ship for a long time, his colors fading to a deep, cloudy grey.

"You need your people," he admitted, turning back to her. "I need you."

Juna looked down at the sand, shrugging helplessly. They reached the boat. Bruce handed Anitonen and Juna in and shoved off. Juna helped him into the boat and watched as he started the motor. When she looked back at the beach, Moki had vanished into the forest.

Juna watched as Anitonen broke her link with Dr. Wu, unclasping his arms carefully to avoid disturbing any of the wires taped to his body.

"He's recovering very well," Anitonen told her. "His heart muscle should be completely regenerated in a couple of days. I've also cleaned out more of his circulatory system."

Juna translated this for Dr. Wu and the assembled medical personnel.

"I feel stronger and more alert," Wu confirmed.

The doctors clustered around the readout of their tests.

"Look at this!" one of them said. "There's a double line here, as though there were two readings instead of one."

"What is this?" Anitonen asked. "Please explain."

"This is the neural readout," Dr. Baker said, after he explained what the graph told them. He pointed to a pair of green lines. "There appears to be a double reading, but then it merges again."

"Yes," Anitonen said, once Juna had translated Dr. Baker's

words, "that is where I linked with him. The line merges as I come into harmony with Dr. Wu."

"And this?" Dr. Baker asked, pointing to another readout. "Why does the heart suddenly slow and then gradually speed up?"

"I was testing it, seeing how the regeneration was proceeding. His heart is much stronger now."

The questions continued. Soon Juna found it impossible to translate the technical terms that each side was using.

"Tell them that it would be much easier if I could show them," Anitonen said, holding her suited arms out as though asking for allu-a.

"But the rules—" Juna said.

"I can't answer any more of their questions with talk," Anitonen responded.

"She said that she can't tell you anything else, but that she can show you," Juna told the doctors. "She's offering to link with you."

Anitonen nudged her. "Tell them I am too tired to do any healing, but I will show them their body from my viewpoint, and show them what I did to Dr. Wu. I can also show them what my body looks like so they will understand my people better."

Juna translated this. The doctors conferred among themselves for a few moments.

"This is—ahm—rather unusual," Dr. Baker said. "We should consult with the Alien Contact team."

"You've got the head of the team right here. Why not ask him?" Juna suggested.

"If one of you is willing to volunteer for this, I have no objections to having you link with Anitonen," Dr. Wu told them. "Allu-a is an amazing experience."

"She wouldn't alter my body in any way?" Dr. Baker asked.

Juna relayed the question to Anitonen.

"No, I promise not to do anything."

"Can we trust her?" Baker asked Juna.

"Dr. Baker, Anitonen is an enkar. Her life would be forfeit if she broke her word," Juna explained. "I've known her for more than four years, and she has always kept her promises, even before she became an enkar."

"I see." He looked appraisingly at Anitonen. "Very well then. I volunteer to link with Anitonen. What do I do?"

Juna guided him to a seat. "Sit down and roll up your sleeves,"

Anitonen touched her shoulder. "Will you monitor us? Your presence will reassure him."

Juna pulled a third chair into the circle. "Anitonen said that I should monitor you. Will you allow me to break quarantine?"

Dr. Baker leaned back and looked over at Dr. Wu. "Well?" he asked.

"I'm still alive after touching her," Wu pointed out.

Baker hesitated for a moment longer, thinking it over. "All right," he said. "Go ahead."

Juna undid her gloves and pushed her sleeves back past her elbows. Anitonen did the same.

"Hold out your arms like this," Juna told him, resting her arms on her thighs, palms up.

He did so. Juna grasped his warm, human arm as Anitonen grasped her other arm, her skin cold and moist and suddenly alien. She felt Baker flinch a bit as Anitonen touched him.

"Are you ready?" Juna asked.

Baker swallowed nervously. "Go ahead," he told her.

Juna nodded at Anitonen and they plunged into the link.

She felt Baker's mingled fear and curiosity as she entered the link. Anitonen moved to enfold him in reassurance. His fear ebbed swiftly. Juna was impressed; it had taken her a long time to get over her fear.

She watched as Anitonen gently began showing Baker his own life rhythms. First, the steady beat of his heart, and the salty metallic taste of his blood. She showed him how the taste differed between the oxygen-rich blood leaving his lungs and the depleted venous blood returning to the lungs. Then they traced his last couple of meals through his digestive system. Anitonen let him experience the irregular, sharp taste of his nerves, transmitting sensation and instructions back and forth between the brain and the rest of his body. Juna could feel the doctor's excitement rising as Anitonen showed him more and more of his body.

Then, as they were exploring his bladder, Juna felt something odd. A tiny cluster of cells in the lining of his bladder was out of harmony. Juna could feel Anitonen waver, tempted to repair the problem; then she moved on. Shortly after that, Juna noticed that Anitonen was tiring, and gently broke the link.

Dr. Baker sat up slowly. "What happened? We linked with Anitonen, and then—"

"I broke the link," Juna told him. "Anitonen was getting tired. It looks like you are too. Try eating something sweet. Sugar helps wake you up after allu-a. That's why the Tendu eat so much honey."

Baker nodded. "There's some electrolyte solution up in the cupboard. That ought to help." One of the nurses handed him a bottle of the solution. He poured some into a glass and held it up. "Can she drink this?" he asked Juna. "It's made up of simple sugars and a few salts."

"I don't know." She handed the glass to Anitonen. "Can you drink this?"

"Let me see." Anitonen stuck her spur into the electrolyte solution. "It should be very helpful." She drank it down, brightening noticeably within a few minutes. "This is excellent for recovering from allu-a," she said. "Even better than our honey."

"There is an irregularity in the cells lining his bladder," she said, pointing her chin in Dr. Baker's direction. "If it is left untreated, the cells will grow too much and eventually spread throughout his body. I could repair it, if he will let me."

Juna translated this.

Dr. Baker's eyes widened. "You mean that cluster of cells was a cancer?"

"A very small one," Juna said. "Anitonen could repair it for you when she's rested. It would only take a few minutes."

"Let me confirm this with some tests," Baker said. "I believe Anitonen, but it would be very valuable to have some independent confirmation."

Juna translated for Anitonen, who nodded. "Let me know when you would like to be healed."

"Thank you," Dr. Baker said. "And thank you for linking with me. I have learned a great deal. It was wonderful to see my body like that, to feel directly so much of what I have been taught and observed indirectly. I wish I could share that with my colleagues and students. If such a resource had been available to me in medical school . . ." He shook his head and smiled.

"I'm glad I was able to help," Anitonen said when Juna translated his words. "And I hope that this will help you too, Eerin. Perhaps now your people will let you out of quarantine."

"It will take time," Juna replied with a shrug. "Though it may take less time now. I think that Dr. Wu's heart attack has changed things."

Thirty

WU'S HEART ATTACK did change things. Four days after it happened, Bremen called Juna into a staff meeting.

"After discussing the situation with doctors Wu and Baker, I have decided to lift your quarantine, and remove your security escort. I think you've proved that you are not a danger to the rest of the crew. I understand that Captain Edison has already assigned you a cabin. You may move into it immediately."

Juna was stunned. "Th-Thank you, sir. I appreciate this," she managed to say.

Bremen smiled. "I apologize for making you wait so long, Dr. Saari, and I thank you for your patience and understanding. You are released from duty for the rest of the day so that you can get settled in your new quarters."

Juna spotted Dr. Baker as she emerged from the meeting.

"Dr. Baker," Juna said, "I wanted to thank you for helping to get me released from quarantine."

"It was no problem. There's absolutely no evidence that you pose any danger to the crew. Actually, Dr. Saari, I'm the one who owes *you* some thanks. I had that spot on my bladder biopsied. It was a very small pre-cancerous lesion, so small they had trouble finding it. They burned it out with a laser, and I wanted to ask you to thank Anitonen for me."

"Of course, Dr. Baker," Juna said. "I'd be happy to. I'm sure she'd be glad to check and make sure that the laser surgery got it all."

"If you could ask her to do that, I'd appreciate it. This allu-a is a fascinating phenomenon."

Juna went back to her quarantine quarters. Laurie stopped by as she was bundling up her few possessions and helped her carry them up to her new cabin. It was a large, airy room with two wide windows looking out on the coastline. Captain Edison had given her a cabin in the quarters reserved for high-level staff.

"Please thank the captain for me," Juna asked Laurie.

There was a knock on the door. It was the captain.

"Looks like you get to thank her yourself," Laurie said, slipping out the door. "See you later."

"Captain," Juna said. "I appreciate the room assignment."

The captain shrugged. "This was one of the few cabins with a bathtub," the captain told her. Dr. Baker mentioned that you suffered from the lack of humidity aboard ship, and I thought this might alleviate it somewhat. Besides, I thought you'd like the view."

Juna smiled. "I do. Thank you, Captain Edison."

"Good," she said. "I'll leave you to get settled."

Getting settled took only half an hour. She had very little to arrange: a few clothes and toiletries, the holograms her father had sent her, a polished na seed from Narmolom, a bamboo knife, and her computers. There was almost no material evidence of the time she had spent among the Tendu. The only changes were in her body and mind.

The bathtub was a Japanese-style *ofuro,* small, square, and deep enough for the water to reach up to her neck. With a sigh of relief, Juna started the water running, slipped out of her clothes, and stepped in. She turned a clear, bright turquoise as the hot water embraced her. Juna relaxed in the hot water and spent the next hour contemplating the joys of indoor plumbing and hot water.

It was nearly dinner time when she emerged from the tub. Someone had delivered a fresh set of uniforms while she was bathing. Juna hung them up, pausing, as she always did, to admire the deep forest green and black dress uniform of the Interstellar Survey. She decided to wear it to dinner, in celebration of her release from quarantine.

She put it on and appraised her reflection in the mirror. The deep green of her uniform clashed oddly with the yellowish celadon of her skin, and her bald head seemed naked and out of proportion to the rest of her trim, neatly clad image. Her features were leaner than she remembered, and her eyes seemed huge without her eyebrows. She looked delicate and fey. She darkened her skin till it was close to the shade of her original, brown skin. It wasn't bad, she decided, just different.

A chime sounded, announcing that the mess hall was open for dinner. Juna closed the wardrobe door, and tugged the sleeves of her shirt out from under the cuffs of her jacket. She was looking forward to sharing a meal with other human beings.

Everyone in the mess hall stood and applauded as Juna walked in. She looked around in amazement.

"Thank you," she said, as the applause died down. "Thank you very much. It's good to be out of quarantine."

She turned and joined the line waiting for food. Laurie came up beside her.

"We've saved you a seat," she said, "over by the window."

"Thanks," Juna replied. She loaded her tray and followed Laurie to a long table near one of the windows. Bruce, Kay, Marguerite, and Patricia were there.

"I've been getting all kinds of requests for time with you," Patricia told her. "Everyone on the ship has questions. Perhaps you should schedule some seminars with various divisions."

"We'll work out some kind of schedule tomorrow," Juna decided.

The talk turned to shipboard gossip. Juna listened intently. She knew very few of the people involved, but it felt familiar and the sheer humanness of it was comforting.

She turned to Bruce. "Tell me more about your nephew," she said.

They spent most of the meal talking about their families. Like her, Bruce came from one of the satellite colonies. His family lived in one of the colonies clustered in the L-4 region.

His parents had died in a shuttle accident, and his sister had married into a line marriage. His in-laws had adopted him as part of their extended family, and he spent most of his leave with his sister's spouses and their children.

Juna told him about her father, how her mother died, how the harrowing experience of the camps had made her feel like an outsider among the sheltered children of the colony. She had joined the Survey, drawn by the thrill of new discoveries as well as the chance to be an outsider among other outsiders. Bruce was here because the pay was good. After another couple of trips, he would have enough saved up to buy a place in one of the better colonies, and maybe even enough for an extra fractional child-right, enabling him to become the father of two children.

Juna smiled wistfully. She had wanted children, but her marriage hadn't worked out. She had been gone too often and too long. Bruce nodded, his warm brown eyes glowing with understanding.

Dinner was drawing to a close when Captain Edison and Dr. Bremen rose and walked to the podium at the front of the mess hall. The crowd grew silent.

"Dr. Saari, would you please come up here?" Bremen asked.

Juna rose and walked to the podium. She felt the weight of the Survey crew's gaze on her, and was suddenly glad that she had chosen to wear her dress greens.

"In recognition of your great service to the Survey, and in honor of the difficulties you have endured, the Survey has decided to promote you to the rank of Research Director," Bremen announced. "Congratulations, Dr. Saari."

Juna turned magenta in astonishment. They had jumped her two full rankings. If she had not been marooned, she might have been promoted to Associate Researcher in another year or two, but this promotion made her one of the youngest Research Directors in the Survey.

Captain Edison handed her a small flat case. Inside were the insignia of her new rank.

"I wasn't expecting this," Juna said. "Thank you. Thank you very much."

"May I help pin them on?" the captain asked.

Juna nodded, and Captain Edison took the little gold galaxies out of the box and pinned them to her collar and chest.

"I'm going to recommend to the Survey that they make this promotion retroactive to the time your flyer went down," the captain told her in an undertone. "It would make quite a difference in your back pay." She smoothed Juna's collar down and stepped back. "Congratulations, Research Director Saari."

"That's very kind of you, Captain Edison."

"The Survey owes it to you for all you've accomplished," the captain told her.

Juna shook Dr. Bremen's hand, then stepped up to the podium. She stood for a moment, looking out over the assembled crew. Alison was standing at the galley door with a towel over one shoulder.

"It's good to be out of quarantine," Juna said. "It's good to be back—" She paused, considering her words. "I would like to thank Dr. Bremen, Captain Edison, Ensign Laurie Kipp, Dr. Paul Wu, Dr. Robert Baker, Dr. Patricia Tanguay, Chef Alison Vladimir, and Technician Bruce Bowles for their trust, support, and friendship." She glanced over at her friends' table and smiled at them. "And thanks to everyone else for coming back to get me."

The crowd laughed in response to her last remark. Juna smiled, waved, and stepped back from the podium. Everyone in the room rose to applaud as she walked back to her table. She was crying so hard by the time she got there that she could hardly see. Patricia handed her a napkin, and helped her sit down. Laurie patted her on the shoulder. She finally felt that she was truly back among her own people.

Then Bruce, who was sitting next to her, reached down to take her hand. Juna slid her hand eagerly into his. It would be the first time that they had ever really touched. She saw him flinch as he felt the moist, alien texture of her skin. She drew her hand back into her lap, fighting to keep a sudden sense of shame from darkening her skin as she realized that despite everything, there was still a deep, uncrossable gulf between her and the rest of her people.

• • •

Juna walked into the Resource Utilization seminar. It was her fifth seminar this week, and she felt tired and drained. Dr. Nazarieff, the director of the Resource Utilization department, greeted her politely, escorting her to the head of the table.

This trip must be frustrating for her, Juna thought. Contact protocols forbid exploitation of a sentient species' planetary resources. It was, she thought with an ironic smile, rather a turnaround. Usually it was the Resource people who were busy and the Contact people who had to sit on their hands. She wondered what they wanted from her.

"Thank you for coming, Dr. Saari," Nazarieff said when they were all assembled. "I know your time is very valuable. I'll get right to the point. This is Gerald Nyimbe, one of my graduate students. Gerald was studying your list of Tendu trade goods, and he thinks that he may have a potential solution to your trade problems. Gerald?"

A tall, slender young African with three rows of tribal cicatrices across his cheeks, rose. "Yes, Dr. Saari," he began in musically accented Standard. "One of the trade goods mentioned in the daily notes of the negotiations was guano, which the Tendu transport from outer islands to use as a fertilizer. In going over the first expedition's reports, I noticed many large seabird colonies located on islands in the subpolar regions. I did some satellite surveys and visited several different sites." He pressed a button on his computer, and a map of the northern subpolar region appeared on the wall. "These three sites have the richest, most accessible guano deposits," he said, indicating three islands in the middle of the northern ocean. "We could harvest them with relatively little disturbance to the local wildlife."

Juna sat up, her weariness forgotten. It looked like an excellent solution to her problems. "What about the Contact Protocols on mining? Won't we be in violation of them?"

"There's an exemption for small amounts of internal trade. We would need permission from the Tendu to proceed with the mining, and there are very strict regulations about environmental degradation that we would have to follow, but we're talking about very small scale, temporary mining here. My most liberal estimates indicate that we can meet our obligations to the village of Lyanan with about 1.5 metric tons of guano. With the equipment we have on hand, we could probably dig up and process that much material in one day."

Juna scrolled through the report on her computer screen, fighting back rising excitement. "This looks very good, Mr. Nyimbe. It may prove to be the solution that we need. I'll talk to the Alien Contact people about it tonight."

It was indeed the solution to the trade problem. Everything fell together with amazing rapidity when Juna introduced the proposal. Once Dr. Wu had confirmed that it wouldn't significantly affect Tendu trading patterns, he gave his approval. After some face-saving hesitations, Lalito also accepted it. By now it was clear that the humans were not going to yield any further on her demands for their technology. Lyanan would receive enough guano to meet its needs for the next two years, cover all the outstanding obligations that the village had incurred in replanting the forest, and still have a small surplus to trade with.

Juna took Anitonen, Ukatonen, Lalito, and Moki up to see the proposed mining site. They stopped briefly at the shuttle base for refueling. Moki made a beeline for the space shuttles as soon as he climbed out of the flyer, and remained there, peppering the amused techs with questions while Juna showed the other Tendu around the shuttle facility. She smiled as she retrieved her errant bami from the bowels of the shuttle.

Moki was fascinated by aircraft of any kind. The bigger it was, the faster it flew, and the farther it went, the more interesting it was to him. Juna's nephew, Danan, was similarly fascinated by planes and shuttles. He was eleven now, she realized with a sudden pang of sadness; she had missed most of his childhood, marooned here with the Tendu. Closing her eyes, she tilted her head back. The sun glowed redly through her eyelids. She wanted to go home.

When she opened her eyes, Moki was looking at her questioningly.

"Let's go," she said.

They walked back to the dock and climbed into the flyer. The Tendu looked out the window intently, ears spread wide in wonder, all the way to the island. The island rose from the dark blue sea like a lost piece of some gigantic jigsaw puzzle. They had chosen this site because of its remoteness. The only creatures that lived there year-round were a few species of flightless birds and some crustaceans. But in the summer, the rocky island was home to millions of nesting seabirds.

Clouds of birds exploded upward as the flyer passed overhead. The pilot set the plane down in a cove on the lee side of the island. While he assembled the landing craft, Juna bundled the Tendu into warmsuits to prevent them from getting hypothermia.

When the boat was ready, Juna opened the door of the flyer. A blast of icy gale-force wind nearly pulled it out of her hand. The Tendu flinched from the cold, their mittened hands fumbling at the hoods of their unfamiliar clothing. She helped them pull up their hoods and tighten them around their faces, then assisted them into the boat as it bucked and heaved on the choppy swell. They huddled in the boat, their faces turned away from the bitter wind. Juna had never seen the Tendu look so miserable before. The pilot beached the boat and Juna hopped out to pull it up out of the swell. She helped the Tendu off between waves. A tumble into this icy water would be disastrous for them.

Juna led the Tendu up a sloping rise to the top of the cliffs, threading their way between colonies of nesting birds, their chicks nearly grown. The birds honked and hissed at her, clacking their beaks together, wings spread, the feathers on their necks and backs raised threateningly. Crushed and mummified corpses of baby birds crunched underfoot. The stench of bird shit and death was overwhelming. Juna fought back a wave of nausea. The Tendu held their mittened hands over their noses.

Already the incredible numbers of birds were thinning. When Juna had visited the island the week before, she had had to wade through a solid tide of black, white, and grey, hissing and fighting furiously at the disruption of their territory. Waves of squabbling birds had spread in their wake, some bloodied from fighting. The noise was deafening. Now you could actually see the ground between the nesting birds, and it was possible to walk between the nests.

They reached the top of the cliff and paused. Spread out before them was a wide plain of packed brown soil, covered with nesting birds. The island had once been a live volcano. Now the crater was entirely filled with guano, which one of the geologists had estimated was over three hundred meters deep. Ukatonen pushed up his sleeves, exposing his spurs, and grabbed a struggling, hissing bird. It threw up on him, its vomit bright pink from the crustaceans it had eaten. He sank a spur into it, and the bird went limp. The other enkar followed suit, picking up birds, and sticking them with their spurs.

"What are they doing?" asked the pilot, as Ukatonen released his captured bird.

"Sampling the cells of these birds. They do that when they see a new or interesting plant or animal. Now they'll have enough information to build a whole new bird if they wanted to."

"Why are they doing it?"

"If you had a chance to fly a new kind of plane, would you do it?" Juna asked the pilot.

He nodded.

"Well," Juna explained, "that's why they do it. No Tendu has ever seen birds like these. They're new and strange to them."

The bird Ukatonen had released woke up and waddled back to its nest, braying in alarm.

Juna found a rock outcropping that sheltered them from the cold wind. She opened the front of her warmsuit, letting in an icy blast of wind, and began explaining the guano mining operation, pointing out where the Survey was going to dig, and how deep they were going to go. The Tendu watched her words intently, then huddled together, conferring among themselves. When they were through, Anitonen turned to her.

"The damage to the rookery will be small. The birds should recover within a year, and the Tendu will profit greatly. This is not perfectly harmonious, but I accept on behalf of the enkar. We ask that you seek approval from the lyali-Tendu, as well, since this negotiation will affect their trade. We also ask for some of the fertilizer as part of our fee for helping to negotiate this trade. We also thank you for taking us here. We have learned much today."

Juna sighed with mingled regret and relief. The treaty was almost concluded, bringing her closer to going home. She glanced at Moki, longing for a solution to his need for her.

The next day the lyali-Tendu came to the landing dock to negotiate their portion of the agreement, floating on their backs so that Juna could see their words. Juna sat with her legs in the water, listening and translating for the suited human negotiators. The sea people were tough traders, and they drove a hard bargain. At last they agreed to accept an amount of fertilizer equal to half the amount the people of Lyanan received, to be delivered to their trading islands up and down the coast. It meant more work for the Survey, but it was certainly possible. Besides, Juna thought with a smile, it was time the Survey did a little work.

The treaty was finalized two days later, at a meeting on the beach attended by representatives from all the concerned parties. The Survey signed a document agreeing to the provisions of the compact, and Anitonen rendered a formal judgment that the Tendu would accept it, signaling this by drawing her name sign on the treaty.

Juna returned from celebrating with the Tendu several hours after sunset. Bruce picked her up in the boat. They rode back in silence. The tropical night air felt like warm milk against her skin. It was a rare, clear night, and the stars shone so brightly that it seemed as though she could reach up and pluck them out of the sky. Night birds flickered like shadows across the stars.

Juna glanced up at Bruce. He was watching her. She closed her eyes, aware of a growing warmth between her thighs, feeling a flush of golden arousal stealing up her back. She stroked her arm; her skin was wet and warm and slimy. She remembered Bruce touching her skin, and flinching away, and her arousal vanished. She had done her best to avoid him since then. The worst part was that she still wanted him.

The boat pulled up to the dock. Juna got out, and started up the steps.

"Juna, wait a minute," Bruce said.

"What is it?"

"I— It's just that you've been so busy with the talks lately. We haven't had much chance to talk. I've missed you."

Juna ducked her head, feeling her skin turn brown with awkward embarrassment. "Thank you, Bruce. I've missed your company too. I like you very much."

"I thought, maybe, there was more to it than just liking me," Bruce said, putting his arms around her. In the darkness, his face was a pale shadow inside his face plate.

"Oh, Bruce," Juna said, fighting the urge to rest her head against his shoulder. "Not while I'm like this."

His embrace tightened. "Why?"

"Because I'm ugly, slimy, alien."

He shook his head. "No."

"Yes," Juna said. "You tried to hold my hand, just after I got out of quarantine. I saw the look on your face when you flinched."

"I'm sorry, Juna," he said. "It just surprised me. Give me a chance. I'll get over it."

Juna shrugged and looked away. "I don't want to be something you have to get over." She slipped out of the warmth of his arms and fled up the stairs. She dogged the lock behind her, stripped off her clothing, and stepped into the soothing warmth of the shower. Finished with the decontamination process, she dressed and headed for the lonely refuge of her cabin. She lay awake for a long time, listening, irrationally hoping that Bruce would come, would apologize, and would hold her.

With the reparations to Lyanan resolved, it was time to turn to negotiating a Contact treaty between the humans and the Survey. The enkar had learned a great deal from the reparation negotiations. They understood what the humans would accept, and they had enough information to begin to define their own needs. What they chiefly needed was time in which to learn more about humans. The Tendu wanted a short-term, highly restricted Contact treaty, allowing very limited and supervised research on the planet, with an emphasis on linguistic and cultural research. All contact with the Tendu would be supervised by the enkar. Trade would be strictly prohibited for the first five years. A second research base could be set up off the coast of one of the enkar reserves. Exploration of the area outside Tendu control required the consent of an enkar in charge of human contact, a position currently shared by Ukatonen and Anitonen.

The treaty was more restrictive than the research people wanted, but it was the Tendu's planet, and the humans had to abide by their wishes.

The treaty took less than a month to draw up. Most of that time was spent on details of grammar and translation. Once the agreement was signed, Juna took a week of leave and went on a fishing trip with Ukatonen, Anitonen, and Moki. They floated down the river, reminiscing. Juna and Moki played and splashed and linked. There was an overlay of sadness to it all, a sense of endings, of last times. Moki clung to her tightly one minute and was withdrawn and sullen the next. Still, Juna enjoyed this quiet time with her Tendu companions.

The last night of the trip, Juna sat up late with Anitonen and Ukatonen.

"I've learned so much, living among the Tendu. There are times when I've wanted to stay here with you forever, but—" Juna stared off into the thick, humid darkness of the jungle. "I miss being human," she said. "I'm tired of being different, tired of feeling like an alien among my own people. I want to touch and be touched, without the other person flinching away."

"Do you want me to change you back?" Anitonen asked. "It wouldn't be hard."

Juna's heart leapt within her at the thought of looking human again. "Oh, Anitonen, that would be wonderful! But I can't change back—the Tendu need me, Moki needs me."

"And you are out of harmony with yourself," Anitonen told her. "You have given us five years of your life. It is enough. Patricia knows enough to serve as a translator now, especially if you help her. It is time to return fully to your people."

"But Moki—" Juna began.

Ukatonen laid her arm on Juna's. "Moki has known that this time would come since you chose him as your bami."

"But what about you?" Juna asked. "If Moki doesn't accept you as his sitik . . ." She trailed off, unable to finish.

"I am responsible for my own judgments," Ukatonen told her. "I will live with the consequences. Even Moki knows that you need your people. Waiting only delays change; it doesn't stop it."

They were right, Juna knew. It was time. Delaying this transformation any further would only prolong her own misery without really making things better for anyone else.

"Will it take long?"

Anitonen shook her head. "I could start the change now. By the time you return to the ship, it will be almost complete. Your hands and feet will take several weeks to return to normal. They will ache while the transition is going on. I can also make it possible for you to go outside without an e-suit. You will be a little out of harmony, your eyes will burn, your nose will run. Once you go back inside, you will feel better. If you like, you can retain your improved eyesight, hearing, and balance."

"That would be good." Juna looked down at Moki, sleeping curled beneath a blanket of leaves. "Should I wake him?"

"It will only hurt him to watch, and he might try to disrupt the link," Anitonen said.

Juna touched Moki lightly; he stirred and rolled over in his sleep. At least this painful waiting would be over for them both. Perhaps Moki would finally bond with Ukatonen. She held her arms out to Anitonen. "Please, en, make me human again."

Moki lay snug in his nest of leaves, listening to the sounds of the forest, not wanting to face the morning. They were going back to the coast today. His sitik would be returning to her people. A cloud of regret passed over his skin. He wanted to stay here and pretend that Eerin's people had not returned and taken her away from him.

He sat up. Eerin's nest was empty. He found her swimming in the cool, clear river. The sun slanted down through the early morning mist in thick golden bars. Moki wanted to memorize this moment, to take it with him when he followed Eerin off-planet. He would miss the jungle. Eerin stood and walked through the shallows toward the beach, shedding brilliant drops of water. Moki clambered down a curtain of vines to greet her.

He ran to embrace his sitik, but stopped a few paces away. Something was wrong. Her skin was cloudy and off color.

"What's wrong?" he asked. "You look sick."

Eerin shook her head. "I'm changing back, Moki. I asked Anitonen to make me human again." Her words were fuzzy round the edges, and it took her longer to say them.

Moki backed away. "No!" he said. "No, no, no, no!"

He turned to flee, but Eerin caught him by the shoulder and turned him back around.

"Moki, please stay," she said. He relaxed, and she released him. "I'm still the same person I was before. Only the outside is changing."

Moki held out his arms, asking for a link. Eerin shook her head. "I can't, Moki. Not by myself. We need someone to monitor me. Let's go ask Ukatonen if he will help."

Ukatonen was sitting on a rock upstream, gutting two big orra fish for breakfast. Eerin asked for him to help them link.

"Let's eat first. Your sitik is probably very hungry."

Eerin nodded. Moki turned brown in shame. He had been selfish, forgetting his sitik's needs.

"Let me help," he said. "What else do we need?"

Ukatonen flickered approval. "You can skin and slice this fish while I go gather some greens."

"What should I do?" Eerin asked.

"Rest and wait for breakfast. Changing is enough work for you today."

"I'll sit with Moki, then."

They sat in wordless companionship while Moki sliced the fish and laid it neatly out on a fresh leaf. Eerin touched his shoulder as he finished. He looked up, ears spread wide.

"Are you angry with me for changing?" Eerin asked.

Moki shook his head as he pitched the fish guts into the undergrowth. He wasn't angry. He just felt empty and hollow inside, like the husk of a deserted na tree. He had dreaded this moment for a long time. Now it was here and he felt only an aching emptiness.

"You need your people," he told her with a shrug. There was nothing else left to say.

"I'm sorry, Moki," she said.

"I know," he replied. "It has to be this way. It's all right."

At least they would be together. He had managed to steal the suit that kept him warm when they went to the island. All he

had to do was get on the shuttle, and it would take him to he
people's ship. He could hide there until it was too late for then
to take him back to the planet. Then they would be together an
everything would be all right.

At last breakfast was over, and Ukatonen held his arms out
ready to link.

"It will be a very short link, Moki. Eerin needs to save he
energy for her change."

Moki rippled acknowledgment. He held out his arms, a clou
of sadness passing over his skin. Eerin clasped his arm an
Ukatonen's. Eerin's spur was soft and mushy-feeling. He trie
to link through her spurs, but all he contacted was a mass o
dying cells.

"Link through her skin, Moki. Her spurs don't work any
more," Ukatonen said.

Moki shifted his grip. He sank his spurs into her skin, an
succeeded in linking. Ukatonen was there, monitoring then
both. He felt Eerin's mix of grief and relief at her transformation. Moki let his love for his sitik rise above his grief. If thi
was to be their last link, he wanted to leave her with goo
feelings. They reached an equilibrium full of bitterswee
longing and love.

The trip downstream passed quietly. Eerin lost the ability to
speak around midmorning. No one said much after that. She
spent most of the day in the water, clinging to the side of the
raft, soothing and softening her dying skin. By the time they
reached the beach where the humans would pick her up, Eerin's
skin was coming off in great patches. She radioed to the
humans' ship, letting them know that she had arrived, then
waded into the ocean, where Anitonen helped her strip away
her remaining Tendu skin. She emerged from the ocean as
someone else, clean and brown and human. Her hands had flat
nails on them instead of claws, and her palms were smooth and
unridged.

Unable to face his sitik's alien appearance, Moki looked
away, out over the slate-colored ocean at the grey clouds, heavy
with rain that blocked the setting sun. He felt like one of those
clouds, grey with grief. Off in the distance, he saw a black
speck rounding the point. It was a boat, coming to take Eerin

way. Even though he knew he would see his sitik again, there was a finality to the boat's approach. Nothing would be the same after she left.

Someone touched him on the shoulder. It was Eerin. She held a stick in one hand.

"I love you, Moki" she drew in skin speech on the damp sand.

Moki nodded. "I love you too," he replied. "My sitik."

Eerin brushed his shoulder, and they stood together on the beach, looking out at the grey ocean and sky, waiting for the boat that would take his sitik away.

At last the boat pulled up onto the beach. Eerin put her gear in the boat, and embraced Ukatonen and Anitonen. Then she turned to Moki and stroked his face. That wordless gesture conveyed everything there was to say. Then she climbed into the boat. Moki watched as it headed out to sea, the waves from its wake washing away the words she had written in the sand.

Thirty-one

AFTER FOUR DAYS of tests, the doctors released Juna from the infirmary. She headed for the communal *osento* to scrub away the smell of the hospital. It was dinnertime, and the baths were deserted. She was grateful for the solitude; she'd had too much clinical poking and prodding lately. A peaceful, quiet bath would soothe her tired spirit and her aching hands and feet.

She took off her clothes, placing them in one of the pink plastic baskets on the shelf, and regarded herself in the mirror. She looked like a gymnast, her body bulging with lean, ropy muscles. She turned, posing and flexing her muscles, laughing with delight at how good she looked. Her hair was still only a thin fuzz on her scalp, and her high, arching eyebrows were barely discernible lines. The lack of eyebrows made her look much younger than her true age. She reached for a towel and washcloth and noticed once again that the faded blue tribal tattoos were gone from her wrists and arms. She frowned. Her mother had taken her to have them done just before everything went wrong. Those tattoos were her last memory of good times spent with her mother. She would have to have them retattooed when she returned to Earth.

She scrubbed herself at one of the low spigots set along one wall, then rinsed off and stepped into the big stone-floored bath with a sigh of pure pleasure. It was wonderful being human again.

She settled deeper into the steaming hot water. Before her transformation, she had avoided the baths. No matter how thoroughly she scrubbed before entering the tub, her skin would still have been alien. She hadn't wanted to pollute the communal waters with her strangeness.

She let her hands float up to the surface. The water was so hot it made her new fingernails ache, but it eased the bone-deep pain in her hands and feet. She could feel occasional sharp twinges as muscle realigned itself along the shrinking bones of her hands and feet. Her hands had already shrunk by a half a centimeter.

Half a centimeter in four days. It amazed the doctors. They were furious with her for undergoing her retransformation in the middle of the jungle instead of under observation in a safe, clinical environment. Juna didn't regret her choice. It had given her a chance to say goodbye to her life among the Tendu in a quiet, dignified manner. The doctors would have plenty of chances to observe the Tendu at work: she had already ensured that.

She took a deep breath and slid underwater to lie fetally curled on the rough black stone floor of the bath, letting the hot water embrace her. She turned her awareness inside, trying to feel her life rhythms, as she had before her transformation. If she concentrated, she could sense them, but it was as if they were behind a veil. She surfaced and stretched out, letting the blissfully hot water buoy her up.

Footsteps thudded dully on the floor of the bathhouse. Juna opened her eyes and sat up.

"Hi there. Want someone to scrub your back?"

"Bruce!"

"Am I disturbing you?" he asked.

"No, not at all," Juna said.

"Then I'll scrub down and join you."

Juna smiled. "I'd like that."

He seated himself on a small wooden stool in front of a spigot and began soaping off. Juna climbed out of the bath, picked up a washcloth, and began scrubbing his back, admiring the smooth curve of his well-muscled shoulders. Bruce left off scrubbing and arched his back under her hands like a pleased cat.

"That feels wonderful," he said. "Don't stop."

She moved lower, scrubbing with one hand, and kneading his muscles with the other, all the way down his back. She hesitated as she reached his buttocks. Bruce turned and began scrubbing her arms and shoulders. She lifted her chin and he moved to her upper chest, the rough washcloth sliding slowly over her skin. She straightened slightly, closing her eyes. Bruce let his hands slide lower, soaping her breasts.

Juna felt a rush of heat spread up her loins; her nipples were turning hard. She opened her eyes and stopped his hands. "What if someone comes in?"

"We won't be disturbed," he told her, with a mischievous grin. "The baths are 'closed for maintenance.' I put the sign up myself. Do you want me to go on?"

She leaned forward and kissed him. His hands, slippery with soap, slid over her back, and up her sides. He cupped her breasts in his large, strong hands, pinching her nipples with his fingers. His tongue slid into her mouth. She met it with her own, reaching down to circle his hard cock with her fingers. He reached up and turned on the shower. They stood under the warm water, still kissing as they rinsed the soap off their bodies.

Bruce slid his hand between her legs, stroking her with firm, gentle fingers. Juna gasped and rested her forehead against his shoulder, turning her hips outward, giving his hand better access. She clung to him as she came repeatedly.

"Please," she said at last. "I've got to lie down."

Bruce spread four bath towels on a dry section of floor, folding the last one to cushion their heads. They lay down. Bruce began kissing his way down her neck to her breasts, sucking her nipples, his hand working in her crotch as she arched again and again in orgasm.

At last she pushed him away. "My turn," she whispered as she moved down to his crotch, smelling his clean, warm, male smell as she took his penis in her mouth.

After several minutes, he moved away. Juna lay back on the

towels, pulled him on top of her, and guided him in, moaning as she felt him slide into her, giving herself up to the ecstasy of sex. It had been so long, so very long. She had forgotten just how good it could be.

Afterwards, they lay together in the hot water of the bath. She stretched and smiled, remembering the feel of his hands on her breasts, wishing that they could have linked so she could share how good it felt.

"What are you thinking?" he whispered.

Juna laughed. "I was just thinking how good it is to have nipples again."

"I wouldn't have minded you without them," he said.

"But it bothered me," she replied.

"I could have gotten used to it, Juna. I was willing to try."

She turned to face him. "I spent nearly five years inside an alien skin, Bruce. I didn't want anyone to have to get used to me. I wanted to be myself again."

Juna looked away across the dark, rippling expanse of the bath. "It was all right before the Survey came back. I was a Tendu among Tendu. I had forgotten how strange I looked. But when the humans returned, I saw myself through their eyes"— she closed her eyes, remembering—"and I knew that I was different. I had changed in ways that made me no longer fully human. I needed to change back. I needed to be fully human again." She rested her head against his chest and smiled. "It feels good to be back in my own skin again."

Juna stepped off the boat and onto the beach, not waiting for the rest of the onshore team. Moki ran to greet her. She picked him up and held him to her.

"It's good to see you," she said, in human speech. She hoped he understood her.

"I missed you," Moki replied in Standard. He took her hand and led her up the path from the beach. "Ukatonen and Anitonen are waiting," he added in Tendu.

Juna sneezed. Her eyes and nose itched as though she were suffering an attack of hay fever. Anitonen had told her that she would react to the alien proteins of the planet, but that they wouldn't kill her. *They'd just make me wish I was dead*, she

thought wryly. The doctors had issued her an emergency
injector kit just in case, though Juna would rather rely on the
Tendu if she had any problems. She hurried up the hill behind
her bami, sneezing. At last they were in the jungle.

Anitonen and Ukatonen were waiting for her. Juna held out
her arms, asking for a link. She sneezed again. Amused ripples
of laughter ran over Anitonen's body.

"You wouldn't think it was so funny if it was happening to
you," Juna muttered.

Ukatonen took her arm and led her over to a nearby tree.
They sat down, and Ukatonen motioned Moki over. "I will
show Moki how to ease your discomfort. That way, he can help
when it bothers you."

They linked. Juna felt the itching in her nose and eyes
subside as Ukatonen showed Moki how to stop her allergic
reaction. When that was done, Moki enfolded her. She was
nearly swamped by the intensity of his emotions—wild happiness at seeing her again, and deep grief at her transformation.
Without her spurs and allu, she was helpless to block him out.
Ukatonen moved to shield her until Moki regained control of
himself. As Moki merged with her, Juna felt his relief at linking
with her again. She had missed him so much. They spiraled
tightly into happiness until Ukatonen broke the link.

Anitonen and the others left to let Lyanan know that the
humans had arrived. Realizing that she wasn't ready to deal
with the Survey team just yet, Juna wandered into the sunbreak
where Bruce had held her while she cried. The glorious
bromeliads that had covered the fallen tree were dying. None of
them had set seed. Whatever pollinator it was that fertilized
these plants couldn't find them so close to the ground. Juna felt
saddened by the sight. Glancing at her wrist chrono, she saw
that she had been keeping the Survey team waiting. She headed
back to the top of the cliff path where the others would be
waiting for her.

Today she was guiding half a dozen Alien Contact specialists
on a visit to the village of Lyanan. It was the first time that any
human, except for Juna, had been to Lyanan's village tree. She
led the Survey team along the familiar path, pointing out
interesting sights along the way. Her voice sounded very loud

in the forest. Birds exploded out of trees, insects and small
animals went silent as they passed. All around her she heard the
pattering of falling leaves as arboreal animals moved into
hiding. It made her feel like an intruder in a once-familiar
house.

At last they reached the village tree. Juna smiled at the other
humans' murmurs of astonishment when they saw the massive
trunk rising into the canopy. She sat down to wait for the
villagers to arrive. The long walk had been hard on her
shrinking feet; they throbbed painfully.

As Lalito and several of the elders on the village council
climbed down to greet them, Juna rose, activating the computer
interface that allowed her to communicate with the Tendu.

"Welcome to Lyanan," Lalito said in formal patterns. "Please
let us escort you inside."

Juna fumbled with the clumsy interface. "Thank you," she
finally managed to say. "We brought a ladder to help us climb
into the village."

She motioned to the others, and they unpacked the long rope
ladder.

Juna smiled as she saw Lalito's ears lift at the sight of the
rope ladder. It was a handsome gift. Not only was it intrinsi-
cally valuable, but it also saved the Tendu considerable effort in
getting the awkward humans up the tree and into the village.

Lalito thanked Juna with gracious formality, then motioned
to some of the bami to hoist the ladder into the canopy. A vine
rope was lowered from the branch above them and tied to the
rope ladder. In less than ten minutes, the ladder was up and
secure.

Juna wadded up the computer and put it back into her pack.
"Follow me," she told the Survey team. "And don't look
down."

Patricia Tanquay came up behind her, followed by the other
A-C specialists. It was a long, painful climb. Juna's hands and
feet pulsated with pain by the time she reached the branch. She
limped to the bowl of the crotch and sat down, tucking her
hands into her armpits, letting the warmth of her body ease the
ache. There was a touch on her shoulder. It was Moki. He held
out his arms to link with her. Juna hesitated, but the pain in her

hands and feet was too much to bear. They clasped hands. Instantly the pain receded. She felt Moki moving through her, soothing the pain, healing the tiny cuts, blisters, and abrasions she had acquired on the walk to the village. Behind it, held tightly under control, she sensed his anguish. Juna was relieved when Moki broke the link, his work done, hating herself both for the relief that she felt and for the guilt that arose each time she felt his grief at her transformation.

"Thank you, Moki. I feel much better," she said aloud, hoping he would understand her. She hated using her translator to communicate with her bami.

"It was good to help," Moki said, touching her shoulder. "We should go now. The others are waiting."

She followed Moki down into the heart of the tree. The Survey team was seated in the doorway of Lalito's room, watching the villagers watch them.

"You lived in a village like this?" one of the A-C specialists asked Juna.

"I mostly lived at Narmolom, which is farther inland, but I spent two months every year here at Lyanan."

"I'm amazed that you didn't break your neck. I get vertigo just looking out the door."

"It was hard at first, but I got used to it. I didn't have much choice," Juna said. She was tired of explaining things over and over again.

Juna and Lalito escorted the scientists slowly down the inside of the trunk, showing them storerooms, living quarters, and even the hives of the tilan bees. The Survey team took samples of everything they could: bits of food, dead tilan bees, honey, even pieces of fiber left over from basket-weaving. They measured the rooms they visited, the height and diameter of the trunk, and the size of the doorways and balconies. The villagers crowded around, watching everything the humans did. Juna felt like a stranger again as she fumbled with the computer, asking questions and translating answers. The Survey team's invasive curiosity made her feel deeply ashamed. Finally, unable to take it any longer, she shut down her translator and handed it to Patricia.

"I'm going up for a breath of fresh air," she said. "You take over for a while."

Juna emerged from the tree with a sigh of relief. The humid air was cool and restless as the afternoon storm approached. She climbed into the middle of the tree's canopy and settled herself in a comfortable crotch. Closing her eyes, she breathed in the sweet, green-scented air of the forest, letting the gentle swaying of the tree soothe her.

The branch she was on vibrated with the motion of an approaching climber. It was Anitonen. Juna shifted to make room on the branch for her. They stared at each other; then Anitonen held out her arms for a link. Juna hesitated, then clasped the enkar's arms.

She could feel Anitonen sorting through the emotions roiling inside her, easing her anger, soothing the pain of her loss. As her pain eased, Juna found herself remembering the ecstasy and release she had felt with Bruce in the baths.

Anitonen broke the link. Her skin flamed briefly golden, reflecting Juna's sexual arousal. Embarrassed and ashamed, Juna looked away, giving Anitonen time to get herself under control.

"Thank you," she said when Anitonen's skin had returned to a neutral shade of green.

"Better?" Anitonen asked.

Juna nodded.

"You mated with Bruce last night."

Juna glanced away, embarrassment heating her cheeks.

Anitonen touched her arm. "Sex takes the place of allu-a for your people, doesn't it?"

Juna shrugged. Sex did many of the same things as linking, but you were always alone inside your own head, no matter how intimate and close you were with your partner. She wished that she hadn't left her computer with Patricia, but then there really was no way to make Anitonen understand. It was too much a part of being human.

"We should go now," Anitonen said. "The others are waiting for you."

Juna followed the enkar down the branch. She moved cautiously, aware that her hands and feet were no longer fully adapted for climbing. The Survey team was assembled in Lalito's room.

"I'm sorry," Juna said. "I just needed some fresh air. Where were we?"

They returned to the landing beach a couple of hours before sunset. The A-C specs settled in the shadow of one of the cliffs and sorted through their samples while they waited for the boat to pick them up. Juna walked down the beach, hand in hand with Moki, glad to be done with the day's work. Patricia fell into step beside them.

"Juna, what happened back there in the village? Why did you take off so suddenly? It was more than needing air, wasn't it?"

Juna looked back up the cliff at the jungle. "I was watching the others taking samples and measuring things, and it bothered me. There they were, in the middle of this amazing village, and they were busy measuring doorways and collecting trash. It just seemed"—she paused, searching for the right words—"so trivial, so foolish. They were so busy studying bits and pieces of the Tendu, when the whole was sitting right there in front of them." She shook her head. "It's a Tendu thing, I guess—the Tendu study the whole system and how it works before they start looking at the bits and pieces that make it up. We humans do the opposite. We take a thing apart and study the pieces, then try to put it together again. I don't think that works when you're studying people."

"It's more than that," Patricia said. "What else is bothering you?"

"It's hard, not being able to talk directly to the Tendu," Juna said. "It makes me feel like I'm stuck behind a thick piece of plexi. It's especially hard with Moki. He needs me so much."

Patricia laid a hand on her arm. "You've been through a lot. Why don't you take some time off?"

"You need me."

"You'll be going home in a couple of months," Patricia told her. "We're going to have to learn to get along without you. Take some leave. Go up to the mother ship, see some tapes, relax. Take Bruce with you. You deserve it, and in my opinion, you need it."

Juna glanced down at Moki and sighed. It was a tempting

thought. She had been working nonstop since the Survey had returned. Besides, she *would* be going home soon. It would be a good idea to let the Survey find out what they still needed to know from her.

"I'll talk to the captain about it."

"Good."

Juna stepped through the shuttle airlock onto the mother ship. An honor guard in dress uniform whistled her aboard. She smiled and blinked back tears. Bruce squeezed her hand. It was good to be back in space. Commander Sussman greeted them warmly and escorted them to a large double cabin.

"With everyone down on the planet, there's plenty of room," the commander said. "And I've told the crew to respect your privacy, so they won't be pestering you with questions. You're on leave, and from what the captain told me, you've earned it."

"Thank you very much, Commander. You've gone to a lot of trouble for us."

Commander Sussman shrugged. "There's not much to do up here except keep the ship ticking over until the supply ship comes through the gate. We're not expecting them for another month and a half."

"When will they be returning to Earth?" Juna asked, hope warring with sadness.

"Two or three weeks after that, maybe longer, depending on the situation downside," the commander told her. "You could be home in five months' time."

"It'll be good to see my family again," Juna said.

"I'm sure it will. Enjoy your leave, Dr. Saari, Technician Bowles."

"Well, I guess I will be going home after all," Juna said when Commander Sussman closed the door. She swallowed back sudden tears.

"What's the matter?" Bruce asked, putting his arms around her. She rested her forehead on his chest, taking comfort from his nearness. He cupped the back of her head in his hand.

"I don't know," she said. "I didn't expect it to be so soon. The standard Research posting is about ten months on-planet and you've only been here for three."

"Juna, this is an important posting. They'll be sending home the set-up crew and whatever technicians they can spare, and bringing in more scientists."

"And you?" Juna asked. "What will you be doing?"

"I'll be going home on the supply ship with you. The scientists are going to have to run their own boats."

"It'll be good to have company on the run home. But—" She looked away, unable to speak through a surge of emotion.

"It's Moki, isn't it?"

Juna nodded, and Bruce gathered her close.

"Juna," he said, lifting her chin gently. "You came up here to forget about all of that for a week. You can worry about it when we go back."

"It's hard," Juna told him.

"Well, I'll do my best to distract you," he said as he moved to kiss her.

Despite her reservations, Juna enjoyed her holiday. They made love, wallowed in the ship's huge *osento*, talked for hours, and explored some virtual-reality worlds together. She visited the commissary, and had the computer spin her some new clothes, then had her newly regrown hair dyed into the pattern of her Tendu name sign. She felt years younger by the end of her leave.

Juna and Bruce were just packing to return when the phone rang.

"Dr. Saari, we found a Tendu on board the shuttle craft, and we need your help. It's in the infirmary."

"I'll be right there," she said. "It's Moki," she told Bruce. "Somehow he got on board the shuttle. He's in the infirmary."

"Let's go, then," Bruce said.

"I'm Dr. Saari, where is the Tendu?" Juna said, when they arrived at the infirmary.

"Right this way. It was unconscious when the crewmen found it in the cargo area. They brought it here just a few minutes ago."

Juna followed the doctor into the hospital ward. Moki was strapped to a gurney.

"It's Moki," she told the doctor. "He's my adopted son." Moki's eyes slit open, at the sound of her voice. Muddy shades of relief and happiness drifted over his skin, but he was too weak to form words. She touched his forehead. It felt cold and his skin was as dry as parchment.

"Call down to the research base, have someone get Anitonen or Ukatonen, and bring them up here. Tell them it's an emergency. He's suffering from hypothermia and dehydration. He needs a hot bath and warm electrolyte solution to drink. Now!"

Juna held him close, warming him with her body heat. "Oh Moki, what have you done?"

A nurse came in. "The bath will be ready in a few more minutes. Here are some hot, moist towels to wrap him in meanwhile."

Juna nodded her thanks. They swathed him in towels, and wheeled him to the bathtub. When the water was ready, they immersed him.

Juna stripped down and climbed into the tub with Moki, cradling him in the hot water. He began to stir again. His eyes opened. He looked at her, and flushed a clear, brilliant turquoise. "On sky ship?" he asked, forming his words with difficulty.

Juna stroked his forehead. "Yes," she said. "You're on the sky ship."

"Cold," he said. "Hungry." Feebly he held his arms out for a link.

Juna shook her head. "No Moki, I can't," she told him, holding up her spurless wrist. Without her allu, she couldn't heal him. Linking would only drain what little strength he still possessed.

"Here, drink this," Juna said, lifting a beaker of warm electrolyte solution to his lips. Moki took a cautious sip, and then began drinking eagerly.

"Good," he said when he was done. He closed his eyes, and drifted in her arms, sleeping in the hot water. After half an hour, the nurses helped her lift him from the tub onto the gurney. Juna roused him, and got him to drink almost a liter of warm electrolyte solution. They settled him in a nest of moist towels warmed by a heating pad. Juna sank into a hard plastic hospital chair to watch over him while he slept.

"Dr. Saari? Dr. Saari?"

Juna stirred groggily, and then awoke. Dr. Wu was standing beside her. Ukatonen hovered just behind Wu's shoulder, his skin ochre with concern.

"Moki! How is he?" Juna asked.

"He's sleeping," Dr. Wu told her. "I've brought Ukatonen to make sure that he's all right. I thought you'd like to be awake while he linked with him. Also, I brought you a translator so you can talk to the Tendu."

"Thank you," Juna said. "I'm glad you came."

Ukatonen touched her on the shoulder. "Our bami is still stubborn," he said in skin speech.

Juna smiled. "He certainly is," she replied through the translator.

"Do you want to link with us?"

Juna nodded, and reached into the warm nest of blankets for Moki's hand. Ukatonen did the same. They grasped hands and linked.

Moki's presence reached for her, enfolding her with a vast sense of relief. Distantly, Juna was aware of Ukatonen moving through Moki, making minor repairs, but she was too caught up with Moki to notice the details. It was wonderful to feel his presence again. Seeing him so weak and helpless had made her realize how much she missed him, and how very happy she was that he was still alive. She felt him responding to her relief, her happiness at seeing him. They spiraled upward into harmony. After so much grief and guilt, it felt like the sun coming out from the clouds.

Juna clung to the link as long as she could. When the link broke, she sat for a moment, her eyes shut, not wanting to lose the completeness she had felt. Moki filled a hollow place in her heart that belonged to no one else. How could she leave him?

She opened her eyes to the outside world.

"He'll be fine," Ukatonen assured her. "He needs a good meal and a day's rest, and then we can take him back down."

Moki clutched her arm. "No," he said in Standard skin speech, "I want to go with you!"

"Moki, I'm afraid that's not possible," Juna told him, her eyes filling with tears. "You have to stay here with Ukatonen."

Wu touched her on the arm. "Clearly Moki wants to stay with you."

Juna nodded, her eyes brimming with tears. "And I want to stay with him, but it's impossible." She looked down at Moki. "I've been hoping that somehow he would accept Ukatonen as his sitik, but now—" She shook her head. "He'll die without me, and if he dies, then Ukatonen will commit suicide."

"We can't let that happen," Wu said. "I don't want to think about how that would affect our relationship with the Tendu."

"I can't stay here," Juna told him. "I need to go home. There's my family. I miss them, and my father needs me."

"You've given more than enough, to both the Survey and the Tendu," Wu agreed.

Ukatonen touched her shoulder. "What are you saying?" he asked.

Juna translated the conversation.

"Take Moki with you," Ukatonen suggested. "For that matter, I'd like to go as well. After all, I am also Moki's sitik. He shouldn't be completely separated from other Tendu."

"Please!" Moki begged, going bright pink with excitement.

Juna shook her head. "It's too cold and dry," she said. "And it's against Contact Protocols."

"There's nothing in the treaty against it," Ukatonen argued, "and if we can change you to fit into our world, why can't we change ourselves to fit into yours? It's risky, but we're both willing to do what we can to adapt."

Moki sat up, ears wide. "Let me go with you!" he pleaded.

Juna looked from Moki to Ukatonen and back again. "It will be hard. You have no idea how hard it will be. My world is so different, so complex," she said. "You'll be too cold, too dry, and everything will seem crazy and confusing. The whole world will feel out of harmony. Some people will be afraid of you, others hostile. You'll have trouble communicating with the ones who are friendly."

"You managed to adapt to us," Moki pointed out.

"I nearly died several times," Juna told him. "I was very unhappy, and I caused a lot of disharmony."

"You're my sitik," Moki said. "I belong wherever you are."

"And what about Ukatonen? He is also your sitik. He would

have to come along. You'll be dragging him into a world of confusion and pain. Are you willing to live with that?"

Moki's ears folded close to his head. Ripples of shame and doubt passed over him.

Ukatonen touched Juna's shoulder. "You don't understand," he said. "I want to go. The Tendu need someone who understands your people. Besides, I want change. Before I met you, I was so bored that I was thinking about dying. I want to see something new and strange, even if I'm cold and uncomfortable—" He paused for a moment. "Even if it kills me, Juna, I want to see your world. Please take us with you. We want to go."

"I can't promise anything, but I'll talk to Dr. Wu and Dr. Bremen about it."

She turned to Wu. "They want to come with me when I go back to Earth."

"Both of them?" Wu asked.

Juna nodded. "They want to go. Moki wants to be with me, and Ukatonen wants to look after Moki and learn more about humans. I tried to talk them out of it." She looked at Moki and shook her head. "They have no idea what they're agreeing to, but they're determined to go. If I didn't feel that it was a matter of life and death for them, I wouldn't ask that they be allowed to come with me."

"Well," Wu said, after a long, thoughtful pause, "we'll have to talk to the captain and Dr. Bremen, but I'll back you on this one."

"Thank you, Dr. Wu," Juna said. "I didn't expect this."

Wu bowed his head for a moment, then looked at her. "A Tendu saved my life. Now I have a chance to save two lives in return. Besides, I agree with Ukatonen. It would be good for them to see us, to learn more about our culture. Who knows what they'll teach us about ourselves?"

Juna opened the door to the observation gallery. It was dark and quiet, lit only by the glow of the planet they orbited. The hush of the air vents and the distant hum of machinery were the only sounds. The two Tendu stepped silently to the wide, curving window. Outside, their world hung below them, vast and brilliant. The black line of the terminator lay on the middle of the ocean, moving almost imperceptibly toward the coast. Moki groped for Juna's hand, unable to take his eyes off the view.

No one said anything for a very long time.

At last Ukatonen turned and touched Juna on the shoulder.

"Thank you," he said. "Before this, I thought that perhaps your people were making it all up; that maybe you were from some northern continent that we didn't know about. Now I see my own world turning beneath me. . . ."

Juna brushed Ukatonen's shoulder. "It's a beautiful world, isn't it?"

"Where's Lyanan?" Moki asked.

Juna pointed out the broad peninsula, just barely visible beneath cloud cover. She remembered the long, difficult trip from Narmolom to Lyanan and back again. From here, she could cover the entire distance with the palm of her hand.

"We've come a long way," she said with a smile.

A soft chime sounded.

"We need to go. They're waiting to take us back down," Juna said.

The two Tendu turned to go with obvious reluctance.

"I hope we'll see it again," Moki said wistfully.

"I hope so too," Juna replied.

Two days later, Juna, Ukatonen, Anitonen, and Moki followed the senior members of the staff into the conference room. Patricia squeezed Juna on the shoulder.

"Good luck," she whispered.

Juna managed a weak, nervous smile. "Thanks," she whispered back.

At last everyone was settled around the table.

Dr. Bremen stood. "Well, you've handed us a rather difficult decision, Dr. Saari."

"Yes, I know," she responded, "but it's important. Unless Moki comes back with me, he'll run off into the forest and go wild again. He might even kill himself. When that happens, Ukatonen will be forced to commit suicide."

"I understand that much from your summary of the situation,

but I don't entirely understand the chain of causality here. You told us during your first briefing that you arranged for Ukatonen to adopt Moki. Now you're saying that won't work?"

"Yes, sir. Parenting is very different among the Tendu. It isn't just a matter of love and affection; there's a physiological bond there too. Moki has bonded with me, with my biochemistry. No one else can substitute for me. He cares for Ukatonen—they are very close—but he needs me. I had hoped he could transfer that physical need to Ukatonen, but he can't. It will be years before he can live without me."

"But why can't he simply become an elder?" Bremen asked.

Juna started to answer, but Ukatonen, who had been following Dr. Tanguay's translation, put a hand on her arm.

"Let me explain," he said.

"Moki is too young to become an elder, and he has been Eerin's sitik too long to adapt to another sitik. Sometimes, if a sitik dies only a month or two after the bami's transformation from a tinka, another elder can be found. But Moki is at a stage where that is impossible. He will need to be with Eerin for another eight or nine years, perhaps even longer."

"Why would you have to die if Moki runs away, Ukatonen?" Dr. Bremen asked.

Ukatonen looked at the translation. "I am an enkar. Anitonen asked me to pass judgment on whether Eerin could adopt Moki. I am responsible for the consequences of my judgment. If this adoption doesn't work out, if Moki is lost to our people, then my judgment was wrong, and I will have to die."

"I see," Bremen said. "That seems rather harsh."

Ukatonen shrugged, another human gesture he had picked up. "I make very good decisions. I have lived almost a thousand of your years."

"What would the diplomatic consequences be if you die?" Wu asked.

Anitonen rose.

"I wish to make a judgment," she said in formal patterns. "Ukatonen and Moki must go with you."

"No!!" Juna cried.

Ironic amusement rippled across Anitonen's skin. "It's too late, Eerin. I have spoken."

"I'm sorry," Dr. Tanguay said. "I didn't understand what Anitonen meant."

Juna translated. "Anitonen has just linked her life to Moki and Ukatonen's. If Ukatonen and Moki don't go, then Anitonen's judgment is wrong, and she must die," Juna explained. "We would lose the two Tendu who know us best. It might take years to catch up again."

"And I don't know how the other enkar would take it if two of their number died as a result of our actions," Wu put in. "It would severely restrict our ability to negotiate."

Bremen shook his head, looking angry. Juna's throat tightened in fear. He didn't like being trapped.

"Dr. Bremen," she said softly. "There's a great deal that we can learn from Ukatonen and Moki if they come with us. They'll be an invaluable source of information to our researchers back home. They can help us prepare people coming out to study this planet. When they come back, they can teach their people about us."

"But the Contact Protocols," Bremen protested. "What about them?"

"We'll abide by them," Ukatonen replied. "We won't teach your people anything that might be harmful to them."

Juna had to fight back a smile at Bremen's amazed expression when he heard the translation. Given what the Tendu were capable of, the humans probably needed the Contact Protocols as much as the Tendu did. Besides, it might not hurt the A-C specs to get a taste of their own medicine.

"There's a provision in the protocols for limited diplomatic missions," Wu said. "I think that we can make a very strong case for it, considering the possible repercussions if we refuse."

"Thank you all," Bremen said. "You've given us a great deal to think about. Dr. Saari. if you and the Tendu could excuse us for a few minutes, while we discuss the situation."

"Certainly, Dr. Bremen." Juna rose and motioned to the Tendu to follow her.

"Well," Ukatonen said. "We've done everything we can."

Juna looked at the three of them. They had staked their lives on this decision. She felt a sudden resolve.

"If they say that you can't come," Juna told them, her throat tight with fear, "then I will stay here with you."

"What about your family?" Ukatonen asked.

"You are my family also. I can't let you die," Juna replied. She brushed Moki's shoulder affectionately, and tried not to think about going home. She was glad that her skin no longer showed her emotions.

Moki took her hand. It was a very human gesture. He looked up at her.

"Thank you, siti."

Juna smiled, feeling the weight of guilt and misery drop from her shoulders. Whatever happened now, Moki would survive, and so would Ukatonen. She looked at Anitonen and bit her lip. Anitonen had risked her life on a dangerous attempt to ensure that Moki and Ukatonen would go with her. There was nothing Juna could do except hope for the best.

"That was a very brave judgment, en," she said. "I hope it isn't proven wrong."

"We'll see," Anitonen responded.

A few minutes later, Patricia stuck her head out the door. "They're done," she said.

They walked back in and took their places.

Bremen stood. "We have decided that Ukatonen will be Special Envoy to Humanity. Moki will be officially listed as his dependent child. I have grave misgivings about this, but—" He shook his head. "You win, Dr. Saari. I only hope you know what you're doing."

Juna felt giddy with relief. She took a deep breath to steady herself and rose to speak.

"Thank you, Dr. Bremen. I'm sure that both our people will gain from this decision."

Bremen adjourned the meeting. Moki and the other Tendu crowded around Juna, their skins vivid blue with relief. Juna took them to the Staff Lounge, where her friends had assembled, waiting for the verdict. Alison met them at the door, a questioning look on her face.

"We did it!" Juna shouted gleefully.

Everyone in the room cheered. Alison popped the cork on a bottle of champagne. "Ad Astra '32," she remarked as she poured. "Your father was hoping there would be something worth celebrating." The galley staff brought out platters of fruit, cheese, and pastries. Moki reached for a pastry, then hesitated, looking at Juna.

"Go ahead, Moki. You'll have to get used to human food eventually," Juna said. "Just eat a little bit, though."

He bit into the crumbly pastry and chewed carefully, eyes shut.

"Well?" Alison asked.

He flushed turquoise and opened his eyes. "I think I'm going to like your world. The food is good."

Juna laughed, then sobered. "I hope everything, else is as good as that cake."

She closed her eyes and leaned back in her chair with a profound sigh of relief. The tragedy she had been dreading for so long had been averted. She was going to get to see her family and keep Moki too. She picked up her glass of champagne, and held it up for a toast.

"To the Tendu, humanity, and the future," she said, and tossed back her father's champagne. It had never tasted sweeter.

Thirty-two

JUNA SAT IN the place of honor at the farewell banquet given by Lyanan. Ukatonen and Moki flanked her. They would be leaving on the shuttle tomorrow afternoon for the Survey ship *Homa Darabi Maru.* It was a huge banquet, so big that it had been moved to the forest floor. Dozens of enkar had come to say goodbye to Ukatonen. Naratonen had brought Ninto. Anitonen had spent almost every minute since then with her tareena. Juna looked at the two of them talking intently, and smiled, glad that they had this opportunity to be together. To her right sat most of the top brass of the *Unity Dow:* Captain Edison, Dr. Bremen, Dr. Wu, and the other department heads. Juna had made sure that the human delegation included the people who had helped her. Dr. Baker, Gerald Nyimbe, and her friends Bruce, Alison, Marguerite, Laurie, Patricia, and Kay sat together watching the proceedings with amazement. Alison had prepared special ration bars and drink boxes full of good wine and fresh juice, so that they had something to eat as well.

When everyone was fed and the food was cleared away, Anitonen rose to speak.

"I want to thank the Tendu of Lyanan for this lavish banquet and for their patience and kind hospitality over the last few months. Without it, we would not have achieved the beginnings of understanding with the humans. We ask you to be patient for a little longer, while we present a new quarbirri."

The villagers of Lyanan stirred, flickers of excitement passing over them. It was quite an honor to host the performance of a quarbirri performed by the enkar. Their village's status would rise.

Ukatonen, Anitonen, Ninto, and Naratonen got up and began putting on rattles and testing musical instruments. They were joined by several other enkar. Wu and the other humans began groping for their recorders. Juna turned to Moki.

"What is this?" she scrawled on her translator.

Moki rippled laughter. "You'll see," he told her.

The villagers started beating drums and shaking rattles. Ukatonen lay down in the middle of the impromptu stage. One of the elders blew on a conch shell, signaling the beginning of the performance.

Anitonen came in from behind the musicians. She saw Ukatonen and stopped, turning deep purple with curiosity. She mimed descending. Ninto and Naratonen followed her. They circled around Ukatonen handling his limbs, exclaiming in excitement at his strange appearance.

Juna laughed, suddenly realizing what this quarbirri was about. It was the story of her arrival among the Tendu. She glanced at the other humans, wondering how long it would take for them to figure it out.

She sat back, reminiscing, as the graceful Tendu moved through the narrative. She heard a burst of surprised laughter from the Survey crew during the digging race. They had finally realized what the story was about.

The quarbirri moved on through her adoption of Moki, her trip down the river, her time in Narmolom, and then through Anitonen's and Ninto's training to become enkar, and the return of the humans. As the story wound to a close, the Tendu began describing the things they had learned from her. They speculated on the changes that might occur as their people learned more about the humans. There was hope, but also caution in their storytelling. Juna smiled. The Tendu would do all right.

The quarbirri closed with a tightly interwoven knot of bodies. Pulses of color passed from one body to the next in perfect synchrony. It symbolized humans and Tendu linking together, achieving harmony. It was a very difficult technical feat. The Tendu in the audience rippled wildly in approval, and the humans joined in with enthusiastic applause. Juna watched through eyes blurry with tears, deeply honored to be the subject of a quarbirri.

When the applause died, she rose. "Thank you," she said, aloud and on her graphics tablet. "I am honored by this quarbirri. I hope that we can negotiate the opportunity to show it to my people. They would learn much from it."

Anitonen stood. "On behalf of everyone who helped create this quarbirri, I give it to your people as a gift that we both can share."

Juna spent the night in the heart of the giant na tree with Moki and the others. She lay awake a long time listening to the familiar night sounds of the village: the rustling as one of the Tendu stirred in his sleep, the faint humming of the tilan bees in the walls, and the occasional creaking sounds of the giant tree shifting in the wind. It would be a long time, if ever, before Juna would hear them again. She was glad that she was going home, but she would miss this world, with its complex, cathedral-like forests and beautiful people.

She thought about Moki and Ukatonen. How would they manage? What would they think of Earth and its colonies? How would her family feel about them? The future was full of questions, but tonight was for thinking about the past. She banished her worries and let the sounds of the great tree lull her to sleep.

The next morning a crowd of Tendu followed them to the beach to see them off. As the launch headed toward them, its wake an arc of white foam, Juna turned to Anitonen.

"Are you sorry you rescued me?" she asked. "You lost so much. Your village, your whole future."

Anitonen touched Juna on the shoulder. "I lost one future, but I gained another one. I think it balances."

"I'll miss you. I'll miss the Tendu."

"You'll come back. We'll see each other again," Anitonen

assured her. "Our people need you too much for you to stay away."

Juna nodded. The boat was nearly at the beach. She stepped forward to help land the boat, then said her formal goodbyes to Lalito, the village council, Ninto, and the enkar. Then she was back to Anitonen. She found she had no words. She held out her arms instead.

They linked, a link that tasted of the sadness of farewells and hopes for the future, reaching a sad, nostalgic harmony. When it was over, she touched Anitonen on the shoulder in a wordless farewell, and then climbed into the waiting boat. Ukatonen and Moki followed her. As they pulled away they flickered goodbyes to the Tendu watching on the shore. Juna kept looking back until the Tendu on the shore had faded into the distance, and all she could see was a pale strip of sand and the endless forest stretching to the horizon.

A Partial Glossary of the Tendu Language

Allu-a—The communion between two or more Tendu involving a deep sharing of physiological state.

Allu—Fleshy red spurs located on the inside of the forearm, and their associated organs, used by the Tendu for allu-a.

Bai—A shortened form of bami, used as an endearment by sitiks when talking to their bami.

Bami—The apprenticed foster child of a Tendu elder, usually chosen by that elder from a pool of immature Tendu known as tinka. A bami is the second, adolescent phase of the Tendu life cycle.

Enkar—A class of Tendu that travels from village to village, rendering judgments.

Ika—A large emergent canopy tree with large blossoms that resemble human hair. It is one of the few trees in the forest that is wind-pollinated.

Jeetho—A large multinucleated mass of cytoplasm derived from any one of several animals. Jeetho is used as a biological substrate for many forms of physiological manipulation requiring the addition of large amounts of tissue, e.g., the regeneration of amputated limbs.

Kenja—A ritual often used to decide precedence among village elders. Many ethnographers note the similarity between this ritual and the "rock-scissors-paper" game used on Earth in several cultures. Many elaborate cultural convergence theories have been put forward to explain this similarity.

Li—A unit of measurement equivalent to three yai. Roughly equivalent to nineteen meters.

Lyali-Tendu—sea Tendu. Those Tendu who live year-round in coastal waters.

Mantu—A large land-dwelling mollusk with an external shell. They average 0.75 meters in length.

Na tree—The giant hollow trees that are the preferred living quarters for land-dwelling Tendu.

Pingar—Any meat that has been pickled, then dried, salted, and chopped fine to keep for travel or emergencies.

Pooo-eet—A fishing bird that lives near the river. During their mating season (also known as the month or "pida" of Pooo-eet) the canopy echoes with their "pooo-eet" calls, prompting many Tendu to go hunting for a little peace and quiet.

Quarbirri—Traditional Tendu dance/narrative art form.

Ruwe-Tendu—The land-dwelling form of the Tendu.

Sitik—An elder Tendu who is the mentor/parent of a sub-adult bami.

Siti—Informal form of sitik, usually used by a bami to his or her sitik.

Tareena—The relationship between two bami who have had the same sitik. It usually occurs after an elder has died without a bami. When this happens, another elder's bami is promoted to fill the spot, and the elder whose bami has been promoted takes another bami. It is a rare relationship. Often hundreds of years can pass without a village having any tareena, and only if there has been a terrible disaster will there be more than one pair in any village.

Tengarra—The Tendu term for a formal judgment rendered by an enkar. The price for such a judgment can be very high, including the requirement that a certain number of elders volunteer to become enkar.

Tilan—A species of bee that lives symbiotically with the na tree, protecting it from leaf-eating insects and some species of vines and other parasitic plants.

Tinka—Juvenile form of Tendu, imprinted on a village. Usually six years and older. A tinka can live as long as fifty years before beginning to age and die.

Trangin—A spiny orange or red-orange fruit slightly larger than a Terran honeydew melon. It smells utterly vile when opened up, but its soft, juicy pink flesh tastes wonderful.

Werrun—The ritual physical transformation by which a Tendu bami becomes an elder.

Yai—A unit of measurement based on the approximate width of a mature canopy tree. It is approximately 6.5 meters in length, though it can vary from region to region (see Tanguay's monograph entitled *Regional Variability in Tendu Units of Measurement* for more information).

Yarram—A species of seaweed that is dried and eaten by the Tendu, it is prized as a source of nutrients scarce in the rain forest, and it is a valued article of trade. It is also a delicacy and is essential for the development of both bami and young elders who have just emerged from werrun.

Yerowe—Any one of several species of highly specialized insects that colonize Tendu villages. They eat vermin and decaying leaf matter found in the Tendu bedding, and lay down chemicals that encourage composting. In short, they keep the Tendu's beds fresh and pleasant.

Author's Note

Earth's rain forests are infinitely more complex, mysterious, and wonderful than anything in this book, and they really exist. Here are some of my favorite books on tropical rain forests and the people who live in them:

Tropical Nature, Adrian Forsyth and Ken Miyata. New York: Charles Scribner's Sons, 1984.

Life Above the Jungle Floor, Donald Perry. New York: Simon and Schuster, 1986.

The Tropical Rain Forest, Marius Jacobs. New York: Springer Verlag, 1988.

Tales of a Shaman's Apprentice, Mark J. Plotkin. New York: Viking Penguin, 1993.

Into the Heart, Kenneth Good with David Chanoff. New York: Simon and Schuster, 1991.

Wonderful as they are, Earth's rain forests are disappearing with amazing and tragic speed. For more information on how to help save the rain forests and the people who live in them, contact these organizations:

Rainforest Action Network
450 Sansome Street, Suite 700
San Francisco, CA 94111
Internet: RAN-INFO@IGC.APC.ORG
Worldwide Web page: URL-HTTP://WWW.RAN.ORG/RAN/

World Wildlife Fund
1250 Twenty-fourth Street, NW
Washington, DC 20037

Cultural Survival
46 Brattle Street
Cambridge, MA 02138